Citadels of Darkover
Darkover® Anthology 19

Edited by
Deborah J. Ross

The Marion Zimmer Bradley Literary Works Trust
PO Box 193473
San Francisco, CA 94119
www.mzbworks.com

Copyright © 2019 by the Marion Zimmer Bradley Literary Works Trust
All Rights Reserved
Darkover® is a registered trademark of the Marion Zimmer Bradley Literary Works Trust

Cover design © 2019 by Dave Smeds

ISBN-13: 978-1-938185-62-5
ISBN-10: 1-938185-62-5

All characters and events in this book are fictitious.

All resemblance to persons living or dead is coincidental.

The scanning, uploading and distribution of this book via the Internet or any other means without the permission of the publisher is illegal, and punishable by law. Please purchase only authorized electronic editions, and do not participate in or encourage the electronic piracy of copyrighted materials. Your support of the author's rights is appreciated.

CONTENTS

Introduction 　by Deborah J. Ross	5
Dancing Lessons 　by Evey Brett	7
Sacrifice 　by Steven Harper	35
Banshee Cry 　by Marella Sands	65
The Katana Matrix 　by Lillian Csernica	84
Siege 　by Diana L. Paxson	113
Sea-Castle 　by Leslie Fish	133
Fire Storm 　by Jane M. H. Bigelow	159
The Dragon Hunter 　by Robin Rowland	181
Fish Nor Fowl 　by Rebecca Fox	204
Dark as Dawn 　by Robin Wayne Bailey	231

The Citadel of Fear   250
    by Barb Caffrey

The Judgment of Widows   263
    by Shariann Lewitt

INTRODUCTION

by Deborah J. Ross

The iconic image of Darkover portrays a castle high in snow-covered mountains, washed red beneath a swollen sun. The combination of elements evokes a place at once romantic and bleak, alien and richly nostalgic. It's a place that beckons us with tales of great feats of heroism and even greater loves. From the beginning of the series (*The Planet Savers*, 1958; *The Sword of Aldones*, 1962; *The Bloody Sun*, 1964), Darkover provided its readers a plentiful supply of castles and fortresses. More than that, in these early novels the planet itself was besieged by the often uneasy re-contact with Terra and its highly technological culture. So it came as no surprise to me when, as I was mulling over possible titles for the next Darkover anthology, I thought of a castle with turrets and towers. It was not just a pile of stones atop a hill but a place that was both fortress and retreat, a stronghold against enemies within and without.

"Citadel" derives derived from the Italian *cittadella,* diminutive of of *cittade,* city, which in turn arises from the Latin *civitas* or citizenship. Dictionary definitions include *a fortress on a commanding height for the defense of a city, a stronghold within or near a city*, and hence, *any strongly fortified place offering safety and refuge*. Archaeological citadels date back to the Indus Valley civilization (1100 BCE – 1300 BCE). In medieval castles, citadels with their high walls offered the last line of defense before the innermost keep.

On Darkover, external architectural forms resemble those of its Terran ancestry, but nothing is ever that simple. A Tower for matrix workers may look like a fortification on the surface but is very different in its function as well as its defenses. Citadels can be psychic, emotional, and cultural as well as military. As with the previous Darkover anthologies I've edited, the wonderfully imaginative authors took the basic concept and spun out stories in diverse and often unexpected directions. Within these pages you'll find citadels of the more traditional, physical variety, but also fortresses of the heart and spirit.

Every anthology I've ever edited, whether by open submission or invitation only, broad in topic or narrowly defined, has developed its own internal structure, with stories frequently echoing one another. My editorial debut, *Lace and Blade*, included two very different stories about Spanish highwaymen (in the second one, two stories featured Chinese generals). I have yet to figure out if this co-incidence is pure chance or the simultaneous emergence of story elements in various creative minds. Putting together "citadel/stronghold/refuge/fortress" and the rich history and landscape of Darkover was bound to result in unexpected and dramatic combinations. I hope you find them as magical as I did.

Finally, a note of farewell: The Marion Zimmer Literary Works Trust holds the trademark for Darkover and has published these anthologies since the first one I edited, *Stars of Darkover* (2013). The Trust has decided to stop publishing new anthologies. They announced the decision in their September 2018 newsletter. While I am sad to lay down this amazing adventure from "the other side of the editorial desk," I am also grateful to the immensely talented, generous authors who have entrusted me with their work and put up with my editorial feedback. Over the years, many have become friends as well as professional colleagues. But most of all, I extend my sincere thanks to you, the readers, who have cherished Darkover over the decades. I hope the stories I've put together here give you the rich rewards of visiting the planet of the Bloody Sun once more, and I hope that you will continue to enjoy that experience through the novels I write for DAW Books under the supervision of the Trust (even if their release dates are a bit further apart).

Adelandeyo, go with the gods.

It's been such a marvelous journey.

Deborah J. Ross

DANCING LESSONS

by Evey Brett

After being persuaded to move to southern Arizona by her Lipizzan mare, Carrma, Evey Brett developed a fondness for the local creepy-crawlies such as snakes, scorpions, tarantulas and Gila monsters, not to mention the coyotes, buzzards and hawks that frequent the area. Evey writes that some of those critters have influenced a number of her stories, including one in *Masques of Darkover* and several in Lethe Press anthologies. When not feeding carrots to her equine mistress, Evey can be found shuffling papers for the city or reading submission stories for *The Magazine of Fantasy and Science Fiction*.

As an editor, I find it no accident that a writer so inspired by one of the "dancing white horses" should pen a story in which hearts also learn to dance.

Going to the midwinter festival at Comyn Castle wasn't my idea of a good time. "They'll have chairs, won't they?"

"I'm sure we'll be able to find you a comfortable seat, but it would be bad form to turn down an invitation from my good friend, *Dom* Ridenow," Captain Maeda said as she inspected my dress uniform. "Besides," she said, giving me a conspiratorial smile, "I want a companion who knows how to keep his mouth shut and isn't going to embarrass me in front of the Darkovan elite. You don't drink, do you, Ethan?"

"Rarely."

"Good. Keep it that way." She brushed a speck of dust from my shoulder. "You look shipshape, Lieutenant. It'll do you good to get out." She sighed, and amended it to, "We both need a night to enjoy ourselves."

It was her attempt to return to normality—or what passed for it these days, since we no longer had a ship of our own and the Space Service had yet to allow either of us to return to duty. So out we went. Comyn Castle was only a stone's throw away, visible from the spaceport control tower, but despite weeks of physical therapy I still found it a trial to travel long distances on prosthetic legs. So Captain Maeda ordered a transport for my sake and we sat in the back, silent as we took in the change of scenery from the Spaceport to Old Thendara.

After a dozen winding, twisted streets, we arrived at Comyn Castle, which was a huge, imposing place—more of a citadel, I thought. Guards stood outside the gate. They accepted our invitation—written in a handsome script on thick, gilt paper—and ushered us inside, where a young page led us to the ballroom.

I was…disappointed. Ordinarily such a scene would have intrigued me. There were colors of every hue, and the cuts of the clothing would have been fascinating once upon a time. I'd always loved beautiful things, whether it was art or movement or clothing, but tonight, the noise and crowd was stifling. I shook off the impulse to tug at my collar, always itchy no matter the fabric treatment, and swallowed the intense disappointment at realizing how even the idea of joy had fled.

"See? I knew you'd like it."

I pasted on my best smile. "Thank you, Captain. I do."

Her enjoyment seemed as forced as mine as we threaded our way through the crowd. Servers offered us filled crystal glasses, and with a tactful question I was provided a sparkling non-alcoholic beverage. Captain Maeda helped herself to a glass of wine, though she sipped it slowly as she searched the gathering for her friend.

The dancing had already begun; men cordially asked the women to dance, although there was one pair of men near the edge who danced together, heedless of anyone watching. This lifted my spirits ever so slightly, although they also reminded me of how alone I now was.

The locals were quite easily discerned from the Terrans, not only because of the dress but also because of their manner. There was a particular sort of etiquette among the Darkovans, one I'd read a little about but had yet to see live. The Terrans thought little of being loud, boisterous and imbibing, but the Darkovans maintained their courtesy. I envied them such control.

I was nearly ready to seek out a chair when the entire hall went silent. A man entered and took a place in the center of the floor. I looked to the captain, who just shrugged. This was no ordinary man; he was thin and graceful with long, silvery hair and had such a presence that nearly everyone in the room turned to look.

The music began, soft and quiet, and the man began to move with an exquisite control I envied. It made me feel all the more clumsy, clomping around on makeshift legs and finding it a trial simply to maintain my balance. Watching this dancer, though, I forgot all that. There was a masculine strength coupled with feminine grace that fascinated me; I'd never seen the two in such fine accord. I'd always loved theater, anything from plays to musicals to opera, but dance always held a special place in my heart. It was the absolute freedom, the way one was entirely at ease with their body and used it to express things words never could.

The music rose and sped up. The man moved accordingly, spinning and twirling, throwing his arms in the air in what could only be described as pure ecstasy. His costume sparkled in the lamplight, creating a hypnotic effect of its own. I could have watched him for the rest of my life and died happy.

But end it did, in a round of enthusiastic applause. I could only stand there, dumb with the thrill and magic of it.

The captain elbowed me, and I clapped, keeping my gaze on the dancer until the last possible moment when the guards escorted him from the floor and through an arched doorway. After that, the Darkovans retook the floor, once again choosing partners and moving in elegant, intricate patterns.

A redheaded man in a gold-trimmed shirt strode over to us. "Captain Maeda. I'm pleased you accepted my invitation."

"I wouldn't miss it, *Dom* Ridenow. Lieutenant Alvarez and I appreciate your hospitality."

"Not at all." He gestured, and a page carrying a basket full of greenery came dashing over. *Dom* Ridenow plucked a modest corsage of evergreen tied with a red ribbon and pinned it to her jacket. "A gift for you at Midwinter Festival, and to honor our blessed Cassilda and the women in our lives."

She smiled, seeming girlishly pleased. I noticed then that all the other women had corsages, too. "You're very kind. Thank you."

"Well, we do like to share our culture with those with an eye for the arts, like your officer here seems to have."

I inclined my head slightly in acknowledgement, still speechless after the performance.

Captain Maeda came to my rescue. "Ethan usually has an eye for the stars, which is why he's my astrogator, but he's also a fine musician and devotee of the arts. That's why I asked him to come along."

"A wise choice." Ridenow grinned. "Would you like to dance, *messire*? I'm sure I can find you a partner who would be happy to show you the steps."

"Perhaps later," I said, trying to think of a gracious way to decline. The artificial legs the Terrans had manufactured for me were not adjusting well. It was an effort to walk; anything more complicated was out of the question.

His eyes narrowed ever so slightly "Forgive me. I should not have presumed. If there is anything I can do to make your visit more comfortable, please don't hesitate to ask."

"Thank you." He and Captain Maeda had been friends for some time; no doubt she'd mentioned my infirmity, although she'd usually been tight-lipped when it came to her crew's personal lives."I've never seen anything like that. It was beautiful. Stunning. I don't have the words to describe it."

"The look of wonderment on your face says enough. I'm glad you enjoyed it. We delight in featuring our oldest dances. Few know all the steps, and those that do are treasured."

I wondered why the dancer had vanished, rather than stay to enjoy his accolades. Perhaps he, too, had a keeper so worried about his comfort and well-being that he couldn't wander alone.

But such thoughts were unfair. I'd saved the captain's life, and in return she felt the need to aid me as much as she could. Honor ran strong among her people, she'd told me once, so she aimed to repay me. Nevertheless, I wondered at the cost. She'd been at my side through the worst of my pain and recuperation, yet she'd shown none of hers. Surely her captain's façade couldn't remain in place forever, but it was all she let me see.

At least here she seemed at ease, freed from her recent grief. I watched the way she interacted with *Dom* Ridenow, more relaxed than I'd seen her since before the accident.

I was just about to excuse myself to find a chair when my right foot started to burn—the foot that was long gone, crushed in a twist of metal. I hadn't brought my painkillers, both because my dress uniform was short on pockets and out of some stupid hope that I wouldn't need them. I had no wish to attract attention to my infirmity, but I needed out of the crowd, away from the press of people so I could wait for the pain to pass.

"Ethan?"

Sharp-eyed as she was, the captain must have suspected my problem. "Forgive me, Captain. I'm finding the room a bit…close."

She raised an eyebrow and was about to speak, but *Dom* Ridenow was already gesturing to me. "May I offer you my assistance in finding a suitable place to retreat? This is not a place I would suggest wandering around alone. It's possible for even those who live here to become lost."

"I would be grateful, sir."

"This way, then. And never fear, Captain Maeda. I will return him to you in due time."

As soon as we were away from the crowd, *Dom* Ridenow offered me an arm and I took it, unable to walk without limping. Every step sent a stabbing pain through my non-existent foot and lower leg. "I'm sorry. I don't mean to be a nuisance."

"Think nothing of it. I would be a poor host if I did not accommodate the needs of my guests. Besides, I'm not all that fond of crowds myself and appreciate an excuse to escape."

I smiled at that. He did seem eager to leave the gathering.

"Not much farther." He led me around a corner and outside to a small, enclosed garden. "Here we are," he said, and deposited me on one of the benches. "This is where our healers and *leroni* grow herbs for their medicines. I've always found it a soothing place. If you'd like, I could send for a *leronis* to help with your discomfort."

"No need. I just need to meditate for a while, and it will pass."

"As you wish. I'll return in a little while to fetch you."

"Thank you, *Dom* Ridenow."

He gave me a nod and departed. At last, I had the peace and quiet I craved, yet I was still distracted. The air was chilly, almost uncomfortably so, and the plants gave off strange, unfamiliar scents.

I took advantage of the solitude to roll up my trousers and remove my artificial legs, which I propped up against the bench. The intense burning feeling didn't stop, but there was a marginal relief at releasing the pressure on my stumps.

Focus on your breathing, the Terran doctors had told me, and given me recordings encouraging me to imagine myself by the sea or some other pretty location to distract me from my pain. Imagery never worked, so I focused on taking long, deep breaths in and out.

The pain had just become bearable when the garden door opened. A man spoke in one of the local dialects, too swiftly for me to catch anything other than the word for *outside*.

I opened my eyes, surprised to see the dancer hurry into the garden. He wasn't alone. Two guardsmen, probably those who'd escorted him from the ballroom, flanked him. He took a deep breath of chilly air, then startled when he realized I was there. "Forgive me, *mestre*," he said in Terran Standard. "I didn't think anyone else would be here."

If he were Terran, no doubt he would have averted his gaze, or looked only at my face. But, being Darkovan, he was utterly unperturbed by my dislocated limbs. "Please stay, if you'd like. I wouldn't mind the company." And not just because looking at him would take my mind off my pain. "I needed a breath of fresh air too."

"Thank you." He sank down onto the bench next to mine. I shivered, even with my thick officer's coat, but here he was, in shirtsleeves, without even a hint of gooseflesh.

"You must be from the Hellers to find this night so pleasant." I'd heard stories of how brutal the weather was in the mountains.

"Nevarsin, actually. Well, near there."

"Ah." I'd read about the monastery and how the denizens managed to control their response to cold. I found it difficult to believe. "This is balmy weather for you, then?"

"It doesn't bother me."

Perhaps not, but I wondered if I was, since all my attempts at small talk were failing. Another few minutes passed in silence before I had the courage to say, "I've never seen anyone dance like that. I could have watched you for hours."

He gave me a shy smile. "You are new to Darkover, are you not? There are likely many things you have not yet seen."

"No doubt my captain will introduce me to a few. We're here for a vacation, of sorts, by invitation of *Dom* Ridenow."

"Ah," was all he said, and I could not judge whether or not I had overstepped.

"Will you be performing again?"

"Not tonight."

"Elsewhere? Do you have recitals?"

I feared I was making a fool of myself, sounding too pleading, but at last he answered. "I have, but not recently, and not in the foreseeable future."

"Oh." This time, I couldn't keep the disappointment from my voice. He'd been the only light in my life, lately, and already it was extinguished. "I was never much of a dancer. Always clumsy, even before…" I gestured at my empty trouser legs.

"Then you had a poor teacher."

"My sister. She didn't have much patience." Our relationship had never been good; I hadn't talked to her in years. "I bet you're a good teacher."

"Some think so. Some do not."

I wondered what he meant by that. "Is that why you have

guards?"

I'd meant to be lighthearted, but that was the wrong question. He stiffened, then forced himself to relax. "My attendance was requested. It is safer for me with an escort."

Requested, or ordered? I was making him uneasy. There was something about him, an air of strangeness. Loneliness. It was easy to recognize, having felt it keenly these past few months. "I wasn't eager to come here, either. My captain insisted on it after…well."

"And now that you're here, what do you think?"

"I think you're the best part, so far."

"You are kind to say so. Is that why you wanted me to stay, *messire?* Merely to ogle?"

Heat sprang to my cheeks, momentarily countering the chill. "I'm sorry. I wished merely to express my admiration. Now that I've done so, I will not keep you. Forgive me if I've been offensive; I've done a lot of reading about your world, but I'm sure I've missed some protocols."

He stood, and I feared he would leave without another word, but he faced me and said quietly, "It is I who should apologize. I know you meant no offense; I am fatigued from my exertions, as well as my company." He nodded slightly at his bodyguards.

"It's completely understandable." I eyed him, wishing I had some of that mind-magic that allegedly ran through Darkovan society's upper echelon. He wasn't just a dancer. There was something more about him, beyond those six-fingered hands that set him apart.

And gods, he was handsome.

"You are so innocent, Terran. Stay that way." He brushed my cheek with a feather-light touch and left me there, shivering with more than cold…

…and free of pain.

Captain Maeda found me the next afternoon, resting in my quarters and reading up on whatever Darkovan cultural files I could dig up. There was plenty of archival information, journals written by anthropologists, scientists and other visitors to

Darkover. A few mentioned dance and how important it was to the people here.

Only men laugh. Only men weep. Only men dance. It was one of their favorite proverbs. So was, *Any time three Darkovans get together, they hold a dance.*

Yet there was nothing at all on the stranger who'd performed the night before. I didn't even know his name.

She leaned against the wall just inside the door. "*Dom* Ridenow sends his regards and hopes you are feeling better."

"That's kind of him."

"He also offered a ride outside the city, if you're interested. He'll arrange some horses."

While it would be better than walking, I wasn't entirely sure I was up to the challenge of dealing with an animal. "I'll probably fall off."

"He promised to be gentle and to lend you his most sedate horse."

This was likely another attempt to get us out of our routine. I owed her my company, I supposed, for all her support. I also wondered if it was because she needed a male escort so her sharing company with a Darkovan noble wouldn't seem improper.

So back to Comyn Castle we went. The skies were overcast, hinting at snow, but Captain Maeda would not be swayed from her adventure. *Dom* Ridenow met us in the courtyard, where grooms held the reins for three horses. At his gesture, a groom urged one of the horses to lie down.

Well. That solved my problem of how to mount. With the groom's assistance, I managed to get a leg over the saddle and then hung on tightly as the horse lurched upright once more. A little fussing with the stirrup lengths, and we were fit to ride.

I admit, I enjoyed the novelty of being astride a horse, and appreciated the animal putting up with my awkwardness. Riding was freeing in a way I had not felt in some time; and instead of two good legs, I had four that carried me down roads and over hills, that reacted to my desires and became a companion in my adventure. Other than a dog in my childhood, I hadn't been around animals at all and enjoyed the novelty.

It was atop a hill while we were admiring the view when I finally had a chance to ask, "Where is the dancer from last night? Does he live in the city?"

"For now, he is a guest at Comyn Castle. We have a Tower there that we use intermittently; he is assisting us with it for a while."

"Tower?" I couldn't imagine what he would be doing there. He didn't seem to be the type to aid in any sort of construction. Designer, perhaps?

"A Tower is like a communications center," Captain Maeda told me. "Their telepaths work there and can send messages to one another. They also study matrix stones and—am I getting this right?"

"It's a simplified answer, but yes," *Dom* Ridenow said. "I spent some time in a Tower myself when I was younger and quite enjoyed it. Nice to be away from the crowds and family duties."

I had a dozen other questions, though none of them seemed polite to ask. I was the third wheel in this outing, anyway, and thought it better to keep what distance I could. They were friends; more than friends, perhaps, but it wasn't my place to pry.

Dinner followed, a lavish meal shared in *Dom* Ridenow's suite. The conversation was pleasant and inclusive, and I enjoyed seeing the captain having a good time. Eventually, though, I had to see to my personal needs and took the opportunity to leave them alone for a little while.

The halls were deserted; this wasn't Council season, so there were few Comyn in residence. *Dom* Ridenow stayed there largely because of its proximity to the Spaceport. So I was surprised to see a familiar, lithe figure and his bodyguards down one of the corridors.

I'm sure I was breaking some protocol to leave so abruptly, not to mention being extremely rude to wander around uninvited, but I couldn't miss my chance to speak to the dancer again.

I was slow, though—frustratingly so, even when I used the walls for support. I lost him after the third turn, and after glancing up and down the halls, I had no idea where to go.

Then I saw his guards walking toward me—and he wasn't with them.

I waited until they passed and went the direction they'd come from, ending up at an ornately carved wooden door. I'd never been very assertive, so it took all my courage to knock on a stranger's door.

After a few moments, a sharp-faced older woman answered. She looked me up and down and frowned. "Are you lost, Terran?"

"I'm sorry to disturb you, but I'm looking for a dancer that went this way. Is he here?"

"You dare refer to our Keeper in such crude terms?"

"Keeper? I'm sorry. I don't even know his name. I just—I saw him dance. That's all I know about him." I put a hand against the doorway, needing the support just to keep standing.

The woman frowned more deeply. "You are out of sorts. If you do not calm yourself, you will disrupt our work."

"Forgive me. I don't mean to be offensive, but I am not used to your customs and I do not know what this place is."

"Obviously." She opened the door wider. "Enter. You may wait in the foyer while I see if Kieran is willing to speak to you."

Kieran. At least now I had a name.

A crackling fire warmed the room, and I selfishly pulled a chair over and sat close to the flames, leeching as much heat as I could. So pleasant was the feeling that I was not aware of how much time passed, or in fact that I wasn't alone.

"You are persistent, Terran."

And there he was, dressed in a loose shirt and pants that spoke of comfort. Indeed, he seemed in his element here, far more at ease than when last I'd seen him. "I was passing by. And it was cold."

"Is your home planet truly so warm? I think I would perish without snow."

"And I fear I will perish *in* the snow." There came an awkward silence, and I again felt the fool. What had I expected when I found him? "You are well?"

"You seem overly concerned."

"I just thought…when the guards…"

"Ah. My protectors."

"Are you in danger?"

He was silent a moment. "I am different."

I desperately wanted to ask him how, why, but had the sense that would be terribly rude. "Are you happy?"

That caught him off guard, and it took him a long time to answer. "Why is that important to you?"

"Because…" I felt silly for saying so, but lying would be worse. "Because other than my captain, you're the only person I've worried about for months. When I saw you before, you seemed…lonely." Or perhaps it was merely my own projection.

"You are kind to be so concerned, but you need have no fear. I am not in danger here, and while I would prefer some things to be other than they are, I am not unhappy."

"Good." It was strange how relieved I was. "I should go. My captain will wonder where I am." Though my legs had begun to ache, and the thought of standing, let alone finding my way back through that maze of corridors was not appealing.

"Word has been sent. You may bide here as long as you need to."

I didn't ask how they'd sent a message. No one had left the room. Maybe it was one of their telepathic messages—or maybe they had another exit and had sent a note with a runner.

"I've asked for some—ah, here we are," he said as a younger woman came in carrying a tray with a carafe, glasses and a plate of cookies. "Thank you, Elorie."

She nodded at him and grinned at me as she began to pour what looked like some type of cider.

"If I am to be here for a while—forgive me if this discomfits you, but I've been upright far too long today." I rolled up my trouser legs, glancing at my hosts to gauge their reaction, and too sore and tired to care if they stared.

They watched—but it was the supportive interest of a friend, not the gazing anywhere but at my abbreviated limbs like most Terrans. I pressed the releases on my false legs and removed them both, along with the socks that covered the ends of my stumps. The skin—still thin and tender—was red. Damn. If I wasn't careful, I'd rub it raw and not be able to wear my legs at all.

"You poor thing! Does it hurt?"

"A little," I admitted.

"I have just the thing. I'll be right back." She hurried off, leaving me a little stunned by her zealousness.

"Elorie is a healer in training. Please excuse her curiosity; she's fascinated by the difference in our methods compared to the Terrans. She will dote on you, if you let her." The statement seemed more of an order than an observation, but I remained loathe to accept assistance. I'd already overstayed my welcome and had no desire to be a burden.

But when she returned with a pleasant-smelling salve, I saw how much pleasure it gave her to be of use so I let her do as she would and helped myself to one of the sweet, crumbling cookies and spiced cider. When she rubbed the abused skin, she was both expert and gentle and didn't leave me feeling like just another patient, the way the Terran therapists did. She ran her thumb along the still-visible scar. "This is recent, isn't it?"

"Eight months ago. Darkover is my first trip since…" Even now, I found it hard to talk about.

"I thought the Terrans were good at saving or re-growing limbs."

"They are. But there was nothing to save, and they decided I was not a good candidate for regrowth." In truth, I hadn't been sure if I could endure the process, despite their reassurances. "I can still feel my legs. My real ones. It's the oddest sensation." When they didn't hurt like hell, at least.

"Really? I've heard such tales, though I haven't seen any cases in person. May I?" she asked, gesturing to a leg, and I assented. She inspected it inside and out, marveling at the construction. The artificial limbs had the shape of human legs and feet, and while the tone matched my flesh, they lacked…hair, for one thing. Real toenails. I was supposed to get an upgrade once my body had gotten used to these, but the adjustment had been slow and not helped by the persistent pain. "They're made well, but they don't seem to fit you."

Somehow, it didn't surprise me that she'd identified my problem so easily. "They take some getting used to."

"Men," she said with an aggrieved look at Kieran. "Always think they have to wear pain like a badge of honor. It's no wonder he didn't want to dance at the festival."

"That's not why—well, not the only reason," I said, ashamed. "I was never very coordinated even when I had feet, so I took up piano and guitar, among other things."

Elorie brightened at that. "We have a harp here. Perhaps you might play for us? I'd love to hear some Terran tunes."

"Yes, please!" My guitar had been lost with the ship, and I'd missed it. Within a few moments, I was provided a small harp-like instrument called a *rryl*. It took a little getting used to because of the various levers, but I was proficient at enough stringed instruments that I was soon plucking out folk tunes from different areas of Terra.

I admit, I purposefully chose tunes with pronounced rhythm, designed to get people moving. It was entirely selfish because I wanted to see Kieran dance. Badly.

It wasn't until I was playing a tango that he rose to his feet and started to sway, and it was all I could do to stay focused enough on the *rryl* to keep my fingers steady.

A strangeness overcame me, as if I, too, was whirling along with Kieran, going faster and faster, overcome with the pure joy of movement. My fingers kept plucking strings, but my mind was elsewhere. Flying.

Dancing.

There came a tune layered over mine, different yet complimentary. The music merged, blended, just as we became one in the dance, although I was not moving at all—

Then, suddenly, everything stopped, and exhaustion swept over me, so profound that I would have dropped the *rryl* had Elorie not snatched it from my hands.

Kieran crouched at my side, eyes full of concern. "Forgive me. I was careless to let you get caught up in rapport."

I wasn't entirely sure what he meant; getting caught up in music was such a natural thing for me that I hadn't thought it out of the ordinary. "I think I've overdone things. If you can communicate with the Spaceport, they'll send a transport for me. I won't be your problem anymore."

"Perhaps I enjoy this sort of problem. Having a musical Terran who is curious rather than close-minded for company is refreshing."

"I'm glad of that, at least."

He smiled. "Stay for the night. Rest. We have rooms to spare."

"Is that wise? He's not even a telepath," said the hawk-faced woman who'd opened the door. She'd wandered in sometime during my playing.

"I am Keeper. I will take responsibility and ensure there is no distraction."

She remained displeased, but gave him a slight nod of acknowledgement. The exchange left me feeling awkward. The offer was kind, if impractical; these rooms were not designed to accommodate anyone with a handicap. "You're kind, but I really should find my captain and head back to the spaceport." Which had the wheelchair I hated, grab bars, physical therapists, and a voice-activated emergency system if I fell and couldn't get up. All amenities I wished I didn't need.

"I wouldn't advise it." He pulled aside the drapes to reveal thick clumps of snow blowing against the panes. "This blizzard will last through the night. Even a Terran transport would have difficulty."

So I was trapped, though a part of me didn't mind at all. For a little while, I'd been free of always having to pretend everything was fine for the captain's sake. I'd remembered what happiness had felt like—and so had Kieran.

"Let's get you settled," Kieran said, and between him and Elorie I managed to get my legs on and walk into a nearby bedroom, which was tidy with a comfortable-looking bed and anything I might need within reach, including a bell, a pitcher of water and a chamber pot.

The bed was warm and welcoming, the sheets scented with something soothing akin to lavender. I was exhausted enough to fall asleep easily, but the strangeness of the evening left my dreams uneasy. I'd thought my terror gone, left behind at the hospital on Vainwal.

I was wrong.

We'd all felt the impact; a sharp thud that had rocked the ship just enough to startle us. Turbulence, we'd figured.

Until the alarms sounded.

The consoles lit up with warnings. I had to yell over the emergency klaxons. "We're losing power and the backups aren't functioning. Whatever hit us sliced into the engines."

The ship lurched, then began losing altitude at an alarming rate. The other crew members dived for their stations, and for a while the only sound was a steady screeching from the alarms.

Captain Maeda stood behind me, reading the screens with grim acceptance. We'd practiced for such emergencies, yet those drills were nothing compared to the reality that we would likely die.

"Right the ship, Lieutenant. Pull us out of the dive."

She may as well have been giving me an order to change course toward Terra, so quiet and calm was she. I'll never know how I managed to right the ship just enough to prevent a complete nosedive. I'd never been one to believe in miracles, but I did then.

We landed on the water, skipping across the surface like a stone. Each bounce threw us across the deck. Pain burst in my head and neck as I slammed against the base of a chair.

Then we hit land, and skidded. There came a horrid screeching of stone tearing through metal as easily as scissors through cloth. I had just enough time to glance up and see a cliff face coming inevitably nearer—and the captain lying too close to the ship's nose.

I dove for her, shoving her out of the way just as we collided with a wall of stone. The ship crumpled, squeezing together like an accordion.

I must have blacked out. When I came to, the air was filled with dust and smoke. Captain Maeda was sitting by me, lightly slapping my face with one hand. She held one arm against her chest, and from the angle I could tell it was broken. "Ethan? Ethan, stay with me. The medics will be here soon."

I didn't know why she sounded so worried. I was fine. At least I thought so, until I tried to move and couldn't. The lower half of my body was trapped beneath a twist of metal and stone.

"Ethan? Look at me. You keep looking right here."

So I looked, too afraid to see the rest of the deck. There were no other voices, no sounds save for the ocean now audible through the ruined walls. They were dead, then. All dead, save for the Captain and I.

We'd ended up trapped on some rocky outcrop out in the ocean and far enough from the populated areas that it took the emergency crews more than an hour to reach us and longer still to send the heavy lifting equipment needed to extricate me. And broken arm and concussion or not, Captain Maeda refused to leave until I was free.

But whatever the medics dosed me with didn't kick in fast enough. They pried apart twisted metal and slid me free.

That's when I saw my legs.

Or rather, what was left of them. Little more than mangled flesh and splintered bone. Until that moment, there hadn't been any pain. Adrenaline, the doctors had told me. Shock. But days after the accident, the image stayed with me. So did the pain even when the doctors did the amputations: a terrible, burning agony that spread through my whole body and—

"Ethan. Wake up. You're safe."

I struggled to open my eyes, but even when I did all I saw was twisted metal and lifeless bodies. My legs felt as if they were on fire and it was all I could do not to scream.

"Look at me, Ethan. Just focus on me."

Look at me. But it wasn't the Captain, this time; it was Kieran, and I couldn't understand why he would be in the middle of a wreck all the way out on Vainwal.

"Good. There you are. Keep looking right at me."

There was an edge to his voice that startled me into doing as he asked. Then he did something strange; he held his hand a few inches above my body and moved it slowly back and forth. There was something in his other hand. A stone? There were strange, sparkling lights in it that made me dizzy.

"Don't look at the starstone. It will make you sick."

"The...what?"

"It's called a starstone." His voice was distant, as though he was only partially listening to me. Elorie was off to the side, watching us, but she, too, seemed withdrawn and far away.

I...drifted. It was the only explanation for the strange, floating sensation. There was an odd tingling sensation that wore away at my fear the way ocean waves sculpt a beach. Through it all came a faint, strange tune, one so foreign I could put a name to neither melody nor rhythm, yet it was soothing all the same.

"Ethan?"

This time, when he said my name, it brought me back to myself—no terrible memories overlaying reality, and no more awful burning throughout my nonexistent limbs. I let out a long, relieved breath and sank back into the pillows. "Is that—what do you call it—*laran*?"

"Yes."

"Is that how you knew I...?"

"Was having a nightmare? Yes. Everyone here could sense it."

"I'm sorry."

"It happens. No one is angry. We're all telepaths here, so there is no hiding what we feel from each other."

"So everyone here saw...felt what I...oh, God." It made me feel suddenly, terribly naked, worse than taking off my legs and being obviously vulnerable. All the terrible things I'd been through, all my anger and grief laid out for all to see.

And all the pain...

"There is no shame in your feelings, however uncomfortable." He wrapped his strange stone in a bit of silk and tucked it away in a pouch that hung from his neck.

"What is that for?"

"It's a crystal that allows me to focus so I can monitor

problems within a body and properly adjust the energy channels. Yours had not adjusted to the loss of your limbs; that's why your brain kept trying to send signals where there was nothing to receive. Another session or two wouldn't hurt—"

"I can help with that," Elorie put in.

"—but the pain should be much less frequent."

"Thank you." I hardly knew what else to say. "Both of you. I'm grateful. You have no idea. The Terran doctors don't have anything so effective."

"You're welcome. Now I will leave you to rest. Your body needs time to adjust."

I watched him, the way he moved, the kindness he emanated. "You're beautiful."

The words dropped before I had a chance to catch them, and to my shame, he stiffened. Elorie let out a little gasp.

"I'm sorry. I didn't mean to—"

For the first time, his voice held an uncomfortable edge. "You are an off-worlder. There are things you do not understand about Darkover, about those who inhabit it."

"Then teach me."

There was his sad, heartbreaking smile. "Darkover is no place for you. Go home, Terran. What you seek does not lie here."

"And what do I seek?" All these mysteries frustrated me no end. "You can heal with this mind-magic of yours. Do you read minds too?"

"You long for beauty, and you think you have found it in me. I am not the means to your end, Terran. I cannot be."

And with that, he let himself out.

In the morning, it was not Kieran who brought me a tray for breakfast, but Elorie, and I couldn't help but notice that she was cooler toward me than she'd been last night. "I'm sorry." I was beginning to feel like an audio file on repeat. "I meant no offense, especially to Kieran. There's so much I don't understand."

She softened at that. "I know, Ethan. Please understand, it's difficult for us, too, but maybe I can help." She seated herself in the chair next to my bed and looked at me earnestly. "Ask what you need. I know you have questions, and I don't think they're about me."

She was right, but since she offered I figured it was best to simply ask. "May I ask why he is different?"

"Kieran? One of his parents was a *chieri*, which is a very ancient and respected race here on Darkover. He's far older than he looks. Legend says that's how *laran* came into our lines, because our ancestors lay with the *chieri*. Like them, he is also *emmasca*. Do you know what that means?"

Not specifically, but I could hazard a guess. "Emasculated? Male, but without...?"

"The preferred term is neuter. Between genders. It's necessary for him as a Keeper because of the way he uses energy. He's partially human, but the part of him that isn't can react strongly to someone he's attuned to emotionally. When that happens, he can shift to either male or female—a process that can take hours, and which causes emotional instability. Some liken the effect to madness. So I beg you—please be careful in your approach toward him. He cares for you, but we—his circle—need him to help us in our work and can't allow him great distractions."

So that was why they'd reacted so poorly; I presented a danger, despite my best intentions. "I will be more careful in the future. No more distractions. I promise."

"You play wonderfully though," she said, and grinned. "You made him happy last night, and we thank you for that."

I hadn't ruined everything, at least. "That's why he has guards, isn't it? To protect him from the crowds?" Again I felt sympathetic toward Kieran, who was stared at and followed wherever he went. I knew the feeling.

Elorie nodded. "Would you like me to work on your legs a little more?"

"Yes, please." They were already itchy, which was an improvement over the burning, but still an annoyance, and I'm sure she was as eager as me to try the treatment.

She'd just finished when the hawk-faced woman rushed in. "*Messire, Dom* Ridenow requests to see you in his suite.

Immediately."

From her face, I knew it was urgent. Something had happened to the captain; there was no other reason he'd send for me like this.

Elorie hurriedly helped me to get dressed and mobile then guided me to the Ridenow wing. Her face was sympathetic as she left me in the sitting room, where *Dom* Ridenow strode in.

"Ethan."

I barely knew the man, but I knew the tone; it was the same the Terran doctors had used when they'd told me my legs couldn't be saved, or that they weren't going to try any further treatments. The captain had used it too, when she'd told me we were the only survivors. I couldn't speak; all I could do was sit there, waiting with a sudden, terrible dread.

"Your captain…Noriko…"

It had been so long since I'd heard anyone call her by her first name. He'd cared for her. They'd been friends.

"Her room was empty when I rose this morning. The Terrans said she hadn't been back, so I sent the guards to search. They found her buried in the snow at the base of one of the walls. She fell from one of the balconies."

He was watching me. Gauging me with that eerie sixth sense he had. I recognized the look now that I'd spent time with Kieran and his friends. "Where is she now?"

"We called the Terrans. They came to fetch her body."

It sunk in, then, what he was trying to tell me. My captain had left me alone on a strange world I didn't understand and certainly didn't fit in. "She fell?"

"We don't know. No one else was up there with her. It's possible she went out for some air and slipped on some ice."

Possible. But why would she venture outside, alone, during a blizzard? The captain never did anything without reason—even if that reason was too awful to contemplate. "You were her friend. Why didn't you stop her?"

"I didn't know."

It was his earnestness that broke me. "You're a damn telepath. How could you not know?"

"I'm only an empath, and not a terribly strong one. I didn't pry. Whatever I sensed from her was on the surface, and there was no hint of..." He went silent, but from the creases in his face I knew he was in at least as much pain as I was. Irrationally, it made me want to twist my verbal knife deeper.

"You should have done something. She was your guest. You were supposed to look after her!" If only because she hadn't allowed me to do it myself—because I'd failed her, too.

His face tightened. He could sense my anger. I was hurting him.

I *wanted* him to hurt.

"Ethan."

I left him there and stumbled blindly through the corridors. He'd been right; this place was a maze. I didn't care. I went left and right and left again, passing carved doors, stone archways. I fell more than once, scraping fingers against the stone walls as I righted myself on shaking legs.

I kept walking anyway. My stumps throbbed inside their manufactured prisons. The pain only made me angrier and gave me the strength to keep walking.

A blast of cold air hit me as I found my way outside onto a large balcony deep with snowdrifts. The doctors had warned me about the limits for my legs. The electronics didn't deal well in extreme temperatures. Wandering around in knee-high snow in frigid air wasn't advisable, and I could already tell the servos were slowing down. Each step was harder and slower than the last.

I plowed forward, heedless of the danger. I had to get to the edge—and when I got there, I saw just how far the drop was. Not enough to make me dizzy, but plenty far enough to cause considerable damage—or worse—should someone go over the edge. The wall was relatively low. It would take much for a man—even a crippled one—to climb over.

"Ethan."

It wasn't *Dom* Ridenow. "Leave me alone." I was too angry, too upset for anyone with that damned mind-magic to be near me, and from what Elorie said, I shouldn't be near Kieran at all.

"I don't think that's a good idea." Kieran draped a heavy, fur-lined cloak around my shoulders. "Come in. You'll freeze to death."

An image of my captain doing just that flashed into my mind. It wasn't hard to imagine her crumpled and broken, all warmth and life draining away. I was the last one from our crew left alive, and I didn't know why. "I shouldn't be here."

Kieran kept a firm grip on my arms. "She brought you to Darkover for a reason."

That wasn't what I'd meant. Not entirely. I didn't know why he'd care, not when I'd been such a distraction.

"Don't worry about that now. I care, Ethan. So do Elorie and *Dom* Ridenow."

I glanced back toward the door. There was the Comyn lord along with Kieran's two bodyguards, keeping a respectable distance. Elorie was there too, wrapped in a cloak of dark blue. She took a couple steps forward but stopped when I flinched. "You should go back to your tower. Both of you." I just wanted him to leave me alone so I didn't end up hurting him, too.

He gave a little sigh of exasperation. "Can you walk?"

Experimentally, I shifted. The reaction was sluggish, but the leg behaved.

Two steps later, it froze completely, and I stood there, tears rimming my eyes, more frustrated and angry and helpless than I'd been when I'd been trapped on the ship. I couldn't move. The red sun gave off such a strange light that I couldn't think, and it was so damnably cold on this planet.

I howled. I didn't care who was listening, or if the whole damned castle had people staring out the windows. The sound was so loud that it bounced off the stone walls and sent a terrible echo around the balcony.

I couldn't even collapse into the snow like I wanted to because my damned legs wouldn't cooperate. My tears were freezing to my cheeks; I hadn't cried since the accident. I'd done my best to be strong for the captain, to be what she'd needed me to be.

And in the end, it hadn't been enough.

Then came the gentlest of touches to my mind. I felt...a word? A feeling? Something, floating in my mind: *Grieve.*

I was no telepath. I'd never shown the barest hint of being able to sense anything out of the ordinary. And yet I *felt* them, all three of them, male, female, and—what *was* Kieran?

And there, at last, I found the beauty I'd been longing for in the joining of emotions—in the sheer need to understand one another and to know that I was not the only one in such deep, desperate pain.

I knew now why the captain had liked *Dom* Ridenow. He was an honorable man, a trait that ran strongly through Darkovan society, but especially within him. Neither was he afraid of his own emotions or anyone else's, although too many could overwhelm him, and he knew the trials of duty and the rare moments of pleasure. He, too, grieved, because he'd failed to save a friend, and in doing so caused another man despair.

Kieran was the strongest and strangest; again I heard that strange, unearthly tune. And for the first time, he let me sense his own loneliness, his own uneasiness at being the odd one out and having to learn new, different ways of living amongst those fully human. He was known for his dancing, and had brought that from his non-human kin, but it had been so long since he'd danced of his own accord, and not out of some formal obligation. I'd given him that, at least, though it was little enough to repay him for his own kindnesses toward me.

And Elorie...she was the warmth, the love and support we all craved and needed, and we drank it up like fine wine. She gave of herself freely, finding her own joy in being of service.

The rapport ended slowly, carefully. Kieran held me, and I was no longer cold. Neither was my grief so crippling that it drove me to madness.

"Learn to walk on your own," he told me when I gazed, stunned, into his silver-gray eyes. "Then I'll teach you to dance."

All I could do was nod, giddy with the knowledge that I wasn't alone.

Not anymore.

The Terrans came for me. Had I been more coherent I would have objected, but after losing one officer I think the Darkovans were afraid of more interplanetary difficulties should they lose another, so they handed me over.

The Terran doctors wouldn't let me wear my legs until the abscesses healed, so I was stuck wheeling myself around in the hated chair. This wouldn't have worked inside Comyn Castle, but I missed it all the same. At least there I'd been an outsider among outsiders and not feeling like an outcast among my own kind. The Spaceport was too clean and sterile, and the Terran lights, yellow instead of the red of the Darkovan sun, burned my eyes.

It took two days before I could bring myself to enter the captain's quarters. She'd left what remained of her possessions to me, save for a couple trinkets she'd wished *Dom* Ridenow to have. Many of her captain's logs were still restricted, and given access only to the Service command, but in her will were the passwords to the private entries in her tablet.

I made myself comfortable on her bed and watched as many as I could. There were things she hadn't told me, like the numerous counselors she'd seen after the accident and the antidepressants she'd been prescribed but refused to take. *Dom* Ridenow was her one link to happiness, during the times she'd enjoyed herself on Vainwal. She'd loved the atmosphere, everything from gravity dancing to walks through the lush surroundings to lying on the beach listening to the waves. She'd needed pleasure, and he'd been happy to be her companion.

But I'd only guessed the edge of her pain. Losing colleagues paled in comparison to losing those under her command along with an entire ship. Our superiors hadn't blamed her; it was a freak accident. Nothing she could have done. Yet she poured out her grief in those entries, and as the days went on, I saw her spiral farther and farther down.

"If it weren't for Ethan, I wouldn't be here," she said bluntly. "He needs me, and I owe him whatever support I can muster. He'll walk again. I'll make sure of it. And he'll have a life where he can be happy. He deserves that."

"So do you," I told her image. But it didn't matter now. She was dead. And I was far from happy.

"I'm going back to Vainwal," *Dom* Ridenow told me one afternoon. We'd taken the horses out again, and this time he'd brought along a hawk to hunt with. I thought it fascinating the way a wild creature would willingly return to his gloved hand.

We were little alike, drawn together only because Captain Maeda had left a gaping absence in both our lives, but I'd come to value his friendship. Save for a few small allowances, such as a kneeling horse, he didn't treat me as a cripple or let my disability become a hindrance. If anything, he encouraged me to far more freedoms than the Terrans, and through him, I'd started to think of Darkover as home. "I'll miss your company."

"Will you stay?"

I'd already checked the opportunities for a transfer once I'd been cleared medically. There were jobs in translation, communications, and even a liaison or two, though I lacked the qualifications for the latter. None of those required the physicality the Service didn't trust me to regain, though it meant I would be grounded for a while. In the end, that was fine. I wasn't ready to be on another ship with another captain. "Probably. Kieran owes me a dancing lesson, after all."

He nodded and lifted his hand. The hawk launched into the air, circling.

For a few months I kept my distance from Kieran. I meant to keep my promise, both to look after myself and to not be a distraction, although I still met with Elorie at Comyn Castle for sessions to heal my legs.

"Much better," she said when we'd finished. "How's the pain?"

"Gone."

"And the bad dreams?"

"Better." Between her and the Terran counselors, the trauma from losing both captain and ship had lessened to a bearable grief, and little by little, I'd been managing to find beauty in the simple, everyday things. I'd gotten a new guitar and Elorie had managed to find me a *rryl* of my own, which helped.

"Good."

She helped me with my prosthetics, new ones since I'd ruined the last pair. These were simpler, less lifelike, but they fit better and didn't have the weight of memory the others did. With these, I could start over. Walk better. Find a future by myself.

"Kieran is leaving soon."

"Oh?"

"Back to the Hellers."

"Oh." I couldn't follow him there; I still coped poorly with the cold weather, and new legs or not I wasn't ready for rough terrain.

"The spring equinox festival is coming up soon. We'll have dancing." There was a spark of mischief in her eyes; I wondered what she was up to.

"I'd better learn, then." I'd hoped Kieran would keep his offer to teach me, but I supposed it wasn't to be. He'd nearly finished his work here and would be needed elsewhere.

"You'd better." She reached for the *rryl* leaning against the wall and plucked a few notes. "Stand up. Close your eyes. This is your first lesson: just listen."

I did as she asked while she played a lively tune not entirely unfamiliar. After a while, I couldn't help but bounce a little to the beat. I was a musician, after all; I had rhythm, if not coordination.

Someone threaded their fingers through mine.

Six fingers.

I opened my eyes and there he was, silvery hair, gray eyes, and I couldn't keep from squeezing his hands with joy.

"I thought it was time for a distraction," Kieran said. "And I had a promise to keep."

"I thought you were leaving."

"I might be persuaded to stay for a while. Someone ought to make sure our newest cultural liaison is comfortable with his duties."

"Was that your doing? I'm not exactly qualified to be any sort of liaison."

"It helps to be—what is your Terran word?—ah. A *celebrity*. Or a Comyn, in *Dom* Ridenow's case. I believe he wrote a letter on your behalf."

"Then thank you to you both."

Elorie hadn't stopped playing, but the song had changed to a calmer, yet no less rhythmic one, and she began to sing with a sweet, lilting voice. I didn't understand the words, but that didn't matter; I knew it was about love.

"Time for your first lesson, I think. Are you ready?"

"Yes. No. I don't know." I'd wanted this more than anything, but now that my chance was here, I was nervous.

"Just follow my lead." He put a hand to my waist…

…and we danced.

SACRIFICE

by Steven Harper

Each of these anthologies stands on its own, welcoming back old friends as well as introducing those new to the world of the Bloody Sun. While an occasional story may refer to previous adventures of the same characters, as an editor I prefer those that require no prior acquaintance. There are always exceptions, however, stories that strike me as so powerful in their own right that they merit a place of their own. One such is the following tale, gritty and poignant, a "Darkover noir" detective story with a romantic twist.

Steven Harper Piziks was born with a name that no one can reliably spell or pronounce, so he often writes under the pen name Steven Harper. He lives in Michigan with his husband and sons. When not at the keyboard, he says, he plays the folk harp, fiddles with video games, and pretends he doesn't talk to the household cats. In the past, he's held jobs as a reporter, theater producer, secretary, and substitute teacher. He maintains that the most interesting thing about him is that he writes books. Most recently, he wrote the Books of Blood and Iron, a fantasy trilogy, for Roc Books.

The girl was fifteen years old and already dead. David North pulled his coat close against the gathering evening chill and squatted next to her. Back alleys were the same whether you were in Taiwan on Terra or Thendara on Darkover—filled with squelching mud and rancid air and soggy garbage. This girl didn't belong in such a place.

She was—had been—pretty enough. Her dark blonde hair was braided instead of held in a butterfly clip, which meant the main adult in her life still saw her as a child. Unusual. Far as North knew, you became an adult on Darkover at age fifteen. Someone in this girl's life was overprotective, even by local standards. Dress and cloak well-made. Copper necklace with a matching bracelet still on neck and wrist, a couple coins still in the pouch at her belt. So she came from a little money, but the killer's motive hadn't been robbery.

The burn that branded itself like sickly flower across her chest and the blaster that lay in the mud several feet away supported the no-robbery theory. You didn't use a blaster in a robbery. It was like using a cannon to swat a mosquito. North leaned over to examine the thing without touching it. Model X-17. Decent power range, adjustable from *what the hell?* to *pearly gates.* Common enough, carried by any number of Terrans. And strictly forbidden outside the spaceport.

"You see why we asked for you," said Loret Ridenow-Castamir. Her own auburn hair was pulled back with a blue butterfly clip that matched her cloak. "Why *I* asked for you."

"Who is she?" North asked. A few steps beyond them both stood a pair of guardsmen, their faces as stern as their pikes.

"Her name is Jaelle Castamir," Loret said. "She's my third cousin twice removed."

"How well did you know her?" North said.

"Not well. Her branch of the family tree is minor nobility with few ties to the Comyn."

"But enough ties to cause trouble," North said.

"A dozen cartloads of it," Loret agreed. "It's bad enough that it happened. Worse that it happened to one of the Comyn, no matter how minor. The Terran who killed her broke the Compact and our treaty with the Terran Empire."

"The killer might be from Darkover," North reminded her. "That blaster is point-and-poof. Anyone could use it."

"What are the chances a Darkovan got hold of a Terran blaster?"

"Just keeping an open mind." He examined Jaelle with quick efficiency with one eye on the setting sun. He wasn't a coroner, but if the fist-sized hole in her chest wasn't the cause of death, North would give his entire stipend to corner hookers. The girl's limbs were starting to show rigor, which meant she had probably died three or four hours ago. There were instruments at the spaceport that would pinpoint her death to the microsecond, but this was technically a Darkovan matter, so North was stuck with Darkovan methods. He took from his pocket a notebook and made a hasty sketch of the crime scene. Darkover didn't go for cameras.

"Who would normally investigate?" North said while he drew.

"The city guard, of course." Loret chewed her lip. "But that blaster involves the Compact, which means the killer is probably involved with the Comyn, which means the guard—"

"—won't investigate lords and ladies," North finished. "I get it. We have politicians in the Empire, too."

"This couldn't come at a worse time," Loret said tightly. "Just when Lord Hastur is negotiating a new accord with the Legate that will grant Darkover access to certain Terran medicines."

"Wow. Major concession from Dan Lawton and the Empire. What did Darkover offer to get that?" North asked idly while his pencil moved across the paper. He didn't really care about batshit bureaucrats, but his subconscious was chewing over something he'd noticed at the scene and hadn't seen fit to tell his waking mind about it, and he needed the distraction until it did.

Loret looked uncomfortable. This got more of North's attention, and he looked at her over his notebook. North could pass for a native easily enough. His ash-blond hair, thick build, and bland features blended easily into a Darkovan crowd. However, at the moment he was wearing a Terran shirt and trousers with a long, heavy coat from the stores at Thendara spaceport, where he currently lived. The clothes and coat looked out of place among the inhabitants of Cottman IV—Darkover, to the natives—who preferred medieval-style tunics and cloaks. And swords. And occasional telepathy. North cocked his head at Loret.

"What did Darkover offer the Empire?" he repeated.

Again, she hesitated, and North's unease grew. Loret was generally unflappable, and she rarely missed a chance to say what was on her mind. Her unease was contagious. At last, she wet her lips.

"*Kireseth* pollen," she said quietly.

North went dead still. Just hearing the name awoke in his gut a hungry worm that gnawed at his insides, made his hands shake just a little. Two years ago back on Terra, North had been a city detective who had discovered his nephew—one among a family of addicts—had overdosed on Kira Ann, a new and highly addictive designer drug. Driven by both guilt and anger, North had tracked the source to Darkover, where he had learned Kira Ann was made from the pollen of *kireseth* flowers. North and Loret had barely stopped one of Loret's relatives from using the drug's addictive powers and its ability to enhance *laran*—telepathy—to take over both Terra and Darkover. In the process, North had been forcibly addicted to Kira Ann. Even with the help of Terran doctors and Darkovan healers, North had endured weeks of painful withdrawal before he'd finally shaken himself free of it. Loret and North had destroyed every speck of Kira Ann in existence, but the stuff still echoed in North's body and brain. Just talking about it awoke an edge of hunger. He snapped his notebook shut.

"Why?" he asked, and his voice was hoarse. "Why in hell?"

"One of your medical scientists thinks he can use *kireseth* pollen to synthesize useful—"

"Useful?" North interrupted. "*Useful?* Jesus! That shit gets off Darkover again, and we're cooked."

"The pollen can't get off Darkover, you know that," Loret said quietly. "When you put *kireseth* pollen on one of your Terran ships and jump, something wrecks it on the molecular level. The pollen has to be treated here, and the new drugs synthesized here."

"That's what happened before. It's a nightmare!" North snapped. "It's—"

"Maybe," Loret jerked her head at the two guards, "we could talk about this another time. We have a dead girl and a Terran weapon."

North pursed his lips. Loret was right. A killer was getting farther and farther away with every passing second. With effort, North brought himself back around to the filthy alley. The thing was still tugging at him.

"I'll need this," he grunted, and wrapped the blaster in one of Loret's handkerchiefs. "Does Thendara have a morgue? She shouldn't be buried until we finish hunting the killer, but she sure as hell can't stay here."

"The family will take her, and they'll want to hold her funeral right away," Loret said doubtfully.

"They may be in for a delay." North put the blaster in his coat pocket and the thing that had been bothering him went *ding* in his head. Finally! He pointed to a spot near the alley wall, a spot that his subconscious had been poking at for several minutes now. "Those footprints have treads on them. Terran shoes."

Loret went over for a look. "So the killer was Terran after all."

"Or was a witness." North took a tape measure from his pocket and ran it over the print. "Forty-one centimeters long. A teen or adult. Probably male." He straightened, and his joints made popcorn noises. He took another look at the girl who had taken her last breath at an age when life was just getting started. "The guards can take the body. Tell them to ask around the neighborhood to see if anyone saw anything and report back to us. You and I have stuff to see and people to do."

He strode from the alley without further comment. Loret spoke with the guards, then hurried to catch up.

Thendara was a city of wood, stone, and thatch. Houses clustered near courtyards like witches around their cauldrons, and a potion of people in tunics, cloaks, and long dresses curled through the streets. Winter was the dominant season, thanks to the weak red sun, and even the short summer was chilly. For all that, North actually liked the place. He had originally intended to go back home after eliminating the source of Kira Ann, but the addiction had forced him to stay and recover with the help of Darkovan healers. During that time, the fresh, unspoiled planet had grown on him. Darkover held a *screw you* attitude toward the Terran Empire that North couldn't help but admire, and its people remained stubbornly attached to their independence, despite the Empire's attempts to lure them—and their telepathic overlords—into the fold. As a reward for North's work and sacrifice, Lord Regis Hastur had handed him an extended visa and even an extended stipend. North had accepted, as much to his own surprise as anyone else's. Now North wandered freely between the Terran spaceport and Thendara, doing a little of this and a little of that, becoming an unofficial envoy to both worlds. This was another reason why news of the trade of *kireseth* pollen for meds had shocked North so deeply. Even an unofficial envoy should know these things.

"Two steps," North said. "We need to find out who owns this blaster, and we need to talk to Jaelle's family. Preferably before they have time to cook up a story."

"And before the sun sets and everyone goes to bed," Loret agreed. "We'll have to investigate the blaster at the spaceport, but you Terrans don't live by the sun and they'll still be awake later. Let's talk the family first."

They were speaking *casta*. North had spent considerable time with tutoring programs, and discovered a talent for the language. As time passed, North found he enjoyed speaking in liquid *casta* syllables. By unspoken agreement, he and Loret spoke *casta* in Thendara and Terran Standard at the spaceport.

"Jaelle was killed in that alley, not just dumped there, so she must live within walking distance," North said. "Do you know where?"

Loret gestured. "It's not far."

They walked in tense silence for a few moments. The red sun slid down to touch the rooftops, tipping them with blood. Then Loret said, "I should have told you."

"How do think this'll help anyone?" North burst out. "Kira Ann was the most addictive, most destructive pot of piss ever invented on this planet. In this *universe*. We almost killed ourselves wiping that shit out. Now Terra is making deals with Darkover for more?"

"They don't want Kira Ann." Loret sighed as they walked. "The lead scientist claims he can make other medicines with *kireseth,* medicines that will save countless lives. That's what the Comyn want."

"What can he make that helps?" North demanded. "Kira Ann was a real killer."

"The researcher thinks he can create a drug to cure threshold sickness among the Comyn-born."

North worked his jaw. Threshold sickness had killed countless Comyn, people who were born with telepathic power, or laran. When these kids became teenagers, they were hit with the devil's double dose—adolescence and new *laran.* The transition was always painful and, too often, deadly.

"You can see why this got our attention," Loret continued quietly. "We already make *kirian* from *kireseth* pollen, but that only helps a little. The Keepers and the Comyn are both highly interested, despite their . . . wariness toward the Empire. It would save so many lives. My family alone has lost three to threshold sickness."

"Basic antibiotics would save even more," North replied. "But those lives wouldn't be Comyn."

"We can debate this all we want," Loret said tightly. "The fact is, the Comyn have allowed the Terran Empire to study *kireseth* pollen at the spaceport in exchange for some of the benefits it could provide. Lord Hastur and Legate Lawton made the decision before I heard about it, and they ignored my appeals. I should have told you about it, but I didn't want to cause you pain over something neither of us can do anything about. One thing we *can* do is find this killer."

North considered this. He liked Loret. She was stuck-up, prissy, and insisted on following even stupid rules just because they were rules. She was also sharp-minded, sharp-tongued, quick to forgive, and fun to argue with over dinner. His best friend on Darkover, or anywhere, though both of them would probably rather die than admit it.

"Find killer now, deal with drug deal later," he said finally with a grudging nod.

"Thank you," Loret replied. "I'll find a way to make it up to you."

North snorted. "I'd like to see that."

Through a back street, they arrived at a wide wooden gate set into a stone wall. It wasn't lost on North that this was a rear entrance, one for servants and deliveries. Loret pounded, and to her plain surprise, a young man opened the gate. He was perhaps nineteen, sharp-faced and foxy-featured, with a mop of red-blond hair.

"Dorn?" Loret said. "Goodness! You've grown since I've seen you last."

"Loret," said Dorn. His voice was quiet and subdued. "We got word from the guard about Jaelle. Are you here on a condolence call already?"

"We're here to find out who attacked her," Loret said. "The weapon was Terran, so I also called on my friend David North. He used to investigate this sort of thing for the *Terranan*." She turned to North. "Dorn is Jaelle's sister, so he's also my third cousin."

"*Vai dom.* I'm sorry for your loss," North said. As a detective on the force back home, he'd rather put his foot through a meat grinder than be the one to tell families about the death of a loved one. It was a bit of a relief that it had already been taken care of.

Dorn nodded an acknowledgment. Grief made his eyes look older and wiser.

"Why are you answering the gate?" Loret asked.

"Mother's in an uproar, and she's keeping the servants busy. Do you need to see her?"

"Earlier is better than later," Loret said.

Dorn gestured them in. Beyond the gateway courtyard lay a tall, thin house with narrow windows and, North figured, a lot of tight spiral staircases. It was a house of secrets, a citadel made for locking in and keeping out. They twisted their way through narrow, windowless corridors to a small door. Dorn put his hand on the latch.

"Will you find out who killed her?" he asked.

"We'll try our best," North said. He'd learned long ago never to make promises.

"Father's not here. It's shearing season, and he's out at the warehouse, inspecting the new fleeces. He probably doesn't even know yet. And Mother will want me to file a Declaration against the killer." Dorn said sadly. "I'll have to do it. Jaelle is—was—my sister. But I never learned much sword work."

"A Declaration?" North asked.

"A Declaration of Intent to Murder," Loret clarified. "Any member of the victim's family has the right to try to kill the murderer, even if it's a Terran, as long as they file with—"

"Department Three," North finished. "I remember now. Jesus."

"We'll try to help, Dorn," Loret said. "Don't worry."

"Wait here." Dorn slipped into the room. A rhythmic thumping thudded on the other side of the door. Loret waited patiently. North was wondering what it would be like to grow up in a house that was both big and confined. He'd lived in small apartments on Terra all his life, but at least he'd had a view of the street. This was living in a cave.

"I haven't seen Dorn since he was eleven or twelve," Loret mused. "He's a man now. Strange to think of him that way."

"This Declaration thing could really mess things up," North observed.

Loret nodded. "Even if the Empire and the Comyn smooth things over after we catch the killer, my cousins could start a fight all over again and stop the drug research anyway."

The thumping in the room ceased, then started up again. The door opened, and Dorn ushered them into the room with, Jesus yes, a window in it. The place was piled with cloth and bright skeins of yarn. In one corner sat a loom and a plump woman with red-brown hair pulled back in a butterfly clip. She worked the loom with hands and feet, zipping the shuttle back and forth with her hands and thumping the pedals with her feet, though her face carried the white, waxy look of someone who had just gotten the worst news imaginable and still didn't know what to do with it. North, who had watched his nephew twist his way through overdose and death, sympathized.

Dorn announced North and Loret to Lady Castamir, then touched Loret's hand and fled.

"Vai domna," Loret said formally.

The woman thumped the loom one more time, then stopped. Her shoulders were tight.

"Cousin Loret," she said, staring at the wall with her back to Loret and North. "You're here to deliver the bad news officially?"

"I'm so sorry, Cousin Cora," Loret said. "I'm not—"

"Is it true she was murdered by a *Terranan?*" Cora interrupted.

"We've only begun investigating," Loret said carefully. "The weapon was *Terranan,* but we don't know who pulled the trigger."

Cora refused to turn around. "And you brought one of the barbarians into our house under these circumstances?" she said to the wall.

Normally, North would have bristled a little, but he'd been on Darkover for quite a while now and he had become used to being called a barbarian, even by people who weren't justifiably upset. *"Domna,"* he said, "we want to find out who did this to her. To you. We know questions hurt, but the longer we delay, the harder it'll be to catch the bastard."

Cora remained silent, still facing the wall. North met Loret's eyes for a moment, then she asked, "Can you think of who might have done this? Did she or your family have any enemies? Anyone who would want to hurt her?"

"We have no enemies." Cora picked up the shuttle and turned it over in her fingers. "We aren't high lords and lofty ladies here. My husband is a wool merchant, and I weave to keep our household together. We have no real fortune or status among the Comyn. We're barely worth noticing. Even you don't acknowledge us."

Loret stiffened as the barb struck home. North hurried on before she could speak. "When did you last see Jaelle?"

"This afternoon. I needed some errands run and she volunteered to go. The market for vegetables, the buttery for cheese. Straight there, straight back. She was a good girl." Cora's voice took on a hard edge that said she was pushing tears away.

"Always a good girl."

"She was fifteen, is that right?" North said.

A nod, still staring at the wall.

"I noticed her hair was in braids instead of held with a clip. Was there a reason for that?"

"She was a good girl," Cora repeated, louder. "There was no hint of scandal about her."

"I'm not here to judge, *domna,*" North said. "I'm here to find her killer. Anything you can tell me—"

Cora slammed the shuttle through the loom and crashed down on the pedals. The loom leaped and snapped. "There was *nothing!*" she snarled. "Now get out! Out!"

North and Loret quickly withdrew, and this time a servant took them to the back gate. For a moment they stood outside in the gathering darkness. North looked up at the spindly rooftops of the house. These people owned a place big enough for a dozen apartments and had servants to show visitors in, but they didn't count as rich because they had to work. Wealth was a point of view, he supposed.

"I'm not a detective," Loret said. "I don't know what to do now."

"There's more to the story, that's obvious," North said. "I didn't say a thing about Jaelle's virtue, but Mom assumed I was thinking about it. They're your family. Any rumors?"

"Like I said, I barely know them."

"But Cora felt you should."

Loret spread her hands. "Cora's branch of the family has no wealth, no *laran*, no connections, and no power, so they're largely ignored. Their only hope to climb is for one of their children to marry up, and now Jaelle is dead. It's hard enough to find a higher match for a low-status girl. For a boy, it's worse. Not only that, murder will create a scandal, and keep matches for Dorn away."

"Even though Jaelle and her family are the victims," North said. "Not surprised. I've seen it before. Still, they're hiding something. If they have no power, why would anyone want to kill their daughter?"

"Maybe it was an accident," Loret said. "We're looking for something nefarious, when it might be just an innocent mistake."

"An accident with a Compact-busting blaster?" North snorted. "Doesn't seem likely. There's more here. I can smell it."

"The citadels of the Comyn are more than physical," Loret agreed. "The physical ones keep invaders out, the metaphorical ones keep secrets in. What do we do next?"

"We need to find out who owns this blaster. Then we—"

Before North could finish, the bolt shot on the other side of the gate and it cracked open. North tensed.

"Who is that?" Loret called.

Dorn slipped through the gate. "I'm glad I caught you," he said. "I don't have much time."

North, already on alert, asked, "What's up? I mean, *vai dom.*"

Dorn cast a glance back at the house. "Mother is grieving badly. We both are. She blames the *Terranan* for Jaelle's death."

"And do you?" Loret asked.

He looked away. North noticed the tear tracks on his face. "I don't know. My sister is dead, my father doesn't even know yet, and I'll have to file a Declaration. When Jaelle's body arrives, we'll have to arrange for a proper funeral. For my little sister."

"I'm very sorry," North repeated. There was nothing else to say.

"Did you have something to tell us?" Loret prompted.

Dorn glanced at the house again. "A couple days ago, I overheard Jaelle talking to one of her friends."

North's hands twitched. "And?"

He took a heavy breath. "She'd met a man of some kind."

"Who?" Loret asked.

"I don't know. I didn't overhear much. She met him in Thendara, and he's…he's a…"

North realized his fingers ached from clenching, and he forced himself to relax. "A…?"

"A *Terranan.*" The word burst from Dorn like a cork from a bottle. Once it was released, more words flowed. "She said she'd met him near the spaceport and he was older and she was in love. Or so she said."

The hair on North's neck went up. Loret gave him a sharp glance, and he knew she was thinking the same thing he was. "How much older?" he asked.

"I don't know," Dorn repeated. "I think Mother suspects something. I think she didn't want Jaelle running off with a barbarian, so she held off declaring Jaelle a woman."

"Does this barbarian have a name?" North interjected. "A description? Anything at all?"

"Jaelle called him *my space man.* That's everything else I know." Dorn lowered his voice, though they were alone at the gate. "Do you think he killed her?"

North touched the hard outline of the blaster in his pocket. "I think we need to find the space man."

"Find him, Cousin Loret," Dorn said, and his voice was angry now. "Find him and make sure the Comyn execute him. He killed my sister."

And he left.

"Jealous lover?" Loret asked when Dorn was gone. "Lovers' quarrel?"

"These Castamirs have no real status," North replied, saying thoughts aloud as they came to him, "so how much trouble will this really cause between Darkover and Terra?"

"A lot," Loret said. "The Comyn will close ranks against Terra. In their—our—view, even the lowest Comyn outranks the highest Terran. Lord Regis will have no choice but to respond. And if Cora makes Dorn file a Declaration, things will become even worse."

North caught the switch from *their* to *our.* Something occurred to him and he glanced at her. "Do you catch flak for being friends with me?"

"You mean trouble?" She pursed her lips. "There are…some who think being friends with a *Terranan* barbarian is a form of treason. And some who think a woman can't be friends with a man unless something untoward is going on."

"And what do you think?"

"I prefer the Terran response," she said. "They can shove it up their asses."

North snorted a laugh. "Is a Terran rubbing off on a real, live Darkovan, *domna?*"

Loret linked arms with him. "In the same way a Darkovan is rubbing off on a real live Terran, sir. And speaking of such things, let's find the owner of that blaster."

It was always a shock for North to go from wood-and-stone Thendara to the metal-and-plastic spaceport. But it was more than just buildings. Thendara lived and breathed. More and more lately, the spaceport lacked a soul. The people of Terra stayed inside as much as possible, glued to screens and VR displays, while the people of Thendara took every chance they could to go outdoors and talk to each other. It was also a jerk to switch from *casta* to Terran Standard.

The spaceport was more like a small city. An outer ring of shops catered to military and travelers, and also to Darkovans who wanted something exotic or who flirted with the forbidden. Next came an inner ring of bland, efficient apartments and homes. And in the center, a spire of headquarters and offices pierced the sky. As skyscrapers went, it was unimpressive, barely a hundred feet high. But on a place like Darkover, it became a citadel that dominated the landscape. It was to this building that North and Loret made their way. Outside, security was all but nonexistent. Terrans didn't worry about attacks from Darkover. If the ordinary populace attacked, it would be with primitive swords and shields, no match for even a single blaster, let alone a city chock full of them. And if the telepathic Comyn declared war on the spaceport…well, *that* attack would end faster than a wino could empty a bottle. So there was no need for border patrols or security in the outer rings. The inner spire, however, still required IDs and cred checks, something that always annoyed North.

"They know who I am on sight," he groused as the guard scanned their thumbprints and let them through the checkpoint into the main building. "But they still want my damn thumb."

"Rules are rules," Loret said, offering up her own thumb with smile. "Who are we seeing again?"

"Sammy. Third floor."

"Good. We can take the stairs like civilized people instead of huddling inside that awful elevator."

"What about efficiency?" North said as they hit the stairwell. "Kinda foolish to climb eight flights five times a day."

"There's efficiency, and there's deficiency," Loret replied. "You Terrans complain you need more exercise, then lazily avoid stairs."

They bickered more about it as they climbed, a relatively new habit North was enjoying. It was just nice to have someone to bicker with. Outside Sammy's office, North paused and said, "I know what you're doing."

"Doing?"

"You're distracting me from thinking about the research into *kireseth* pollen."

"Ah. I was hoping it wasn't obvious, but you're the detective." She drew him away from the door by the elbow. Other people, most of them in black Terran uniforms with stars blazing across their sleeves, passed them in the utilitarian hallway. North and Loret ignored them, but kept their voices down. "How *do* you feel about all this, North?"

He started to answer, then paused and grimaced. Saying the word *kireseth* aloud a moment ago had awoken echoes of the addiction again. Almost everyone in North's POS family had been an alcoholic or an addict, and North grown up swearing he would never touch a drop or flick a needle. He had remained pure to that promise despite all the odds—until Ferrick Alton had poured Kira Ann down North's throat and addicted him in a single dose. The horrific sweetness of that memory still followed him. In the end, Ferrick had been handed over to the Keepers for justice. They had scoured his mind clean of all thought and memory so he could spend his remaining days as a simple-minded stable worker. He'd been stopped and punished. But North had been left to deal with the aftermath, with the shakes and sweats and screams that Terran doctors and Darkovan healers could barely lessen, and the lingering hunger that still dogged him, probably would for the rest of his life. North had saved two planets from addicted slavery, and he'd sacrificed everything he had to do it. The thought of watching another fool poke the *kireseth* bear awoke both fear and rage in his gut. Since he'd left the alley, he'd kept all this at arm's length by focusing on Jaelle's killer, but Loret had brought the problem snarling back to him. A glance at her expression told him she understood every one of his thoughts, and that without touching the matrix chained at her neck. His poker face needed some work.

"The research has nothing to do with you," Loret said quietly. "It's not your fault, it's not your responsibility, it's not your worry."

"They're *coming* for me," he blurted out.

"Who is?"

"The Kira Ann dealers." He waved vaguely. "Ferrick Alton. I shoot awake at night with that damned Alton face leering over me, and he's pulling my mouth open like a dog's, and he's pouring his poison into it, and I can't move or stop him." Cold anxiety gripped his stomach. North was panting now, and sweat gathered at his hairline. "I expect him around every corner or down every street. It never stops."

Loret made an expression North couldn't read this time. "You never told me this."

"I've never told anyone," North said. "Too hard to say aloud. But now this investigation…" He trailed off.

"We know of this on Darkover. We call it *estres bella*. War stress. Your body can't let go of the terrible thing that happened to you, which forces your mind to relive it. We could talk to Lord Regis, or maybe a Keeper who could—"

North's communicator chittered loudly in the hard hallway. He held up a finger and checked the readout. Loret, ever nosy, peered over his shoulder, and her eyes widened. Dan Lawton.

"Why is the Legate calling you?" she asked in a hushed voice, as if Lawton might overhear.

"I have a feeling. Don't let him see you," North said, and accepted the call. Lawton appeared on the little screen. He was a red-headed man whose mother hailed from Darkover, and his strong features would have fit in at any Comyn Council meeting.

He'd been offered a seat on the Council, North happened to know, but Lawton had turned it down.

"Dan!" North breezed. "What's hanging?"

"You use his first name?" Loret mouthed at him, and North stepped on her foot.

"Dave," Lawton said from the screen. "Enjoying the fall weather in Thendara today?"

"Wet and cold is wild and crisp," North replied amiably, but Lawton had made his point—he knew North had been in Thendara. Not that visiting Thendara was illegal or even vaguely frowned upon. But when the Legate bothered to know something about you, it was time for you to be bothered. "What's going on?"

"Loret Ridenow-Castamir roped you into checking out that girl's death," Lawton said. "I want you to drop it."

Loret's mouth fell open. North drew on his poker face. "That so?"

"Things between the Empire and Thendara are delicate—"

"When are they not?" North drawled.

"—and I don't need a Terran messing with a purely Darkovan matter just now," Lawton finished.

"The killer was probably Terran," North said.

"Do you have evidence of that?"

"I will soon."

"Meaning you don't." Lawton cracked his knuckles, which told North he was uneasy. "Leave it."

"Why?"

"Because I'm the Legate and I damn well told you to."

North's ire rose. "You don't have the authority to—"

"Actually, I do. As the Legate, I'm in charge of everyone and everything at this spaceport. To be blunt, I'm king around here." Lawton leaned forward, and his nose ballooned into ugly prominence on the screen. "Let me make myself clear, Mr. North. Continue this investigation, and I'll have you shipped back to Terra in shackles. Got that?"

The ire tightened North's jaw. "This is about the research, isn't it? You're worried I'm going to turn up something that'll hurt your pet pollen project."

The Legate's voice turned to icy sandpaper. "Walk away, Mr. North."

"Mr. North? What happened to Dave, Dan?"

"Right now I'm not your good friend Dan. I'm the asshole Legate Lawton, and I'm ordering you to end your investigation."

North stared at him for a long time, then finally said, "Fine. I'll drop it."

"Thank you." Lawton's tone softened. "Look, Dave, I know how hard it is for you to—"

"Save it for the Council. Mr. Lawton." North snapped off the communicator.

"Zandru!" Loret swore. "I can't believe the Legate is interfering with this."

"Believe it." North sucked at his teeth. "He's getting pissed on from a higher pay grade, and rather than push back, he's pissing on me. The Empire wants that *kireseth* stuff."

Loret shook her head and turned to walk away. North stopped her. "Where are you going?"

"Downstairs. Without you on the case, I'll have to hunt the killer on my own."

He sighed. "I'm not dropping the case, Loret."

"You're not?" she asked in genuine surprise. "I don't understand. You received a direct order."

North leaned insouciantly against the wall. "That's partly why I'm not dropping it."

"Sometimes I don't understand you at all," Loret said with kind exasperation. "You fight for the law, but you break it for justice."

"Law and justice aren't the same thing."

"We're being pulled in two directions," Loret observed. "A killer or a cure. Law or chaos. Orders or choice."

"Darkover or Terra," North added with a rare smile.

"Which would you want?" she asked pointedly. "Darkover or Terra?"

The question caught him off-guard. For a moment he saw himself dressed in a cloak and tunic with a sword at his belt. He snorted. "I don't have to make that choice."

"You will one day," Loret predicted. "Choices have a way of coming for us all. But what about the other part?"

"Other part?"

"You said you're still hunting the killer in part because Legate Lawson told you not to. What's the other part? It wouldn't be that finding the killer might wreck the research into *kireseth*, would it?"

"The other part," North said firmly, "is to catch the slime who seduced and killed a teenage girl. It'll take time for word to get around that Dan kicked me off the case. Let's talk to Sammy."

They entered the office. Sammy Baxter was a short, round man who looked exactly like the bureaucrat he was. North had actually gone to school with Sammy on Terra and had been surprised at running into him here. With a cop's instinct, North had cultivated their thin acquaintance into an actual friendship just for moments like this.

"Sammy!" North said with forced cheer. "You're here late!"

Sammy gave him the usual *working hard/hardly working* response, and North made the rest of the required small talk while Loret waited.

"So what brings you?" Sammy asked at last.

North set the blaster on Lenny's desk. "Someone used this to kill a girl in Thendara. I'm unofficially helping the Comyn look into it. Can you run the registration?"

"Sure. Two seconds." Sammy leaned over to read the number inscribed on the blaster's barrel, then poked at his computer. North held his breath. There was a chance Lawton would have sent a message around already.

Sammy's computer pinged. "Got it. The blaster belongs to a guy named Benton Messer."

Loret made a small sound, which she turned into a cough. North cut his eyes to her, then back to Sammy. "You got an address?"

North waited until they were in the relative privacy of the stairwell before turning on Loret. "What's up? I saw your reaction to the name."

Loret exhaled hard. "Dr. Benton Messer. He's the one who's experimenting on *kireseth*."

"Jesus." North ran a hand through his ash-blond hair and wondered if it was thinning. One more stupid thing to worry about. "Okay, we gotta get over there. Now. Before he gets wind of this and rabbits."

"The Legate must have known," Loret mused as they hustled out of the building. "It's why he ordered you off the case. He chose research over justice."

"Maybe," North said. "Or maybe he's getting orders from someone *else* who chose research over justice. Let's talk to Messer."

Still in the shadow of the spaceport citadel, they trotted across the port to the ring of efficient homes and apartments. North found them flat and dull as old beer compared to the quirky, hand-built homes in Thendara. Those houses had character. They expressed the person inside. In Thendara, you could tell something about a house's owner at a glance, by the colors they chose, by the flowers they planted, by the repairs they made or ignored. Even the spindly Castamir house told its own story. These Terran houses were as functional as a stack of shipping containers, and only half as interesting.

Benton Messer's building was a set of row houses crushed tightly together to save space and maximize efficiency. Before North could ring the bell, Loret took his elbow again.

"Maybe you should wait outside," she said. "I can talk to Dr. Messer alone, and we can tell the Legate that Sammy gave us the information before he kicked you off the case. We can get a Keeper to look at your *estres*, and—"

"No." North worked his jaw. "I'm going to see this through. Lawton can shove it up his ass. It's about justice."

"The fact that justice might also kill the *kireseth* research has nothing to do with it?" Loret asked.

"You keep asking that. What are *you* thinking? Back in Thendara, you wanted to find the killer, too. Now you're hesitating."

Loret set her mouth hard. "Threshold sickness took two of my cousins and one of my brothers. More will die in the decades—centuries—to come. We have a chance to stop that if we let Jaelle's death go. Jaelle is already dead, and arresting Benton Messer won't change that."

"Another way to look at it is that Benton Messer can screw around with a teenage girl, kill her, and walk away just because he might have a cure for threshold sickness."

"Yes," she said tightly. "I don't know the answer, North. I truly have no idea what the right thing to do is."

"I think that's the first time I've heard you say that."

Loret shook her head hard. "Should we drop this or not? The killer is your countryman. North. I'll...let you decide."

North hesitated. Hundreds or thousands of future lives could be saved if he walked away, let Jaelle be a sacrifice on an altar of science. Then his resolve hardened. No one should be allowed to commit murder; no one should be allowed to get away with it. He tapped Messer's door chime, and Loret's face fell.

Benton Messer opened the door. Messer was a balding man of average height. Brown eyes, hooked nose, thin lips, five o'clock shadow. North's first thought was that he didn't look like a killer, though few killers did. He was buttoning up his shirt, and North guessed he'd been getting undressed for bed when Loret rang.

"Can I help you?" he asked. North noted the unease in his voice, but that could have been because of the late hour.

North gave his and Loret's names. "If you're Benton Messer, we need to ask you some questions."

"What about?" he asked, still uneasy.

"It might be better if we had more privacy," Loret interjected. "May we?"

Messer grudgingly ushered them into the living room, a plain, uninteresting room, sparsely furnished. North took a stiff seat. This man had seduced a fifteen-year-old and killed her.

"Can I get you tea or coffee?" Messer offered.

"Let's get right to it." North reached for his pocket. "Do you recognize—"

"Dad?" A hallway led away from the living room, and a kid was standing at the threshold. He was maybe sixteen or seventeen, not bad-looking, still in his day clothes. "Who's here?"

"Nothing you need to worry about, Rick," Messer said. "Go get ready for bed."

North flicked a glance at Rick Messer, then back at Benton Messer. He looked down at the man's feet. At that moment, North's communicator buzzed with a text message. It was from the Legate.

I told you to drop it, the message read. *Stay where you are until security arrives.*

North put his poker face back on.

"This is your son?" Loret asked, not noticing the message.

"He is," Messer confirmed shortly. "Rick—bed."

Rick slowly turned away and slunk down the hall. North listened hard for the sounds of running feet or maybe even a siren, but he only heard a door shut a little too hard.

"Now," Messer said, "what's this about?"

"I like your shoes," North said abruptly. "They're old, but clean. You're careful with them. Don't see that much these days."

"Oh?" Messer extended a foot in confusion. "They're good leather, and expensive. I take care of all my things."

"All?" North produced the blaster. "What about this, sir?"

Messer paled. "Oh, Jesus."

"It was found at the site of a murder this afternoon in Thendara," Loret said. "It's registered to you."

There was a brief pause. Messer glanced at the hallway, then broke. "All right. Yes. It was me."

"So you seduced Jaelle Castamir," North said. "Then you killed her."

"I...I...did." Messer licked his lips. "God help me, I did. We had a fight, and I lost my temper."

Loret shot North a look. North ignored her. "Funny thing about this murder," he said. "The killer shot Jaelle three times. Obliterated her head and chest, even part of her arm."

"Yeah. I said I lost my temper." Messer held out his hands. "You can arrest me now."

Loret caught what had just happened, what was wrong with Messer's confession. She looked toward North, who studiously ignored her.

"No, Mr. Messer," North said. "It's not you."

"But it is!" A frantic look came over his face. "It was! I did it! I confessed."

North raised his voice. "Come on out, kid."

From hallway crept Rick Messer, his face a white mask of terror. "I'm sorry!" he said in a broken voice. "I didn't mean—"

"Shut up, Rick!" Messer dashed over to his son and grabbed his shoulder. "Don't say a word."

"You still have mud on your shoes from the alley, Rick," North said quietly. "And I can see at a glance that your dad's feet are way smaller than yours. What's your size, son? Forty-one centimeters?"

"It's not true," Messer blustered. "You don't know what the hell you're talking about."

"You can't take the blame for him," Loret said to Messer, also quietly. "As much you wish to."

"Don't hurt my dad!" Rick cried. He was trembling all over. "I did it! It was me."

The fight seemed to go out of Messer then, and he slumped into a chair, head down. Rick remained in the hallway entrance. "Tell us what happened," Loret said.

"We met in Thendara," Rick choked out. "Jaelle was fascinated with Terra and our technology. She called me her space man. I was a little older than her, but only a year and a half. Her parents are really strict, and it was hard for us to meet. She invented errands so we could see each other."

"How did it happen?" North asked.

"I...I was showing off. Being her space man. Jaelle wanted to see a real Terran weapon, so I stole Dad's and met her in the alley." Tears were running down his face now. "I must have been holding it wrong, because the next thing I knew..."

"Maybe it was an accident," Loret said in North's memory.

"We're looking for something nefarious, when it might be just an innocent mistake." North's heart twisted in his chest, and he felt a grim nausea. It was a stupid accident, nothing more. It had already wrecked Jaelle's life and ripped up her family. Now it was going to destroy this one. How much justice was there to find here?

"I panicked and ran," Rick finished in a choked voice. "I didn't notice I'd dropped the blaster until I got home. But I killed her. It was me."

"Zandru." Loret put a hand to her mouth. "It *was* an accident."

"How do you know for sure?" North asked sharply.

She tapped the matrix on its chain around her neck. "I can feel it. He's telling the truth. The guilt is crushing him."

"I'm seeing it over and over." Rick slumped into a chair, his head in his hands. "I loved her, and she's dead because of me."

"What'll happen now?" Messer asked.

"By our laws, your son is an adult," Loret said. "He'll be tried for murder. Even if the Council lets him live, Jaelle's brother Dorn will demand the right to hunt Rick until one of them kills the other."

Rick went pale. Messer clenched his fists. "No! We'll leave the planet. Go somewhere else. Hang the pollen research."

"If the Comyn Council demands blood, the Legate won't let you leave," Loret said. "The Empire's treaty with Darkover—"

Someone pounded at the door. Rick jumped, and Benton bolted to his feet. "They're going to arrest Rick!" he said. "Please! It was an accident. Tell them it was me!"

"I get it," North said. "A father will sacrifice anything for his son."

More pounding.

"I'm sorry, Dad." Rick was in tears now. "I'm so sorry. I'd do anything to—"

"Quiet," North said, and handed the blaster to a confused Loret. Then he opened the door. Four black-clad TE security officers boiled into the room. Loret stuffed the pistol into her dress pocket. Rick shrank away.

"David North," said one of the officers, "you're under arrest for violating a directive from the Legate," said one of the officers.

In seconds, North was cuffed and hustled out the door, leaving the others behind.

Justice at the spaceport was swift. No judge, no jury. Just Lawton in his office with Loret pale behind him.

"I told you to drop it, and you didn't," Lawton said. North didn't bother asking how Lawton had found out so fast. There were any number of ways. "Do you have anything to say before sentencing?"

North glanced at Loret. Her mouth was set hard. The choices pulled North in opposite and unpleasant directions. Law against justice. Fair against unfair. Darkover against Terra. The words *I know who the killer is* formed in his throat. Then he looked at Loret again, her face filled with hope and sorrow.

North kept his expression flat. Lawton would almost certainly have learned from Sammy that Benton Messer owned the blaster that had killed Jaelle, and Lawton would almost certainly have come to the understandable, but false, conclusion that his little research scientist was the killer. If this "fact" got out, the Comyn would certainly call for Benton's head, and Dorn would file his Declaration. No more research. No more drugs.

North could also tell Lawton that the killer was actually Benton's son, Rick. North couldn't see Benton Messer wanting to stay on Darkover after his son was executed—or on the receiving end of a Declaration. Either way, the project would be over.

And a whole mess of Darkovan teenagers would die of threshold sickness.

Jaelle had died in an accident. There was no justice to be had in an accident, and trying Rick Messer for murder would condemn some of Loret's future family to death.

And Loret would be hurt. His best friend. She would undergo fear and pain every bit as bad as he had with the *kireseth*. His gut and his heart tightened. That was really the center of it all, the reason he did anything. Unexpected emotion swelled in him and thickened his throat. Loret had saved him from Ferrick Alton, had found a way for him to stay on Darkover, had given him a *family*. She had helped him. She had spoken for him. And now he had to help her, even if it meant losing her.

"Well?" Lawton asked sharply.

With a final glance at Loret, North said, "I've got nothing to say."

Loret touched the matrix on the silver chain around her neck with a shaky hand as Lawton's voice went stiff with formal regret.

"Very well," he said. "David North, for disobeying my order, you are hereby ordered to leave Cottman IV on the first available ship. If you ever return, you will be punished to the fullest extent of the law."

The cell wasn't bad, as cells went. Clean. Bare white walls on all sides. One wall formed of good old iron bars. North sat on the bed, waiting with a cop's patience. It was all over but the paperwork.

Sometime later, Loret stepped into view. She grasped the bars, and North looked up at her. He was surprised at how glad he was to see her, then surprised at his own surprise. Why wouldn't he be glad to see his own best friend? Especially when this was probably the last time he'd ever see her.

"New house?" Loret asked.

"Yeah. Cool digs," he said grimly. "But I could use a housekeeper."

She dropped the pretense of banter. "Why, David? You could have told the Legate. Since Benton Messer wasn't the killer after all, Lawton would have let your deportation drop. He likes you, even when you make him angry."

"You could have said something," North pointed out.

"I'm not being exiled over a lie." She leaned toward him, stopped only by the bars. "Why didn't you speak?"

North changed the subject. "What's happened to Rick?"

"Not a thing. After the officers took you, I left. As far as I know, nothing's changed for Rick or his father. Benton Messer will be back in his lab tomorrow morning."

"Good," North said with a nod. "What about your cousins?"

Loret set her mouth. "They're being…compensated. On the condition that they drop the Declaration idea and let Jaelle's death go. For the good of future generations. They've agreed."

"That'll have to do," North said.

"But why did *you* keep quiet?" Loret repeated. "You said you wanted justice."

"Yeah." North sighed. "But I figured on balance, we should save the kids."

"Even though it means losing—"

North spread his hands to interrupt her. "Guess so."

"You're making yourself into a sacrifice."

He snorted. "Maybe it's just a garden-variety martyr complex. When I get back to Terra, I'll see a shrink about it."

"And I'll never see you again."

"I know." He got up and took one of her hands through the bars. "Somewhere, when I wasn't looking, Darkover turned into home. I don't want to leave it. I don't want to leave *you*. You're…" He had to force himself to keep speaking. "You're the best friend a guy could have. And the best sidekick."

Her eyes filled with tears, and she put her hand over his. "I always thought *you* were the sidekick."

Loret's touch almost crushed him, so he forced a laugh. "Who's telling this story, lady? You or me?"

"At this point, I think I'm telling it," said a new voice.

Loret snatched her hand back in surprise. Into the holding area strode a tall man in a rich blue tunic with a sword at his belt. His hair was white, but his face was young. North recognized Regis Hastur. Loret bowed.

"Vai dom," she said, with North echoing her a moment later.

"You're in some trouble, *Dom* North," Regis said.

North gave him a wary look. "Seems so."

"And I've spoken to the Legate," Regis added.

"Have you?" North remained careful, but hope flared. It would be just like Regis Hastur to reckon himself a white knight and ride to North's rescue.

Regis leaned toward him, and North noticed the matrix around his neck. "I can't undo what the Legate has done, and I can't blame him for doing his duty. He's under orders from his own superiors."

North slumped a little. Well, he could still find work as a private investigator or security consultant on Terra. He could get a shithole apartment somewhere, and live the rest of his shithole life. The life of a sacrifice.

"So I'm in the shit," he said, slumping into himself.

"Indeed." Regis held up a finger. "But Darkover owes you several debts. You saved our world from destruction, you saved us from Kira Ann, and now you're involved in the attempt to end threshold sickness. So. I'm here to make you an offer."

The last word brought North quietly alert again. "An offer?"

"You can stay on Darkover," Regis said, "under one condition."

"And that is?" Loret asked before North could do it.

Regis said, "You have to swear fealty to the Comyn."

There was a pause. A breath of air wafted through the room. Loret clutched her own matrix chain.

"Fealty," North repeated. "What would that mean, exactly?"

"You would renounce your Terran heritage and become a citizen of Thendara under my rule," Regis explained. "You would live as a man of Darkover for the rest of your life and obey the Comyn in all things. And as a convicted criminal, you would never set foot on Empire soil again. Including the spaceport."

Law against justice. Fair against unfair. Darkover against Terra.

"A different kind of sacrifice," Loret murmured.

North thought of the cold, bleak Thendara winters. Of the weak red sun. Of the new language and strange customs. He also thought of stubborn people in quirky houses. Of liquid syllables rolling off his tongue. Of Loret.

"Done," said David North.

"You can stay here for now," Loret said.

North set down the small satchel containing his few belongings. The room was on the top floor of a three-story boardinghouse run by a married couple who were distantly related to Loret, as everyone on Darkover seemed to be. The place was simple and chilly, heated only by the chimney. A bed, a table, and a hard chair were the only furniture, but the sheets were crisp and clean, and the quilt was thick.

"It's perfect," North said. He drew aside the worn curtain at the room's only window. The thatched rooftops of Thendara stretched into the distance, and near the horizon poked the tower citadel of the spaceport.

"How do you feel?" Loret asked.

They were speaking *casta,* of course, and North wondered if he'd ever speak Terran Standard again. He continued to stare out the window. "You want the truth?"

"Always."

"I feel like I've escaped. Like I never have to go back."

"You don't have to because you can't," Loret said briskly. "The stipend from Lord Regis should do you until you find another way to earn your bread. In the meantime, we'll have to look for a proper place for you to live. And a proper woman for you to marry."

"Whoa whoa whoa!" North put out his hands. "Slow down! No one said anything about getting married."

She cocked her head. "And how will you get along without someone to take care of your house? Do you know how to cook and clean in the proper ways? Sew your clothes? Bear your children?"

"No one said anything about children, either!"

"You're on Darkover now," she said. "Scandalous for a man of your age to go without a wife and heirs to carry on his line."

"Now look—"

"Come to think of it," she continued, ignoring him, "my cousin Arlida lost her husband three or four years ago, and she might be ready to marry again. You need an experienced woman."

"No! No cousins! Your family is big enough."

"It's getting bigger," Loret said, and dropped her hands to her sides. "I'm getting married, you know."

This caught North like a club upside the head. "You're…what?"

"Getting married." She gave a solemn nod. "To Dorn."

"Married?" North spluttered. "But…you…"

"The family has to be compensated, both for the death of their daughter and for their silence. My family has more status with the Comyn. Dorn's chance to marry up."

"He's a lot younger than you. And your cousin!"

"He's a grown man. And my *third* cousin. It'll be strange at first, but we'll get used to it. A small price to pay if it means my children won't have threshold sickness."

"Jesus." North dropped to the bed. "I don't know what to say."

Loret gave a wan smile. "How about congratulations?"

"Thank you," North said quickly.

"For what?"

"You went to Lord Regis. Darkover almost never offers sanctuary to *Terranan,* but you persuaded him."

Loret shook a finger at him. "We're friends. Best friends. And that's what best friends do."

"Well…thank you."

"You're welcome. To celebrate, let's argue about something over dinner. You pick the topic."

With shared smiles, they turned away from the window and the spaceport, ever distant and far away.

BANSHEE CRY

by Marella Sands

Marella Sands writes, "This story grew out of a desire to feature banshees, horses, and arranged marriages in the same tale, partly because I've always been intrigued by the banshees of Darkover." My introduction to her work came through her submission to *Gifts of Darkover* (2014), "Stonefell Gift." Who was this writer, I wondered, who could weave a story with such subtlety and finesse that the ending was inevitable, surprising, and deeply moving? Since then I have had the privilege of editing a number of her stories, each one a treasure. "Banshee Cry" continues that tradition.

Currently Marella is at work rewriting a novel that is straight fiction with no fantastical elements. She is ready to schedule a yellow fever vaccination so that she can travel to Ghana, and is working on developing a moderate command of Twi so that she can talk to the locals in Accra in something besides English. Her new cat is named in Twi: Afia is the name given to females born (or, in this case, adopted) on a Friday. Marella's Twi name would be Akosua, as she was born on a Sunday.

Rory MacAran wanted to be in the stable with his horse. That was where he felt most at home. The large beasts were sometimes more like family to him than his parents.

But today was the day he was to meet his future bride. He took a deep breath of the cool late spring air and let it out slowly to ease his anxiety. Marriage was something Rory had always known was in his future, and had pushed aside as a boring detail that would straighten itself out somehow. Now the future had arrived, and the dreaded first meeting with his intended was upon him. A murky possibility had come starkly into focus, and he did not like the feeling at all.

His mother had insisted he wear his best clothing, even though the shirt was a bit thin for the spring cold here in the foothills of the Hellers. Still, she was his mother, so he wore it. He had complemented it with the jacket he had received at Midwinter and the new boots his father had had made after his growth spurt a few months ago. All in all, he looked every inch the MacAran: powerful and competent, just as the MacAran heir should be. And yet he was miserable.

He had never met Camilla of Scathfell before. Though her family had always been invited to the Midsummer festivities at Falconsward, Lady Scathfell had been too ill to travel for years. Her husband and family had become reclusive while the lady had battled her ailment. She had died over the winter, and so, for the first time in years, Lord Scathfell was venturing out of his holding, this time to bring his daughter to live at Falconsward until she was old enough to marry.

The age of marriage was a bit fuzzy as far as Rory was concerned, but he was glad the fact Camilla was only fourteen meant the date was still at some undetermined time in the future. There was still time to be himself before becoming a husband and, perhaps someday, a father. And then, some day, the Lord of Falconsward.

Rory's parents, Lord and Lady MacAran, stood at the top of the steps that led down to the main courtyard. Rory, who had dawdled while deciding whether or not to braid his hair back and had finally decided not to, dashed up just as the gate opened to allow their guests.

"Stand up straight," his mother insisted. "Remember your manners."

Rory bit his tongue. He was sixteen! He didn't need his mother to remind him of things like manners. Hadn't she and his tutors taught him for years how to behave, how to dance, how to converse at dinner? He knew his manners.

It wasn't his fault he'd rather be with the horses.

Lord Scathfell rode in first on his horse, a proud roan that Rory quickly realized was one of Falconsward's own, followed by his aides, and then, at last, by a young woman and a girl on horses small enough they were dwarfed by the men's mounts. Rory's mother always rode a horse the same size as any other; Rory wondered if things were different in Scathfell.

Lord Scathfell dismounted and turned to help the young woman off her horse, then the girl. The young woman looked much like the lord, but was too old to be Camilla. She must be a cousin or niece who had come after Lady Scathfell's death to help raise the lord's daughter.

As the young woman stepped aside, the lord helped the girl down from her pony-sized mount. The girl held on to the saddle's pommel as though her life depended on it, and almost sank to her knees as her father placed her on the ground.

Was she afraid of horses? Rory's heart lurched as he thought, *Maybe she can't even ride well!*

How could he marry someone who couldn't ride a horse? Worse, how could someone be Lady of Falconsward and not be a horsewoman, or a hawkmistress? The MacArans were talented around animals, often forming telepathic rapports with them. If this girl were too frightened to be around animals much, her life at Falconsward would be grim indeed.

Lord Scathfell and his daughter came toward the MacArans.

"Lord Scathfell, my friend, it has been too long," said Rory's father. He walked forward with hands outstretched.

Lord Scathfell took the MacAran's hands. "The Scathfells are grateful for your hospitality." Then the men broke into identical broad smiles. "Darrell, it's been too long."

"It has," said the MacAran. The two men shared a bear hug.

"And here is my daughter, Camilla," said Lord Scathfell with obvious pride.

The young woman stepped aside and gestured for the girl to step forward. She did, appearing reluctant to do so. Rory peered at her curiously, but a pert nose and a wisp of bright red hair were all that stuck out from the hood the girl wore.

"Now, child, let them see you," said her father.

The girl pushed her hood back. She had bright green eyes and a small chain of freckles across each cheek. Her delicate heart-shaped face was pale and her eyes narrowed slightly in...fear? Anticipation? Anxiety? The girl smiled slightly but the smile did not lift the tension on her face.

Rory's mother held out her hand to the girl. "My dear, you are most welcome here. I know you have had a hard winter, and I hope you can find some peace and rest here with us."

"Thank you, Lady MacAran," said Camilla. Her voice was low and sweet and Rory instantly liked it. The horses would, too.

"And this is my son, Rory," said his mother. She gestured for Rory to come closer.

He did and bowed slightly. "Welcome to Falconsward."

Camilla smiled slightly again and bowed in return. But her smile still did not reach beyond the corners of her mouth. Rory could judge nothing of her inner thoughts or feelings at all. Camilla kept her hands still and moved no more than necessary; she was almost doll-like in her inexpressiveness and passivity.

Rory had not expected her to be loud or brash; that would hardly have been tolerated by her parents, no matter how sick her mother had been, but she seemed far too insipid to be worthy to be a future mistress of Falconsward.

"Well, let's get inside where it's warmer, and a meal has been prepared for us," said the MacAran. "I have some fine musicians to entertain us while we eat."

The families moved inside while servants took the horses and pack animals to the stable. The Scathfells' gear had already been hauled into the house to the guests' chambers.

Rory watched Camilla walk behind her parents, her manner calm and demure. But her downcast eyes seemed to hide a secret, as if she might not be as dull as she seemed. Rory wondered how he was supposed to get to know this girl and learn if they could manage to like each other well enough to marry.

Lunch was, as far as Rory was concerned, a disaster. He had been seated by Camilla, of course, so that they could chat. The MacAran and Lord Scathfell were mindful of no one but themselves and in renewing their old friendship, so long interrupted by Lady Scathfell's inability to travel, and his mother chatted with the young woman, Camilla's cousin Tessa, who had been brought along as a chaperone. That left Rory and his intended bride.

"Tell me about Scathfell," said Rory while they ate. "I hear it can be lovely at Midsummer with the way it is positioned in the valley overlooking the lower slopes."

"Yes, it has quite the view," said Camilla without emotion. "When the flowers are in bloom, we often eat outside on a veranda near the family's quarters so that we can enjoy the beauty."

"That sounds lovely."

Camilla said dutifully, "Falconsward is also quite appealing."

"Yes," said Rory. "The snow was especially thick this winter, but it's melting nicely off the pastures. Soon you'll be able to see horses wherever you look. And we raise hunting hawks as well. Do you hunt?"

Camilla gave that same smile, the one that appeared plastered on her face and gave away nothing she was actually thinking. "No, my lord, I do not wish to take part in killing things."

"But we must kill to eat."

Camilla merely took another bite of her food. "That is true. But I do not wish to be the one to do the killing. I suppose you hunt? And ride?"

"Yes," said Rory. "My horse is just three years old now, and I have been training him myself. He has known no other trainer or rider than me. I can take you to the stable later to meet him. He's not one of the blacks that we raise to sell. He's a bit short and stocky and can have a mean streak sometimes, so you have to watch out for his teeth, but he's the strongest and smartest horse in the whole stable!"

"He sounds like a fine animal. You are fortunate to have him."

"We will find a horse for you, too," Rory promised. "The future Lady MacAran should ride a well-bred animal worthy of her."

Camilla bowed her head. "As you wish, my lord."

Her voice was calm but Rory caught the hint of a sob in it.

How could Camilla be saddened by the thought of getting a beautiful horse of her very own? Especially when she could have that instead of something that looked half-grown and underfed?

A roar of laughter from the lords drew everyone's attention. Rory realized his father had been indulging in his hawking stories again, which everyone always seemed to find so amusing. In fact, Lord Scathfell was nearly doubled over with laughter, while Camilla's cousin giggled delicately behind her hand. Rory's mother gazed at her husband with a mixture of exasperation and love.

"What about the stories we've heard lately?" asked Lord Scathfell. "They say the banshees have come down from the high passes because of a harsh winter in the Far Hellers. We thought we heard one on the way here, but I wasn't sure."

"If you had heard a banshee, you would know it," said the MacAran. "No one can mistake that sound for another."

"We are safe enough here," added Rory's mother. "The banshees, even in the years when they come down from the passes, don't come this far. And they never approach human habitations. Even if they *did* come, and they *were* here, they could not harm you while you were safe here in the house, only frighten you with their cries."

Tessa looked pale but Lord Scathfell looked mollified. Camilla merely dabbed at her lips with a napkin and did not respond at all to the behavior of the others, or react to the news about the banshees.

Rory soul quailed, but he reminded himself that Camilla was a guest at another's home for the first time in years. She was surely just being extra careful to be polite.

While the others started off on stories of what this year's Midsummer celebration might be like, Rory considered his intended bride. He might be stuck with her at his side for the rest of his life, which, at the moment, was not a tasteful proposition. The two of them might not have the passion of the bard's romances, but they should at least be friends. He sincerely wanted to like her, and for her to like him back. The obvious affection between his parents was something Rory always admired, and secretly feared he would never have.

"What is your horse's name?" he asked.

"Lovely."

That seemed an odd name, but at least she was engaging in conversation. "I call my horse Champion, because I know he's going to be a great horse one day when he's fully trained. What is the story of your horse's name?"

Camilla gave the tiniest shrug. "Merely that when she was presented to me, I said, *how lovely*, and that's what everyone started calling her. She really is a sweet thing. I shall miss her."

That startled Rory. "Miss her? Why? She didn't look old. Is she ill?"

Camilla shook her head. "No, but when my father leaves for home, he will take Lovely back with him. He says I must get used to Falconsward ways, and Lovely will have no place here."

For the first time, Rory's heart went out to his intended. No matter that Lovely was an odd name, or that the horse was undersized. He would be heartbroken, not to mention, incensed, to be parted forever from Champion by anything less than Zandru's Hells. Why would Lord Scathfell make his daughter give up her family, her home, *and* her horse? That seemed outrageously cruel.

Of course, as his mother often reminded him, many people didn't feel for animals the way the MacArans did. Perhaps Lord Scathfell felt one animal was interchangeable with another. Rory had heard about such people; he had just never encountered any. He had been glad to offer his intended a mount worthy of her, but he would never have separated her from an animal she loved. A person could be fond of more than one horse at a time.

After lunch, the group retired to a veranda where they could look over the horse pastures. Some of the blacks gamboled around the field nearest them, while a few roans and bays grazed on the outskirts, displaying only the occasional bared tooth or raised hoof toward the rambunctious blacks.

Camilla sat by Rory, hands clasped inside a muff as if it were fully winter and not late spring. She looked out at the green fields without any expression. Whether she was terrified, annoyed, angry, or even cautiously hopeful, Rory could not tell.

"Will you come to see the horses with me, lady?" he asked, wondering if she might be more open when her father and chaperone were not close enough to overhear.

"I would love to," said Tessa.

Rory bristled. "I am hardly going to behave badly toward my intended bride between here and the pasture fence, which you can clearly see from here. She needs no chaperone to see the horses."

"Still, Tessa is here and would like to go," said the MacAran. "Take both the ladies along for a stroll."

Rory bowed his head, knowing he couldn't go against his father's express wishes. Camilla made no comment as she rose and followed him down the stairs to the courtyard, and across to the pasture fence. Tessa, however, prattled on the whole time.

"Oh, this is just perfect," she said, for about the tenth time. "Such weather, and, oh! the views of the Hellers. I thought no place was more beautiful than Scathfell. And look at that hawk!" She pointed toward a yard where the hawkmaster was training a young ladies' hawk, which Rory's mother had thought to give as a gift to Camilla. Rory would have to tell his mother that was a bad idea. "How beautiful. Are they all so pretty? I hear you train good hawks here. And, see, the courtyard here is in good repair; the one at home could use some attention..."

How anyone endured much time with Tessa was beyond Rory's comprehension. She barely drew breath in between one inane utterance and another, nor did she pause after raising a question, as if she expected no one to answer her. Perhaps that was why Camilla was so quiet; she had learned to keep her attention elsewhere so that her cousin did not drive her mad with drivel.

Rory tried to call one of his favorites, a rugged bay named Morning who was trusted to train babies to ride, but the horse put her ears back at Tessa's incessant chatter and remained by the fence some yards away. Camilla merely stared into the distance and said nothing.

Eventually, Rory led the women back to the others, heavy of heart and thinking dark thoughts about his future with the silent Camilla.

That evening, Rory's mother visited his room and sat by his bed while he finished tidying up his room, which his mother insisted he do each night so that each new day "started afresh and neat." It was also a task she forbade the servants to perform for him, because she said he should do something for himself every day, just as the Bearer of Burdens would wish.

"I thought the day went well," she said, as she brushed a few stray hairs back from her face. Her blond braids were untouched yet by gray, even though she was nearly forty and had endured multiple miscarriages. Rory was her only living child. "How do you like the girl?"

The girl. As if she were a broodmare for breeding, and not a person.

"How can you talk about her like that?" he asked. "She's not a *thing*. It might be better if she were; then I could ignore her. But how can I know if I even *like* her if she will barely speak to me?"

His mother smiled. "You're right, of course. When I first came to Falconsward, I was terrified. I had heard of the MacArans and their powerful gifts with animals, and I expected my husband to be some half-man half-hawk who could, I don't know, do magical things, perhaps even fly! And then he was a handsome young man, brash and bold, but still awkward and hopeful, and no wild creature at all. No doubt Camilla has heard stories about the MacArans and is nervous about living here."

"What stories do you think she has heard about me?" asked Rory tentatively. He had some ability with animals, especially horses, but nothing like his father, who could literally meld his mind with the mind of hawk or horse or chervine. Rory had some hope he might grow into more power, but at sixteen, he was rapidly losing that hope. What if the servants, or the neighbors, were gossiping about his lack of powers?

"I don't see what stories she could have heard," said his mother as she rose gracefully from her chair. "Other than you are a handsome young lad with a bright future and a loving family. What else could she desire?"

She left the room before Rory could work up the courage to ask what *she* had desired when she had first ridden into Falconsward.

Rory tossed and turned but sleep eluded him. He kept seeing Camilla's blank stare as she looked out over the pastures of the land where her future lay, and her lack of reaction to either Tessa's rambling or Rory's attempts to coax Morning close enough to be stroked.

He wanted, no, he *needed* to be at the stables. The stables were home in ways his own room simply wasn't. Rory put on thick pants and shirt and a heavy jacket to combat the cold of the spring night, and tiptoed down through the halls until he reached a side door that would give him access to the yard and stable. He had long ago mastered the technique of opening the door slowly enough to keep it from making enough noise to wake everyone.

He didn't breathe deeply and freely until he stood in front of Champion's stall. The horse rather negligently put his nose over the rail to be petted, and Rory complied. The horse's nose was velvety smooth and his breath warm on Rory's face.

Champion was restless and kept twisting his head to look at something at the far end of the stable. Rory listened carefully but heard nothing out of the ordinary. He placed his face against Champion's and mustered what little *laran* he had. The horse could sense another person in the stable, someone the horse didn't know. The person wasn't frightening, just alien.

Rory patted the horse in thanks and called out. "I know you're there. Come on out."

After a few moments, a small, heavily cloaked figure, crept out of the shadows. The way she moved and the fiery red hair streaming out from under the cloak gave away her identity.

"Camilla," said Rory with a slight bow. "I wasn't expecting to see you in the stables."

She came closer, displaying no more emotion than she had earlier. "I wanted to see Lovely before my father takes her home."

"What if I asked him to let her remain?"

Camilla hesitated. For the first time, Rory saw indecision on her face.

"I would like that..." she said. But she slammed down the mask once again. "It is up to my father, however. She is only a horse."

"But surely your father will be here for some time," said Rory. "After all these years, this is his first visit outside his own home. He'll stay more than one night!"

Camilla looked back at a stall which must be Lovely's. "It is difficult for him to be away from my mother."

Rory stopped himself from blurting out *but your mother's dead*.

"I know it sounds strange," Camilla continued, "but he took care of her for so long. He barely left her bedside the last few months of her life, didn't even notice the rest of us, not for any reason, not ever. Now that she's gone, he goes to her grave every day. I swear he talks to her more than he talks to me, or the steward, or anyone. And she's the one that can't hear him."

Rory suddenly realized, *Tessa's staying, too*. That way, Lord Scathfell could disencumber himself from two family members and be alone in his holding with his dead wife. Rory shuddered in horror. Lord Scathfell had seemed cheerful enough this afternoon; he had managed to hide his grief, at least briefly. Long enough to come here, drop off his remaining living family, and disappear again back into his living death.

"Then he should certainly leave Lovely here with you," said Rory. "We'll find a way to ask him to make sure that happens."

"You are too kind."

"I hope you will be happy here," he said, thinking desperately how he could make Falconsward somewhere Camilla would be glad to call home. Even if they had to share it with the garrulous Tessa.

She shrugged.

"If you don't like to be around the hawks, perhaps Lovely can help you get more used to being around horses," he said, aware he was blathering on much like Tessa. Perhaps that was why Tessa never shut up: she wanted to do anything to fill the silence Camilla cloaked herself with as heavily as she cloaked her body. "You could learn to train them, if you like. My mother doesn't do that, but my father's mother did. Or, do you like to sew? Or embroider? My mother is good at those things."

Camilla's expression did not change. "I am sure I will find something to do."

"But what do you *want* to do?" asked Rory in frustration. "Don't you want to be happy? Don't you want a home?"

An expression finally crossed Camilla's face. It might have been fear. Or anger. It was gone before Rory could identify it.

"Who doesn't?" she finally said.

"This could be your home," said Rory. "We don't have to marry for years. We have time to do things together, and be friends, and find out what our life might hold. We can make plans, and learn what makes the other happy."

"I know what my life will hold," said Camilla. "I will be your wife, and bear your children. I will preside over Midsummer celebrations, and Midwinter festivals. And one day, I will be buried wherever it is you place your lords and ladies. My life will hold no surprises."

"And no joy, either? That is a grim future!"

"I do not ask for any joy. The Bearer of Burdens knows I have the strength to endure, and that is enough."

Rory's heart almost failed him, and he reached out for her. "My lady…Camilla…how can I tell you that I would do anything to make you happy, if I only knew what it was."

She said again, "You are too kind."

"Damn kindness to Zandru's Nine Hells!" he exclaimed.

Camilla's eyes widened in shock. "My lord!"

"*Kindness* is a start, but it is not enough. I will have no wife that is not happy with me," he said. "I will only marry the woman who comes to our marriage with hope, and who looks forward to years at my side. How could I endure anything else? How could you?"

Before she could reply, a bloodcurdling screech filled the

stable. Champion whinnied in fear and pressed his head against Rory's chest. The other horses in the stable made panicked sounds and stomped their hooves.

One high-pitched scream filled the air from the far stall.

"Lovely!" said Camilla. She ran to the stall, where the horse was throwing herself against the sides of her stall in terror. Camilla reached for the latch.

"Camilla, don't!"

But she didn't listen.

As soon as the latch lifted and the door swung aside, Lovely bolted out of the stall. Startled grooms, who had come rushing in as soon as the horses had started stamping and screaming, flung themselves out of the mare's way.

Camilla ran after her horse.

"Young lady, stay inside!" shouted one of the grooms. "The banshees won't come near the stable."

But Camilla would not heed, and Rory could not blame her. If Champion were out in the dark, helpless before hungry banshees, would he cower in the house? Or would he try to save his horse? The answer was obvious.

Rory grabbed a rope and ran after her. "Tell my father where I've gone," he said to the grooms as he dashed by them.

Despite the fact that Camilla was weighed down by a dress and a heavy cloak, she was quick enough on her feet that Rory had difficulty following her. Rory ran across the courtyard and around the mews, listening for Camilla calling out to her horse.

The horrific scream of the huge flightless bird echoed throughout Falconsward. Dark windows began lighting up with candles as people awakened and placed lights on their sills to ward off the terrifying creatures, who were notoriously averse to light.

Rory had never seen a banshee, nor had anyone he had ever met, because they rarely came this far down from the tree line where they normally lived. But in particularly cold weather, or long frigid springs, they occasionally wandered beyond their normal habitat, and everyone knew what to do when they came.

Snow began to fall. Rory was grateful; it meant he might be

able to track Camilla, and that his father's men would also be able to track him. With torch-bearing reinforcements behind him, the banshees would surely retreat back to the darkness, no matter how hungry they were.

The moons gave enough light that Rory could find his way around the fields beyond the mews, aided by his intimate knowledge of the land. He had run and played throughout the fields his entire life. He knew every hillock, and every rock. He was only afraid that Camilla would hurt herself in her quest to find Lovely, and that he might miss her in the dark.

"Camilla!" he called out.

The cries ahead of him of "Lovely!" grew fainter. Camilla was clearly running headlong into the dark without care. Rory redoubled his efforts to catch up with her.

Rory got to the fence line, but was greeted by a gaping hole. Timbers had been shattered and pushed aside. Rory's heart froze. The banshees had been inside the pasture.

But the tracks in the snow were of hoof and foot, and led out, beyond the fence. Either the banshees had gotten into the pasture before the snowfall, or they had turned back after destroying it due to the lights in the windows.

Either way, Camilla and Lovely were outside the fence line, and Camilla was his first concern. No one else knew where she was; it was up to Rory to find her and bring her home safely. Rory would let the grooms and his father's staff worry about any banshees that might have gotten inside.

Rory stopped to listen and consider which way the tracks led. If he could hear something, or figure out where Lovely might be going, he could cut off horse and owner rather than simply follow where they had already been.

The tracks led up the slope, away from the house and road. Rory knew where the horse would end up if she kept up in this direction. He could get there first. He turned aside and did his best to ignore the cry of the banshee from farther up the slope. The sound seemed to wrap around every nerve and pull at each one of them, making fear surge through his veins and sending icy tendrils, far colder than any snowfall, into his organs and mind.

But Camilla was out in this. He had to find her. Rory pushed ahead.

"Camilla!"

Rory heard a hue and cry behind him: someone else had found the destroyed fence. He glanced back once, and saw a field of torches and milling men in the pasture. The rest of the denizens of Falconsward, man and beast alike, were safe. Rory turned away from the scene and plunged further into the night.

"Camilla!"

"Here!"

Finally. Rory ran around a large boulder and found Camilla and a trembling Lovely in a shelter formed by several large rocks and overhanging branches. The horse was trying to bolt past Camilla, who kept herself between the beast and freedom.

"Thank the Bearer of Burdens you're all right," he said.

Camilla ignored him. "I can't catch her."

Rory held out the rope and approached slowly. "I can get her. Just don't let her get past you."

Despite her fear, the mare did not strike out with teeth or hooves and Rory was able to get the rope around her neck. Camilla wrapped her arms around the horse and whispered to her and the horse visibly calmed.

"How did you find me?" she asked when she lifted her head from the horse moments later.

"Tracked you in the snow," he said. "Now, we need to get back before the banshees find us."

"Get back?" asked Camilla with some heat. "I'm not going back!"

"You want to be eaten by a banshee?"

"No," she said. She grabbed the rope from him. "I don't know where we'll go, but Lovely and I are leaving. There has to be somewhere other than Falconsward and Scathfell in the world, somewhere I can became a ladies maid or…or even a *barragana*. But not here."

"Are we so horrible?" he asked, astounded. "What did we do? What did I do to make you hate us so much?"

Camilla stepped back from him and clutched the rope to her

chest. "Nothing. I only know that my father wants to get rid of me. I considered jumping from the walls of the manor, or sneaking enough sleeping drugs from the apothecary to make sure I never woke again. I won't live like a prisoner anymore. I won't live at all."

Rory was at a loss. "You're not a prisoner! You're the daughter of Lord Scathfell and will one day be Lady of Falconsward."

"So what?" she said, her anger flaring. "I've been kept shut in a house for years while my father did nothing but wait on my mother, who was out of her mind from illness, and who had gone mad after repeated stillbirths and childbirthing injuries. Now my father wants to send me off to suffer the same fate somewhere else, among strangers, and even my Lovely can't be with me while I endure years of marriage and eventual illness and death."

"But look at my mother," said Rory. "She's alive, and healthy, and happy."

"And has had borne four dead children. My father told me. She might not be mad yet, but she will be one day."

Rory was stunned. He had never considered that his intended bride would be so unhappy about the prospect of marriage to him, and for such a reason! But if he'd been raised in Lord Scathfell's household, perhaps he, too, would think the only fate for a lord's wife was the dreary and tragic one of Lady Scathfell.

"Our life together does not have to be like that," he said.

"We won't have a life together," she said bitterly.

A banshee's scream interrupted them. It was close by. Lovely neighed in terror and Camilla nearly went to her knees. Rory turned around and thought he saw movement in the darkness.

"We certainly won't have a life together if we don't get back to Falconsward," he said.

Another movement. At least two banshees stood between the humans and safety. Maybe more.

They were trapped. Rory's heart beat quickly as he tried to keep his panic at bay. All they needed was for one more banshee to scream and he knew he would, too. And then what? The birds would likely fall on the three of them, their phosphorescent beaks darting into and out of their flesh, ripping muscle from bone, tearing apart organs...

Rory forced his mind away from such morbid thoughts. They weren't dead yet.

Could *laran* be used to control banshees the way it was used with horses and hawks? He wasn't very strong, but he should at least try.

"Lady," he said. "before we either escape this or die trying, I would pledge to you that I will marry you only if you decide, after living at Falconsward for a year, that you wish to enter that state with me."

"You are wasting what little time we have left," she said with a sob. "I'm only sorry Lovely will die with us."

"There's a chance we will die," he said, "but I won't die a craven and shallow man who thinks of the agreement our parents made as final, and you my property." He held out his hand. "Take my hand and my pledge. I will not marry you against your will. In return, you agree to live here for one year, and judge at that time whether or not you will remain. If you choose to go, I will not stop you, nor allow my parents to stop you. That is my promise to you."

Camilla hesitated. Then she stepped forward and held out her hand. "Very well. I pledge to live in Falconsward for one year, and make my decision at that time."

She took his hand. And suddenly, Rory felt the mind of Lovely more clearly than he had ever felt Champion's. Other minds surrounded him, too. Hungry, dark minds that had tracked him by scent and were here to kill and eat.

Rory had heard of the gift of telepaths who could increase others' powers, but he had not known it was found in the Scathfell line. *Catalyst telepath*.

"What is it?" asked Camilla. Her eyes widened. Whatever this bond felt like from her side, she had clearly felt something.

"I think...you are helping me. Don't let go of my hand!"

Rory clutched Camilla's hand and turned toward the banshees. He held out his free hand and thought of himself as a huge predator with giant claws and razor-sharp teeth. *You are afraid of me. You are afraid. Fear me!*

The minds of the banshees became confused. Where was the easy meal they had just scented?

Rory did not stop. The pressure built up behind his eyes, but he did not relent. The strength he drew from Camilla helped; she was afraid herself, but he could sense she had a deep well of iron will to draw on, afraid or not.

Fear! Fear me! I am going to eat you! Be afraid!

The banshees milled about, butting each other with their beaks as they swung their heads from side to side.

Be afraid! I am coming for you. I am coming. I am Fear! Fear! Fear!

Rory gathered what strength he could from his own mind and Camilla's and threw it at the birds so hard he thought his skull might burst from the strain. In the background, he felt a cool tendril of support and comfort from Camilla's mind, and it helped him hold on one moment longer.

Then he was exhausted. His mind could do no more, as untrained as he was. But it had been enough. The birds backed away, then ran. In the distance, Rory heard the shouts of men and glimpsed the flicker of torches. Rescue had arrived. Rory's knees wobbled in relief.

His connection with Camilla faded, but not before he felt a curious warmth come across the bond, a warmth he would have liked to explore But he knew the time wasn't right. There was no need to rush, especially now that he had Camilla's word she would give him, and Falconsward, a year.

He would have let go of Camilla's hand, but she held on tightly. "Are they gone?" she asked.

"Yes."

"You drove them away."

Rory ignored his aching head and kissed Camilla's hand. "*We* did. And we also have rescuers to thank. I don't know if it was more us, or them, but at least together, we scared away the banshees."

"It was you," said Camilla. For the first time in Rory's presence, a quirky smile spread across her face. "And me, too."

She dropped his hand.

"My pledge will not change," said Rory. "You are not a piece of property to be wed to me against your will. If you stay, and choose to be my lady, I will honor you my entire life."

She said nothing, but her face now showed contemplation and respect rather than anger and despair, or worse, nothing at all.

"Rory!" shouted the MacAran from down the slope. "Camilla!"

"We're here!" Rory yelled back. "We are safe."

"Yes," said Camilla softly. "We are."

THE KATANA MATRIX

by Lillian Csernica

Many tales of Darkover begin with the arrival of a stranger, an off-worlder, or a Darkovan returning home. The character then provides the vehicle for we the readers to explore this world, so different from yet so unlike our own. In the best of these tales, the protagonist is more than a mere cipher but a person with history and goals of her own. Darkover often challenges the hero to the limit, for good or ill or healing, as in this tale. At the same time, these encounters can also send ripples of change through the hidebound aristocracy of the Domains. Lillian Csernica says, "I knew one way to really upset the men of Darkover would be to make my main character a woman with a sword. I'm fond of Japanese history and culture, so it seemed quite natural to create Nakatomi Madoka, a female mercenary from a long line of samurai. The villain of the story who hires her has no idea he's about to grab a tiger by the tail."

    Lillian Csernica has published over forty short stories in such markets as *Weird Tales*, *Fantastic Stories*, and *Killing It Softly 1 and 2*. Her nonfiction how-to titles include *The Writer's Spellbook* and *The Fright Factory*. Born in San Diego, Ms. Csernica is a genuine California native. History is her passion, jewelry making her hobby, and glass blowing the next item on her Bucket List. She currently resides in the Santa Cruz mountains with her husband, two sons, and three cats. Visit her at lillian888.wordpress.com.

Madoka spotted the client as soon as he walked in. He wore grubby work pants, a secondhand shirt in well-washed gray, a battered leather jacket and boots. A few days' growth of beard stubble matched his dark brown hair. He kept his hands in his jacket pockets and his shoulders hunched in an effort to conceal his height. Not a bad performance. He could have walked out of any of the service bays in the spaceport's civilian docking area.

Madoka preferred to meet new clients in the Four Moons Cafe. It stayed open at all hours, catering to Trade City and spaceport workers. Terrans and other off-worlders were just common enough to give her some protective camouflage. She wore a sleeveless knee length tunic of green silk figured with clusters of bamboo. Her long black hair she'd braided and bound at the nape of her neck with her mother's jade hair clasp. The odds of meeting another Japanese, especially on Darkover, were quite low. Not many residents of the Edo Enclave on Samarra traveled off-world. Along with the other ancient traditions of their culture, Madoka's people preserved their insistence on marrying only those of *samurai* blood who possessed the required documentation. That was one of the main reasons she'd chosen to leave.

At the counter the client ordered tea and a wedge of fruit pie. As he turned from the counter he scanned the room, taking in the two dozen round tables with their matching chairs in a lovely shade of midnight blue. Madoka sat in the corner farthest from the counter, forcing the client to walk toward her. Round paper lanterns in green, purple, blue-green, and white hung from the ceiling, paying homage to the real moons and lighting the client's path.

The subtle arrogance in his stride. The auburn highlights shining through the temporary hair dye. The beard color too closely matched to the hair. The prickle along Madoka's nerves that alerted her to the presence of danger.

The client was Comyn.

He stopped a few feet from her table. "*Mestra* Nakatomi?"

"*Messire* Gavin?"

"I am. Thank you for agreeing to this meeting."

With a tilt of her head Madoka offered him the seat across from her. "I was told the matter is urgent."

"It is." He set the tea and pie on the table and took his seat. "The deadline is two tendays from receipt of the demand. That gives us fourteen days from now."

"Delivery, recovery, or acquisition?"

The Comyn's expression turned stony. "Recovery."

"Ah." Madoka's estimation of her fee doubled. "I sense a scorched-earth policy."

"We don't tolerate our people being victimized this way."

That voice of feudal authority. So much like her father. Madoka gave the Comyn a long, measuring look. "Your people have never been victims."

"Says the Terran."

Silence hung between them so cold it should have frozen the Comyn's tea.

"*Messire*," said Madoka, "you asked for this meeting. If your politics are going to be a problem, I have other appointments to keep."

"My apologies, *mestra*."

"May I see the demand?"

"Why?"

"This is Darkover. The paper, ink, and penmanship will tell me important details about who we're going to meet."

The Comyn brought an envelope out of his jacket's inner pocket. Madoka took the envelope between her left thumb and forefinger. Quality paper. She opened the envelope and sniffed. The lack of chemical smell told her the ink had been mixed the old-fashioned way by rubbing a stick of pressed ink on a wet inkstone. She gripped the message itself with the thumb and forefinger of her right hand and slid it out.

> *We have Anndra Ridenow. Send one man with pack animals bearing Ridenow's weight in copper to the foot of the Kilghard Hills. You have two ten-days. Deliver the copper or expect Ridenow's head.*

Madoka turned the envelope upside down. The small bulge inside fell out. A scrap of green brocade, gilt-edged and patterned with yellow flowers. At the center of each bloom sat a tiny orange gem.

"Have you confirmed this with the family? Ridenow is

definitely missing?"

"*Mestra* Nakatomi, would I go to the effort of contacting you just for some prank?"

"You might, *messire*. It's been my experience that people with wealth and power often have a strange sense of humor." Madoka laid aside the ransom demand and smoothed out the piece of brocade. "The Kilghard Hills. They're probably using Sain Scarp as their base camp. They're old Rumal's descendants, by heart if not by blood."

"You seem to know quite a lot of Darkover's history."

"I was raised on history, on the lessons it teaches and the patterns it reveals." She stopped stroking the brocade and looked him in the eye. "What exactly do you want me to do?"

"Find him. Free him. Bring him to Thendara."

"So. A round trip from here to the Hellers. Extracting one person. The strong likelihood of armed combat."

"Correct. I will be joining you."

Another bad sign. "Are you responsible for your personal safety? Or is that part of my duties?"

"I am quite capable of protecting myself."

"You don't plan on bringing an escort, I hope?"

"The fewer we are, the faster we travel."

"Good to know you're a practical man."

"You have no idea."

His disguise gave Madoka some idea. He was no stranger to traveling incognito. She tucked the ransom demand and the bit of brocade back into the envelope.

"You know Helvetia?"

"I do."

"Once I receive confirmation of payment, we move out."

"Not acceptable. I'm authorized to approve payment once my cousin is delivered to me safe and whole."

Madoka weighed the pros and cons of walking away. This Comyn would want things done his way at every turn. If she didn't given him exactly what he wanted for his money, he'd badmouth her all over Darkover, possibly the entire Empire.

"*Messire* Gavin," she began. "You must know my reputation

or you wouldn't have asked for the meeting. Given the kind of people who can afford to hire me, I wouldn't survive long if I didn't honor my commitments."

"Anndra's life depends on moving fast and striking hard." The Comyn let all of his natural arrogance show in his glare. "Surely you can understand my caution."

"I understand this negotiation is about power, not money. If you hire me, you stand back and let me use the skills you're paying for."

"You can't mean to do this alone. Who will you bring with you?"

"A reliable team I've worked with often enough to trust them."

"I need to know who they are. If I'm paying them, I deserve that much."

"You're not paying them. I am. You pay me."

The Comyn stared into her eyes. If he was trying anything with *laran*, he'd get nowhere. Growing up under her father's imperious glare had hardened Madoka to such tricks.

"You pride yourself on your reputation for success," the Comyn said, "on your amazing record of never getting caught."

"That's right."

"But you did get caught once, didn't you, *Mestra* Nakatomi?" The Comyn smiled. "Three years ago you received a dishonorable discharge from the Spaceforce for aiding and abetting smugglers."

Madoka's heart stuttered. This Comyn had better connections than she'd realized. "Everybody has a past."

"You like to work on Darkover. Your last three contracts have been here."

"What's your point?"

"Mercenaries have their place, but thieves and traitors are universally despised. The right word in the right ear and you'll be both arrested and deported. You will never set foot on Darkover again."

The ring of absolute sincerity in his voice made Madoka sick with thwarted fury. Another man determined to make her do things his way no matter how much she suffered. Just like her father, determined to make her into the son she'd never be. Just like her partner, Conrad. He'd maneuvered her into giving him the Spaceforce quartermaster information he needed to tip off the smugglers.

"Fine. I prefer to work with Free Amazons."

"Why?"

"Because most men are more trouble than they're worth."

"Very well." The Comyn drank the last of his tea. "As a gesture of good faith, I will see to it half of your fee is deposited within the next few hours. Be ready to leave as soon as it clears."

Madoka watched him walk out of the cafe. *Dom* Gavin might think he was clever, but by hiring an off-world mercenary he'd already revealed one very useful fact. Whatever he was really up to, he wanted to keep other Comyn out of it.

A bitter wind blew down from Scaravel Pass. Kyrrdis shed its murky blue-green moonlight across the dull brown hillside. Madoka hunkered down behind a patch of scrub. A shirt and pants of the sturdy green cloth woven by the mountain folk topped with a dark brown cloak helped her blend into the landscape. Fifty feet away stood the back of the guard tower. Arrow slits in the crumbling masonry allowed the faint glimmer of lantern light to brighten the darkness. A shadow slid away from the tower. Moments later, Raziya n'ha Sandel crept up beside Madoka. In the usual dark brown clothing favored by Amazons, with the hood of her cloak drawn up to hide her golden braid, she was almost invisible.

"How many guards?" Madoka murmured.

"Two upstairs, four downstairs."

"Anybody on patrol?"

"Two. They're on the far side of what's left of the wall."

"Where is our target sleeping?"

"He's in the upper story. It's the only part of the *forst* with four walls and a roof."

"Mountain granite. Wonderful." Madoka shook her head. "I knew I should have brought more black powder."

"Explosives? Really?" Gavin scowled. "Why not just start a forest fire and drive them all out that way? Bad enough we've ridden into bandit territory with nothing but women."

"They're not 'women'," Madoka said. "They're Free Amazons. Don't make me explain this again."

Gavin's eyes, that eerie silver-gray, narrowed. "Kindly bear in mind we are working against a deadline."

"Sain Scarp was a fortress back in old Rumal's day." Madoka looked up at the broken wall of granite blocks jutting out from the hilltop above them. "Now we've got eight bandits holed up in a two-story stone hut. Not the biggest challenge I've ever faced."

Madoka slid down the side of the ravine. Gavin followed her. Raziya's fellow Amazons had made a cold camp with four tents surrounding a circle of fist-sized stones. That would have been their fire pit had they been certain the smoke would not betray their presence. Anja, the rounder, cheerier Amazon with a wealth of gray curls had prepared a meal of brown bread, cold meat, and slices of pale cheese. Madoka sat cross-legged on a saddle blanket spread out on the stony ground. Anja began handing round the wooden dishes that held each portion.

Raziya accepted her dish and sat beside Madoka. She bit into a cooked rabbit leg and chewed, frowning. "I'm still wondering what in Zandru's hells a Ridenow was doing on the far side of the Hellers."

Gavin stared at her across the cold fire pit, those silvery eyes gleaming in the dusk. "What makes you think *Dom* Anndra was that far north?"

Madoka drank a long swallow of watered wine. "Gayla, tell the man what you heard."

A thin Amazon with straw-colored hair cut short above her ears looked over from checking her horse's saddle girth.

"The men here have no liking for this place. They wish they hadn't come, no matter what riches they were promised."

"Who did the promising?" Gavin asked.

"It's a family matter. None of them would say more."

"What happened to your cousin's escort?" Madoka asked. "He would have had one, wouldn't he?"

Gavin shrugged. "It's not unknown for a lad his age to do some traveling on his own."

"Over the Wall Around the World?" Madoka asked. "And at this time of year, when the sun fades early? And all by his little red-headed self?"

"I hired you to find him and get him away from the bandits who captured him. That's all you need to know."

"*Dom* Gavin," Raziya said, "by our reckoning these bandits caught the Ridenow at least two weeks ago. That's how long it would take a man riding two, maybe three, horses to get from here to the Ridenow Domain."

"What's your point, *mestra?*"

"These men have been here not more than a tenday."

"How can you tell?"

"Trail sign is too fresh. Not enough horse droppings piled up. Only one latrine pit dug so far. Not enough trash, scraps, or bones from supplies they've used up."

"Bandits are messy *gre'zuin*." Madoka tossed the rind from her cheese into the fire pit. "They don't care because they'll just move on."

"This is all fascinating, but what does it prove?"

Madoka smiled. "Ridenow has no idea these bandits have their boy. You knew, so that means one of two things. Either you had him taken, or you intercepted the ransom demand."

Gavin shot to his feet. All four Amazons closed in, trapping him in a ring of bared steel.

"I am Gavin Mikhail Lanart-Alton," Gavin said. "From the Alton Domain. Stand down or learn why even Comyn fear the Alton Gift."

Madoka got to her feet. "Look around, Lord Alton. It's just you and us out here. I'm guessing whoever sent you to fetch *Dom* Anndra won't be in a hurry to risk discovery by making sure you come out of this all right."

"Loyalty among Comyn is legendary. We do not betray our kinsmen."

"Does the name Aldaran mean anything to you? Barred from becoming a recognized Domain for the despicable act of allowing Terrans to set foot on Darkover?"

"And rightly so."

"I really don't care who lives or dies among you Comyn as long as we complete the job and my people get paid."

"You have taken pains to point out how isolated and vulnerable you believe me to be." Gavin eased back down onto his seat on the other blanket. "What do you want?"

"Tell me the truth." Madoka leaned forward to stare right into those silvery eyes. "Are we here to rescue *Dom* Anndra or to kill him?"

"You can't kill Anndra. Not until I get the answers I need."

"Interrogation? No problem. I can't guarantee he'll survive it."

Gavin shot her a look of contempt. "I'm a telepath. I hardly need your barbaric methods."

"Fine. The half you've already paid can be my fee for getting you this far." She stood up. "Break camp. We're done here."

"*Mestra* Nakatomi. Surely you're not walking out on a contract only half-finished?"

"When the client won't tell me what the contract really is, I decide when I'm done."

Gavin blew out a long breath. "Very well. Stay. I need your services to 'extract' Anndra. What happens from there depends entirely on how he answers my questions."

A night bird twittered from the rooftop of the guard tower. The cry of a mud-rabbit snapped up by a hungry predator rose just above the wind.

"Follow me." Madoka whispered. "The Amazons will clear the way. Let me do the fighting."

Gavin nodded. "Agreed."

Madoka kept to the shadows cast by the tower as Kyrrdis, the blue-green moon, crept higher. A knotted rope slapped down against the wall. Madoka tugged at the strap that secured her *katana* in its scabbard across her back, patted the bandolier draped over her left shoulder, then grabbed the rope with both hands and planted her feet against the mortared stones. Out in front of the guard tower a tree crashed down, spooking the bandits' horses. The clatter and jingle of harness betrayed their frantic rearing and plunging. Sleepy voices cursed.

"Jaken! Damn you, Jaken! Are you asleep out there?"

Madoka climbed up to the wooden platform atop the tower where Gayla waited. The slim Amazon bent down and held out one hand. Madoka clasped wrists with her and Gayla hauled her the rest of the way. Gavin clambered onto the roof behind her.

The bandit who'd been acting as lookout lay in a spreading pool of his own blood. Madoka squatted down beside the body. Shirt and pants made of good quality cloth. Boots and belt cut from matched leather. Hands somewhat roughened from handling reins. Nails trimmed and clean.

"Quite a tidy bunch of bandits," she muttered. "One might think they were something else entirely."

Keeping low, Madoka led Gavin across the roof to the trapdoor where Anja sat, using her bulk to thwart the efforts of the bandits below. The clamor out in front of the guard tower grew louder with sudden shouts and a scream.

"Boran! We've got Ama—"

The warning was silenced by a meaty thud.

At Madoka's nod, Anja rolled off the trapdoor. It burst open and a man's head popped up. Anja slammed her heavy fry pan down on the man's skull, cracking it like a nutshell. He dropped out of sight. Anja peered down after him, then looked up at Madoka and nodded. Madoka jumped down through the trapdoor to land on a tabletop, scattering bottles of *firi* and a deck of playing cards.

"Stop! Or the Comyn dies!"

In the far corner, another well-dressed "bandit" had his back to the wall with his captive held before him like a shield. The "bandit" had one fist buried in the captive's red hair, pulling his head back. The red hair, fine clothing, and lack of any wounds or even bruises told Madoka she'd found Anndra Ridenow.

Madoka froze where she crouched on the tabletop, right hand gripping the hilt of her *katana*, left hand resting at her belt.

"Easy now," she said. "You want that fellow alive. Spilling

Comyn blood means a bad death for all of us."

"Who are you?" asked the man holding Ridenow. "Why are you here?"

"He might be Anndra Ridenow, but you are no bandit." Madoka stepped down onto the seat of a chair, and from there to the floor. "I'm guessing you're his escort, trying to blend in with the local bad boys."

"Did the Dealer send you?" Ridenow asked. "We were supposed to meet at the rendezvous point."

Aware that Gavin still perched on the rooftop next to the open trap door, Madoka chose an easy answer. "The Dealer changed the plan once he found out you were holed up in Rumal's ruins."

"I don't believe you. In his dealings with the Comyn, the Dealer would never send a woman, much less a woman with a sword!"

"More fool him, then."

The door burst open. Another "bandit" stumbled in backward, one sleeve soaked in blood. Raziya charged in after him. She snatched up a chair and swung it hard, slamming the man against the wall.

"Free Amazons?" The man holding Ridenow stepped to the side and pushed him into the corner. He sheathed his dagger and drew his sword. "Stay back, *Dom* Anndra!"

The bandit Raziya hit spun away from the wall, coming for Madoka with a big knife in his hand. Madoka reached back and drew her *katana* in one smooth slash that cut the bandit from shoulder to hip. On the backswing she sliced straight across his belly.

"Stop that!" Ridenow cried. "I'm not being held captive!"

Gayla staggered in, left arm cradled in her right, her features pinched with pain. "All clear. Danna is calming the horses."

Ridenow's guard lunged toward her. Madoka's left hand snapped forward. A gleam of silver streaked through the air and buried itself in the man's throat.

"Marcus!" Ridenow fell to his knees beside his guard. "Damn you, you Terran bitch!"

Gavin swung down through the trapdoor, landing just behind

Ridenow. He threw one arm around Ridenow's chest and jammed a Terran syringe into his neck.

"Where is it?"

Ridenow hung limp in Gavin's grip. "*Reish. Reish* to you, Gavin." He giggled. "Gavin, King of *Reish*."

"What did you do to him?" Madoka asked. "Why is he babbling about horse droppings?"

"I told you, I need answers." Gavin's silvery eyes narrowed. "Anndra, tell me. Where is it?"

Ridenow winced, teeth bared as he shook his head.

Raziya stepped up beside Madoka. "He's trying to pry the answers out of Ridenow's mind. He must be an Alton."

"And that makes the drug *kirian*."

Madoka flicked the blood from her blade with a practiced snap of her wrist, then sheathed it. She put two fingers into her mouth and blew a sharp whistle. Anja looked down through the trap door. Danna came running from outside. Gayla stayed by the door.

"We have a problem," Madoka said. "*Dom* Anndra claims he's not a captive. That he was waiting for word about a meeting." She shot a glare at Gavin. "*Dom* Gavin appears to be after something he believes *Dom* Anndra has taken possession of. Whether or not either of them has any right to whatever it is has yet to be determined."

She slapped the hilt of her katana twice.

The Amazons flanked Gavin, daggers ready. Anja tossed the knotted rope down to Raziya. She threw it around Gavin's ankles and hauled backward, jerking his feet out from under him and dumping him on his backside. Anger burst forth in a stinging tide, leaving a scalding pain inside Madoka's mind. Freed from Gavin's grip, Ridenow sprawled on his side. Gavin rolled over onto his belly. Before he could get up, Anja planted a boot between his shoulder blades. Madoka put an end to his telepathic assault with one hard kick to the back of his head.

Ridenow struggled up onto his feet and ran for the door, staggering under the influence of the *kirian*. He threw his weight against Gayla, driving her wounded arm into the doorframe. She cursed him in blistering *cahuenga* and tried to grab him with her good hand. He shoved her aside and disappeared down the hallway.

Madoka ran after him.

Anndra Ridenow burst out of the tower doorway and made straight for the nearest horse. Madoka expected him to wheel around and take the trail back to the road that led to Thendara. Instead he drew his own sword and kicked the horse, making the stallion burst into a thundering gallop right at her. Madoka plucked a sparkflower from her bandolier, twisted the small pink tube, then tossed the sparkflower at the horse. It hit the dirt in front of the stallion. Crimson and purple sparks erupted, spinning into the image of a lotus blossom. Ridenow's horse reared, fighting to turn aside. Ridenow struggled one-handed with the reins. The horse shook its great head, jerking Ridenow half out of the saddle, then jinked sideways. Thrown off balance, Ridenow tumbled forward over the horse's shoulder.

Mindful of the answers worth so much to Gavin Alton, Madoka kicked the sword out of Ridenow's hand. Ridenow wobbled to his feet. His fingers closed on Madoka's bandolier. He jerked her to him, driving his fist into her solar plexus to force the breath out of her. Madoka slammed the heel of her hand against Ridenow's nose. He flinched back with a yelp of pain. She broke his grip on her bandolier and spun to her left, using a foot sweep to scythe his legs out from under him. Muddled with pain and the effects of the *kirian*, Ridenow rolled away from her, toward the latrine pit.

Madoka hurried forward to stop him before she had to ask the Amazons to haul him out of the pit. Ridenow rolled back and flung his arms around her knees, toppling her across him. Their combined weight sent them both tumbling over the edge into the foul reek of the latrine pit. Madoka landed on top. Her weight shoved Ridenow down under the surface of the soupy muck. The stench left her dizzy and sick. She thrust both hands down into the mire and closed her fists in the front of Ridenow's tunic. She dragged him up onto his feet. He cursed and spat and wiped at the blood running from his broken nose.

"Enough," Madoka said. "I was hired to get you out of here."

"Gavin—kill—" Ridenow fought for breath, straining to inhale. "Kill—you, too."

His knees buckled. Ridenow yanked at his collar, then fell face first into the mire. Madoka grabbed the back of Ridenow's sword belt and a fistful of his tunic. Hands slipping, footing unsure, she hauled backward and dragged him upright, then pinned him against the wall of the pit. No heartbeat. She pressed her hands over Ridenow's heart and pumped as well as the awkward leverage allowed. Pinching his nose shut, she blew three breaths into his mouth. Still nothing. Weakened by the *kirian*, his breathing hampered by the broken nose, Anndra Ridenow was dead.

So much for Gavin's precious answers. And so much for the other half of her fee.

Madoka swiped the back of her hand across her eyes, trying to clear her vision. The adrenalin burn drained away, leaving her sick and shaking. She kept her *katana* ready in her right hand and fumbled her way along the side of the pit on her left. Every step through the knee-deep sludge brought fresh fumes bursting upward. She gripped the hilt of her dagger in her left hand and jabbed it into the wall of the pit, searching for some strata beneath the topsoil dense enough to support the pitons she carried. Six or seven of those would give the footholds she needed to climb out. On the fifth stab, the point of her dagger hit something solid. Madoka pushed the point deeper. The tip slid away to the side. She pried away enough soil to reveal a glint of gold. More digging left a scrap of cloth hanging out of the hole. The high moon shed its blue-green rays on a band of fine embroidery. In the center of each tiny flower glittered an orange gem.

Madoka pulled on the cloth. A heavy weight held it trapped. More digging freed a lump that fit into the palm of her hand, rolled up in a strip of cloth torn from Ridenow's tunic. What had he hidden here, and why? She unwrapped the cloth. Inside it lay a raw chunky crystal fresh from the belly of the planet.

A rope hit her shoulder.

"Up," said Raziya.

Madoka wiped her *katana* and dagger, sheathed both, then stuffed the crystal inside her blouse. It nestled against her belly just above her belt. She grabbed the rope and climbed out of the pit, then staggered over to one of the buckets used for watering the horses. She hoisted the full bucket up and dumped it over her head. The water rinsed away at least some of the filth. Danna pressed a cloth into her hand. Madoka scrubbed her face clean, then stared around her.

"Where's that lying prick of a Comyn?"

"Gayla and Anja have him tied up across a saddle." Danna looked around. "Where's the one you chased?"

"Dead."

"You killed him?" Raziya asked.

"The *kirian* killed him."

"Did you get any of those answers?"

"I got more than that."

The cool night air had begun to clear Madoka's head. She brought out the crystal. Deep inside, a spark glimmered. More appeared, gathering into ribbons of light. They twined and danced, drawing her inward, lighting up the cold darkness that filled her spirit. Down in the depths, something like a sparkflower bloomed.

Madoka's guts roiled, doubling her over. Dizziness made the night spin around her. Voices in her head. Not her thoughts. Raziya, angry at Gavin, ready to bury both him and the crystal in the same deep hole. Danna, angry about Gayla getting wounded. Pain tore through Madoka, pushing up and out of her in a shriek.

"Madoka!" Raziya grabbed her by the shoulders. "What is *wrong* with you? Everything living thing in the Hellers must have heard that!"

Danna caught Raziya by the arm. "It's that crystal she's holding. Look at it glow!"

Colored lights danced around Madoka. She tried to grab one.

"We have to get her to a Tower," Raziya said. "Only Keepers know what to do with crystals that size."

Four days' hard riding took them south from Sain Scarp over Scaravel Pass and southeast to Neskaya. Between the nausea and the hallucinations, Madoka clung to the reins and did her best to stay in the saddle. The world kept turning gray. Pinpricks of light flashed everywhere around her. Sleep left her writhing in a world of mists and whispers. By the third day Raziya had to buy the biggest horse they could find and mount up with Madoka sitting in front of her. Only the Amazon's arms on either side of her kept Madoka from tumbling out of the saddle.

"Peace, *mestra*. All will be well."

Madoka opened her eyes. A girl sat beside her, thin and pretty with long red hair. She dabbed at Madoka's sweaty face with a cool cloth, then held a porcelain cup to her lips. "Drink a little, *mestra*. You are quite weak."

Madoka took a sip of tea. Her belly heaved. She rolled away from the girl and retched, bringing up nothing but bile. The glittering pinpricks appeared again, filling the air. Madoka fell back against her pillow.

"Raziya?"

"Here." A hand clasped her right hand and held it tight. "Can you sit up?"

Strong arms lifted her. Someone else stuffed pillows behind her back.

"*Mestra*," another voice said. "I am Linora Aillard, Keeper of this Tower. You show every symptom of threshold sickness. I am here to help you recover."

Madoka stared up at the figure bending over her. Red robes. Red veil hiding the face, if there was a face. Another hallucination? A Keeper. A Tower. Not Nevarsin, unless they were in the guest house. Not Arilinn. Too far away. Neskaya?

"Where's the magic rock?"

"You're still holding it," Raziya said.

Madoka became aware of the ache in her left hand. Her fingers gripped the blue crystal so tightly the ache extended halfway up her forearm.

"Be at peace, *mestra*," the Keeper said. "Listen to my voice. I shall guide you."

Alarm bells clanged in Madoka's mind. Red robes. Danger. Keepers. Keep your hands off. Touching a Keeper was punishable by death. Keepers knew all about matrix technology. Ribbons of blue light fell across the Keeper's red robes, striping them in purple. Purple in Japanese was *murasaki*. Lady Murasaki Shikibu wrote *The Tale of Genji* about a prince who wandered around seducing noblewomen. Charming but faithless.

"*Dom* Gavin," Madoka said. "Where is he?"

"Here, *Mestra* Nakatomi." He stood at the foot of her bed, looking remarkably civil. "I am so relieved to see you awake and alert. Threshold sickness often occurs when Comyn coming into puberty experience the awakening of their *laran*."

"I am not Comyn."

"We are in your debt, *Mestra* Nakatomi," the Keeper said. "You stumbled upon the secret of *Dom* Anndra's journey north."

Madoka glared at Gavin. "And how much of this secret did you already know?"

"The Towers had picked up a brief signal from the Tramontana region," Gavin said. "A burst of matrix crystal energy without any signature belonging to a known Comyn."

"Why would a Ridenow go looking for that kind of trouble?"

"Our exact question," Gavin said. "Anndra was an empath. The Ridenow Gift wouldn't be of much use at such a distance."

"And yet he found the crystal and brought it back over the Hellers." Madoka frowned. "What I really want to know is why the magic rock decided I'm its favorite person."

"Let go, *mestra*," said the Keeper. "All that you love, all that you fear. All that binds the crystal to you."

Binding. Attachment. The First Noble Truth: Everyone suffers. Attachment leads to suffering. Was Madoka too attached to something? The crystal, but she hadn't chosen that. The crystal was outside. What lay inside? What held Madoka with chains so mighty she was slave to the attachment?

Madoka shut her eyes, fighting her way past the pain echoing through every nerve in her body. There were rules about matrix crystals. Every Comyn had his or her own little one. Once they got their crystal, nobody else touched it. If they did, it could cripple or even kill them. Ridenow must have known how to prevent the crystal from choosing someone before he arrived at his destination.

"Once upon a time," she said, "a Comyn and a Terran joined forces to stop a bandit king from stealing the power of a matrix crystal." Madoka nodded to herself. "The Terran had been captured by the bandit king who thought the Terran was a Comyn heir able to make use of the crystal. Does this story sound at all familiar, *Dom* Gavin?"

"Ancient history. Irrelevant."

"Quite relevant. Your ancestor, Kennard Alton, and the Terran Larry Montray decided it was better to destroy the crystal than risk the devastation it could cause." Madoka smiled. "Collateral damage: Kennard Alton's crystal was destroyed."

"What's your point, *mestra?*"

"You can't kill me. You can't separate me from the crystal. And you sure as hell can't let me just walk out of here with it." On familiar ground again, Madoka felt stronger. "Whatever happens next, my cooperation is essential. How much is that worth to you?"

"Curing your threshold sickness. Making sure you don't lose your mind before you can recover. And above all, not telling the Comyn Council you murdered Anndra Ridenow."

"I didn't kill him. *You* shot him up with *kirian*. *You* made him too weak and disoriented to walk a straight line. He fell into the latrine pit and drowned."

"So you say. Have you any witnesses?"

"I have witnesses to you jumping Anndra Ridenow from behind, injecting him with *kirian*, then trying to read his mind by force."

"Only a Comyn is qualified to bring such charges."

"I'm guessing if it comes down to your word against mine, they'll believe the person holding the magic rock."

"The crystal has taken possession of something deep within you," the Keeper said. "You know this to be true. All Comyn wear their crystals around their necks."

"Slave collars," Madoka muttered. So tired. Tired of fighting all the time. "I'm nobody's slave!"

"Let go. Let go of the cause of your pain, your sorrow, source of the chains that bind you to the crystal."

Pain. Madoka fell down a well of memory, back to a time when her mother was still alive, when Madoka was very small. Her mother loved her, brushing her hair, bringing her little toys, always smiling. Her father.... Never more than a nod to acknowledge a birthday or a perfect score or even just a greeting.

When her brother Tomohiro arrived to ruin Madoka's world, their father filled the house with lucky bamboo and showered their mother with jade. Every one of Tomohiro's birthdays meant feasts and treats and celebrations. Madoka's birthdays brought one red envelope, perhaps a new doll. Tomohiro. Spoiled, lazy, stupid and clumsy and arrogant. He got away with anything and everything, blaming all his faults on Madoka. Her good grades, her judo skills, any achievement great or small was dismissed in order to spare Tomohiro's feelings.

"Your father refused to love you, Madoka," the Keeper murmured. "Why? You were the best at any subject you chose."

"Never enough." Hot tears ran down Madoka's cheeks. "Never good enough."

"Your search has led you here, to Darkover. To a crystal from the Ages of Chaos. You yearn to prove how worthy of love you truly are. The crystal knows this."

All those years of pain and rage and disappointment. All the punishments she'd suffered for Tomohiro's bad behavior. She won the Samarra World Kendo Championship. Her father complained about the expense of sending her to that city, paying her lodging, shipping the trophy home again. Tomohiro began growing illegal herbs in a garden shed and selling them to his friends, turning them into addicts and dealers. He put the whole family in danger of arrest and prosecution. When Madoka discovered the plants and told their mother, nothing happened. The shed disappeared one night, and their father set Tomohiro up in his own landscaping business.

"You've done great things, Madoka," the Keeper said. "Time to rest. Time to heal. Release the past. Break the chains that bind you to this crystal, this symbol of all your father has withheld from you."

The crystal. Madoka raised her left hand. In the shifting gray mists, the blue crystal shone, its glow stabbing through the murk. The ribbons of light inside it rippled like the silks of her mother's antique kimono.

"Are you my enemy?" Madoka asked.

I am yours. Friend or enemy, that choice is also yours.

"Let go," the Keeper insisted. "You are not meant to carry such a burden. Leave that duty to us."

Duty. Loyalty.

"Raziya?" Madoka closed her right hand. Raziya no longer held it. "Raziya? Where are you?"

"Fight!" The faint sound of Raziya's voice reached Madoka through the mists. "Fight!"

In a world of gray uncertainty, Madoka reached for what she knew. The crystal in her hand flared, sending out a long shaft of blue light. It revealed five figures, two on each side of her and one right in front.

"Hands off the Amazon!" Madoka bellowed. "I'll gut every one of you!"

Searing pain shot through Madoka's head, ripping at her concentration.

"Worthless creature!" The Keeper's voice now rang with scorn. "Unworthy. Unwanted. Unloved. Yield the crystal to those meant to possess it!"

Madoka stared at the *katana* she held, a sword forged of pure blue light. The gray mists surrounding her resolved into her room in her father's house on Samarra. *Tatami* mats. A futon. Her books and clothing and trophies and everything that made her world bearable when she was still in school. She'd just come home from winning the Championship. There on her desk sat a handmade pawlonia wood case, long enough to hold only one particular object. Madoka opened the case to discover an antique *katana*. Not just some souvenir from a trip to the old country.

This was an actual weapon of war.

"Do you like it, Doki-*chan?*"

In the doorway stood her father, dressed in a somber gray *yukata* with an *obi* striped in black and white wrapped around his thin waist. The use of her childhood nickname didn't shock Madoka half so much as her father's smile. An actual smile.

"You thought this came from your mother, didn't you?"

"Hai, Oto-san."

"That was for the best. Tomo-*kun* would have seen only its material worth and thrown a tantrum."

"I—don't understand."

"I know. You are so strong, my daughter. No fear, even in the cradle. No matter what the challenge, you were determined to succeed."

Was that pride in her father's voice? Now she knew she was hallucinating.

"Doki-*chan*, I could leave you on your own because you didn't need me. Tomohiro got most of my attention because he is weak. I had to keep watch over him to prevent even greater acts of shameful self-indulgence."

Old pain brought the sting of tears. "I worked so hard. My hands bled. I broke my arm in kendo practice! You never said a word."

"You did not need my praise, child. The whole world could see your strength and your skill."

"I did need it. I needed it so much!"

"Words fade." Her father extended one hand toward the *katana*. "Better to give you the gift that would prove my confidence in you as the rightful heir to our family's history."

Madoka took hold of the hilt, lifting the *katana* into the light. Perfect balance. As she studied it, she sucked in a painful gasp.

"A Sukezane! Oh, Papa, a real Sukezane!"

"*Hai.* There are older *katana* to be had, but this one seemed the best for you."

At once all the shattered pieces of Madoka's heart came back together in a sudden fusion of light and love and peace.

"*Domo arigato gozaimasu, Oto-san.*" She bowed. "I will do

my best to be worthy of your confidence."

"I know you will, my daughter. Should you wish to come home, even for just a visit, know that you will be more than welcome."

The scene faded, leaving Madoka standing in the gray mist, holding the *katana* of light.

"Father!" she shouted. "See me now! See Nakatomi Madoka fight as our ancestors fought!"

She lunged, skewering the figure to her left. Pivot. Slash. A scream, to her right. Hot spikes pierced her bones. Ice crystals clogged her lungs. She held tight to the hilt of the *katana*, dismissing the illusions. The blue blade flashed and stabbed and burned its way through the gray mists.

"Too much!" The Keeper's voice. "She's too strong!"

"We've got to get that crystal," said Dom Gavin.

"I am Nakatomi Madoka, daughter of fifty generations of *samurai!* Know me, and know that I will not be defeated!"

The Keeper screamed. The power of her will faded.

"Madoka!" Raziya's voice. "Stop!"

Madoka opened her eyes to find herself on her feet. The cot where she'd lain had been knocked over. Bodies lay slumped on the floor. Two on her left, two on her right. At her feet lay the red-haired girl, the one who brought tea and cool cloths. Madoka stared around her at the wreckage of the room. In her hands she held only the crystal. Her father's *katana* hung in its scabbard from a hook on the wall.

"What have I done?"

"You saved us." Raziya leaned against one wall. At her feet lay two of the Tower guards. She limped over to Madoka. The Amazon's clothing was torn. Blood stained one pant leg. A bruise darkened her cheek. "They tried to take the crystal from you."

"What did I *do?*"

"You fought them. In that place where Tower sorcerers work their magic."

Madoka knelt beside the girl and brushed aside the silky red hair that covered her face.

"*Dom* Gavin abandoned this child to a danger the Keeper herself refused to face?" She stood up. "Where have they gone?"

"Comyn Castle in Thendara. They mean to alert all Comyn."

"Then we ride for Thendara." Madoka stuffed the crystal down inside her blouse. She slung her father's *katana* across her back. "They need to know *Dom* Gavin and his pet Keeper are traitors."

Madoka reined in outside the tower that housed the Crystal Chamber, meeting place of the Comyn Council. Getting inside the gates of Comyn Castle had been easy. She wore a black leather jerkin over a burgundy tunic and black leggings with high black boots. Between her cover story and the power of the crystal itself, no one got in her way. Raziya and Danna pulled up on either side of her.

Madoka dismounted and adjusted the hang of her *katana* across her back. It now lay rolled inside a small decorative wall-hanging, scabbard and all. A length of parchment ornamented with patterns of maple leaves further disguised the sheathed *katana*. Madoka had bought the cheap piece of art at a shop near Thendara House while Raziya took Gayla and Anja inside to receive the medical care they needed. They could have gone to the Guildhouse in Neskaya, but they wanted to go home. Madoka knew that feeling all too well. While she'd been busy shopping, Danna stitched together a pouch from the length of oiled silk Madoka used to wrap up her throwing stars. Tan silk, patterned with green turtles, those symbols of longevity.

Now the pouch protected the crystal. Madoka touched the crystal where it nestled once again inside her tunic. She felt a kinship with turtles. When danger threatened, they could withdraw into their shells. Most enemies would give up and hunt some easier prey. Madoka sought her prey inside the Crystal Chamber itself. Gavin Alton would not escape her by hiding within its walls.

The House Guard in their uniforms of green and black stepped forward as Madoka approached the tower doors.

"What brings two Free Amazons and you, *mestra*, to Comyn

Castle?"

"I have business with *Dom* Gavin Alton," Madoka said. "He asked me to meet him here, him and the Keeper from Neskaya Tower."

The guard in the more elaborate uniform looked her over. "Have you any proof of this?"

Madoka smiled, flexing her will and feeling a corresponding surge of power from the crystal. "How could I know which Tower the Keeper is from had not *Dom* Gavin himself told me?"

"What's that on your back, *mestra?*"

"A scroll."

"A message, then? That big?"

"It's a work of art meant to be given to the one worthy of the owner's highest regard." Madoka's voice held the solid sincerity of absolute truth. "Keep me standing out here and the parchment might well dry out to the point of becoming brittle. When *Dom* Gavin unrolls it, imagine his distress when cracks appear and spoil the gift."

The two guards behind their commander exchanged a glance. Madoka knew that look. This was a problem for somebody higher up in authority.

"The Amazons stay out here," the higher-ranking guard said.

"They were hired to protect the scroll. Where it goes, they go."

"There is no place safer than inside Comyn Castle."

"Have you ever tried to stop a Free Amazon from honoring a contract she'd sworn to carry out?"

The guard started to speak, swallowed, then shook his head.

"Don't start now. Once I put this scroll into the hands of *Dom* Gavin himself, the contract will be complete."

"I will have *Dom* Gavin informed of your arrival. The Council is currently in session, so—"

"Just let us come inside out of the sun. *Dom* Gavin can take delivery and we can be on our way."

The guard's head bobbed up and down in a nod. His right arm jerked upward in a gesture that made the other two guards open the Tower doors.

"Many thanks, *messire*." Madoka walked past him into the cool blue interior of the tower. Raziya and Gayla followed her.

Word passed quickly, just as Madoka had hoped it would. People dressed in the colors of the Seven Domains drifted in from various parts of the tower and through the main doors, curious enough to catch a glimpse of two Free Amazons with a Terran. Soon Gavin Alton himself appeared. He made it halfway down the winding stairway when he spotted Madoka. His eyes widened. His teeth clenched. He spun around and ran back up the stairs, shoving his way through the onlookers. Madoka chased him to the Crystal Chamber itself. Two more of the House Guard stood before the doors, backs straight and eyes front.

"Stop her!" Gavin yelled. "She's a Terran! An assassin!"

The guard on the left reached for his sword. The guard on the right opened the doors ahead of Gavin. Madoka quickened her stride and dove beneath the left guard's arm while it was still bent in the act of drawing his sword. She slid across the polished stone floor and cleared the doorway just as the House Guard inside slammed the doors shut behind her.

Madoka flung up one hand to shield her eyes from the rainbow brilliance blinding her. It took precious moments for her sight to clear and her brain to register the full glory of the Crystal Chamber. Eight walls. Each of the Seven Domains displayed its own banner, and beneath it that family sat in rows of tiered seats. A good-looking man with flame red hair and a stern expression stared down at Madoka from his throne. He wore silver and blue, Hastur colors. Regis Hastur himself?

Gavin kept running, putting himself on the opposite side of the Chamber, under the green and black banner of the Alton Domain.

"What madness is this?" Regis Hastur demanded. "*Dom* Gavin, who is this woman?"

"I am Nakatomi Madoka." She got to her feet. "Daughter of Nakatomi Masahiro, son of fifty generations of *samurai*." She stabbed an accusing finger at *Dom* Gavin. "Lord Hastur, I come to tell you that man is a traitor to the Comyn and to Darkover itself."

"Lies!" Gavin stalked forward. "She's a Terran assassin, a hired killer. Even now she wears a sword, here, in the Crystal Chamber itself!"

Regis Hastur beckoned the Honor Guard. Six of them surrounded Madoka. She held up both hands in a gesture of peace. "Hear me out, Lord Hastur. I bring you absolute proof."

"Show us this proof."

"Lord Hastur!" Gavin lunged between Madoka and Regis Hastur. "I beg you, take care! For all we know she has some Terran weapon!"

"*Dom* Gavin plays a good game of misdirection, Lord Hastur. Let me prove my sincerity." Madoka freed the clasp on the strap holding her *katana* across her back. The bundle fell to the floor. She unbuckled her belt and let it drop, then caught the silk pouch as it fell out from under her tunic. "In here lies proof of everything I come to tell you."

She opened the pouch and spilled the crystal out onto the palm of her left hand. The Crystal Chamber erupted in shouts and cries and harsh gasps of wonder. Regis Hastur rose from his seat.

"I will have order!"

The uproar settled down. Regis Hastur remained standing.

"How did a Terran come to possess a matrix crystal of that size?"

"Ask *Dom* Gavin, Lord Hastur. He hired me to help him take it from the Comyn who found it."

All eyes turned to Gavin. As he drew breath to speak, Madoka thrust out her right hand at the Keeper from Neskaya Tower where she stood among the Aillards in all their scarlet and grey finery.

"Ask *her* what she knows, what she's seen today, and what *Dom* Gavin convinced her to do to me. To *me*, the one this crystal has chosen!"

Fresh uproar made the crystal walls ring with echoes. Madoka held the crystal up over her head and turned a complete circle, staring into the eyes of all the Comyn around her. Light streamed from the crystal, reflecting off of the crystalline walls, taking all sounds and turning them into a song of recognition.

"Hear me, Comyn of Darkover. Every one of you knows this crystal is real, as real as those that almost destroyed your planet during the Ages of Chaos." Madoka approached Regis Hastur, cradling the crystal in both hands. "Lord Hastur, I come to you as an ally. *Dom* Gavin killed Anndra Ridenow, who discovered this crystal somewhere north of Tramontana."

"Anndra?" A Comyn lord in the orange, green and gold of Ridenow shot up out of his seat. "You saw Anndra?"

"Only briefly, Lord Ridenow," Madoka said. "*Dom* Gavin made me believe *Dom* Anndra was being held captive at Sain Scarp. The truth is he was on his way to Thendara, to present this crystal to the Comyn Council."

Regis Hastur frowned. "How did you, a Terran, key into a crystal this powerful?"

"Word should reach you very soon about the crisis at Neskaya Tower. The Tower circle is dead. You have *Dom* Gavin and that blood-soaked bitch of a Keeper to thank for it!"

"You killed them!" the Keeper screamed. "Threshold sickness, Lord Hastur. She went mad and killed them all!"

"Elora?" cried a Comyn woman dressed in the black and silver of Ardais. "Is my Elora dead?"

"Silence." Regis Hastur stared down into Madoka's eyes. He looked up at the coruscations of rainbow light streaming from all sides, called to the heart of the crystal Madoka held.

"It's true," he said. "You have keyed into the crystal. How is this possible?"

"The crystal reached out to me from the place where *Dom* Anndra had hidden it. I did not ask for this."

"Lord Hastur," Dom Gavin said, "I tell you she stole it from *Dom* Anndra! She—"

"I tell you *Dom* Gavin injected Dom Anndra with *kirian*," Madoka said, "using a Terran syringe!"

"*Kirian*." Lord Hastur turned that silvery stare on Gavin. "You used Terran medical equipment to inject *kirian* into an unwilling subject outside of a Tower and without a Keeper on hand?"

Gavin bowed before Regis Hastur's rising fury. "Lord Hastur—"

"Such a concentrated dose of *kirian* could easily kill a man!" Regis Hastur turned to Madoka. "How exactly did Anndra Ridenow die?"

"He couldn't breathe, Lord Hastur. I tried to help him, to use the emergency rescue breathing, but he was too weak." She faced the Ridenows and bowed. "I am sorry for your loss."

"Liar!" Gavin snapped. "Lord Hastur, *Dom* Anndra meant to deliver the crystal to the Terrans. He plotted—"

"You dare blame the dead?" Madoka fought the urge to bring forth the *katana* of light and kill *Dom* Gavin where he stood. "You'd lay your crimes at the feet of the man you murdered?"

A blast of scorching hatred swept the Chamber. Rage poured from Gavin like boiling oil. Madoka stood her ground against the Alton Gift. The *katana* of light appeared in her hands.

"A sword!" cried a voice among the Comyn.

"A matrix sword," cried another. "Kin to the Sword of Aldones!"

Madoka stepped back with her right foot, bent her knees, and brought the hilt level with her jaw.

"Say the word, Lord Hastur, and I will execute this traitor."

"*Mestra* Nakatomi," Regis Hastur said. "I am grateful for your kind offer of assistance. For the moment I will have both *Dom* Gavin and the Keeper confined to separate chambers while the Council investigates these charges."

"As you wish."

Madoka let the *katana* of light fade. Better that Gavin live to suffer the punishments the Comyn inflicted on their own. As much as it would have gratified her to kill him, the death she brought was much quicker than he deserved. After the House Guard had removed both Dom Gavin and the Keeper, Regis Hastur took his seat.

"*Mestra* Nakatomi. Where do you come from?"

"I was born on Samarra, in the Edo Enclave."

"Have you family there?"

Old habit made a denial spring to mind. Madoka hesitated.

"My father, Lord Hastur. I have made a home for myself on Darkover."

The graciousness of his smile astonished and confused her. Madoka assumed the Comyn would never let her leave Darkover. They couldn't kill her, but they could make her stay unpleasant.

"*Mestra* Nakatomi, you have been through a terrible ordeal. On behalf of my caste, I offer sincere apologies." Murmurs rippled through the Chamber as Regis Hastur stepped forward to face her. "Although we come from different worlds and different traditions, we are not enemies. Your mastery of this ancient starstone demonstrates the power of your Gift, as your integrity speaks for the quality of your character."

"*Vai dom*, thank you," she said, since a response seemed to be called for. "However, this does not solve the dilemma before us. The crystal must stay with people who know how to contain its power and use it properly, yes? To do so I must be trained, but only Comyn are allowed that training."

Old doubts rose up in her mind: *I'm an off-worlder, a commoner. Unworthy.* Then, as if the katana itself became luminous, a beacon and mirror, she heard her father's words. *"Worthy . . . You do not need my praise, child. The whole world can see your strength and your skill."*

Her vision cleared, and she held her head high. Regis Hastur was speaking again.

"*Laran* runs strongest in the Comyn, true, but is not exclusive to us. More than that, it is increasingly rare, so we cannot afford to lose even a single person possessing it. I foresee a time when Darkover's future may depend upon *all* her resources."

"Are you–are you proposing to offer me a home among you?"

"Not only a home, but a place of honor, where all your Gifts will be celebrated. You will enrich us, and we you. That is, if you truly wish it."

"I've already risked my life three times to bring this crystal to you, Lord Hastur." Madoka sank to one knee, holding up the crystal in both hands. "Can you think of any greater proof of my sincerity?"

SIEGE

by Diana L. Paxson

We think of citadels as fortifications with high walls, built for defense and protection. But any place can become a citadel when danger rushes upon us. And who better to manage a siege than a group of Renunciates, women trained to rely upon their own resourcefulness and courage? Diana L. Paxson's work has appeared in almost every Darkover anthology, as well as *Sword and Sorceress* and *Lace and Blade*, two other anthologies I've had the honor to edit. Here, the skill of her story-telling shines through in this memorable tale.

Diana L. Paxson is the author of twenty-nine novels, including the books that continue Marion Zimmer Bradley's Avalon series. She has also written ninety short stories, including appearances in most of Marion's Darkover anthologies. She is currently working on a novel about the first century German seeress, Veleda.

Gali's first warning was the "whyfft" of the arrow flashing by her ear. She hauled back on her stag-pony's reins as the merchant who was riding ahead of her screamed and fell backward, clutching at the black feathers that had sprouted suddenly from his breast.

"Take cover!" came a shout came from the front of the line. The arrows were coming from a patch of brush on the slope ahead of them. Beyond, the red sun turned the clouds a deeper scarlet as it descended toward the tree-clad summits of the Kilghard hills.

The pack train dissolved into a wild scurry of men and animals crowding toward the half-ruined buildings on the other side of the trail. Gali booted her own beast into a shambling gallop. Martina, the other Free Amazon in the caravan, was already urging her mount after them.

A wall loomed ahead, remainder of one of the many forts left from the Ages of Chaos in these hills. Beyond ancient gate-posts she glimpsed a courtyard and the rough walls of the old keep within.

"In here!" Martina gestured toward the gate "Leave the animals!"

Save your breath to get yourself to safety! thought Gali as they stampeded through. This was her first job as a courier, but that was no reason for the older woman to treat her like a child. *Or a* Terranan...She had been born and raised at Thendara House, but she was Festival-begotten, and on this pale-skinned planet her toast-colored complexion and dark, kinky hair marked her as alien.

The ruined keep loomed up before her. Gali scrambled out of the saddle, using the pony's bulk to shield as she jerked her pack free. Most of the animals were already milling around the yard, the men crowding into the only building that still had a roof, a long, low structure next to the tower. The breath went out of her in a startled "oof" as a portly merchant shoved past, knocking her against the tower wall. She grabbed for the hilt of her Amazon not-quite-a-sword and swore as a pack-beast plunged between them, its load swaying dangerously. It squealed, kicking, as an arrow struck its flank, and she jumped back, coughing in the dust kicked up by feet and hooves.

"Anyone with a weapon, follow me!" came a shout from behind her. Still shocked at being attacked by a weapon allowed only for hunting game, to know that someone was taking charge eased a fear she had not recognized. But why should reivers care about the Compact that forbade men to fight with distance weapons when they had committed so many other crimes?

Through the dust-clouds dim shapes were moving. Gali recognized the caravan guards and fell in behind them, sword in hand. The ruins were in better repair than they had appeared from outside, the walls around the courtyard more than man-high. If they could hold the gate they might keep their foes from getting in.

I can do this, she told herself, though her heart was hammering in her chest, or what were all those training sessions at the Guildhouse for?

The arrows had ceased to fall. Over the heads of the men in front of her she saw their attackers coming down the hill. There must be nearly two dozen of them, a rag-tag band of bearded fellows in mismatched clothes and gear, but though their garments were grimy, their weapons gleamed red in the last light of the sun.

Captain MacAran and his guardsmen were already dragging a wagon across the gateway. The others scurried to reinforce it.

"Surrender!" came a bellow from the big, fair-haired man in the lead. With his left hand he brandished a sword. The right was encased in a metal gauntlet with closed fist and spikes jutting from the knuckles.

"It's Ranald Wrong-Hand!" Gali recognized the voice of Captain MacAran, leader of the guards who had been hired to protect them from situations like this."Right here in the no-man's-land between Armida and Serrais! Last I heard, he was still in Shainsa, Zandru damn his soul!"

"On what terms?" The quavering voice belonged to *Mestre* Andres Cardrow, the leader of the caravan.

"Your lives—" Ranald laughed again. "You've found a nice bolt-hole, but it's a foolish rabbit-horn that dives down a burrow with no back door."

"When we don't turn up at Serrais, *Dom* Kester will come!" *Mestre* Andres replied.

"You think those lousy Comyn gonna save you?" One of the reivers sneered. "Ridenow's swilling Terran whisky in Thendara. Alton's off-planet somewhere, and only the gods know what he be drinking there."

"Come out, and we give you your lives." The leader growled. In the fading light the reivers were hulking demon-shapes emerging from the spiky silhouette the Kilghard Hills thrust against a purple sky.

"And our goods?" cried Giorgio Varney, who sold spider-silk. He was answered by a burst of laughter from Ranald's men.

The medicines Martina and I are taking to Serrais are for women's ills, thought Gali, *no use to these scum.* They would be more interested in her body than her possessions. The Renunciate's oath to lie with a man only "at my own time and season" meant little when you were a prisoner.

"We're safe here," Kyril MacRae, the spice merchant, gripped *Mestre* Andres' arm. "And we have shelter. Let them kick their heels outside the gate for a time."

The caravan leader turned to the captain. "Can we hold?"

"If we barricade the gate, and they care about losing men." MacAran replied in a low voice.

"We're waiting..." called the big, scar-faced fellow who seemed to be Ranald's right-hand man.

"We have to discuss this," *Mestre* Andres answered him. "'tis not my decision alone."

"I give you 'till morning..." there was an odd note in the bandit leader's laugh. "See how well you like your fortress when you've spent a night within its walls."

"Are you all right?"

Gali stilled at Martina's whisper, then sighed. They had laid out their bedrolls in a corner of the building where the folk of the caravan had taken refuge. Some of the scribblings on the walls showed it had been used as a barracks; it still had most of its roof, a fireplace, and some rough tables and chairs. The snores of the other survivors echoed from walls of rough stone.

"I'm sorry if I woke you," she replied. "I was just trying—"

"...to find a comfortable position?" Martina snorted. She was a big woman with a sometimes crude sense of humor, good at outdoor work and missions for the Guildhouse. This time, mentoring Gali on her first trip out as a courier had been added to her tasks. "Why do you always apologize? We are lying on a stone floor in an abandoned fortress, besieged by reivers who will rape us if they can. There *are* no comfortable positions here."

"I'm sorry..." Gali began, then shut her lips on the words, realizing that she was doing it again. *The truth is, I am sorry to be alive*, she thought then. *When she saw I was going to look like one of the Terranan, my mother should have left me at the Spacemen's Orphanage.*

"I can't sleep, either," Martina whispered. "And after hours of listening to men arguing I thought I would drop right off, since all their chest-pounding only served to confirm what we already knew."

Gali nodded. "There is still water in the well. We have a few days' food for humans, or longer if we start killing the packbeasts, and since we are nearly out of fodder, we may have to do that, anyway."

"But to carry the goods away the bandits need those animals alive," Martina replied. "So Wrong-Hand has to attack."

Gali sighed. "I saw at least two dozen outlaws out there. Captain MacAran only has ten guards, and I would be surprised if as many as four of the merchants know how to use their swords..."

"Four, plus us—" the other woman replied.

Gali shook her head. "Do you really think our long knives will be much use against bandit blades?"

"Do *you* always have to look at the gloomy side of things?"

I've never seen much reason to do anything else, Gali thought bitterly. Her mother had called her Margali after a Terran woman who was one of the legends of the Thendara Guildhouse, but she had never dared claim more than a part of that name. Darkover's relationship to the Terran Empire had varied over the years, but since the Yellow Plague, prejudice against the *Terranan* had been running high. Despite her full-Terran birth, Margali n'ha Ysabet had been able to pass as Darkovan in a way that Gali n'ha Simone, though she had been brought up in the Guildhouse, would never be able to do.

When I took the Renunciate's oath I thought I could win a place for myself. Even if we get out of here, I will never belong.

"The world goes as it will, not as you or I would have it," Martina said finally. "Look at it this way—if they kill us, at least we will not starve. And laughing or weeping we need sleep, so get some rest if you can." She patted Gali's shoulder, then pulled up her blankets and turned over.

For a time Gali lay listening to the snores coming from the men bedded down in the other part of the room, but eventually sleep took her as well.

In the deep hours of the night, she dreamed.

Someone was calling her.

She wandered through what seemed endless passages. At first they were as dusty as the room in which she lay, but as she went on, the floor grew smoother, and sometimes when she reached out she felt the textured weave of tapestry instead of rough stone.

But these were only minor distractions. As Gali moved on, ever more clearly she could hear the call. "*Help me…*"

Morning brought a fight between two of the guards. Gali snapped awake when she heard the shouts, thinking the outlaws were attacking, and was not sure whether to be angry or relieved when she heard Captain MacAran swearing at his men. He was a big, black-bearded man whose voice showed that even his usually even temper could be strained. She should not have been surprised that one of the combatants was Karlo, a cocky fellow with curly dark hair and a young man's first wispy beard. Like Gali he was on his first trip with a caravan. He had already tried to grab her, only desisting when Martina set hand to the hilt of her sword, and picked a quarrel with Tomas Kinnair, a nervous little man who was hoping to trade Terran cloth for Dry Towner spices in Serrais.

As the merchants set a cauldron boiling to cook breakfast there were more hard words. Apparently no one had slept well. Even Martina's sense of humor seemed muted today. Gali's head ached. Wrong-Hand had warned them, she remembered, cradling the mug of tea between her palms. What did he know?

She was just finishing her porridge when a shout from the gate was echoed by the harsh blat of a horn. The men had spent the previous evening fortifying the entrance with wagons braced by boards and fallen stones. Porridge bowls went rolling as people reached for their weapons. On the other side of the makeshift barrier they could see Ranald and his henchman, who were mounted, and the points of a dozen spears.

"Well, now," said the leader, eyeing the barricade. "This be a poor sort of welcome!"

"'Tis no welcome at all!" *Mestre* Andres said boldly. "What we have, we will hold!"

For a moment the outlaw stared at him. Then he grinned. "I think not, but my men are bored. Maybe they give you some exercise." The hoof beats faded as he galloped back up the hill.

Captain MacAran was already shouting orders. The leather-armored guards, spears ready, spread out and those merchants who were armed fell in behind them.

"You two!" the captain's gaze lit on the Amazons. "You look like you can climb. Get yourselves up in the tower and yell if they try one of the walls."

Gali eyed the structure behind her. The tower loomed above the old barracks, three stories tall, part of its top blasted by wind or wizardry. Beyond it lay more ruins. She noticed that men passing that way instinctively avoided them. Suddenly the tower seemed a refuge, and she hurried to follow Martina inside. The ground floor was partially blocked by old boards and other trash, but the plank ceiling and the ladder seemed to be in relatively good repair.

On the second level half the wall was gone, but the ladder remained. When Gali emerged from below, Martina was already leaning over the parapet that still rimmed part of the top, the cropped strands of her graying hair lifting in the breeze.

"Not very secure, is it, but at least we have a good view!"

Gali's head cleared as she drew in deep breaths of the fresh air. Except at the front, the ground fell away sharply on every side.

"They'll have to attack the gate. I don't see how anyone could scale those walls. What will we do if they succeed?"

Martina pointed at the ladder. "Hit each man over the head as he appears? And leap to our deaths if they get past—"

A shout focused their attention below. Wrong-Hand was

marshalling his men. The horn blatted and they rushed forward, but the spearmen were ready, jabbing through openings in the barrier as the enemy surged against it, their boiled-leather caps and back-and-breast plates repelling the arrows that were falling from the sky. Watching from the top of the tower, Gali could almost fancy she was looking at one of the puppet shows they put on at festivals, where tiny figures jerked and bounced before a painted screen.

And then the reiver horn blared once more. The men of the caravan cheered as the attackers began to back away.

"We didn't drive them off," said Captain MacAran, setting down his emptied cup. "They withdrew." Dinner was finished, and conversation had returned to the events of the day. Gali spooned up the last of her soup, wishing the dull ache in her head had not started again. Martina had gotten out her kit to mend a seam in her belt-pouch, but she sat with eyes closed, needle and waxed thread beside her. She had always seemed so confident, but now Gali could see dark circles beneath her eyes.

This isn't right, she frowned. *Or am I being a child, expecting everyone else to be perfect so they can take care of me?*

"Do you mean they'll be back again?" asked *Mestre* Andres. Some of the guards began to laugh.

"Sure as the sun rises," the captain replied. "Though they may not wait for the sun. I do not think they will press a real attack during the night, but we must turn out for every alarm."

"And who do you think will tire first?" muttered the spice merchant. "They only need a few men to wake us while the others slumber."

"Spawn of *kyorebni*," hissed one of the other men. "Did you see how their leader laid out poor Kendry?" He nodded toward the man who lay on piled cloaks by the fireplace. A single blow from the outlaw chieftain had smashed his shoulder.

"Wrong-Hand indeed!" exclaimed Kyril, who had contributed some of his silk to bind the wound. "Does that gauntlet even come off?"

"In the Merchant's Guild they say his hand was warped by

magic," said *Mestre* Andres, "some device from the ancient days that he found in a ruin. When he tried to use it, the thing melted his bones."

At those words it seemed to Gali that a shiver passed through them all. Conversations faltered. Everyone sought their blankets, and soon she heard only an occasional moan from the man who lay by the fire.

This time, sleep came quickly, but in the depths of the night, Gali dreamed again.

Once more she moved through a maze of passages. Was she remembering the ruins she had seen from the top of the towers? These corridors seemed carved from the bedrock of the hill.

Once more she heard the murmurs. When they ceased, she found herself in a chamber whose pillars were hewn from living stone. On a table light glowed from a box about a foot long and a little less than that high, carved of some pale, translucent stone.

Gali moved toward it—

—and jerked awake, shaking, to the sound of shouting and the clash of arms.

It was morning, and the outlaws were attacking once more.

The same pattern continued for the next five days. The bandits would attack at dawn, and sometimes again in the afternoon. But despite their threats, they never appeared until the sun was in the sky.

As food supplies lessened, tempers were growing shorter as well. Not surprising, perhaps, when they were all cooped up together and under constant strain. She had hoped their shared danger would bring them together. Surely everyone understood that solidarity was their only defense, but quarrels broke out, when people talked to each other at all, and only Captain MacAran's authority kept blows from leading to blades.

On the fifth day, the man who had been punched by Wrong-Hand died.

"That blow should not have killed him," said Martina, settling down with her back against the parapet that edged the intact part of the tower. The day had dawned cloudy. If it stormed, the tower would become an uncomfortable refuge.

"It must have been the spikes," Gali replied. "You saw the punctures. The gods only know what filth was on that glove." The spider-silk merchant was the closest they had to a healer, and she had helped him to treat the man. First the holes had grown red and puffy, then dark streaks began to spread beneath the skin.

"Dirty wounds can go bad that way," said Martina. Gali nodded, but she could not help wondering if some evil magic in the gauntlet itself had poisoned the wounds.

For a time they sat in silence, listening to the wind.

"Gods, how I want to get out of here!" Martina exclaimed.

"If you could go anywhere, where would you choose?"

The older woman laughed. "There is a lovely inn at Neskaya. I stayed there after I escorted a girl from Thendara to start training at the Tower. She was from a family of leather-workers, but there must have been Comyn blood in her line somewhere. She had hair like new copper, and she could snap her fingers and spark a candle flame."

Gali nodded. For a child on Darkover the idea that some unsuspected heritage might give her such powers was a common fantasy.

"And you would like to see her again?" she asked. Martina had no lover in the Guildhouse, and Gali had never thought to wonder what her romantic history might be.

"Not her—" Martina laughed. "Such a little bit of a thing she was, I'd have been afraid I'd break her. No, I'm remembering one of the maids at the inn. We had a few lusty nights together, and I dreamed for years of going back, asking her to help me set up a place of our own. She's probably married with six children by now."

They had their very own tower here, thought Gali, but if it held any magic it was very different from what the matrix mechanics taught in the Towers. And it was the blood of Terra, not that of the Comyn, that flowed in *her* veins.

"And what about you?" the other woman said then.

"I might go off-planet..." Gali's father had been a

hydroponics engineer, rotated away soon after she was born. But he had registered her as his child. If she chose to claim Terran citizenship, she could seek a new life on another world.

"To Terra?" Martina's eyes widened, then focused, as if really *seeing* her companion for the first time, and she gave a little laugh. "Of course, I keep forgetting that you have the right to choose."

Now it was Gali's turn to stare. Did the other woman really see her as just another Guild-sister? Did they all?

"It's just a thought I have sometimes," she said abruptly and got to her feet.

The view had not changed much, except that more color was leached from the landscape by the lowering clouds. Beyond the gorge that backed the fortress rocky cliffs were crowned with resin-trees. In the other direction, hill and pasture sloped toward the valley where the Carthon River rolled.

A few curses drifted up from below. Old Rafael, the drover, was organizing men to tend the pack-beasts penned against the far wall. Captain MacAran's black horse threw up its head and snorted as it scented the water, echoed by the bleating of the chervines.

As the water-bearers swung wide around the ruins, she looked at them more closely, trying to make some sense of the jumble of room and passageway. One large space might have been a common room, but what about that collection of squares, and the darker rectangle nearby? She leaned over, peering down.

There was something about that space… Her gaze seemed to sink into the shadow, as if it were calling her.

She started as Martina's hand closed on her arm.

"Don't you fall over the side!" The other woman gave her a shake. "We just buried one man. I don't want to have to bury you as well."

Gali shook her head, surprised to find she felt only gratitude that her companion cared. *What I saw doesn't matter,* she told herself, but as she sat down again, her deeper mind replied, *There's something important down there.*

A drop of moisture splashed her hand. It was beginning to

rain.

When she felt the touch, Gali thought she had backed into one of the tables. Another day was ending, and the people of the caravan had gathered for a meager evening meal. Then the pressure became a pinch. She whirled, astonishment exploding into fury as Karlo snatched his hand back and grinned.

"Nice butt in those Free Amazon breeches—" he began, but her blade was out. It might not be a proper sword, but at such close quarters it was long enough to score a white scratch across his leather vest as he leaped out of the way, lust turning to alarm.

"Hey now—" one of the other men stepped between them. "That's no way to behave!"

"She drew on me!" Karlo pointed, seeking support from the men who were turning to see what the commotion was. "The bitch drew steel!"

"You groped me!" Gali gasped.

"A friendly pat—" said one man. "Wear a skirt if you don't want men to appreciate your ass!"

Now all the men were babbling. Gali set her back against the table, bared sword still gripped in her hand. Eyes flashing, Martina joined her.

"She should take it as a compliment—" said someone.

"Sooty-dark as one o' the forge-folk she is! Who would want her if there was anything better to hand?" another man chimed in.

Gali felt a flush further darken her skin. Sometimes children had pointed at her in Thendara, but the city saw enough strangers that she did not attract too much attention there.

"You leave her be!" snapped Martina. Her hand was on her hilt, though she had not drawn her blade. A deep grumble came from the men who faced them, and Gali's anger was replaced by a chill of fear.

"What's all this?" Men turned as Captain MacAran elbowed his way through the crowd.

"That lout assaulted my companion," Martina said stiffly. The captain turned to Karlo. "I don't see any blood—"

"But she—" the young man started to protest.

"Those bitches all alike, makin' trouble," came a mutter from behind him. "Should never have let 'em out on their own."

"Boys with no manners should go back to their mothers," said Kyril.

"An' men that don't know you need to keep the bitches in line should stay home," someone replied.

At MacAran's glare, the men began to back away, but tension still throbbed in the room.

"All right—" The captain turned back to the women. "You two take first watch. Give these fools time to simmer down. And you, bully-boy, will take mid-watch, so sleep while you can!"

The rain had ceased, but a restless wind moaned among the stones, whipping the clouds across the sky. It was the kind of weather that encouraged strange imaginings. At the beginning of the siege, old Rafael had entertained them with bits of local lore picked up on his many journeys through this land. During the Ages of Chaos, the Kilghards had been a constant battle ground. The hills were studded with ruins, and the hunters and herders who roamed here were happy to share their tales of less tangible survivals from the ancient days. One of the most disturbing was the tale of the White Lady of the Fells whose mere glance brought death. Requests for stories had ceased after Kendry died, but when Gali saw someone start at a shadow, she knew that people were remembering.

Wrapped in their cloaks, the two women settled where they could see the gate beyond the broken side of the tower. On the hillside behind it the bandits' fire made a golden glow, and from time to time the wind would carry a snatch of raucous song

"I didn't do anything to encourage him!" murmured Gali. "He stared at me a lot, but I didn't talk to him."

"I believe you, *bredilla*," Martina replied. "Some men think it an invitation if you do no more than meet their gaze. Now you understand why we hire out in pairs."

Gali remembered how she had resented the other woman's authority, as if she wasn't considered good enough to go out alone. "Is it always like this when we take outside employment?"

Martina shook her head. "There are always some who assume any Renunciate pair are lovers and will joke about it, but if we do our share of the work and seek no special treatment, most men will leave us alone."

"I suppose so," Gali admitted after awhile. "They were polite enough until we got stuck in here. We're all on edge, and afraid…"

"And frightened men do crazy things—" the other woman agreed. The day before, one of the merchants had snapped and made a run for the gate, getting most of the way over the barricade before outlaw arrows pinned him to its timbers. His body was still there.

Gali gazed out across the quiet landscape. The smallest of the moons, pearly Mormallor, rode high, and mauve Idriel was just lifting above the trees.

"Do you think Wrong-Hand will attack tomorrow?" she asked.

"Yes." Martina sighed. "But do I think they will really try to get in?" She shook her head. "They've had time enough to fetch a log from the mountains and ram it through our barrier. But why should they risk their skins? No, I think they are doing just enough to keep us pinned down here, waiting for desperation to deliver us into their hands."

"Like poor *Mestre* Niccolo." Gali replied. The merchant who ran had gotten too far for the defenders to help him without getting skewered themselves, and he took a long time to die.

The thought was enough to stifle conversation, and they sat in silence until Mormallor had set and it was time for the watch to change.

Gali had expected to be too tired for dreaming, but in the darkest hour she found herself underground once more, in the room that was lit by the stone casket's glow.

"*Take me…*" sang the voice she had heard before. "*Set me free…*"

Was this some spell from the Ages of Chaos, like the thing that had cursed the outlaw chieftain's hand?

She was still wondering when she began to hear men's voices. As she opened her eyes, the glow coming from the box was replaced by orange sunlight shafting through the slatted shutters of the room in which she lay.

Her dream chilled her soul. But could it be worse, she wondered, than what she faced in the waking world?

"We've lost another chervine," said Rafael, gnarled hand furrowing his white hair. The pack-animals had eaten all the fodder they had carried, and every sprig of green within the walls. Their moaning complaint was almost constant now.

"Then we know what tonight's dinner will be..." one of the men replied. He was echoed by a bitter laugh. Everyone knew that the supplies of human food were getting low as well.

That morning the reivers had made a half-hearted attempt to force the gate and then withdrawn, leaving a token watcher to trade insults with the caravan guard stationed on the other side, and *Mestre* Andres had called a meeting.

"We can live on our animals 'till Liriel wanes and swells to full once more," said Kyril. "But when we finish gnawing the bones of Captain MacAran's horse, we'll be no better off than we are now."

By that time they might be ready to eat each other, thought Gali, remembering some of Rafael's tales. The waistband of her breeches was looser now. That thought put the events of the night before in a different perspective. She and Karlo were not the only ones who were fighting. Morale was ebbing even faster than their store of food.

"Worse." The captain looked at *Mestre* Andres. "We have protected the goods entrusted to us, but I think we have reached a point when we must think of ourselves. The outlaws offered us our lives. It's time to find out if that offer still holds."

"And lose all our goods?" exclaimed someone.

"Can we trust their word?" said another.

"And will they look on us as merchants or merchandise," murmured Martina into Gali's ear, "to be raped and then taken to the Dry Towns to be sold?"

The meeting broke up shortly thereafter, debate still sparking between the hold-outs and those who wanted to surrender. Gali didn't much like either choice, but even if there was nothing to eat someone needed to bring water to the animals, and it was her turn.

She had passed the first ruined building when she sensed movement behind her and whirled, water from her brimming pail splashing the ground.

Karlo stepped out from the shadows, his cloak draped over his arm. "Saw your name for this duty on the roster," he said smugly. "Thought I might catch ye here!"

"Really? I didn't know you could read..." She saw his face go red and smiled.

She took an inadvertent step back as he moved closer, stopped as her shoulder brushed stone. He had chosen his ground cleverly, trapping her in the angle formed by two walls. Beyond the shorter one were more ruins, and the dark opening she had seen from the tower.

"Read, *and* think!" he spat. "I've a cloak to trap that toothpick you're carrying, and the others are yelling at each other so loud no one will hear ye scream, so why don't ye just set down that pail an' we'll both have a little fun?"

"I would rather," she snarled, "lie down with a *cralmac*!"

"Or a reiver?" Surprisingly, he laughed. "I expect ye'll be doin' that soon. But I'll be dead, an' I want a memory to cheer me as I go."

For a moment, Gali almost pitied him. *But what memories will go with me?* she thought then. *No...*

"Let me do something with this pail," she answered, and saw a tell-tale easing in his stance.

Water sprayed in a glistening arc as she threw. The pail clanged at his feet, tripping him as she shoved past. Sputtering, he charged after her, but she was already rounding the corner and stumbling down into the dark.

Gali stopped, chest heaving, and leaned against the smooth wall. It was cool here, and quiet, even Karlo's ravings only a faint vibration in the stone. Most of the men had been made wary by Rafael's stories, and she did not think that even his lust would drive him follow her here. She looked around her, using the faint illumination that cracks in the ceiling admitted from the world above.

I am not afraid, she thought, recognizing an image of interlaced *kireseth* blooms carved into the wall, *because I have been here before...*

Gali moved carefully onward, guided by memories from her dreams, spiraling downward until the dimming daylight was replaced by a colder illumination that came from below. *Here is the tapestry of Hastur and Cassilda that I saw, and here, the niche with the statue of a standing warrior. Around this bend I will find the room with the columns...* She slowed, her heart thudding in her breast, though she could not tell if it was with anticipation or fear.

She recognized, cool beneath her feet, the polished jasper floor. And there on the stone table was the box, its glowing surface carved with inscriptions in a language she did not know.

"Help me..." It was the voice she had heard in her dreams.

"And what will happen if I do?" Even in Thendara there had been stories about what happened to people who meddled with artifacts from the ancient days. A trained matrix mechanic might be able to handle such things, but she was only a Free Amazon, and half a Terran at that.

"*Listen!*" the voice replied. "*Move to the corner, and tell me what you hear—*"

That was not what she had expected. Frowning, Gali took a few steps and halted as a trick of the room's acoustics brought her a babble of angry voices from above. She heard Captain MacAran giving orders, and then the clash of swords.

"*The merchants are fighting each other,*" said the voice. "*Half of them are trying to get over the barricade, and the reivers are attacking it from the other side. When they meet, what do you think will happen? Help me, and I will help you.*"

Slowly, Gali turned. "What—" She swallowed. "What do you want me to do?"

"Open the box..."

Gali touched the top. The carved stone was cool beneath her hand. It did not feel evil, but how would she know?

"Ranald Wrong-Hand sought the power to harm, and harm is what he received. What do you seek?" The voice answered her unspoken question.

Gali shook her head. "I don't know!"

"I think you do."

As the light from the box grew brighter, thought grew clear.

"I want to know who I am and where I belong!"

"Open the box and take me out into the light of day."

She was shaking. She could not do it. But from that carven surface flowed a compelling appeal. Gali pressed, and the top sprang open, releasing a flood of light into the room. Within lay a diadem fashioned of some white metal, set with a single stone big enough to rest in the palm of one's hand. In its depths she recognized the intense blue flicker of a matrix crystal, though she had never seen one so large.

With trembling fingers she lifted out the diadem. The metal tingled slightly against her skin.

"Put me on...and save your friend!"

Gali could not resist the compulsion. She felt pressure as the cool metal bound her brow, followed by a tickling sensation in her head that triggered a cascade of memories. Then came a moment of dizzying descent that severed her physical senses from her will. But even as she felt her limbs obeying the command to leave the room, a part of her mind remained apart, observing as she made her way up through the passageways and out into the light of day.

Pain! Fury! Fear!

In the courtyard, unleashed emotions raged as men fought and fell. Gali observed without feeling them, shielded by a white blaze that challenged the rosy light of day.

The reivers, attacking, were the first to see. "The White Lady! The White Lady comes!" they cried, as swords flashed back that light and dropped from nerveless hands.

Ranald Wrong-Hand, raising his gauntlet to guard, screamed as the bright metal flared to incandescence. For a moment the warped bones of the limb within were visible, then they too were consumed. Still screaming, the outlaw chieftain fell, and the scar-faced lieutenant shouted to the survivors to flee.

By then, the men of the caravan who still lived had seen as well. They dropped to their knees or stood swaying as their remaining enemies scrambled up the hill and away. Captain MacAran began to look for his guardsmen. *Mestre* Andres sat weeping. Gali, still a passenger in her own body, noted Karlo, a great wound across his breast, lying lifeless on the ground. But he was not the one she wanted to see.

"Gali! You're alive!" Martina was hobbling toward her, leaning on a broken spear. "Merciful Avarra!" She stopped short, staring.

Gali tried to answer, but her lips would not obey. She felt a rush of sensation as the Other within her took a deep breath of clean air.

"It has been so long, so long," came that thought that was not her own. *"This body is young, healthy. I could rule this land as I did before!"*

"No." As Gali replied, she felt something trying to invade the space that held her soul.

"I'm half Terran, not one of your red-haired Comyn girls," she thought, *"and this body belongs to* me!"

Her awareness reeled beneath a blast of rage, but she resisted until it faded through grief to acceptance. Gali sensed the other woman's sadness as for the last time she contemplated the lovely shape of the hills against the sky.

"Now, set me free."

It was time to stop being a passenger. As Gali bent her whole mind to the task she found the power to move her arm. Then Martina's hand was beneath hers, lifting it to the diadem. As it touched, the older woman yelped and let go, but Gali's spasming fingers had closed on the metal band, jerking it off to spin free.

As it hit the ground Gali's legs gave way. Swearing, Martina caught and eased her down.

"Get me a hammer, a rock, something hard," Gali whispered as the light grew. From the diadem she felt an unstable pulse of power.

Martina's eyes widened. She stared wildly around her and seized a cobblestone.

"Go free!" breathed Gali, raising the rock and smashing it down on the shimmering stone. As it shattered, vision was extinguished by a blinding glare. For a moment the world whirled in a maelstrom of mingled grief and joy. Then light and emotion together vanished away.

But the earth was still shaking. She put out a hand for balance as a tremor passed through the ground. Then she heard a rumble from the tower. One stone popped out, then another. The walls crumbled, stones arching outward to bounce across the courtyard in a thunder of falling rock until with a last shudder, all was still.

The pack-animals, bellowing, were dashing around their pen. The tower was a heap of rubble. *All* the walls were down. The humans found themselves the only upright figures in a devastation of scattered stone.

"Thank the gods you are still alive!" Martina exclaimed, looking at the distorted tangle of metal surrounded by glittering shards.

"Maybe my Terran blood protected me," whispered Gali. "She took over my body, but I was still there, riding along inside."

"*She?*" Martina struggled to her feet and offered Gali her hand.

"The White Lady—" Gali looked down at her own brown arm and laughed. "Imprisoned by her own sorceries."

"And now she is free," said Martina. Her rugged features creased in a smile.

And I can go where I want to go, thought Gali, *and be what I want to be.*

SEA-CASTLE

by Leslie Fish

Leslie Fish fell in love with science fiction at the age of eight, mostly through EC Comics and the movie "Destination Moon." Born and raised in a boring, respectable suburb of Newark, New Jersey, she swore that she would lead an adventurous life or die trying. As a result, she became a war-protester, a folksinger, an industrial pirate, a union organizer, a go-go dancer, a dominatrix, and a science fiction writer. She's best known for her several albums of science fiction folk-music, or filk, which are available from Amazon or in the dealers' rooms of science fiction conventions. She currently lives in a farming town in Arizona, along with her husband Rasty, an orchard of exotic fruit-trees, and her experimental breed of super-smart Silverdust cats. About "Sea-Castle," she writes, "This story deals with yet another of Darkover's non-human intelligent species, this time a rare one that's almost never been studied before."

Unlike some of the other stories in this anthology, "Sea-Castle" is remarkable for not focusing on violent conflict but the gradual nourishing of understanding, trust, and ultimately, love.

The net was heavy and hard to manage alone, but Ian dragged it into the skiff without snagging or tearing a single strand. Only as he untied the line from the short dock did he pause to look back at the house.

It stood as it always had, a little round tower of hand-laid mortarless flat stones, with narrow wood-shuttered windows and a central chimney on top—the chimney that stood on the hand-built fireplace in the middle of the interior dividing wall, but with no smoke emerging now, and only a resting shorebird perched on its rim. Even in the light of the first warm day of spring, the house looked so sad, small, and empty...

...And why not? he thought bitterly. *There's no one left but me...*

That brought up sour memories of Anndra and Stefan, arguing with him even as they packed up to leave, snapping that with Mother now dead—and Father long dead—there was no reason to stay any longer, dragging up fish out of the Bay of Dalereuth day after day, carting them off to the market-dock or the smoke-house in town for the variable—and usually poor—prices they earned.

Anndra had only said, bluntly, that he was sick of the life of a small-boat fisherman and wanted to see the greater world and make a better living. Stefan's complaint had been longer and more telling; that he meant to go inland or down the sea-coast road and take service at some great lord's house, or army, and eat more than fish and sea-bird and sea-weed every day—which really wasn't fair, because they could have kept Mother's kitchen-garden growing if they'd bothered. Worse had been their scorn for their little brother, that he was content to live as their ancestors had lived for time out of mind.

By now Ian's outrage had faded to a distant sorrow and bewilderment. How could his brothers not feel any love for the old stone house that, as his father had described in great detail, their MacRae ancestors had built centuries ago? How could they not feel the pull and majesty of the sea, where their family had made their living for more generations than anyone could remember? How could they so easily forget Mother as soon as she was buried, turn their backs on all the tales she'd told and the warnings she'd given, and hurry off to the cities chasing rumors of wealth and supposed wonders? Had they no sense of family, or history? Did they have no love?

With a sigh, Ian pulled in the hitch-line and coiled it in the bow. He took up the oars and steered away from the dock, out into the open water, letting himself feel the mood of the sea.

There was calm water above, but beneath lay a churning restlessness: a crossing of deep tides that grumbled against the shore and drove the fish further out, into the safer waters. Out there, no less than five kilometers, were a string of sea-mounts that drew close enough to the surface for sunlight to penetrate and feed the growth of broadweed, which in turn fed and sheltered fish of several breeds. Ian knew, as surely as he recognized the taste of the seaward wind, that the fish would be there. He knew he could fill the net quickly, and the water-box, and return in time to row down to the market-dock in town. Ian set his attention to straightening the net and securing its line. A familiar caw drew his eyes upward, where a lone shorebird circled.

As he watched, it settled neatly at the bow-post and folded its wings, showing all intent to stay there. *Odd,* Ian puzzled. Except when migrating, shorebirds never fared very far out to sea. From the bandings on its tail-feathers, he could swear it was the same bird that he'd seen perched on the chimney back home. Perhaps it was a regular visitor, used to picking up reliable meals from the MacRae household and expecting that the family boat would provide food this morning, too. "Well, come along, then," he chuckled. "Fish you'll have, soon enough—and any companion is welcome."

Ian turned back to his work with a lighter heart, and soon had the net stretched out and ready for casting. He could tell from the sound and feel of the sea that the sea-mounts were close ahead, and yes, thick shoals of fish were gathered there. He could drop his anchor and cast his net very soon now...

The shorebird leaped up off the bow, screaming.

An instant later Ian heard/felt that deep restlessness in the sea gathering itself and rushing toward a point—no, a line—in the sea-bed behind him: a rumbling, a shaking, a burst of pressure—*Upwelling!* he realized, as he felt the fish scattering frantically, fleeing. He looked back and saw it: a rogue wave, enormous, bigger than he'd ever seen or heard of, crested with a crown of foam, reaching for the sky and rushing straight toward him.

Ian lunged for the tiller and held it hard, desperate to keep the skiff's stern pointed straight toward the oncoming mountain of water. He remembered, from Father's old tales, that he had a chance to ride out the wave if he could just keep at the right angle to it. Sea and sky tilted as the monster rushed under him, lifting the boat, stern-first. Ian braced his feet against the water-box and held the tiller straight with all the strength in his body. Another wrenching, the skiff fell flat and the pressure on the tiller slacked. Ian saw nothing ahead of him but sky. *I'm on the crest!* he realized dizzily.

The skiff was safe for the moment, riding the crest of the rogue wave, but—like the legendary skier who rode the avalanche—he had no choice as to where, or how long, it would carry him.

All Ian could think to do was tie down the tiller, crawl forward and secure the net. The wave showed no sign of slacking, and the feel and sound of the sea was unchanged. Ian settled in the bow, where he could at least look down and see the face of the wave slanting away before him and the surface of the sea a dizzying distance below that. He guessed that he was well past the sea-mounts by now, far out into the Bay of Dalereuth, possibly further out than any sailor had ever gone. How far would the wave run? He'd heard legends of great waves that could run halfway—or even all the way—around the world. How would he ever get home again?

As he watched the hypnotic sight of the water running below, Ian began to wonder why people knew so little about the sea. Yes, the weather was always treacherous and usually rough, the water prone to ferocious storms and—as now—huge rogue waves, but if his little skiff could survive, why not a bigger boat? Back on the mainland there was no shortage of timber; he'd seen huge trees in the forest north of town that could supply wood for a ship 100 meters long. Why had no one but fishermen, like his family, ever ventured out on the sea? Why had none of them ever ventured far, no more than ten kilometers at most? The threat of storms and huge waves didn't explain it. It was as if the vast majority of humans had long ago chosen to turn their backs on the sea and never think of it again. His brothers, he knew, had minds like that. But why? He couldn't understand it.

And the wave rolled on, and on. Hours passed, bringing hunger and thirst. Ian crawled back to the stern cabinet, drew a cup of clean water from the keg anchored there, and took one of the oilcloth-wrapped packets of dried fish. As he ate he thanked all the gods in agreement that he'd always kept up the tradition of keeping the cabinet full-stocked. There was food and drink enough to sustain him for a tenday, easily. Hopefully, the wave would exhaust itself before then. He wondered how he would sleep when night came. The thick blanket in the fore-cabinet would keep him warm enough, but the thought of himself snoring peaceably while his skiff raced along on the top of the mountain of moving water made him laugh.

He was halfway through the dried fish when a familiar caw drew his attention to the bow. As he watched, scarcely believing, a shorebird came angling downward, flailing its wings gamely, to land on the bow-post. Yes, it was the same bird, the dark-grey bands on its tail-feathers were unmistakable.

"You followed me all this way?" Ian marveled. "Are you that greedy for easy food?"

He held out the chunk of dried fish. The bird took a single delicate peck, and then graciously left him the rest.

Not hungry, Ian considered as he chewed the last of the fish. *If not for food, why did he follow me?*

As if in answer, the bird turned around and faced out toward the oncoming sea. Idly curious, Ian unbuttoned his belt-bag and pulled out the folding spy-glass. It took awhile to adjust to the altered angle of the sea and look toward the horizon.

Yes! There was a rigid unchanging shape there, just visible above the edge of the sea, dark and solid: an island.

And the skiff was headed straight toward it.

Ian's flare of hope changed into a shock of alarm. If the edge of the island was a stone cliff, or even a pile of boulders, the boat would be smashed like a bug under a rock. He searched the edge of the island frantically, looking for some kind of beach or low shore. If he couldn't find any, he'd have to discover some means of steering the skiff along the top of the wave, row it east or west somehow, get past the end of the island—and keep riding the wave, hopefully weakened by then…

In fact, that was his best hope to get free of it.

Ian stuffed the spy-glass back in his pouch, scrambled to the stern and re-set the tiller. Then crawled to the waist of the boat, pulled up the oars, set them in the locks and clamped the locks shut, put their blades in the water and push-pulled to starboard. It was incredibly hard, like hauling against packed sand, but the nose of the skiff shifted a finger-width to the right.

The shorebird gave a caw that sounded almost triumphant, and flapped into the sky. At ten meters up, it turned and began circling the skiff.

Thanks for your help, Ian thought, as he hauled on the oars again. Yes, the skiff was turning, but so slowly against all that weight of water. Could he get it turned in time? How close now was the island?

He glanced down at the sea—and saw something changed. There seemed to be lumps bobbing in the water rushing toward him. *Fish?* he wondered, though they didn't have the look or feel of fish. And now the island was visible without the spy-glass. *Too close!* Ian concentrated on hauling the oars. His shoulders ached.

Then the arms came out of the water.

They were pale human arms, followed by pale human heads with long varicolored hair. They clutched the port-side gunwales of the skiff, ahead of the sweep of his oar, and pushed. He felt the skiff turn, much further than his own efforts could move it. A quick glance to starboard astern showed more gripping hands—with webbed fingers—pushing. They had come to help him, these creatures.

Selkies!

What else could they be? Everyone who lived on the seacoast knew the legend, but nobody living had ever seen one. Mother had said that her grandfather swore to his dying day that he had seen a Selkie once, but he was known to be fond of drink, so no one believed him.

And here was the legend, come to life—dozens of them—helping him save his skiff from destruction.

Now the skiff faced across the arched length of the monster wave, and the Selkies let go of the gunwales and slipped backward in the water. Ian lifted the oars, scrambled back to the tiller and re-tied it straight, then crawled forward and bent to the oars again. One of the Selkies gave a complex trilling call, and most of them darted to the skiff's stern. Ian felt the nudge that added to his effort, looked back and saw that as many Selkies as could crowd close had pressed their hands to the stern gunwale and were pushing again. As he turned forward Ian saw one of the Selkies lunge up, almost completely out of the water, reach into the bow and grab the hitching-line, then slip back into the sea. Even as he bent to the oars, Ian saw the line slide around in front of the bow, and then go taut. *Pull and push,* he understood, as he worked the oars. The skiff moved faster.

But the island was close now, very close, and the wave was still rushing toward it. Ian's heart sank as he realized there was no time to reach the end of the shore, and the isle's coastline was a tumbled slope of wave-washed boulders. He rowed harder, desperately scanning the shore for a change.

And there: just a hundred meters, maybe less, at the foot of a hill, there was a pebbled beach. If he could turn again, at just the right moment... No time to change the tiller.

But the Selkies knew! Quick as darting fish, as the bow came parallel to the edge of the beach, they changed position again. Even as Ian push-pulled the oars, they slipped to the sides of the skiff and helped it turn again. The skiff came about landward, facing clear beach, Ian shipped the oars fast, all the Selkies dashed to the stern, and then the surf was roaring close and there was no more time.

Ian dropped to the scuppers and curled up fast, feeling/hearing the bottom of the wave catch on the rising shore and the top crest over it. The howling of stone and water filled all creation, and the wave rushed up the beach, arched over and crashed into seething chaos that carried skiff and Selkies and all up to the top of the pebble-slope and further, up the hill, into salt-grass and brush, losing force at last, and finally sinking into foam.

Before Ian could even raise his head, the Selkies were swarming around the boat, pulling the hitch-line and gunwales, pushing the stern, making certain that the skiff wasn't sucked back into the withdrawing water. He thought to grab the anchor and, with a shout of warning, throw it out ahead of the bow. The boat held in place while the retreating water howled in frustration and sank away. Ian sat up in time to see the Selkies go wallowing after it into the muddy and grumbling sea.

The lone shorebird settled on the bow-post and cawed in satisfaction.

No, not all the Selkies were gone. One of them—clearly female, her modesty preserved only by her long hair, which looked as if had been deliberately placed—sat waiting on the coarse grass, calmly watching him. He noticed that one lock of her pale hair had been braided, with something—it looked to be a round stone—woven into it, and one hand was stroking the braid. She looked very human, save for her webbed fingers, and her elongated splayed feet that resembled nothing so much as two halves of a fish's tail. Ian wondered if she could walk on those, or only swim.

He pulled himself shakily out of the skiff, gave the Selkie a brief bow, and said: "By all the gods in agreement, Sea-Lady, I thank you for my life—and my boat."

The Selkie woman clutched her braid, visibly concentrated, and said—slowly: "We. Need. Your help."

Ian's first thought was: *Can I rest awhile first?* What he said was: "What help, Lady?"

For answer, she swept her arm wide, uphill, indicating the top of the island. Ian climbed on tottering feet up the slope, past the flattened and uprooted brush, up to the stony crest of the hill. There he looked up and down the length of the island, and saw what the monster wave had done.

Except for the central hill, the island was long and thin and fairly low—and the wave had swept it bare. Save for the thin band of soil and scrubby brush around the hilltop, nothing remained but wet, bare and jumbled rock. At only one spot, perhaps 30 meters away, was a roughly round area of flat stone, maybe 50 meters across before it fell away to the jumbled slopes on either side. An oddity: between the stones on the slopes lay deposits of mud that was oddly pale, almost white.

What is it that I am supposed to see? Ian wondered, giving a questioning look back to the Selkie.

She furrowed her brow in thought—just like a human—and gripped her braid. Ian got the strong impression that she thought in terms of images, clusters of sounds and scents and...*feel*, the way he could feel the mood of the sea—and it took her effort to translate these into discrete words, to speak like a human.

He also knew, as surely as he knew that the sea behind him was calm and sated, that the round pebble braided into the Selkie's hair was a deep and glittering blue: a *laran*-stone, such as landside sorcerers used. She used it to enhance her sea-sense—so much like his own—to communicate with beings other than Selkies.

As if in confirmation, the shorebird circled down to perch on the ground between his feet and gave a cheerful caw.

The Selkie pointed toward the bare stone platform and pronounced: "Rookery."

Understanding came in a flood. This island was where the local shorebirds came in their migration, came here to mate and breed and raise their chicks. Before the ruin of the wave there had been topsoil here, and sheltering brush: enough flat and covered ground on the island to host countless thousands of birds. That white mud between the now-bare stones was guano from generations of birds; it had fertilized the topsoil and drained down in the summer rains into the sea, where it fed the algae and broadweed that in turn fed and sheltered the stone-worms and sea-flies and fish—which fed the birds and the larger fish, which fed the Selkies and other creatures of the sea. The guano from the birds washed as far off as the sea-mounts, which accounted for their abundant sea-life. All of this depended on the roosting birds.

And now there was no safe place, no shelter, for all those birds when their season came. A few hundred, perhaps, could crowd into the surviving brush on the central hill, but for the rest—thousands and thousands—there was nothing but the bare and jagged stone.

Ian spread his hands helplessly, and turned back to the Selkie-maid. "Speaker," he named her, "What can I do?"

Speaker clutched her stone and concentrated again.

This time the message was a simple image: his family's house on the mainland, as seen from the sea—in fact, seen from several angles, and seasons, and times. He saw Father patching the roof and himself, a small boy, solemnly handing up tools and baskets full of tiles. He saw storms battering at that plain stone wall, exhausting themselves while the stones stood firm. He saw a vague image of that circular stone wall being built, by people he didn't recognize but who had a familiar look, and knew that the memory was very old. He saw, with a peculiar intensity, the building of the narrow windows.

…Windows, gaps…

Right there, he understood what Speaker wanted. He imagined it as a single image: a round roofless tower with a thick, sea-proof, stone wall—and regular gaps in the wall, all the way around and all the way up—*small gaps, fit for shorebird nests*—a rookery tower.

And more… His thoughts skipped ahead. The rocks of the island where the same flat-sided stone as on the mainland shore; he could fill the rough gaps, build nest-spaces, all over the island. He knew the technique of splitting one rock with another, chipping stone into shape, making a flat surface and rough walls and roofing them with another large stone. He could do it, make spaces for thousands of nests, enough to house all the birds of the migration. How much time would it take?

"I'll need help," he told Speaker, "Help to carry the stones, and chip them… And for now, I'll need to rest. And how shall I eat, or find drinking-water?"

He paced his way back to the stranded skiff, too weary to think further, and there he found that somebody—*oh, the Selkies of course. Who else?*—had pulled out the sail and propped it into a small tent beside the boat. They had also thoughtfully dug out his camp-blanket and spread it under the tent. Wordlessly grateful, Ian crawled into the tent, pulled off his boots, curled up in the blanket and fell asleep within minutes.

His last thought was the realization that the Selkies had been watching his family for a very long time.

Waking came slowly, but with complete memory. Ian crawled out of the tent into a warm and sunny dawn, feeling his salt-stiffened clothes as rigid as armor. After a moment's thought he stripped them off, intending to rinse them in the sea and dry them spread straight in the sun; there was no point being modest in front of the Selkies, who were as naked as fish.

When he got to his feet, Ian saw immense change. The pebble-beach was gone, washed away by the rogue wave as might be expected, but the slope of heavier rocks remained—and the sleepy ocean seemed to be slowly rolling the pebbles back. More interesting was the number of Selkies working among the stones. They were sorting the rocks by size, pulling the bigger slabs up the hill to leave them near the flat area, and piling the smaller slabs to one side. The work was difficult for them, with their broad fin-feet not designed for walking. Still others, he noted were crouched over the assembled slabs, holding smaller stones and using them as hammers to chip the rough ends of the slabs somewhat smooth. Ian realized they had learned this from him, by way of Speaker—or else from his ancestors, by way of Speaker's mentor. *What else have they learned from us?* he wondered, thinking of Mother's vegetable garden.

On the other side of the skiff Ian saw that the Selkies had gathered driftwood into a tidy pile. Speaker, after a glance at him, clutched the stone in her braid and concentrated on the pile. As he watched, a thin stream of smoke rose up from the wood. Firestarting, he knew, was not something the Selkies could have learned by themselves. What use did they have for fire? He looked further, saw some cleaned and skewered bluefish waiting to be cooked, and understood. He also saw his waterskin lying nearby, looking full. Speaker wordlessly held out the skin for him, and Ian uncorked it and took an experimental sip. Yes, the water was fresh, with a faint taste of fish. He handed it back, considering that Selkies intended to pay him well for his work.

The water on the wave-ward side of the island was too thick with mud and debris to consider for rinsing his clothes. Ian abandoned them in the skiff and resigned himself to going naked for the unforeseeable future—though his boots might be useful. He sincerely hoped the weather would stay warm and dry.

A dozen Selkies were waiting for him, watching, beside the pile of stones. Ian wondered briefly how long they could stay out in the sunlight, whether their skins would suffer, and if they'd have to retreat to the sea often during the day—then set the thought aside as he decided where to set the first slab. He strained to lift the stone, and two Selkies hurried to help him, walking with an odd high-stepping gait to raise their long fin-feet clear of the ground.

The other Selkies stood up to watch, and began singing among themselves. Singing it definitely was, ranging from notes so high they made Ian's teeth quiver to others so low he mainly felt them through the ground under his feet. He moved as carefully as he could, aiming for a particular spot on the edge of the flat ground, and the Selkies followed, watching. Once he set the slab on the ground and turned back for another, the other Selkies went to the pile and began picking up more stones of the same size, copying him. As he and his two assistants set the second slab by the end of the first, he saw the other crews likewise placing stones end-for-end.

Ian wondered how much Speaker had conveyed to them about the tower's construction. There was no need to leave gaps for the rains to wash out the guano; the rough-finished stones, not sealed with mortar, wouldn't block water flowing. The question was how far up to start making the nest-niches, and how thick to make the wall so it would stand through storms and future rogue waves. Had Speaker thought of that?

By the time the sun was a quarter of the way up the sky, Ian and his crew had finished half of the first course of stones and all of them were visibly drooping with fatigue. A trilling call came from behind him, and Ian turned to see Speaker approaching with the water-skin in one hand and three skewers of roasted bluefish in the other. The working Selkies finished their tasks quickly and hurried past her, heading for the slope. He understood that they were going down to the sea, where they could rest in the water, and no doubt food had been prepared for them, too.

Ian sat down on the nearest slab and rubbed his tired feet while Speaker came up and sat down beside him. She wordlessly handed him the water first, and then the first skewered fish. It had, he noted, been cooked stuffed with broadweed, very like Mother's recipe, and it was delicious. After a few bites, Ian pointed to the half-circle of stone slabs. "It will need a second, inner ring of stones to keep it strong," he said, hoping she understood. "The labor is hard for your folk. How soon can they return? How long can they work?"

Speaker clutched her braid and handed him another skewered fish before she spoke. "More come soon. Fresh. Work another quarter-sun sky. Then more again."

Ian understood. "Four shifts per day?" That was understandable.

"And night," Speaker corrected. "Moonlight. We see clearly."

"Eight shifts..." Ian marveled. "All day and night? But I can't see well by moonlight, and I need to sleep."

Speaker gave him a very human smile. "You show by day. We copy by night."

Ian thought about that, and noticed a new crew of Selkies approaching. They were bringing more stones up from the slope. A further glance at the hill showed two Selkie-maids bringing more driftwood up to the fire, and two more carrying what looked like a metal pot and another water-skin: no doubt salvage from other shipwrecks. From further down the slope came the steady sound of stone chipping stone. He finished the second fish and reached for the third.

By noon, and a meal of steamed rock-crab, the first circle of stone slabs was completed. Ian was careful to leave a gap — wide enough for a man or Selkie to walk through, narrow enough that a single long slab could serve as lintel—facing the path to the slope. Ian explained, between bites of excellent crab, that the tower must have a doorway to let in the Selkies too if ever they needed shelter from a bad storm. Speaker nodded acceptance, explaining in words and visions that Selkies had no fear but welcome for the fresh-water-from-the-sky, and caught it in intricate cisterns on the other slope of the central hill, but they appreciated shelter from hard winds. The completed tower would also be welcome at birthing-times. Ian frowned at the thought of a Selkie-maid birthing her babe on ground covered with guano, and altered his plans for the tower so as to place the nest-niches only in the outside of the wall. Also, guessing that the Selkies would finish the inner rank of stones by the day's end, he explained how the next course of slabs must lie crosswise atop the first, so as to clench the first two rings in place. In fact, he would start on that work with the fourth shift, just to show them how it should be done if indeed the Selkie crews worked through the night. "And I will tell also," Speaker promised, as the third shift approached.

Ian also showed the fourth shift how to leave the nesting-niches—shorter slabs, matched even with the edge of the inside course, but leaving gaps to the outside—at every third crosswise stone. The Selkies caught the idea quickly.

As the sun sank into the horizon and Speaker's trill sounded up from below, Ian gratefully followed the retreating shift across to the hill and down the slope, aching in every muscle but greatly content. The basic shape of the rookery-tower was set and solid. If the Selkies were indeed as clever as he thought, they could probably finish it for themselves, and further such walls as well. In the long shadows of dusk the little cooking-fire twinkled brightly and Ian dragged his weary footsteps that way.

Speaker sat by the fire, and next to her was another female, much older, likewise with a lumpy braid in her hair—*Mother? Teacher?*—who was dipping her fingers into a cupshell full of what appeared to be ointment, and rubbing it on the foot of a weary-looking male Selkie. Ian winced in sympathy, thinking of the stress and pain that hauling and laying stones would cause to a foot never made for walking.

He came up to the fire and sat down beside Speaker, who wordlessly dipped an empty cupshell into the bubbling iron pot and brought it up filled with what appeared to be stew. She handed it to him, and he saw that it was indeed a delicious-smelling stew of fanshell-meat, cuts of assorted fish, broadweed and sea-celery. Ian blew it cool, sipped a mouthful, and found it flavored as well with touches of nameless spices. He couldn't remember ever eating a finer dish. Speaker handed him another water-skin, lest he burn his tongue eating too fast, then took up a pair of sticks and pulled the pot off the fire. She and the other Selkies took up shells and fed themselves a few mouthfuls of the stew, treating it like a rare and odd experimental dish. Ian wondered, as he emptied his shell and reached to refill it, if the Selkies normally ever ate cooked food. If not, then where had Speaker—or possibly her teacher—learned of it?

When the pot was emptied, and Ian thoroughly full, the Selkie laborer got up and limped away toward the sea, leaving Ian alone with Speaker and the older female, who looked at him expectantly. He could understand why; yes, he had questions he hoped they could answer.

"Whence came the Selkies?" he asked. "How did your folk begin? Were your ancestors brought here by the Star-folk, as our legends say that ours were?"

Speaker glanced at Old Woman and clutched her braid before she answered. "Legends. Tell us. We were made here. From landsfolk... Humans."

Ian gaped at her. "...How?"

Speaker frowned in concentration, picking precise words. Old Woman stroked her own braid encouragingly. "Very long ago," Speaker managed, "In the Very Bad Times on land..."

Ian knew she meant what humans called the Ages of Chaos. Oh yes, there were many legends about those days.

"Some feared...all land...would be ruined." Another glance at Old Woman. "Some say...landsfolk sorcerers...changed some landsfolk...to Selkies...so some would survive. Others say...it was the Beautiful Ones...who changed them...same reason."

Ian nodded slowly, seeing what sense this made. It explained why there were no other warm-blooded creatures in the sea. It would also explain another old tale. "Legend," he said slowly, "Tells of a fisherman who had a Selkie wife. She gave him three children. When they were old enough, she went back to the sea." He bit off his next question, replacing it with: "Is that tale true?"

It was Old Woman who answered: "True tale. True."

Ian's next question was inevitable. "What became of those children?"

Old Woman only raised a hand and pointed to him.

Speaker confirmed: "MacRae. And others."

Ian let out his breath in a rush, understanding everything now: his sea-sense, his love for the sea—though his brothers hadn't inherited that—and the Selkies watching his family for so long. And why they had come specifically to him for help when they saw the wave approaching, knowing what it would do, knowing he had the skills to save them.

"I will never leave the sea," he promised, then amended: "But I can't stay here, not after the cold weather comes. I must go back to the shore then, to the round house on the mainland."

The two Selkie women nodded in grim understanding. "The birds...come then," Speaker said. "The rookery. Finished?"

Ian looked up at the two visible moons rising, listened to the steady clinking of unseen Selkies chipping stone, and glanced at the line of human-like silhouettes carrying stones up the hill—so many of them, straining to do labor their bodies weren't designed for. He was awed by their dedication. But how long could they keep at it?

"I'll know by morning," he said. "I think... the tower at least. Other nesting-walls... I don't know."

The Selkie women exchanged another look, doubtless calculating how many birds that would house, how much the interlocking life of the sea would be diminished. "Rest now," Speaker told him. "Rest well. Dawn comes soon."

Ian dutifully got up and paced carefully down to the skiff, noticing that his clothes had been spread out on the farther gunwales, and were dry. The Selkies had thought of everything. He smiled as he crawled into the tent and wrapped the blanket around him.

Sleep fell on him quickly.

Dawn brought waking to many surprises. For one thing, the hill and the slope to the sea rang with sound: many trilling voices, the constant clink of chipping stone, and a moderately distant cawing of hopeful birds. Ian pulled himself out from under the sail and saw an altered landscape.

There were many more Selkies than he had seen yesterday—hundreds of them—and not all of them looked the same. Taller and heavier and darker ones were dragging flat rocks up onto the slope, where a horde of smaller and pale and slender ones hammered and chipped the stones into fairly smooth-ended uniform slabs which their larger cousins—with, he noted, feet wrapped in tough sedge—then carried up to the crest and along the path to the tower. The slope was no longer bare stone, but dusted with rock-chips. As Ian stretched his stiff muscles, he toyed with the thought that if the sea never brought back the pebbles, nonetheless, by the end of summer the slope might end in a beach of coarse sand.

That thought brought his attention down to the sea. The water looked cleaner this morning, though quiet and calm, but there was what looked like a stone-ringed tide pool to one side, and there hadn't been one before. As he pondered that, the Selkies noticed him and set up a cheerful trilling that was enough like a salute to be embarrassing. Ian waved briefly, then turned away toward where the cook-fire had been last night.

Sure enough, the fire was burning merrily and the driftwood pile beside it was higher. Speaker sat nearby, holding three skewers of fish in the fire. She smiled and waved him toward her, and he hurried that way.

As he chewed on his welcome breakfast, Ian asked where all the new Selkies had come from. "Everywhere," Speaker said, gesturing vaguely toward the sea. "Summoned. Come to help."

"Did you call every Selkie in the Bay of Dalercuth?" he chuckled.

"No. Only one in four." She sounded perfectly serious. "More come soon, from the far south waters, from the deeps to east. More come…to work, by turns…to end of summer."

Ian nodded, quietly amazed at the sheer extent of the

unknown domains of the sea. "Why did they build that tide pool?" he said, pointing with an emptied skewer.

"Food stores." Speaker gestured out to sea. "Look."

Ian looked out at the quiet waters, and after a moment saw heads bobbing. As they drew closer he saw that they were a line of half a dozen Selkies, swimming laboriously, towing something behind them. They came up to the edge of the slope beside the pool, and he realized that they were towing a net which was full of fish. With a neatly coordinated effort, they lifted the net and dumped the live and wriggling fish into the pool. "Oh, of course!" he laughed. "You need large stores to feed that construction crew!" ...*And they can't hunt while they're working.*

The fishing crew swam back from the pool, took the net and spread it out at the bottom of the slope. As they began picking it over, pulling out bits of weed and searching for snags, Ian recognized that net. He gave a pained look at the skiff and saw that, yes, it was empty. "Well, you're welcome," he grumbled. "'Tis good to know that I'm still of some use, now that you have your tasks so well in hand."

"Much use!" Speaker said urgently, clutching his arm. "Difficulties. Only you can solve. My people…never…have built with stone. We need you!"

"All right." Ian picked up another filled water-skin—this one, he realized, made of a very large fish-bladder—and paced off to the rookery site.

Three days later, the rookery-tower was finished. Ian took a long look at its ragged but stable top, then led his crew along the crest of the island to look for other spots to fill. There were, he saw, other crews already working. For a good two hundred meters to either side of the tower were small groups of Selkies busy with slabs and smaller rocks, or even baskets of pebbles, filling the narrow cracks between boulders, leveling gaps, laying slabs and building small rookery-walls. Oh yes, they had learned quickly.

At the end of third quarter-shift, with his small wall half-built, Ian was surprised to see Speaker coming toward him, a basket on her arm. Saying nothing, she led him not down to the fire but into the finished tower.

The first thing he noticed was that the floor was covered with fresh feather-sedge, soft and springy. The second thing he saw was that they were alone. Speaker sat down in the middle of the tower, set down the basket and pulled away the broadweed cover, revealing a freshly-steamed crab, a small water-skin, and more broadweed. "Feast," she said. "Celebrate."

They ate and drank in companionable silence while Ian idly studied the inner wall of the tower. It was sturdy and sound, right enough, and would stand through anything except possibly a bigger wave than the one that had brought him here, which he couldn't imagine. He hadn't counted the nest-niches, but there had to be well over a hundred. There were close to another hundred already in the gap-nests and small walls outside.

"We're going to do it," he said, as he turned to hand the last crab-leg to Speaker.

Then he saw she was clutching her braid, and smiling. An instant later he felt/saw the image in her mind. It left him gaping in amazement. She smiled, set the crab-leg aside, reached out and ran her long-fingered hand down his chest. That one touch was enough to break his paralysis.

Yes, he thought. *Yes...* He lay down on the feather-sedge, and she lay down beside him. He noticed that she smelled of the sea, and after that there were no words for a long time.

When Ian wakened it was near sundown. Speaker sat beside him, eating the last crab-leg. *"A fire, a meal, and a bed"...* he recalled. It seemed perfectly fitting that they were lawfully mated, and that they would lie in a tower he had built—as his ancestors had built the little round house on the shore. Could he live here, always, among the Selkies?

No, he remembered. He wouldn't survive the winter at sea, in a roofless house, with no winter clothing nor blankets nor a steady fire, and not when the birds would need the land.

"I must go home at the end of summer," he told her, feeling his heart ache.

Speaker pondered that, then reached into the basket, pawed the shore-weed aside and brought out a little box made of two halves of a fanshell. She opened it to reveal two small strings and a little blue pebble. It was a clear, glittering blue—unmistakably a sorcerers' stone.

"You touch," she said. "Only you."

Understanding, he picked up the little stone and held it in the palm of his hand.

At first all he felt was Speaker's presence, and awareness of the other Selkies some distance away, and the sea beyond that. Then the sensitivity deepened, and he felt a sense of immense time and a vast weight of water—and a thin feeling of another person, quite young, washed away by all that water and time.

Where did this come from? Ian wondered. *How did you find it?*

Old shipwreck. Speaker gave him an image of a ruined ship, long covered with weeds and sea-worms and shellfish, a dark space inside it, skeletons and small blue gems clustered in one tilted corner. *Old knowledge.* A trilling song played through his mind, a teaching-ballad about the blue pebbles, and a faint image of the legendary Beautiful Ones. It wasn't very distinct, and Ian understood that there was some knowledge the Selkies must keep for themselves.

Ian remembered, amused, that he was thoughtlessly naked. Pockets, he remembered, were not very trustworthy at sea. The small strings were too short to fit around his neck, and anyway, there was no hole in the pebble. *How shall I carry it?* he wondered.

For answer, he felt Speaker running her fingers through his hair. He heard her chuckle.

It was five years later that Anndra MacRae returned to the old town, marching in along the shore road. He stopped first at the tavern, and measured out his coins carefully before ordering a modest cup of mulled wine. The main room was crowded, as might be expected at the end of winter, and his there were three other men—with the unmistakable look of fishermen—at the table with the nearest spare seat.

"So, how's the fishing?" he asked over his cup.

"Good. Aye, very good," the three agreed. "Have ye lived here before, then?"

"Oh, aye," Anndra laughed. "I'm Anndra MacRae, and I was born here. Do none of you recognize me?"

The three men fell suddenly silent, glancing at each other, and one of them made a surreptitious protection-sign. "MacRae?" another ventured to ask, "Any relative of Ian?"

"Indeed," Anndra frowned. "I'm his elder brother. Why, what's become of him? Is he…dead?"

"Oh no," the men hastened to assure him. "He's well, and lives in the same old house. He has great luck at the fishing. Very good luck. Aye, even in winter. He never comes home with an empty net. Some say…" There was that exchange of looks again. "His luck is catching, that he's the cause of the town's flourishing."

"Amazing," Anndra laughed in relief. "I never really thought he could manage the skiff alone." Indeed, he'd thought that Ian would have to give up and take work in town, at best.

Again, those looks were traded around the table. "He…does na' always sail alone," one man murmured. "He has…a wife." The other two glared at him.

"What, Ian married?" Anndra marveled, wondering which of the local girls would have married a boy with such poor prospects. "Is she from hereabouts?"

More silence, more looks, and finally: "Nay, she's a…foreigner. She does na' speak well." One man ventured, "He brought her back after a whole summer's voyage," and then shut up quickly.

"Ah, well, that makes sense," Anndra chuckled into his cup. "I suppose I should drop in and congratulate him, then."

"Oh, aye," the other men agreed. "Just… Do na' be affrighted by the birds."

"Birds?"

"The shorebirds cluster 'round that house." The men buried their mouths in their cups, and couldn't be persuaded to say anything more.

Puzzled, Anndra finished his drink, made a brief farewell and set out along the old well-known road.

Eventually he saw the house, and understood what the man in the tavern had meant about the shorebirds. There must have been a dozen of them perched on the roof, and they rose up squalling loudly as they saw him coming. He noticed also that Mother's old garden, though fallow now, looked well-kept and even enlarged. At least Ian and his family were eating well.

The birds circled and cawed as he walked up to the door and knocked on it. "'Tis I, Anndra," he announced, a little doubtful of his welcome.

"Come in," called a familiar voice—stronger and deeper than he remembered, but not angry at least. Anndra pulled the latch-cord and pushed the door open.

The old main room was warmer than he remembered, there was a cheery fire in the old fireplace and a good supply of wood and sea-coal in the basket nearby. There was also a kettle hung over the fire with savory-smelling steam nudging the lid. There was a small forest of herbs and vegetables hanging from the roof-beams, and...yes, that was a small water-box holding live fish by the window.

Just rising from one of the old chairs by the fire was Ian, true enough, but how changed! He stood taller, and was notably more muscular, and his hair was long and braided. One of the braids was lumpy, and Anndra wondered if Ian had taken up the old family custom of hiding valuable coins in his hair.

In the other chair sat a woman, wrapped from the waist down in a blanket, though her chair was set further from the fire. She was pale, but not in the fashion of the Dry-Towners: near-white of hair, gray of eye, and with a face that looked as if it had never seen the sun—milk-pale, all over—and with an angled, elfin face. Her hands were tucked under the edge of the blanket, and she looked as shy as any high-born inland lady.

"What, Anndra! Ye've come home then?" Ian strode forward, smiling, hand extended.

"Nay, I'm only visiting on my way east." Anndra clasped the

proffered hand, noting that it was more calloused than he remembered. "I thought to drop in and see how you fared. You look well, I see."

"Aye." Ian dropped his hand and went to fetch a stool. "Ye'll not be staying long, then?" Though the words sounded warm, there was something unwelcoming about them.

"Nay, I'm hastening off to a lord's service, hoping to be first in line." Anndra carefully avoided asking if he could stay the night. The house felt...strange, and he could reach the next town well before dusk if he tried. "I see ye've done well. And married, I hear?"

"Aye." There was something stiff in Ian's smile. "This is my wife, Sylvie."

The woman gave him a slight smile, and a proper nod of greeting, but said nothing.

"Milady," Anndra said in his best formal manner, just to take no chances, "In the name of our ancestors, I welcome you to the family of MacRae."

The woman smiled wider, looking genuinely...amused. She still said nothing.

Anndra bowed—formally, formally—and turned to take a seat on the stool. "Congratulations, wee brother. Wherever did you find such a beauty? There were none like her hereabouts when I left."

"Oh, away to the south...east," Ian said airily, not quite meeting his brother's eyes. He'd never been a good liar. "But what of you, Anndra? Where have you been these last five years? And what have you been a-doing? And what's become of Stefan?"

"Ah, we parted company some twenty kilometers west, and I haven't heard from him since. I took off to the northwest, and worked at all manner of trades..." Anndra glibly related the story he'd planned to give his next employer, all the while wondering about Ian's wife. He'd never heard that the folk along the east coast of the Bay of Dalereuth looked so utterly pale: the opposite, if anything. And they spoke a perfectly understandable dialect.

But there were other people he'd heard of in his travels, folk who weren't entirely—or even remotely—human. ...*Could she be a* chieri*?!*

"Ah, but where are my manners?" Ian broke in suddenly. "Let me fetch you a bowl; the stew should be done enough. We've nothing to drink but water, but I can boil up some herbal tea..."

"Nay, water will do," Anndra hastened to say, wondering what herbs Ian might use. "I had enough of that rusty wine down at the tavern, and their hard bread too. I'm full."

While Ian fetched a cup, and a dipper of water from a tall jar near the window, Anndra took the opportunity to smile at the wordless Sylvie. "And tell me, milady," he said quickly, "How grow the forests in your land?"

For an instant she looked bewildered. "For...ests?" she quavered.

Not a chieri, Anndra decided. The *chieri* were always seen in forests. But what did that leave?

Ian came back with the cup of water, asking: "So, what work are you seeking eastward?"

"Some lordling wants more foresters," Anndra said, neatly covering his question to Sylvie. "And there's never enough of fire-watchers, though the pay varies..."

Right then came a squall and a thump from the back room. The door swung open and out ran a pair of toddlers. In the lead was a girl of perhaps four, followed by a clumsy-stepping boy of no more than two. They wore nothing but breechclouts, and Anndra saw that they had unusually long feet, very broad across the toes. "Mama!" the girl howled self-righteously, "He bit me!" The boy giggled.

The woman started up automatically, but Ian hurried ahead of her and caught both children. "Enough, tots!" he snapped. "Don't bother our guest. You're supposed to be napping." He picked them both up and carried them, protesting noisily, off into the back room.

But Anndra had been watching Sylvie, and saw that the blanket had fallen partly away from her legs, briefly showing her near foot. She twitched it back under cover quickly, but not so fast that Anndra didn't get to see that her foot was definitely the wrong shape: far too long and broad across the toes. *More like half a fish's tail...*

The hair rose up on the back of his neck as he recalled another of Mother's old stories. Yes, there was another legendary creature which his brother's wife might be.

He covered his shock with a laugh. "Ah, children!" he chortled, "They need such constant watching. If they're not asleep, they're constantly toddling about, getting into everything..."

Sylvie favored him with a smile and a vigorous nod.

At that point Ian came back, grumbling about "...they never listen," and giving Ian a nervous glance.

"Congratulations again, brother," Anndra smiled, smiled. "Two healthy children already! Aye, ye've done well for yourself indeed. I'm most glad to see it." He swigged down the water, which was clean and cool, plotting one last proof. "Ah, but I need be off soon if I'm to reach Grassdale before dark. Sorry I can't stay longer."

He set down the cup, stood up and tossed Ian a brief salute—then turned and formally offered his hand to Sylvie. "*M'sera*, I bid you good fortune, and pray you be always happy with my brother."

The woman hesitated a moment, then drew out her near hand—which was wearing a knitted mitten—and reached to touch Anndra's fingers.

He took the opportunity to clasp her whole hand firmly, and felt that her fingers were very long—and there were soft ridges between them, like folded skin.

A Selkie! He let go quickly, bowed and turned away. *They're real!* "Farewell, Ian. Perhaps I'll see you again in less than another five years. Nay bother, I'll see myself out."

He heard Ian's puzzled farewell following as he slipped out the door and pulled it shut behind him. The shorebirds were back, perched on the roof again, but they were silent now.

Anndra paced away as fast as he could without actually running. Indeed he'd reach Grassdale before dark, and pay whatever he must for sleeping-room at the inn, or any place where no shorebird could peep in, if indeed they ever came that far from the sea.

A Selkie-woman! he marveled again, thinking of the old tale of the fisherman and his Selkie wife. That legend hadn't mentioned her use of shorebirds as guards, or her ability to bring luck at fishing; he had something to add to the story.

It occurred to him that his luck had changed, too. He now had a tale which would garner him free drinks for the rest of his life.

FIRE STORM

by Jane M. H. Bigelow

This sweet, sad love story weaves together elements that recur in the earlier Darkover novels, particularly the Ages of Chaos tale, *Stormqueen*. *Laran* carries the potential for great benefit, but also great harm, and Marion Zimmer Bradley's stories emphasized over and over again the risks of well-intentioned use resulting in disastrous consequences (for both the user, recipient, and environment itself). Marion pointed out that bringing rain to one region might create a drought in another. Perhaps that dry area might lack the water with which to combat a wildfire, one of the enduring dangers in those areas of the Domains that depended heavily upon their forests. But fire, like *laran*, and like the yearning of the human heart, is never simple.

Jane M. H. Bigelow had her first professional publication in *Free Amazons of Darkover*. Since then, she has published a fantasy novel, *Talisman*, as well as short stories and short nonfiction on such topics as gardening in Ancient Egypt. Her short story, "The Golden Ruse" appeared in *Luxor: Gods, Grit and Glory*. She is currently working on a mystery set in 17th century France. Jane is a retired reference librarian, a job which encouraged her to go on being curious about everything and exposed her to a rich variety of people. She lives in Denver, Colorado, with her husband and two spoiled cats.

Melisendra Delleray sat frowning at the sky, her embroidery neglected in her lap. To the south, clouds piled up against the Hyades mountains, bunched at the ridge line like sheep at a gate. Was it foolish to hope that they'd climb past the ridge and bring rain to Caer Anailh?

It didn't *feel* as if they would, nor did it look that way. There was barely enough wind to lift the dry leaves in the courtyard below. The clouds bunched at the ridge line like sheep at a gate. And so the barley would go on withering in the few fields that were level enough to grow it, and the fire danger would go higher than it already was.

Every house in the village kept its largest bucket filled with water, ready to douse any errant spark. The guards of Caer Anailh scanned the lands around for any wisp of smoke outside its few streets. The lands just outside the village had been cleared of brush. Nothing was ever allowed to grow within yards of the castle, even in these peaceful times. They had done what they could.

"Melisendra!" By her tone, *Domna* Adrianna had spoken to her before. Melisendra looked away from the window to find the old lord's sister staring at her with one eyebrow raised. Giggles sparked all through the circle of women.

"I'm sorry, *domna*," Melisendra said. "I was thinking about the fire danger."

"As are we all! But there's nothing you can do about it, Melisendra, and you *can* finish that nightgown yoke in time for *Damisela* Felicia's wedding if you apply yourself. You embroider so nicely when you turn your mind to it, my dear." She came over and lifted the finely woven linex from Melisendra's lap and examined the clusters of tightly wound knots that made up the flowers. "This is lovely." Smiling, she handed it back.

There's the sweetie to make up for the slap. Melisendra murmured her thanks. It was true, and she knew it, but it was nice to be recognized for it. She lowered her eyes modestly to the delicate sprays of flowers. The work was tediously slow, but the effect was elegant.

"We'll stitch for your wedding soon, I expect," added *Domna* Adrianna.

Not likely. Melisendra didn't think she was ugly, but no one would marry her for her looks. Brown hair with only the faintest hint of red, if the sun struck it just right. Gray eyes. Middling height, and a build that kind persons called "sturdy." No one was going to marry her for her family connections, either. Her father's family had been scant help to her widowed mother, and had cast them off completely when Caitlin remarried to a commoner. Melisendra kept her mother's domain name of Delleray simply to avoid being thought without family.

It must be marriage someday, she supposed. She had no intention of seeking a position in a Tower, even if any were willing to train her *laran*. Her sister Janelle had gone to one of the best–only Arilinn itself was more revered–and what had that gained her but an early death?

It was a good thing, thought Melisendra, that she was clever with her needle. She turned back to her work.

Caer Anailh was a small castle, and its lands were scarcely more than one narrow valley. This room at the top of the keep was ample for every woman of rank, and two skillful commoners besides. Even young Carla had been set to simple stitching. Her stitches were surprisingly even for a girl of nine years.

They were needed. *Dom* Marcus' daughter Felicia's wedding was planned in scandalous haste.

Felicia was well-named, and lucky in her father. His kindness was known all the way to Dalereuth. The castle was full of *Dom* Marcus's rescues, orphaned children and orphaned animals alike. How could such a man be harsh to his own daughter? He could not.

The bride-to-be sat by the northern window, its cool light falling gently onto her work. She smiled as she did the black work on cuffs for a shirt for her betrothed.

Good for her, thought Melisendra. She'd have the husband she wanted. Melisendra doubted that old *Dom* Marcus Syrtis-Leynier would have given his only daughter to a third son of a minor family of the MacArans if his hand hadn't been forced. Ann'dra MacAran was a handsome man and a lovely singer, but he brought neither lands nor influence to the marriage.

"This is so boring," Carla complained. She was ignored.

"Bo-ring." she added. "Boring boring bore," she sang softly, "O....bore," and dropped a fifth on the last word. The child could carry a tune–and make one up.

"Stop whining," said Serafina.

Poor child, thought Melisendra. She'd had nothing *but* the boring parts, long plain seams, and the gossip couldn't do much to amuse a child who didn't even know most of the adults mentioned. "Here," she said. "Finish that hem, and I'll show you how to do a counted thread pattern. You can put it on the neck of your dress for the wedding."

Carla looked thoughtful. "With the bright green floss?"

At *Domna* Adrianna's nod, Melisendra agreed. Carla stitched away with dedication.

Melisendra rubbed at her forehead, just above the eyebrows. It seemed unfair to have the headache that an impending storm always gave without getting any rain. The chatter in the room felt even more annoying than usual, and louder. Also less meaningful, if such a thing were possible. Never mind. Push the needle through, twist the thread around it, finish the knot. The steady rhythm was soothing.

Someone whispered, "Away with the Fair Folk again, with a storm coming on."

Someone else said, "If she'd make the rain come here, I'd never tell how it happened."

A very young voice cried out, "That would be dangerous!"

Yes, it would. Melisendra pretended that she hadn't heard. Rumor had it that there was Rockraven blood in her family if you went back far enough. Though the stories of the Aldaran disaster had faded to legends, the taint was still there. Better to be thought devoid of *laran* than to be associated with the talent of moving storms.

She'd never figured out how the rumor had reached Caer Anailh. They were far enough from everyone except the other lordlings of this hand-shaped cluster of valleys that she'd thought she would be safely anonymous. No such luck. She'd been here for over a year now, but only the wedding scandal had completely displaced her in gossip, and that not always.

"Stephanie," said *Domna* Adrianna.

"I was only joking!"

Domna Adrianna frowned. "We don't joke about some things,

Damisela Stephanie. Legends exist to teach us truths, like the legend of Alanna the Gossip. Also, you are frightening young Carla."

Melisendra suspected that *Domna* Adrianna made up some of the legends she mentioned. Few people were willing to challenge her; for one thing, she always came up with something long in response. Stephanie muttered an apology–to Adrianna, not Melisendra.

Melisendra dodged back out of the path of four kitchen staff carrying a long plank table top out into the wellspring courtyard. More kitchen staff hauled trestles and benches into place. As soon as they stepped back from a bench, someone thumped down on it.

Groups of firefighters stumbled in, dragging picks and mattocks. Two men leaned their axes carefully against the courtyard wall with a sigh that could be heard at the other side.

Four of the *Comhi-Letzii* claimed one corner for their own. Melisendra was both glad and worried to see them: glad because they had the reputation of being some of the best, and worried that help was needed from outside the linked clans of the Five Valleys.

Melisendra dodged again around a group of three men as she tried to get to the trestle tables with her pitcher and cups. Two other ladies of the castle had come to help, though *Damisela* Stephanie didn't look as though she liked it much. Melisendra felt she'd fetch and carry willingly for anyone who'd helped to surround the latest fire before it reached the village. The stone huts wouldn't burn, but the livestock pens and the gardens surely would.

She turned to the trio she'd just dodged. "Is the fire out?"

One rasped out a laugh. "Would we be here if it wasn't?"

The other snapped, "Fool, be nice to the lady with the drinks." He smiled at her. "It's under control, *damisela*."

Which was not, she noted, the same as "out."

Thunder rumbled in the distance. The whole courtyard fell quiet as people listened hopefully. Melisendra's temples throbbed in time with the thunder.

Young *Dom* Stefan flung himself down onto a bench and grabbed a flagon of watered wine. "It's hitting all around us," he said when he'd downed half of it. "Why can't *we* get any rain?" His eyes shone green in a face masked with dust and smoke.

Green as grass, or as grass had been back in the spring. Even the brush by the creek now looked more gray than green. The forested mountainsides looked like a cloak nibbled by moths. So far, they'd managed to keep the fires from spreading, but most of the men in the courtyard looked exhausted. That one there just sat, head in his hands.

She took a chunk of barley bread, spread it with soft cheese from a pot, and handed it to him. "Here, eat a little before you sleep," she said to him. Obediently, he took a bite and chewed. When she looked back, he was slumped over the table, snoring.

A short while later, kitchen workers began dismantling the trestle tables to make room for pallets for firefighters from other villages. *Domna* Adrianna shooed all three of her young ladies upstairs.

In the solar, it was still quite light enough for plain sewing. Melisendra's needle flashed in and out of a skirt length of smooth, dark green wool. The chatter in the room faded into the background.

She could sense rain on the wind, together with the metallic scent of lightning. If only she could sort out the one from the other, like sorting out tangled embroidery floss! The lightning flashed bright as her needle among the gray lines of rain that fell to the east.

Why not give the storm just a little push? Just this once. It would give the firefighters a chance to sleep for more than a few hours. They must have that soon. No man could go forever on only a few hours' rest, nor any woman either.

Just a little nudge... Should it be push, or pull? It would be such a relief to stretch her awareness out, like a muscle cramped from long inactivity.

No. She had promised the old *leronis* who tested her that she wouldn't be lured into using this poisoned gift. "It's dangerous as the flower-drug," the *leronis* had warned. "You start out thinking that one little time won't do any harm. It will."

But Melisendra still felt the pattern of the storm. It was trying to come over the ridge as if it were a person with conscious desires. What was stopping it? If she could move *that*, change that, then maybe she could bring the rain without breaking her promise. She clutched her starstone through her undertunic and the stone's silken bag and strained to sense the nature of the barrier. Something shivered in her mind.

No. I will mind my work, and keep away from this. She clenched her jaw hard. Winds soared upwards in the next valley.

In the room, Carla coughed again. A chorus of coughs followed. The constant dust and smoke were plaguing everyone.

I dare not.

The scent of rain came in, carried over the metallic tang that meant lightning. Surely, with it already so close–

A dagger of lightning struck blindingly close to the castle. Thunder boomed.

Women shrieked. Serafina ran and tried to hide under one of the little tables that held sewing supplies. She crouched there, sobbing. Outside, men shouted words scattered by the wind. Wind carrying ash and dust rushed through the windows.

"The shutters!" Could anyone hear her? She could barely hear herself. Melisendra forced her way to the window and began hauling one shutter closed against the force of the wind.

Below her, she could see that one section of the outer wall had collapsed. Melisendra didn't envy the men the task of getting that repaired. *But there's no fire.* And no rain, either.

Domna Adrianna joined her, and between the two of them they wrestled first one and then the other shutter closed and latched.

"*Damiselas*! Close the rest," Adrianna commanded. Only the bride-to-be managed to pull herself together enough to assist with the second window. The remaining two windows, being on the side away from the wind, were easier.

In near-darkness, they groped their way over scattered chairs to the center of the room. The branch of candles had fallen off the central table in the confusion, but she managed to find it. *Domna* Adrianna fished flint and a tiny bit of steel from her housewife's pocket and managed to coax a small spark; the crying woman went into hysterics.

"Hush, now, it's only a bit of light so that we can see our way," she said. Then, "Here. Hold this." She handed the candle to Melisendra, strode over to Serafina, and hauled her upright. "Stop that." She spoke calmly, almost too softly for Melisendra to hear her, but the shrieks died away into hiccuping sobs, and then quiet.

Two more stones thudded to the ground outside.

That went well, didn't it? Evanda and Avarra, I was only thinking about doing anything, just daydreaming.

No one must know.

The storm outside rumbled away, drifting east and north. The storm in her thoughts stayed with her. *I didn't do anything! I kept my promise!* But had she? Was just longing to move the storm as dangerous as actually doing it?

In that case, why not try it?

Oh, nonsense–and dangerous nonsense at that. It was a warning, not permission. Melisendra forced her attention back to the tasks of cleaning up and storing things away. At least the delicate embroideries had been safely stowed away earlier! The long, dark green skirt would be fine with just a little brushing. But where was her needle? She shook the skirt out again, more vigorously. No needle.

Domna Adrianna was staring at her, one sandy eyebrow raised. In order to do the delicate knots that made up the flowers, Melisendra had been trusted with one of the few metal needles. She'd kept on using it for the plain work, liking its smooth slide better than the best polished bone.

She crouched beside her chair, groping under it, and winced as she found the needle the hard way. "Ah, here it is." Melisendra held it up. Her hand trembled.

"Well, that's something to be thankful for! But *chiya*, you're quite pale! Let's leave the rest for tomorrow. We're losing the light, and we're all weary." The solar emptied quickly.

Domna Adrianna drew Melisendra aside. "My dear, a moment's word, if I may."

"Of course, *domna*. I would value your wisdom." Melisendra could just picture herself saying anything else.

"You mean no harm, I'm certain, and I doubt that anyone save I has noticed it yet."

Now Melisendra was truly puzzled.

"Ah, yes, I thought so! You don't even know what I'm talking about, do you, *chiya?*"

Well, maybe from Adrianna's viewpoint, a woman of 19 looked like a child. "Forgive me, *domna*, but I don't."

"That's to your credit." Adrianna paused to clear her throat. "This constant smoke! How I wish–but never mind that. My dear, I saw you looking at *Dom* Stefan today in the courtyard."

Now it became more clear. Melisendra restricted herself to a respectful nod.

"And well, my dear, I was young once!"

No doubt. She could hardly have sprung into being gray-haired and gaunt.

"He *is* a handsome lad, but he isn't for you. Not that you wouldn't honor any man with your grace and talents—"

Oh, this was not to be borne. "But the heir to Caer Anailh must make a higher match than one of the sewing-women? Thank you for your wisdom, *domna*, but I know that. And truly, I do not aim so high." Nor did she. In fact, she took good care not to be alone with the young lord. There were rumors, and she had her reputation to think of.

There came a touch to her arm, feather-light. "*Damisela* Melisendra, I knew your mother. I speak to you now as she might have spoken, had she been here."

"She is not dead, *domna,* only living in Caer Donn with her second husband." Melisendra saw the older woman flinch. "Who is a kind and clever man, even if not of the Comyn."

"I offer no insult!"

"Nor do I wish to take what is not offered." Melisendra said. "I didn't mean to offend, either, *domna*. As you said, we are all tired."

It took no great gift to see the question in Adrianna's eyes. People dreamed up such terrible things if she didn't explain, that she'd long since worked out a short answer. "I was turned 16 when they met. That's too old to acquire a stepfather, or at least it was for me. His ways and mine don't agree well, but Mama seems happy, and I'm glad to have her so."

"You're a good daughter, Melisendra. And of course this way, there is some hope of a good marriage for you."

She had to laugh. The woman never gave up. "*Domna*, are good marriages only among the Comyn?"

"For those born into it, yes. I mean no disparagement of your mother, but she did you no favors there."

Melisendra decided that it was time to yawn very widely, and then apologize on her way to bed.

She woke the next day as every day, to the smell of smoke. On good days, it was distant. Some days it hung so heavy that it was hard to breathe. The healer and every assistant she could train went heavy-eyed among the old people and the babies, easing their struggles where they could. There had been two funerals last week, a baby who had scarcely breathed at all and *Mestra* Marja, who'd been assistant cook in the days of the old *domna*.

Melisendra slid out of her narrow bed under the window. She had it all to herself, another kindness to be grateful for! To be sure, it was drafty in the winter, but one mustn't be picky.

She clambered up into the window embrasure and enjoyed the privilege of being the first one awake. How quiet it was!

First of the ladies, anyway. Below in the kitchen courtyard, someone was scolding. "No, no, *no*, Eliane! Evanda and Avarra, stop mooning about like a sheep in fuzzyweed and control those geese! They've eaten most of the bugs, and they're digging up plants. That's *Mestre* Daffyd's own herb garden. "

The girl was sniffling quietly and holding her arm. "I can't!"

"Yes, you can. I did at your age."

A goose nip could sting, Melisendra knew. For pity's sake, the child wasn't much taller than some of the ganders! How was she supposed to control them?

"Here," said the old woman. Melisendra leaned her head out the window to watch. An older woman took the willow switch from the girl and gently tapped the geese into a lumpy sort of line. "You have to get them under control, Eliane. Otherwise they rush around and bite people. Now they know that you know what to do, you'll be fine. Take them over to the water now."

She handed the switch back. Melisendra watched as the girl herded the geese off to wherever they were supposed to go. One made a dash off to the side, but the girl got it back in line.

Melisendra pulled her head back in. That's what I need, she thought. Someone to tell me how to get my geese in line. Though I think it will take more than a willow switch.

She wished she could find someone. Her sense of the weather currents was getting harder to ignore, and the headaches were nearly constant. She'd had a little training as a girl; her *laran* had seemed too slight to need more.

Caer Anailh had no resident *leronis*. Pairs would come by from time to time to test youngsters, or if summoned in cases of bad threshold sickness. *Domna* Adrianna could deal with simple cases. Some of the great lords had *leroni* to help fight fires, but little lands like this one were left with mattock and axe and bucket brigade.

And a sewing-woman who could change the weather if she were brave enough. But I promised not to. Nor can I be released from my promise. The vai leronis died barely a year after she tested me. Poor, fretful old lady, I hope she has a calm existence now.

Melisendra sensed the storm brewing in the south as clearly as she could see the geese waddling through the archway. It roiled against the knife edge of the MacKenzie Ridge, looping back on itself, strands of air tangling as it struggled to rise higher. The back of her neck ached as though it might snap.

If the storm would just top that ridge, it could flow down into the valley and drown the fire. The clouds billowed higher, blood-red in the rising sun. Lightning flared within them.

Someone touched her shoulder. "Meli? Are you well?"

She turned to see Carla looking at her worriedly. Even now in late summer, Carla clutched a shawl around her shoulders in the morning air. How the girl was going to get through winter when it came, Melisendra had no idea.

"You were frowning so," offered Carla. That was courteous, to let Melisendra know that she hadn't been broadcasting thoughts. She'd learned in a hard school to keep them to herself, but Carla didn't know that.

"Oh, sorry! I was thinking hard, and that makes me frown. I'm well. How are you this fine morning?"

Carla looked quickly back at the rest of the room. No one else had her eyes open yet. Softly, she asked, "Is this as warm as it ever gets?"

'I'm afraid so. But cheer up, you'll get used to it. Here, borrow a shawl for now and I'll teach you to knit when we've time." The girl had better get used to it. *Dom* Marcus had taken her in out of kindness and in memory of her parents, both cousins of his. What a long journey, from a holding that lay south almost to Dalereuth itself, for a girl so young! A cousin had escorted her, but even so, it meant leaving home and kin behind. The girl was tall enough to look older than her nine years, with fine red-gold hair and pale eyes. So far, she seemed unaware of how pretty she was.

The days wore on, and no rain fell. Lightning started twos and threes of small fires that had to be put out before they could join together. First all the men who were out helping neighboring lands were called home. Then any task that could be scanted, was, aside from the preparations for the wedding. It would be a modest feast.

The barley was just coming ripe. Whoever could be spared from firefighting was soon out scything it and carrying the scant stalks of grain into the stone drying barn. The walls were close-laid granite; its roof was made of finely split slate. No flame could touch grain stored there unless it managed to come in through the vents. Harvesting this early risked mold, but leaving it the fields risked losing it to fire.

It began to seem almost normal to have smoke in the air, and the rumble of thunder most afternoons. Melisendra began to spend as much time mending work clothes, and stitching new ones, as she did embroidering.

The next day two fires merged into a massive blaze. The *coridom* came to where they were all eating breakfast and began commandeering ladies who were young and fit enough to do courier duty. After frowning at Melisendra for a moment, he nodded at her.

"Not this one," protested *Domna* Adrianna. "I need her for the embroidery on *Damisela* Felicia's gown! The wedding's in a week!" She gripped Melisendra's sleeve.

"And I need anyone able to carry water to the fire line, even undersized waiting-women. If that fire breaks through into the arroyo that leads to the fields, your young lady can whistle for her wedding feast. She won't need a fancy gown if the whole valley's burned."

No, she wouldn't. Melisendra gently pried her sleeve loose from *Domna* Adrianna's grasp. "I think I'd better carry water, *domna*."

"Indeed she should," said a voice from behind them both. "I don't wish to have anyone working on my dress today, Lady Aunt," Felicia said. She added, with a laugh, "We can postpone the wedding a *few* days without disaster."

Adrianna wailed, "Those clever hands, carrying buckets!"

"No worries," said the *coridom*. "We'll send her up with bladders of it in a pack. Buckets slosh too much. It'd be half dust and ash by the time she got there."

"Give her a carry-belt of comfrey, too," called a healer.

Climbing up the hill, Melisendra was glad to have her hands free. The newly-hacked path up to the fire was so steep in places that she needed to grab at the roots of trees to keep from sliding back down. She'd slide onto the hands of the next person in the line if she did. The pack straps sawed at her shoulders.

She reached up again, groping for some help.

A rough hand seized hers and helped her up onto a narrow ledge. "Here you are, then!" A young man with bright blue eyes and the blackest hair she'd ever seen smiled at her. "Good job!"

Melisendra repressed the urge to say, "Woof." He was an interesting-looking man, and she'd seen too few smiles to discourage one now. His made the corners of his eyes crinkle.

He hoisted the pack to let her slide out of the straps and handed it on to a crop-haired woman. "Stefan's line. Take a swig yourself." The woman trotted off up the slope easily as a chervine.

They stood on the edge of old-growth forest. Two-man tents were squeezed into a tight line along one edge, led by an open-sided healers' tent. Flames hadn't reached the camp, but the heat and the sound of them had. Her skin prickled.

"Sit down and rest before you try to go back down," the man who'd helped her said. "It's more dangerous than coming up, believe it or not." He waved at a folding stool no one was using just then, and turned back to help another person up over the edge.

"I'd better deliver this first," she said to his back.

Just outside the healers' tent, a woman was doing triage. "Great, thanks," she said as she took the packet. "Now go sit down a bit."

Did she look so terrible, that everyone told her to go sit down? Well then, she would. For a miracle, the folding stool was still unoccupied. Melisendra had a small leather bottle of water at her waist. She drank some of it down, grimacing at the taste of leather. People popped up over the edge of the ledge like puppets in a show, hauling their burdens of water and food and medical supplies. The firefighting chemicals had been exhausted a week ago. No one knew how long it would take to get more.

The man who'd helped her pulled several others up that last difficult pitch. When he wasn't doing that, he directed supplies and personnel. He never seemed to stop moving.

At last a quiet moment came. "Whew!" He grinned at Melisendra. "No, no, don't get up. I'm used to sitting on a log, whenever I get a chance to sit at all."

"You don't get that often, I think."

"Not often. I'm in charge of logistics here–name's Alaric, by the way. This fire's a brute, the way it keeps popping up small ones well away from the main blaze."

"I'm Melisendra." Since he gave no family name, it seemed rude to add hers. Anyway, she'd probably never see him again. He must be from one of the farther valleys; she'd remember if she'd seen him before. "I sew for the family, mostly embroidery."

"That's delicate work," he commented. He moved to push his hair off his forehead, and she saw that his shirt was torn at the collar.

"I wish I had needle and thread with me. I could fix that." Then she blushed to have looked at a man closely enough to notice the state of his shirt.

Politely, he looked away. "That's kind of you," he said, and fidgeted the pieces together as best he could. Neither of them looked at the other for the next few minutes. They spoke of common things, the barley harvest and the rumors of strange new people in Caer Donn. Both thought it wildly unlikely that they had come from the stars.

It was oddly relaxing to sit here beside this stranger who seemed not to care for any of the posturing and struggle for position that plagued even so small a court as Caer Anailh. She felt as though she could talk with him of more serious things, and be heard. Everyone else here was much too busy to stare at them and wonder.

A man so covered in soot that Melisendra couldn't have said *what* he looked like loped into the camp. "Alaric! Have those diggers shown up yet?"

He rose. "This was a welcome respite, *damisela*, but I must get back to my work." He hesitated, then, "When the fire's been beaten back, my men and I will rest at the castle. Perhaps we'll meet again."

"That would please me." Would it? Could it be the same, back in the castle with all those other people? One could hope. For now, she had that trek down the mountain before her, and no doubt she'd be needed somewhere after that.

"Evanda and Avarra bless your work, Alaric," she said.

He was right about it being trickier to go down. It was much harder to keep her balance on the steep trail when her feet wanted to follow it down just as fast as she could–no, faster than that. She heard a shout and a crash. "Slow down up there!" called a man's voice below her.

Word passed up the line that a boy had fallen. He was hobbling down with the help of two others, one before and one behind.

"Could've been worse," said a gray-haired woman in shortened skirts who was next in line to Melisendra. "Saw a man break his leg on a hill like this once. The work it was to get him down in a litter, and how the poor thing screamed!" She seemed to know where to put her feet without even looking. That calf-length skirt might help, thought Melisendra. She kilted her own skirts up higher, and crept on down the mountainside.

The man at the bottom of the trail took one look at her and said, "Thank you, *damisela*. Go rest now. Arravant's sent us some help." She limped away, feeling grateful and ashamed at the same time. One trip. That granny she'd spoken with was probably on her way back up by now.

Someone handed her a bread roll with cheese in it, and to her surprise she found she was hungry. Someone else handed around a bowl of apples, the first of the year. The sweet tang tasted better than anything else she had ever eaten.

There was no shortage of work to take the place of her usual embroidery. She could help clean herbs and strip the leaves sitting down, and she did. No need to know one herb from another, she was assured. That was a good thing, Melisendra thought. She could tell hairy from shiny, but that was about it. Then they began to run short of some of those, also, and where was more calendula to come from, this time of the year? Some must be left to set seed.

Her head felt stuffed with dry leaves. "Get some water, and a nap," said one of the healers. "This will go on for more than today. And if the fire flares up, you may be needed in the night."

The women's dormitory was still empty when she reached it. She stripped down, bundled her filthy clothes off into the corner by her bed, and got a quick wash with the water from the common pitcher. Her hair would just have to wait—maybe quite awhile. There were more urgent needs for water. Then, clothed in her spare shift, she lay down and was instantly asleep.

Melisendra never knew what woke her, early the next morning. Did she smell the fire coming closer, or was that only the stink of her own hair? She'd wrapped a scarf over it—not tightly enough, evidently. The fire couldn't be as close as it smelled. The entire castle would have been rousted out to help pull water from the wells as long as it lasted. She turned over again, trying to find a place where the sheets weren't sweaty.

A sleepy voice from one of the beds near the door asked, "What's the matter with you?"

"Sorry," she said. Maybe if she got up and went to the solarium, she could see where the fire was. If she for herself that the fire was no closer, she'd believe it.

But it was closer. Somehow, unlike any fire she'd ever heard of, it had moved downhill. As she watched, a resin-tree on the edge of the forest exploded into a moving cloud of sparks. A flurry of new fires began where they landed. "Oh, Evarra," she murmured. Had the fighters been able to escape? What of the granny?

In the distance, lines of falling rain glinted blood-red in the first light. They were surely no more than one valley over. *But they're not here.*

Melisendra could feel the storm moving towards her. It strained against...something. The flames, roaring upward above the line of the hills themselves?

People would die if the fire spread more. It was likely that some already had, just from the smoke. A strange calm flowed into her mind. Was her life more precious than theirs?

No. And I might not die. I am no delicate lady of impeccable ancestry, only Melisendra of nowhere in particular.

She hauled a chair with arms over to the window. The scrape of its legs against the stone floor sounded very loud. Someone had left a shawl behind; she wrapped it around herself. The old *leronis* had told her about the care that Tower workers took to make their bodies as comfortable as possible when they did demanding work.

They had monitors. She had no one. Who could she possibly ask to take this risk with her? Who could she trust believe that she could do it, and not just summon help to keep her from trying? *She* wasn't at all sure that she could do it.

Something in the storm called, "Now!" The river of wind wanted to flow down into the valley; she could sense that. Something was blocking the notch in the valley wall.

She was. Somehow, she was keeping the rain from the valley. Had her fear done this?

She said aloud, "I am sorry, *vai leronis,* most humbly sorry. I must take back my pledge."

She felt the old wall of her promise give way in her mind, much as the wall around the castle had collapsed that day of the lightning. The day she'd thought, "Why not try?" but flinched from the attempt. Today she would not flinch.

The first thing was to know what she had to deal with. How could she tell where to stop? She felt a stretch and pull as if she were still climbing the mountain, still trying to reach farther than her body was willing to go. A roar of wind filled her ears and light flared behind her closed eyelids. It was all too much! She had no words to think of this, no pattern to make sense of it.

Too much. She sat clutching her shawl around her in spite of the rising heat. There seemed to be two shawls now, how strange! She'd worry about that later.

Gently, now.

Slowly, delicately, like a seamstress untangling a skein of spidersilk floss, she found the places where only a few lines of the storm's pattern tangled with farther-flung nets of other storms. The winds flowed on the lines, tracing their curves. The clouds sailed on the winds like great birds.

And birds could be guided.

Or birds could bite you, if you came too close.

She pictured the clouds as great white geese on a river of wind. Could she picture a stick? But what would be large enough? She tried to imagine it. Lightning sizzled between the clouds. The cloud-geese flapped their wings and pecked.

Melisendra could feel blood bead up on the skin of her arms.

The stick clung to her hand, searing along her palm. Yet it was her invention, this stick. *No. I began you and I can end you.* She knew well enough what her hand looked like, after seeing it during all those hours of stitching! She need only hold it clear in her mind, in spite of the wind and the trembling lines of storm–she must just focus. Just!

And yet, it worked. Melisendra grinned as the stick faded. The pain didn't, but never mind that.

If she could guide the river, the birds would follow. The winds poured down into the valley. Rain clouds came tumbling with them, racing to be first.

Now she saw both with her eyes and her *laran*. Rain was falling on the village and the mountains alike. Shouts of delight and fear mingled as people scrambled to get under cover. Someone yelled "Move, damnit!" and a chervine belled. The village streets were becoming streams.

Torrents of rain pounded the remaining unharvested barley flat. A cowshed sagged and tumbled down; cows bellowed in panic. A tangle of nut trees rolled up against a bridge and lodged against its supports. Water surged behind them. Underneath what her eyes saw, Melisendra sensed the struggle between the water and the bridge. The lines that bound the bridge together convulsed.

She reached out towards the bridge, nudging at the trees. Pick, pull, slide–yes, like the children's game. One tree raced downstream, followed by two others. Yes, she could do this! The currents of the storm thrummed along her nerves like low notes of music.

A line of copper arched along the mountainside. The path hacked up to the fire had become a stream–no, a waterfall. It shone in the slight of fire and rising sun. And in it someone's body tumbled helplessly.

A slurry of mud and water raced down the mountain. *Please,* she thought without being at all sure who she pleaded with, *Please, I need to control it. I called it; I must guide it. This is too much rain for our little valley.*

Her imagined geese were gone now. There was only a roiling gray mass of rain too dense to see through, too convoluted to guide.

There, a swath of storm-lines curved down from the notch in the ridge. She reached out to push them along it instead.

Years ago, a cousin had let her ride his prize mare. They all three had cause to regret that. The mare had been far stronger than her delicate lines made her look. The storm fought Melisendra in much the same way as she strove to pull it off to one side, to make it flow along the crest of the valley wall.

"Melisendra!" Someone shook her shoulder. "Melisendra, wake up."

What nonsense. I'm wide awake. I just have to get out of the rain.

Small hands grabbed her arms and yanked her forward, out of the chair.

Stupid, don't distract me. I must focus. Is it moving away? A long roll of thunder echoed into the next valley. *Yes.* But she was tangled in the storm-skeins now, and she could not get enough breath to break free. She gasped for air, and felt water instead. Rain entered her mouth and her nose. There was no air, yet wind tore through the room. Cold, so cold!

Melisendra felt a stabbing pain in one hand.

Stabbing, indeed. A bone needle protruded from her thumb. Melisendra choked, and gasped. The horrible feeling of drowning receded.

Carla stood in front of her, holding both Melisendra's wrists. The girl let out a squeak as Melisendra toppled forward.

The window sill was just within reach. Melisendra clung to it as Carla scampered back. "I'm awake now," Melisendra said through chattering teeth. "Could you just push that chair over here?"

Carla did so. "Here, you'll be warm now," she said as she bundled both shawls around Melisendra's shoulders. "Just sit still while I fetch food and drink."

She did not return alone. *Domna* Adrianna followed her,

bearing a steaming pitcher of sweetened cider and a slab of nut-bread soaked in honey.

"First, you eat and drink." She hauled a low table over, one-handed. "Drink," she repeated, and placed the cup in Melisendra's shaking hand. She braced it with her own hand.

"We will have to discuss this later," Adrianna said. "Preferably with a *leronis* present. In fact, I hope milord will insist on it."

Melisendra drank, ate a hunk of the gooey bread, and drank again. "Is it bad?"

"Depends on what you mean by that. The fire's out, I'll say that for you. *Chiya*, why did you not ask for help?"

"Nobody's supposed to know," Melisendra said, somewhat thickly. "And who could I ask for help?"

"A child, evidently."

"She didn't ask me! I just knew." Carla drew herself erect. "Everybody thinks I'm just a child and don't know anything. I knew Melisendra needed help." She nodded briskly.

"Yes," said Melisendra. "Yes, you did. You are wise beyond your years."

Over Carla's head, she met Adrianna's eyes. "Will you speak of this?"

"Only to *Dom* Marcus. You know I must tell him."

Melisendra nodded silently.

"Don't look so sad, *chiya*. He'll know you meant to save us. And perhaps a *leronis* can help you with this gift."

"The last one didn't."

"Ah? Well, they're not all alike either."

One could hope.

Melisendra had not meant to enter the audience chamber at the same time as *Dom* Marcus and his son Stefan, only to cross it as a short cut between the solar and the kitchens. She knew that the old lord had sent for a *leronis*. Until the messenger had time to go to Corandolis, and return with someone willing to make the journey, she could avoid his notice.

She was glad of the delay. He had been more merciful than

she had any right to expect, but she couldn't expect him to forgive her for causing such ruinous floods. Now she walked softly along the far wall of the room, hoping to escape notice.

The *coridom* was with them, giving his report. "All in all, *vai dom*, it could have been worse," he said. "We'll be short on barley before the next harvest, but if we can keep the early harvest from rot, no one will starve. *Mestre* Derek means to hold a giant cattle-roast to use up all the beef that can't be turned into jerky before it spoils. And for a miracle, there was only one death."

Melisendra slowed her steps, stopped, and reached out to touch the wall. She had seen someone's body fall from the mountainside, too far away to be certain whether it was a man or a woman. She had spent the last two days not thinking about who it might have been. Fear and dread arose in her mind like the roar of the storm.

Dom Marcus sighed. "Even one is a great loss. Who was it?"

"The fire crew chief, Alaric from West Cliff."

Melisendra turned her face to the wall and silently wept.

THE DRAGON HUNTER

by Robin Rowland

In all the years I've edited Darkover anthologies (and read the ones that came before), I have never encountered a story that involved Darkovan paleontology. I love dinosaurs, as does every Darkover fan I know. The combination is so magical, I wonder why no one wrote about them before. (Of course, maybe someone has and I just never came across it.) I was delighted to receive this tale from Robin Rowland, who adds his own particular twist.

Robin Rowland lives in Kitimat, British Columbia, a town in a northern mountain valley, which he says has a microclimate that closely resembles Darkover. Before retiring to his old home town, he spent 30 years as a news producer and photographer for Canada's television networks. In 1995, he co-wrote *Researching on the Internet*, the first computer manual on how to search the internet. He is mostly a non-fiction author, specializing in historical investigation, including two books on Canada's Prohibition gangsters.

"There are no dinosaurs on Darkover nor—what are those giant fossil lobsters on Hawkesbury's Planet?"

"*Hawkesburia exocrustacea duodecapoda hosnioia agnusdei*," I replied.

"Yeah. Right. The eight-clawed bone crusher. Nor are there any dragons."

It had taken me seven days after I landed to get a ten-minute late afternoon appointment with Fletcher Giblin, Deputy Legate for Scientific and Engineering Affairs, at Terran Empire Headquarters. The windows in his eleventh-floor office overlooked the landing field, the concrete glowing purplish in the

Bloody Sun.

"A contractor for the Leonard Bowey Foundation for Planetary Evolution." Giblin snorted. "You're on a fools' errand, Owens." He looked at his com-tab and shook his head. "You have a Master's degree but no Ph.D. Why not, young man?"

"The budget at Empire University cut the number of grad students," I said. "Exo-paleontology is not a high priority. The contract means I get to work in my field, then send out more applications."

I thought, I'm by myself at the far end of the galaxy while my friends are boasting about their fossil finds.

"One: Didn't whoever sent you actually read any of the fifty odd years of geology reports and scholarly papers about this place? The tectonic plate movement that built those huge mountain ranges means that any fossils were likely destroyed. Or if the fossils exist on mountain slopes, they are probably nothing more than sea shells and are totally inaccessible because the mountains are snow covered year-round. Two: It would require permission from Comyn Council and they have never granted access to archaeologists. Will never. So, I am not going to try explain to the ruling council of this backward planet that believes they are native to this world what a fossil hunter does."

"Paleontologist."

"You're here for three months, so find something else to do and stay out of my hair. And what *is* that you're wearing on your tunic?"

"It's the red dragon of Wales. I grew up in a little town on the coast called Tywyn."

"That's going to be the only dragon you see on Darkover. Goodbye."

I stood.

"Don't ever tell the natives that you're a fossil hunter."

"Paleontologist."

I opened his office door.

"One more thing. If you're going to go out to the Trade City, you have to attend cultural sensitivity training. If the Comyn Council granted you access tomorrow, which won't happen, you'll need the full 'Beyond Thendara' course that lasts three months and by the time the three months are up, you'll be lifting out of here. Explore Trade City," he concluded. "Don't give me any trouble. The Spaceport library is excellent."

I rented the cheapest possible room in the Sky Harbor Hotel, a hole in the wall single with no windows on the central corridor. It was a strain on my expense account. Maybe he was right and I was on a fool's errand. Yet anything was possible. I truly believed that. I remembered one amazing grad summer in the Rockies working on the Burgess Shale, those beautiful, pure, high-resolution fossils from the Cambrian Explosion.

Giblin was deliberately baiting me. He would have known from my file that my undergrad third year field season had been on Hawkesbury's Planet.

Hawkesbury's Planet. A blazing white sun—always too hot. But I had barely noticed the sweat dripping from my forehead as I spent the days on my knees using an ultrafine laser pick to expose the delicate exoskeleton of what in life must have been a nightmare.

On a rare day off, I was wandering in the street market when a flash of green caught my eye. It was just a pendant hanging by a chain—green Hawkesbury amber, like thousands of others. Or so I thought. When I looked closer, I saw a distorted fossil, a cross between a seahorse and a dragonfly. The reverse caught the light of the sun—and then the fossil resembled a Welsh dragon.

Even with the weight limitations for fourth class interstellar passage, I kept the pendant in a small pocket in my carry-on.

I called up Cultural Sensitivity Training on the com-tab. A three-hour course for crew and passengers who weren't going to go beyond the Trade City. A three-day course for longer-term Empire staff and visitors. The three-month course, limited to those with permits who were going beyond Thendara. The next three-day course started in the morning. I signed up.

I approached the instructor, Melora n'ha Mesyr, at the end of the afternoon session. "In class, there was this reference to a Darkovan saying, 'It is ill done to keep a dragon to roast your meat.' Are dragons on Darkover?"

"That saying reaches back to the Ages of Chaos," Melora answered. "There are ancient tales of creatures called dragons. Any reliable information is lost, so there are no definitive descriptions. There are some rocks called Dragon's Eggs, but they are just that, rocks. Darkover is not the best place for..." she looked at her com-tab. "Paleo....that kind of exploration. What are you going to do for the next three months?"

"The Foundation has a mandate to enhance scientific understanding," I explained. "I am hoping there are fossils in the marketplace."

"In the marketplace?"

"On almost all worlds with intelligent beings..." I was going to say *in pre-scientific eras* but caught myself in time "...legends grow up around fossil discoveries. Fossils are often sold in marketplaces as jewelry, as charms, or as interesting types of rock. If I make a discovery there might be a chance that the Comyn Council would issue a permit."

"You'll most likely find something on Kyrrdis Way—there are jewelers and gem dealers just off the main marketplace," Melora said. "It may be expensive. The price often triples for someone carrying interstellar credits. Then there's the Night Market on the east side. Just don't wander into any of the side streets. That's the Thieves' Market and dangerous. You are more likely to be robbed and perhaps killed. It isn't worth risking your life for a couple of rocks.

"To be honest, young man," she added, "even if you find a *fossil*, it is unlikely that the Council would grant you permission. I would be wary of letting you look for such things."

I passed the exam and was issued an exit pass.

Even though it was summer, the forecast was for icy rain. I didn't want to look too *Terranan,* but the weather gave me no choice, so it had be my trusty faded blue T-Level All Hab-Planet All-Weather field jacket with the red and white Simon Fraser U logo, where I did my Masters, and the high viz yellow stripes down each side. I put the green pendant from Hawkesbury's

Planet around my neck under my Welsh Dragon tunic, both for good luck.

The wind was driving the rain along the narrow streets. I spotted a deep alcove between two stone buildings where I could check my map.

"Watch out!" came a cry in accented, barely understandable *cahuenga*.

I collided head-on into a man coming out of the alcove. I fumbled for the word from my language immersion. "Sorry."

I found myself looking into the blue eyes of a young Darkovan, perhaps a year or two younger than me. His eyes widened in surprise, his pale freckled wet face framed by a ragged tartan hood. There was a smell of old wet wool that reminded me of rainy days in the Tywyn Valley back home, combined with tangy oily scent, likely waterproofing.

"You're a *Terranan*."

"Yes. I am," I replied, slowly to get the words right. "I am completely at fault. I wasn't looking where I was going,"

"I too am sorry," he said slowly, choosing his words carefully. "I was looking the wrong way. I must go." His pronunciation seemed as bad as mine, yet there arose an unspoken connection: we understood each other. "Be careful, *Terranan*, you might trip on the cobbles." He ran off into the rain. The connection was suddenly gone, like an airlock slamming shut.

Kyrrdis Way turned out to be a disappointment. Guards with hooded rain capes huddled in doorways. The buildings closest to the main street were like fortresses, with bars on the windows and doors. At the largest, a black metal sculpture vibrated in the driving wind, the universal three balls of a pawnbroker. The next shop had a polished copper representation of Darkover's bloody sun. Signs in Empire Standard read, "We buy all forms of metal. Top prices." On a metal-poor planet, one where copper was the most valued, these buildings must be those of metal smiths.

Further down I found the gem shops and jewelers. Each time the proprietors' faces lit up when they saw my Terran garb. Here I found beautiful sparkling gems, including the famous Darkover star sapphires, all kinds of gold, silver and copper settings, rings, necklaces, small crowns, brooches, and raw stones as well. But nothing close to what I was looking for. I asked about amber, about fossils, only to be met with expressions of quickly-masked scorn. Without giving offense by saying so aloud, the shopkeepers made it plain that no respectable person bothered with such things.

Back on the street a symphony of smells of baking bread, aromatic spices, and roasting meat struck me. I was starving. Where Kyrrdis Way opened into Market Square I spied a sign depicting a white horse frozen in a gallop across a green field with purple mountains in the background.

Melora had told me, "Look for the White Horse Tavern. It's one of the best places to eat in Thendara. Good plain Darkovan food."

"This way, *via dom*." Speaking Terran Standard, the greeter ushered me into the dining room. It was hard to hear him over the cacophony of voices. "You have not been here before? Are you from the latest ship?"

"Yes, the latest ship."

"We share tables during bad weather," he shouted. "Is that all right?" Before I could say yes, he began to lead me among the maze of tables. Most of the customers were Darkovan, but I recognized a couple of off-duty Space Force guards.

At the very back, at a small table, a Darkovan man bent over his meat pie. The greeter pulled back the second chair. When I sat down, the diner looked up. My eyes met the blue eyes of the young man I had encountered near the alcove.

"Hello again, *Terranan*. I see you are indeed smart enough to come out of the rain."

A server approached our table with a pictograph menu.

"Let me order for you." My companion spoke slowly, pronouncing each word carefully. "The *Terranan* is newly arrived. A mug of *jaco*, the spiced mud-rabbit pie, and honey cakes." He turned to me. "That's what I had, it's very good and it's cheap." He took a spoon and gulped down another chunk of his pie.

"Thank you. Please stop calling me *Terranan*. My name is Rhodri ab Brymor Owens."

He looked up. "Dominic Ansaldo," he replied with his mouth almost full. "Of the Vale of Valiante. It's good to meet you Ryoodari. I am only in Thendara for a couple of days and have much to do, so I unfortunately do not have the time to savor this lunch."

Dominic finished his pie and was about to lift the mug of *jaco*. "What is that on your tunic?" he asked. "Is it some kind of monster?" With that question he looked more like a curious kid. *I think I can like this guy,* I thought.

"It is the *Y Ddraig Goch,*" I replied. "The Red Dragon of Wales."

He frowned just a little. "A dragon," He thought for a second. "Excuse me if I am being rude, but is there a story of this dragon?"

"Wales is an ancient country on Terra. It is where I grew up. In the tale a king wanted to build a castle on a mountain. Try as they might, after it was built each day, at night it fell down. So the king sent for the most powerful wizards in the land. They looked into their visions and told him that beneath the mountain two dragons were trapped and when they fought, the ground shook. That brought down the castle walls. The king had his men dig a tunnel. Both dragons escaped from their underground prison. One was white and one was red. They continued their battle in the sky. The red dragon won, and the white dragon fled. The king built his castle and the red dragon remained to protect Wales. That's the short version."

The server arrived with a steaming mug of *jaco*, a plate with an aromatic crusty pie, and a smaller plate with the two honey cakes.

Dominic drained his mug. "I thank you for the tale and your time. Enjoy your lunch." He walked away just like that.

After my meal, I went to explore the market. I thought I spotted Dominic in a leather shop but couldn't be sure. No place sold anything close to what I was looking for. It was a disappointing day, except for that chance meeting.

My hotel room was only slightly bigger than a fourth-class single berth on a star liner. It was little different from the cramped rooms when, in my student days, I'd come back after an exhilarating day in the field and lie in the dark on a lonely cot. I had good friends and amazing colleagues but there was always something—or someone— missing.

I had a fleeting image, probably my imagination, of Dominic in a small room in a tavern. His bed had an intricately carved headboard and tartan blankets.

I got up and accessed the Darkovan database.

Vale of Valiante.

No matches. No fuzzy matches. Possible translation, "Valley of the Valiant."

The next day was hot. This time what I wore resembled local clothing, heavy-duty field work pants combined with a loose-sleeved shirt I'd bought in the Oriel IV spaceport.

The streets and market were busier than before. I browsed the stalls but again no one sold rocks, either raw or polished. People kept staring at me. At first, I thought it was because I was obviously Terran. A haughty Comyn woman asked me, "What is it you wear around your neck, Terran? Why isn't it in a silk bag?" She meant the green pendant, visible in my open neckline. It must resemble the legendary blue starstones that the telepaths were reported to wear. I buttoned up the shirt and headed back to the Terran Zone.

I refused to accept failure, however. I might get lucky. With all this talk of Darkovan telepathy, I was wondering if there might be something to my granny's tales of second sight.

The Night Market was a series of stalls, lit mostly by torches that burned a fragrant wood, and also by candles or lanterns, the bright lights dancing on the faces of the crowds. Stalls with knives and swords attracted young men. One with the long knives favored by the Free Amazons brought members of that order and some young men as well. Other merchants sold cloth or leather goods. I thought I spotted Dominic haggling with a merchant that sold trail clothing, but he disappeared before I could make my way over. There were food stalls. Stalls that sold pots and pans. Again, I found nothing resembling a fossil.

The Thieves Market was almost as crowded as the Night Market, but the crowd was different, poorer, and roughly dressed. I was about to leave when I spotted a table near the entrance to an alley, lit by a dozen red wax candles. An ancient woman in a tartan shawl sat on a stool with wooden crates filled with small, flat stones.

"You want a charm, *Terranan*?" she said. "Good luck charm? Curse charm for that man in the *Terranan* tower? Charm to keep you safe in a fight?" She looked at me. "A love charm, perhaps?" She searched through a box as I studied the display. Not what I'd hoped for, only eroded sandstone, slate, or shale.

"This is the one you want." She handed me a grayish stone about half the size of my palm. There were two painted figures, and the stars of a constellation. "Gareth and Donnell," she chuckled, "The *Bredu*. This charm will find you the man you have sought all your life." Her grey eyes danced. With her white hair I had no way of finding out if she had had red hair and *laran*, but somehow she knew what I wanted.

"That will be one *reis*," she said firmly.

My granny's second sight prompted me to say. "But you sell them to Thendarans for five *sekels*." She paled for a second and then grinned. I laughed. "I know," I said, "The price for *Terranan*," and handed her the coin.

I slipped the charm in my pocket and turned to head back. "Wait," she called out. She handed me another stone, one with a horned chervine. "You'll need this," she said. "The safe travel charm, for tomorrow you begin your journey. No charge."

Back at the hotel, I spied a notice that a ship was due in two days. Was this the journey she'd spoken of? Should I cut my losses, return to Terra, file a report, and hope the Foundation would award me with a new contract?

I spent a couple of vital credits to call up the Empire newsfeed. A new species of plesiosaur was found in my old stomping ground, Dorset's Jurassic Coast. There was the accidental discovery of fossils on an uninhabited part of Keef. The government of the pleasure planet was already anticipating an increase in tourist credits—and hiring paleontologists. If I was going to leave, however, it was worth it to have one more lunch at the White Horse Tavern.

The greeter once again led me past the tables, but to my surprise he turned and took me through a door to a small private dining room. I was so surprised that I bumped into the greeter. Sitting at a table was Dominic Ansaldo.

"I knew you would come today," he said. "I have already ordered the best of the lunch menu." He handed me a glass of golden liquid. "Syrtis cider. Don't worry, it won't get you drunk. It is good to keep a clear head when speaking of serious matters."

I thought, he isn't trying to seduce me.

"You search for dragon bones."

The cider went down the wrong way. "Dragon bones?"

"I saw in your mind when we first met in the rain, you look for dragon bones. I've watched you search the merchants and markets, even the Thieves Market. You do not ask, you just look. You seek dragon bones."

"You know of dragon bones?" Does that mean there are fossils on Darkover?

"Perhaps. Your thoughts betray you, Rhodri ab Brymor Owens. You were sent across the stars to find ancient bones and found none. You keep it deep inside but you are a desperate, disappointed man. What can disappoint so much in one as a young as I am? No matter. I can take you to dragon bones. First, you must swear that everything I tell you must be secret. If what I tell you is not what you seek, then you will have had superb lunch and you can return to the stars. If I have what you seek, then tomorrow I will take you. But it must, must, be secret. Swear on that green stone that is around your neck. I will know if you lie."

"This is not a starstone, even one from off world."

"In that stone is the same dragon that is on your tunic. The dragon of your people's castle."

The skeptical scientist in me replied, "It's just an insect fossil from Hawkesbury's, nothing more."

I saw that spark in those blue eyes. This time they seemed to be looking into my mind. "You think it *is* a dragon. And that green stone channels your thoughts."

I put both hands on the pendant. "I swear I will keep everything you say secret."

I meant it. Then came a stray thought, If this guy is right, I can find a similar geology elsewhere and keep my promise. I instantly tried to suppress that idea.

He reached into his pocket and pulled out a piece of flat stone, the finest small fossil I had seen in my life. It was an iridescent winged insect, so detailed it could almost fly away from the table. Even the colours had been preserved, unless a fluke of mineralization had created those brilliant hues.

"Is this what you seek?" he asked.

My heart skipped a beat. All I could do was nod. Again there was a spark in his blue eyes that reached mine.

"This comes from the Vale of Valiante. We usually do not speak of the Vale to outsiders. I have decided to break that custom for the sake of my grandfather. Only to you, the seeker of dragon bones."

Lunch arrived. He was silent as we ate a sort of frittata with a salad of leaves and flowers on the side. I was becoming impatient as we finished the ice melon desert.

"My grandparents raised me." Dominic picked up his story. "As I know your grandparents raised you while your mother and father roamed the stars. These beast stones are so many in our valley that they are children's playthings."

I almost choked a piece of ice melon but managed to cover it up with a cough. Fossils so many that they were children's playthings? And how did he know my grandparents raised me?

"My grandfather began collecting them as boy. He wants to know how they were made. He has seen at least sixty-eight winters. So if he is to know before he dies, I will bring you to him and you will tell him. That is my price for our bargain. But this must, *must* be secret. Swear again."

A second time, and this time eagerly, I swore.

"Return to the spaceport," he said. "Get whatever you need for a long journey. When we leave Thendara you must look like us." He smiled that seductive smile. "You are about my size, so you may wear my clothing. Show me your map. Here, at the Emerald Grasshopper Inn, we will meet. In four hours."

I didn't have much to bring. My field clothing could blend in and I wasn't going without the under-fleece. On my bed I laid out the exo-paleontology field multi-sensor, latest generation, that my father had sent me as a graduation gift. Beside it was my Search and Rescue light/megaphone that could either fit in the palm of my hand or be configured as a head lamp. I had always carried it since I was seventeen when I took a course in Snowdonia in North Wales.

I was already breaking the rules by leaving Thendara without authorization. Could I smuggle the tech past gate security? There was one other thing I always travelled with, a battered sensor-blocking bag that when I was five had held toy dinosaurs, also from my soldier father. It was obsolete even then, now a century old. I put the field multi sensor and the SAR light in the bag. On a whim, for luck, I added the travel charm

The man looking into the mirror the next morning would not be recognized as *Terranan*. I was wearing a rough homespun wool shirt and pants with battered riding boots. I also wore Dominic's spare tartan travel jacket. My sandy brown hair with its reddish-brown highlights was an unruly mop.

"Now that looks better." Dominic laughed, coming up behind me. "I have for you the finishing touch."

He handed me a large knife in a leather sheath engraved with spirals. "It's the knife you were eyeing in the marketplace. You need a weapon and you can't handle a sword. A man without a sword or knife doesn't look right."

I reached out to take the knife. In that moment our fingers touched. This time it was more than a spark, it was a flow of energy. I knew then that I could never betray Dominic, no matter how much I was tempted. I knew one more thing: His decision to buy the knife was purely practical but more than that. Darkovan lovers—*bredu*—exchanged knives. If that old woman was right, if time and the stars aligned, one day I would have to find a knife for Dominic.

"We start in an hour," he said in a husky voice. "Meanwhile, don't talk too much. Your accent is strange and you still get words wrong." He stopped. "You *can* ride a horse, can't you?"

"Yes, in the mountains of Terra."

The horses that Dominic brought from the stables were not what I expected. They were mountain-bred, with an insulating coat of tightly curled hair. Dominic said, "The white one is mine, 'Riannar,' which means *starlight* in the Vale dialect. I am going to give you the reddish one, 'Saayor,' which means *wise woman*. She's easier with new riders." The other three carried packs.

Saayor was not as easy as Dominic said. I was used to Terran Quarter Horses but not anything smaller. I almost fell off getting into the saddle, had to have Dominic lengthen the stirrups, and the first couple of times she turned too wide when I tried the reins.

"*Barleto*," one of guests yelled. To my consternation, Dominic laughed.

We first took the road to Armida in Alton country, and that night we had a travel shelter to ourselves. "I am sorry I laughed," Dominic said. "It is so funny to hear someone call a *Terranan* a country bumpkin."

"That's okay."

"Stiff and saddle sore?"

"Yes."

"You'll get better as we go on."

On the second day, we came to a creek with a stone bridge. Without guidance from Dominic, Riannar turned off the road down to the creek and along a narrow, almost hidden trail. High above us, a hawk rode thermal air currents.

Each day in the wilderness of Darkover, I felt more and more as if my ancestors' ancient DNA was being revitalized. I wanted to believe that Dominic was interested in me, not just dragon bones and beast stones. I couldn't be sure. The three-day course for visitors to Thendara hadn't touched on relationships and sexual customs. Was Dominic thinking the same thing? What did he know about the customs of the Empire?

We slept side by side. Each night we huddled closer together, but nothing more.

On the sixth day after we left the Armida road, the trail got steeper, the track narrower, and the forest thicker. A pair of large black birds, local raven equivalents, dove and soared just above our heads.

About an hour after we had stopped for our noon meal, the horses, of their own accord, began to pick up the pace. After another hour, we looked down upon a valley surrounded by towering snow-covered peaks.

"That, Rhodri, my friend, is the Vale of Valiante. That is our citadel."

In the middle of the valley a rocky hill dominated the landscape. On the crest of that hill was indeed a citadel, shining pale purple in the red sun. At the base of that hill was a village, with sturdy buildings and smoke rising from chimneys.

The horses quickly began to descend the slope. Emerging from a grove of blue-leafed trees I got a better look at the village with its scattered buildings, houses, and barns.

"Something is wrong." Dominic kicked Riannar into a trot.

"How do you know?"

"My *laran*."

A couple of minutes later, we saw a man on a horse galloping toward us.

Dominic yelled, "Iain!"

Now he and the pack horses were galloping. Saayor raced to follow, as I hung on.

The man Iain pulled up his horse as we approached. I could see at once that he was related to Dominic, perhaps a younger brother. Iain broke into a brief smile as Dominic pulled up beside him. Neither said an audible word. In a microsecond, the smiles turned to desperate expressions.

"It's my grandfather!" Dominic told me. "He went up to the citadel and hasn't come out. There's a search team looking for him."

Together we raced into the village, where Dominic dropped the reins of the pack horses. He and Iain pushed their horses up the slope to the citadel. Saayor was keeping pace.

We reached the gateway arch. "We'll be in the old throne room through that door," Dominic said. "You tie up our horses. Then follow us."

I had a moment of joy, knowing that Dominic trusted me with the horses. I also felt his growing fear.

I tied the three horses to a hitching post and took a quick look around. The citadel was old, half a ruin, and the roof was long gone, but the cobble stones had been swept clean. I had never seen anything like the stratified sedimentary rock that comprised the citadel walls. Layer after layer of thin blue stripes ranged from pale to navy, interspersed with brilliant green blue and embedded in grey, probably slate.

I passed through the stone arch, carved with a leaf and branch pattern. Moss covered the corridor. It too was striped sedimentary rock. A large room opened ahead of me, brightly lit by the rays of Darkover's red sun. On the far wall, protected by a faded, fraying awning along the length of the wall, was mounted an articulated skeleton embedded in clean rock matrix.

I could have sworn it was the second cousin of a Terran mosasaur.

Only then did I notice the semi-circle of people, including Dominic and Iain, around a second arched doorway; listening to a man at the centre. I knew immediately from my own search and rescue training that this was the universal "stop, assess, plan, repeat," SAR session, whether in a society with sensors and satellites or horses and *laran*.

The man in the centre, obviously the SAR incident commander, stopped his briefing and looked at me. "Who are you?"

"*Dom* Felix, this is my friend Rhodri ab Brymor," Dominic said.

Felix pointed to me. "We don't have time for newcomers. You stay here and don't get in the way."

"I can help, sir," I blurted. "*Dom* Felix, as incident commander, please know that I am fully trained in search and rescue, five years' experience. Let me help." Everyone was staring at me, including Dominic. I realized I said the words "incident commander" and "search and rescue" not in *cahuenga*, for I did not know the equivalent, but in Terran Standard.

"He speaks the truth," a woman said. "I know his thoughts. He is schooled in rescues, but not here. Somewhere else." Then she paled. "He is *Terranan*."

"Thyra, our wisest Elder," Dominic whispered to me. "She has the most powerful *laran* in the Vale."

"You can find no trace of old *Dom* Kieran?" Felix asked.

Thyra's face showed anger and frustration. "I know he is down in the caverns beneath the citadel, but where, exactly?" she said. "It's this cursed *laran* fog. I cannot make sense of anything because of the stones."

"Search your assigned areas. Do it quietly. Listen for any sounds." Felix turned to Dominic. "Dominic, you search the north wing. If you take the *Terranan* with you, don't let him get lost. I will go to the watch tower with Thyra. She may sense something from there."

Felix turned to me. "I don't care what you did on Terra. This is Darkover. You do everything Dominic tells you."

A middle-aged woman handed out burning reed torches. Dominic led me down a passageway.

"What is *laran* fog?" I asked

"What do you know about *laran*?"

"Darkovan telepathy, just what's in all the planetary guides."

"Here, down these stairs. For most of us, and more so for the powerful, *laran* is, in most circumstances, clear—sort of like looking out on a sunny day. The stones do something to the *laran*.... Images are blurred or fade in and out. For those whose minds can speak over distances it is hard to understand one another. It is like when fog suddenly comes down from the mountains. That's why we call it *laran* fog. The deeper in the caverns, the worse it is."

I remembered the cultural sensitivity lecture, where Melora n'ha Mesyr had told us that Darkovans believed the *Terranan* overly dependent on technology. Now I wondered if they were overly dependent on *laran*.

Dominic, who clearly knew the citadel, took me through a maze of corridors, our torches lighting the way. When the torches had burned down to half their original length, he stopped. He used his free hand to rub his temple.

"He's not here." Then: "Do you have a headache, Rod?"

I'd been ignoring the nagging pain behind my eyes. "A slight one."

"You must have some *laran*, my friend. The stones can also bring *laran* headaches. There's nothing more we can do here."

Back in the throne room, the mood was glum. "What more can we do?" Iain said. "It's getting late, it will be dark soon."

It was then, almost subconsciously, I made the decision I had been pondering since we began the search. "Let me try something," I said in my horrible *cahuenga*.

They stared at me.

I slipped off my knapsack and dumped out the remains of a crumbling travel cake, my rain cape, and the sensor block bag. I took out the field multi-sensor unit, civilian Exo-Paleontology version of Special Forces tech. About the size of a larger com-tab, it featured artificial intelligence together with a McKechnie scanner, particle penetration sensors, ground penetrating radar, ultrasound and acoustic sensors, infrared heat sensitive sensors, the classic Yelnu probe, and a video recorder. The unit was built to detect fossils, but the manufacturers had added a search and rescue capability. I knew by showing the Darkovans advanced tech I was breaking every law on a Class D Closed World. I didn't care.

"Maybe *Terranan* tech can help," I said. "*Vai domna,* show me where your *laran* senses are strongest for Dominic's grandfather."

She thought for a moment. "Toward the west, I think. I am

not sure."

Time was urgently short, but I had to let the sensor do its initial sweep. That took about two minutes, although it seemed longer, to build up a basic image of the citadel that probably was as foggy as their degraded *laran*.

"Now we'll go," I said. "Just myself, the *laran* lady, and Dominic."

Carrying a torch, Dominic led me down another stone corridor. I concentrated on watching the sensor. Thyra followed with her own torch. The multi-sensor was slowly building data. The maze of corridors appeared in low resolution pale green on a dark background.

At one point I stumbled over a loose flagstone and brushed against the wall. I had flash of vision: an island in a sea.

From time to time Thyra said, "Stop." Each time she shook her head. Each time the sensor indicated no high-level life forms.

We turned a corner, Thyra said, "I sense him now. Farther down... No. I've lost him."

Just then the screen displayed, "Compiling," It refreshed and a new, crystal-clear image of the citadel appeared. The corridors were bright green, three-dimensional layers of lines; yellows, purples and greys displayed differences in the composition and thickness of the stone walls.

It took Thyra and Dominic just seconds to recognize the configuration of the citadel. As Dominic looked closer, his hand grazed my arm. Again, there was a spark of intimacy. I felt his fears for his grandfather.

Thyra reached out and touched the edge of the sensor. "Can you make that thing larger?" She pointed to one section. "This may be where I may have sensed *Dom* Kieran."

I pushed the enhance slider to its fullest extent. We spotted a faint blue dot, still fuzzy. One last button, "Analyze." It took too many seconds. "Life form. Insufficient data for definite conclusion. Possible Terran *Homo sapiens*, confidence 34 per cent."

"That's it," she said. "The cliff gate. You old fool, Kieran, what were you doing there?"

Dominic said. "Get the others. I am going to the cliff gate." As he raced down the corridor, the flames from his torch threw dancing shows on the walls until he disappeared.

It took many minutes, along corridors, back to the throne room, along more corridors and then on a narrow cliffside trail for the rescue team to reach the cliff gate. Iain carried a folded-up stretcher. It was getting dark; the last arc of the huge red sun was setting behind the mountains.

Dominic was waiting. I took the SAR light from my pack. In the bright white of my headlamp and the flickering orange of the torches, we saw a pile of shattered rock, plain grey volcanic tuff, blocking the front of the narrow gate.

I pointed my multi-sensor. The acoustic sensor detected slow breathing and a rapidly beating heart. "He's alive."

"Headache's almost gone," Dominic said. "Thyra?"

She looked at the sensor at the blue icon. "Yes, I know where that is. Form a circle."

I watched as the Darkovans joined hands. In just moments, the rocks blocking the entrance fell away, creating a space large enough for Felix and his team to enter.

"Can I use your light, Rhodri?" Felix asked. I handed it to him and he was first through the gap in the stones.

Then the sensor beeped. I looked down, astonished. It displayed "34 fossils found." The AI had been working in background during our search for Kieran. The sea monster in the throne room had been bright red. The other 33 indicators were orange—showing possible fish or other sea creatures. There were many more dots in pale peach, indicating the algorithm couldn't give a definite conclusion. That usually meant small shells or invertebrates.

Meanwhile, the rescuers were pulling themselves out from the gap. Moments later, the elderly man was carefully brought out on the stretcher.

Kieran was taken to the Thyra's house, so she could monitor his condition. Dominic led upstairs to a room where the moment I lay down on the huge bed, I was instantly asleep. I dreamt once, briefly, of an island in a sea.

I awoke much later. From the light in the windows, it must have been noon. A tray beside my bed held three kinds of cheese, thick slices of bread packed with dried fruit and a mug of steaming hot *jaco*. An hour later Dominic suggested we go for a walk. It was a warm day, an afternoon breeze wafting down from the pinkish peaks.

"Grandfather is already up and about—and anxious to meet you." Dominic said.

"He's recovered already?

Dominic nodded. "He's always been a determined man—and although he was trapped by the rock fall, his injuries were slight, or so he says. Thyra is monitoring him. He wants to meet at the foot of the citadel trail."

In the light of the bloody sun, the stones of the citadel were marked by thin lines of purplish blue patterns like vines after the leaves have fallen. Waiting for us was a white-haired man, Kieran, sitting on a large, old stone block. He was flanked by Felix and Thyra. The stone was grey and brown volcanic tuft. No blue lines.

"Grandfather this is…"

"Your *Terranan* dragon-hunter friend. I thank you, Rhodri ab Brymor Owens, for helping rescue last me last night… Yes, I know your name. I do have *laran,* but it is weak. Since I was a boy I have always sensed old, very old, echoes of life in our beast stones." He looked at Thyra and Felix. "To others they are curiosities."

"I can barely feel the echoes, myself," Dominic said. "When I first met you, when we bumped heads, I knew at once that you had *laran* that could help *Dom* Kieran."

"You are obsessed with our beast stones," Felix said. "Why?"

"Sir, I only found why myself this morning. My second sight is not powerful, but I think I can show you in a vision."

I grasped Dominic's grasped hand as I put the other on the stone.

"After all the years, it was only when I came to Darkover, did I finally know why I am, as you say, a dragon hunter. Like

Kieran, I sense history in stone. The rocks 'talk' to me."

Dominic reached out to the others. We formed a circle. Kieran held my other hand. In that moment I—no, we–were transported back in time...

...A five-year-old boy holding the hand of his long-absent hero-father, back on leave. A three-day excursion to London to see the Natural History Museum, then crossing Cromwell Road to see the Exo-Paleontology Museum. Lights from opal-like giant fossil "clam" shells from Samara singing...

...Student field work. Under the blazing sun of Hawkesbury's Planet, on the steep uplifted slopes of the Rockies, finding wonders of the Burgess Shale millennia after the first discovery, combining Search and Rescue training in northern British Columbia with a trip to see the fossils of Driftwood Canyon and Tumbler Ridge, on the planet Shinyanga co-discovering a skeleton of a new species of flying raptor...

...Disappointment. We regret to inform you that due to high number of applicants, Empire University is unable to offer you a position as a PhD Candidate in Exo-Paleontology...

Kieran gently pressed my fingers into a groove in that old stone, and I *saw*...

...One hundred million years ago, a rift on the floor of Darkover's ocean opened, beginning the tectonic forces that created chain after chain of offshore volcanic islands, islands that, pushed toward the mainland, would later gave birth to the Hellers...

...Sixty million years ago, a super volcano exploded, spreading billions of tons of volcanic ash, falling in layers tens to hundreds of meters thick. Forty-five million years ago, a volcanic island chain emerged from the old caldera. Ancient ash created shallow seas and island wetlands—and superfine layers of ash meant perfectly preserved fossils...

...In those wetlands was a "bog-orchid" with blue flowers, an evolutionary ancestor of *kireseth*. Over ten million more years, the bog-orchid flourished, growing only on those few islands—what would become the Vale—generation after generation dying into the mud, building up layer upon layer, covered from time to time by volcanic ash...

...When the islands collided with the mainland, rock was compressed, folded, changed. Like coal on Terra, the remains of those reeds metamorphosed into the blue layers in the citadel stones, a mineral that interfered with *laran*...

I opened my eyes. We were back in the afternoon sun of the Vale of Valiante. As others let go, Dominic continued to grasp my hand. Everyone was quiet for—I felt it was an eternity.

"I had no idea our home was so ancient," Felix said.

"Amazing," Dominic said.

"You must come back to our house," Kieran said. "To tell me about the creatures in my collection."

Yes. I just had to see and study Kieran's collection. Then another thought: What do I do? The rulers of this world do not want anything to do with paleontologists.

"Rhodri," Thyra said. "Centuries ago, in the Ages of Chaos, our ancestors fled the wars. Our scouts discovered this isolated valley. We needed a citadel to overlook the pass. We quarried stone from a mountainside. Only when the citadel was complete, when our families came, did we discover the citadel interfered with even the most powerful *laran*. *Laran* does work—though not well—where the roof is open to the air," she said.

Can I write a peer reviewed paleontology paper when half the research is telepathic?

"In the rest of the Vale, *laran* works, except close to outcrops of the blue stones. We knew then that in those terrible times such a discovery would be so tempting that all the Domains would seek to conquer the Vale. In the Ages of Chaos, we cut ourselves off from the Domains. The wars lasted for centuries. We only ventured out of the Vale when we had to. It was more than a hundred years after the time of Varzil the Good that we learned about the Compact."

There is nothing more than I want to do than study the fossils, first Kieran's, then the sea monster and other treasures I cannot yet imagine. There's obviously a lifetime's work here.

Felix said, "From centuries ago, we have felt safe in the Vale. We have our own ways and customs, which we want to preserve.

We have chosen not to be part of the Domains. Even today we often play the country bumpkins, so as not to arouse suspicion. We have no desire to be involved in the politics of the Comyn. But now the arrival of the *Terranan* has changed everything on Darkover—and, I believe, perhaps not for the better."

Am I welcome?

Kieran, despite his "weak" *laran,* sensed my thought. "Lad, of course, you're welcome. You have just shown us that this world is countless ages old. Darkover is always changing. The Vale will have to change. But we will decide how it will change. I have a feeling that you—our dragon hunter—will stay here for many years—and help us decide what to change and what not to."

Really, I thought. What about Dominic?

Dominic grabbed my face in both hands. "*Barleto,*" he said. "I didn't just bring you here because you can sense the beast stones. Of course, I saw you looking for me in the markets. But you're the first *Terranan* I've met in my life. I could not be sure about you or your strange customs. If you were a born Darkovan, I am sure our journey up the mountains would have been, shall I say, a lot more fun."

"Dominic, I am going to have to learn a lot more about cultural sensitivity." He frowned for a second, then realized I had made a joke. We both started to laugh.

FISH NOR FOWL

by Rebecca Fox

Rebecca (Becky) Fox is a Kentuckian by happy accident and an Arizonan by birth. She has sold short stories to a number of anthologies, and someday–if she can stop being distracted by horses, wild birds, Walt Disney World, and the Internet for long enough–she may actually finish a novel. In her "other life", she's a field biologist and an associate professor of biology at a private four-year college, and enjoys pointing out to her students that the dinosaurs are in fact alive and well and eating at your bird feeder. Becky shares her life with three parrots, a Jack Russell terrier who makes no secret whatsoever of being an evil genius in a dog suit, and a big goofy gray thoroughbred gelding who was once the world's worst racehorse. She blogs intermittently at bluebird_of_something.dreamwidth.org.

Becky's story echoes and embellishes the central question of the early Darkover novels: how can the culture of the Domains with its mind-based sciences survive re-integration with a highly technological Empire? With people to whom the Compact, which saved Darkover from cataclysmic psychic weapons, is only a superstition?

I have chosen the worst possible time to come home to Darkover. The thought, and heart-pounding sense of impending disaster that followed hard on its heels, struck Miralys Ridenow so abruptly that she simply stopped short in the middle of the arrivals concourse of the Thendara Spaceport. The *Terranan* tourist following in her wake plowed into her hard enough to make her stumble. Through the brief contact, Miralys could feel his irritation.

The man, dressed head-to-toe in brand new—and expensive-looking—cold weather gear, didn't bother to so much as offer to help her up. "Damned rustic," he muttered under his breath as he stepped around Miralys and her tumbled luggage with an expression of distaste.

Fuming, Miralys scrambled to her feet. But before she could open her mouth to deliver a stinging rebuke, another woman intervened. "You'll find you'll get along better in Thendara, sirrah, if you learn to watch where you're going." The woman's voice was friendly enough, but her dark eyes, set under a short-cropped cap of curls in a face the color of the drink the *Terranan* called *café au lait,* were steely. The man reddened–whether with embarrassment or with fury, it was hard to say—and quickened his steps, and the woman chuckled faintly.

The woman's expression warmed considerably when she turned to Miralys. "And given that you're the only Darkovan woman on that shuttle, I'm guessing that you must be my new translator. I'm glad Cultural Reconciliation managed to get you here from Idyllwild before the storms cut us off for the winter, though I hope they left you a few minutes to pack before spiriting you away." The woman held out a neatly manicured hand tattooed with a pattern of stylized leaves. "Interim Legate Neemah Bell. Do you shake hands?"

Warmed by the Interim Legate's courtesy, Miralys reinforced her psychic shields and took her hand with a smile. The other woman's hand was warm and dry, and her grip was firm. "Miralys Ridenow. I didn't expect you to come to the spaceport personally, Interim Legate."

"Call me Neemah, please. Look, I'm so desperate for someone with any real fluency in *casta* that I would have flown the damned ship to Idyllwild to fetch you myself. Coming to meet you in person is the least I can do." She gave Miralys a weary grin and hefted one of her travel cases. "Let's get you to your lodging. I'm sure you're exhausted. Space travel is no one's idea of a good time."

Miralys gathered the rest of her luggage and fell into step beside the Interim Legate. She hadn't remembered Thendara Spaceport as being so small, or as looking so shabby. "There are any number of Darkovans who speak *casta,* you know. And many of them would be more than willing to lend their services to the Legation."

"But there aren't any number of *casta*-speaking Darkovans with two masters' degrees from the university on Vainwal and top marks on the Civil Service exam." There was a wry smile lurking in the corners of Neemah Bell's eyes. "And given the mess the late, lamented Legate Hamilton left me with, I'm going to need every bit of that at my disposal. Legates are supposed to request a replacement and retire in an orderly fashion, not drop dead while playing cards on a restday afternoon." She sighed heavily. "The Comyn Council is insisting that their agreements were with Legate Hamilton, not with the Terran Empire. As far as the Council is concerned, they and I are starting on square one."

Miralys blurted her next words without thinking. "The Council doesn't know you, Interim Legate. And no doubt they feel like the Terran Empire is insulting them by sending a woman to take Legate Hamilton's place." Appalled at what she'd just said, bald-faced, to a woman she hardly knew, however true it happened to be, Miralys bit her lip.

Neemah Bell gave a humorless chuckle. "Do you know, Miralys Ridenow, that you are the first person to be completely straight with me about that? Cultural Reconciliation keeps pussyfooting around it like they're either afraid they're going to hurt my feelings by telling me the truth, or else they don't want me thinking badly of the Comyn Council." She strode into a waiting lift and held the door for Miralys. "And I thought I told you to call me Neemah. We're going to be spending entirely too much time together to stand on formality with each other."

"Neemah," Miralys agreed hesitantly, and stepped into the lift after the Interim Legate, feeling rather as if she had just put her feet on a fraying tightrope. For a moment, her vision blurred and doubled, and as the lift doors slid shut, the unnerving sense of imminent doom that had never quite left her coiled around her throat like an icy snake.

Miralys told herself firmly it was simple anxiety. It had been twelve standard years since her feet last touched Darkovan soil, after all. A lot could change in all that time.

Miralys had never imagined it was possible to come home and still feel homesick.

The Legation had quartered her at a Darkovan-owned women's hostel in Thendara Trade City. Miralys was sure whoever had made the arrangement had intended it as a gesture of cultural sensitivity and tried to take it in the spirit in which it was meant. They couldn't have known how unnerving she found Trade City, with its haphazard, unpredictable patchwork of traditional Darkovan buildings and *Terranan* technology. At night, neon light from the sign above the entrance of the tavern across the square streamed through her bedroom window, and the building shook from time to time with the roar of shuttles landing and taking off at the spaceport.

On her first restday on Darkover, she bundled up warmly and walked to the open-air market that stood on the invisible, but very real, border between Trade City and Old Thendara, hoping to distract herself. She glanced up at the bulk of Comyn Castle glowering over the city, and beyond it the soaring metal skeleton of the big launch gantry at the spaceport. Once that gantry had seemed impossibly huge to Miralys, a symbol of all the possibilities that waited for her in the stars beyond Darkover. Now she knew that it was hardly large enough to accommodate a medium-sized lander from one of the Big Ships. The spaceport at Vainwal had fifteen gantries twice that size, and it wasn't even a major transit hub.

A few desultory snowflakes drifted down from a cloud-choked sky. Soon enough, winter would close in on them in earnest. There wouldn't be many more chances to enjoy the market until spring. Surely buying something pretty would dispel some of her gloom. Miralys squared her shoulders and quickened her step, resolving to spend the afternoon enjoying herself.

Miralys was regarding a bolt of finely woven russet wool when she heard a voice behind her familiar enough to make her start.

"Miralys Ridenow! I thought you said you were never coming home!"

Miralys set the bolt back down on the counter of the clothman's stall and turned. Sure enough, Amalie Delleray was bearing down on her, a broad smile creasing her wide, homely face.

"I was young," Miralys said as they embraced, laughing and blinking back tears all at once. "The young say a lot of really stupid things. We were all a lot younger then," she added softly. Amalie's eyes were bracketed by lines Miralys didn't remember, her bright copper hair shot through with iron gray.

"My grandfather used to say that the only thing that never stops marching is time. Oh, *breda*, it's so good to see you." Amalie gave her another hard squeeze before releasing her. "And I can hear you wondering how in the gods' name I recognized you from behind. *Chiya,* after all those years we spent at Neskaya Tower, I'd recognize you in a *Terranan* space suit!"

Miralys couldn't help but chuckle. "I might have said I'd never come home, but I can't imagine *you* ever leaving Neskaya, Amalie. What are you doing here in Thendara?"

Grief and bitterness flashed across the other woman's face like a brief summer squall. "Keeper Ruanna died two winters ago. Little Viviana is still far too young to take her place."

"The circle is broken?" Miralys tried not to feel the horror of it.

Amalie closed her eyes for a moment before squaring her shoulders. "Donal and I came here to Thendara. He's paxman to Garin Ardais now."

"And Byrna?" Byrna Castamir had been the closest thing to a mother Miralys had ever known.

Amalie hesitated a moment, searching for something in Miralys's face.

Swallowing back tears, Miralys pressed a hand to her mouth. She couldn't bear to think—

"Oh, no, it's nothing like that, little sister. Byrna is alive and well. She insisted on staying right there at Neskaya with the *kyrri*. Said she was too damned old to pick up her entire life and move."

"It's the only home she really remembers." On her most homesick nights, Miralys had looked up at the stars wherever she was and comforted herself by imaging life at Neskaya, going on just as it always had.

Suddenly Amalie smiled determinedly. "But this is hardly fitting discussion for a celebration, *chiya*. You've come home to us at last, and that deserves some recognition." She laced her arm through Miralys's. "For the rest of today, we'll only think of happy things."

They were halfway through a steaming bowl of mulled wine at a little inn in Old City when Amalie turned to Miralys with a quizzical expression.

"Do the *Terranan* ever ask you about the Towers?"

Miralys felt muzzy and relaxed. The question took her by surprise. "Sometimes," she admitted, tipping her head to one side. "They're curious. I can hardly blame them."

"What do you tell them? I know you swore that oath to Keeper Ruanna before she let you leave for," Amalie made a helpless, half-frustrated gesture skyward, "out there."

Miralys put on her most innocent face. "I tell them we practice meditation, like the *cristoforos*."

For some reason, that struck both of them as uproariously funny.

The first day of the new work period started pleasantly enough. Miralys spent the morning giving a language lesson to the newest staffers in Cultural Reconciliation and Security. Teaching was a task she'd enjoyed from her earliest days in graduate school.

When the class decamped to the Legation cafeteria for lunch, one of the security officers, a tall, dark-haired woman with an engaging freckled face, hung back. "Do you mind if I join you for lunch, Ms. Ridenow? I just got here on the *Valiant* two days ago, and I don't really know anybody yet."

"Not at all." Miralys couldn't resist smiling at her. "I haven't been here much longer than you. And you can call me Miralys, really." It would be nice to have a real friend at the Legation.

"Officer Jennifer Petrie," the other woman said. "But then you know that already, since you're teaching our class. I'm sorry. I'm a little… awkward sometimes, you know. It's why I'm in Security instead of Cultural Reconciliation."

Miralys laughed and took the proffered hand. As she did, she had a strange instant of doubled vision, and the oddest sense that someone else was looking through her eyes. Before she had a chance to wonder about it, the bizarre sensation had faded. *Probably I'm just hungry. It's been a long morning, after all.* "It's all right. I don't mind awkward."

They were halfway through their meal when Officer Petrie set down her fork and regarded Miralys seriously. "I hope this isn't a personal question. They told us in our training that Darkovans don't really like to leave home. But you went to Vainwal and then you joined the Civil Service. Why?"

Miralys paused, a spoonful of soup halfway to her mouth, remembering the two years she'd spent at Neskaya Tower. How the closeness and telepathic rapport her foster-father had spoken so fondly of had begun to feel stifling and claustrophobic, how— much as she loved Donal and Amalie and Byrna—she'd longed for more than an instant or two of privacy and the chance to have thoughts she knew were wholly her own. Teenage folly, some of it, but even now the thought of going back to a Tower filled Miralys with an urge to find a berth on the nearest starship and never come back. Finally she drew a deep breath and said, "There aren't a lot of roles open to women on Darkover. I didn't fit into any of them very well."

"Well," Officer Petrie said, "I think you fit here pretty well. Mind if I eat with you after class tomorrow?"

Miralys couldn't help but grin.

Unfortunately, after such a pleasant start, the day took a decidedly sour turn. An hour after lunch, Miralys accompanied the Interim Legate to Comyn Castle for a meeting to discuss the status of three *Terranan* researchers who were currently mewed up at the Legation, unable to move forward with their work. Legate Hamilton had extracted a promise from the Hastur to allow them access to the villages in the Kilghard Hills, but with Hamilton's death that promise was null and void.

And it looked likely to stay that way, Miralys reflected when she saw they'd been relegated to one of the outermost reception chambers and that the Hastur had sent Miralys's cousin, Kyro Aillard, as his representative. Miralys liked Kyro well enough: as children growing up together in Comyn Castle, they'd played together in this very chamber more times than she could count, and he'd sent her frequent letters while she was studying on Vainwal. For a time, they'd even talked about marriage. But Kyro was a younger son, and while he nominally sat on the Comyn Council, he had neither political standing nor any real authority to make decisions.

Something felt strangely off from the moment Kyro set foot in the room. He paused for a moment in the doorway, a vague, distracted look on his face, and frowned when he met Miralys's eyes. At the same instant her vision blurred in the same odd way it had at lunch. Miralys didn't really care for *Terranan* physicians, but she was beginning to wonder if she should speak to one. By the time her vision cleared, Kyro seemed to have gathered himself. He strode briskly to the chair at the head of the table, and waved Miralys and the Interim Legate into seats without bothering to offer them refreshment. From the look on Neemah Bell's face, she knew enough of Darkovan culture to be well-aware of the snub.

Still, one had to go through the motions.

The motions largely involved a lot of shouting, both on Neemah Bell's part and on Kyro's, while Miralys did the delicate dance of translating faithfully while attempting not to give offense to either party. In the end, they were all exhausted and no closer to a resolution than they'd been when they started. Miralys wondered why the Hastur had even bothered to let them arrange this meeting when he could more easily have sent them a firm *no* by messenger.

"Well, that was a waste of two hours," Neemah Bell muttered as she got to her feet wearily. "I can't imagine what harm having three well-trained musicologists loose on Darkover can possibly do. You'd think I was asking to set Terran Intelligence's entire propaganda arm free to do as they liked."

Miralys shrugged helplessly and stood a beat behind the Interim Legate. It was impossible to explain the Darkovan distrust of their *Terranan* cousins to anyone who wasn't Darkovan. But before she could follow Neemah Bell into the hallway, Kyro caught her arm. The touch was entirely unexpected. They were neither married nor closely related, and she was a grown woman.

Miralys froze, more offended than she'd expected by the minor impropriety. "Kyro, *bredu*, what are you playing at?"

"I've heard *Terranan* women don't mind being touched. That's what you are these days, isn't it? I'm told you have the passport to prove it and everything." His expression as at once vicious and oddly blank.

All Miralys could do was gape at him. This wasn't the boy she'd known practically from babyhood, and it certainly wasn't the young man who had written her monthly letters for years. The one who, mere weeks ago, had professed his delight that she was coming home at last.

"And when you go back to the Terran Zone where you belong, you can tell that *Terranan* cow of yours that we are done letting you *Terranan* spread your filth outside Thendara."

By the time Miralys got back to her tiny suite of rooms in the women's hostel it was all she could do to yank off her boots and shrug out of her clothes. Leaving her skirt in an untidy heap on the floor, she peeled the bed coverlet back just far enough to admit her weary body and crawled into bed in her shift and stockings without bothering to unpin her hair.

Some hours later, shouts from the tavern across the square awakened her. The room was chilly. The orange and pink neon light pouring in through a crack in the curtains cast strange shadows. Miralys squinted at the dial of the wrist chronometer she'd tossed across the bedside table. Just past midnight, local time. Another damned bar brawl. Probably spacers on layover.

She wondered if the *Terranan* would ever learn to mind their manners. Grumbling, she pulled the covers back over herself and closed her eyes.

And all at once the sense of utter *wrongness* she'd felt at Comyn Castle descended on her, only this time it was so thick it threatened to strangle her.

The shouting grew louder, but it was so distorted by distance and window glass she couldn't make out what was being said.

Driven by that unnerving feeling, Miralys set her feet on the floor and lunged toward the door, groping for her dressing gown with one hand and her boots with the other. There would be no getting back to sleep tonight.

She shoved her feet into the fur-lined boots and plunged down the stairs to the street while she was still tying the belt of her fur-lined dressing gown. She'd worry about the sight she made, half-dressed with her hair mussed and coming loose from its pins, later.

The cold that greeted her when she stumbled out onto the street drove the air from her lungs, but Miralys hardly felt it. The scene that confronted her would burn itself forever into her memory.

In the center of the square, ringed by helpless bystanders, a red-headed young man holding a short sword faced off with a tall *Terranan* woman wearing the uniform of a security officer from the Legation. The pitiless yellow light from the *Terranan* street lamps that illuminated the streets of the Trade City threw their faces into harsh relief. Their expressions, she would think later, were oddly blank. With a shock she recognized Officer Petrie and a young man she'd seen once or twice when she visited Comyn Castle with the Interim Legate. Coryn, she thought his name was.

And then Miralys's saw the sleek silver object in Officer Petrie's hand and recoiled in horror. *No, no, it can't be. Not energy weapons. Not here. The Compact forbids it. Surely she knows.* Staggering backwards, Miralys fetched up against the wall of the hostel. Officer Petrie leveled the snub-nosed weapon at the young swordsman's chest. Miralys tried to call to her, but the sound died in her throat.

"Coryn! Coryn, *no!*" Another young man on the edge of the crowd lunged forward, only to be held back by his comrades. "Let me go, you sacks of chervine dung!"

Oblivious to his friend, Coryn lunged at Officer Petrie, snarling curses. His flat expression never changed. Time seemed to slow. Miralys tried to look away and found that she couldn't.

The smothering sense of utter wrongness intensified, driving Miralys to her knees. Panting, she pressed shaking hands to her temples.

For the briefest of instants, an image skittered through her mind. Officer Petrie and young Coryn, depending from strings like a pair of grotesque marionettes.

Petrie leveled her weapon at the young man. Her expression was as vacant as his. Her finger closed on the trigger.

A bolt of pain as intense as the flash of blue light that leapt from the weapon's muzzle to lodge in young Coryn's side lanced through Miralys's head. She crumpled onto the cobblestones and knew nothing more.

"*Breda? Breda*, can you hear me?" The woman's voice seemed to come from a million miles away. For a long terrifying moment, the words were nothing but sounds without sense. "Gods, she's half-frozen. Donal, I may need you to monitor."

"She wasn't supposed to get hurt. You said—" That was a man's voice.

"Donal, hush. This isn't the time or the place."

Miralys opened her eyes slowly. Icy cobblestones pressed painfully into her back. Her head throbbed. Two startlingly familiar faces swam into focus above her. Wincing, she sat up. Amalie steadied her and Donal crouched down to take Miralys's hands, scanning her with the same gentle, practiced efficiency she remembered. Donal was more stoop-shouldered than she remembered, and his hair was thinning.

"I'm all right, *bredu.*" Why was it that his touch filled her with unease?

"You're in shock," Donal said gently. His rumbling baritone

was as soothing as Miralys remembered. He did not sound as shaken as he certainly must be. "I think we all are. But it would be worse for you, I think, with the Ridenow Gift."

Amalie's eyes widened in horrified realization. "Did you feel—"

"I felt—I'm not sure *what* I felt." Miralys closed her eyes, shivering with the memory of that nauseating sense of *wrongness*.

Donal frowned, then got to his feet and reached down to help Miralys up. "Come, *chiya*, let us take you home and tend you. You need a stiff dose of *kirian* brandy and a good night's sleep."

The square was near empty and unnaturally still. A few guardsmen prowled the perimeter. Only a dark stain remained where young Coryn had fallen. Miralys's stomach roiled. She bit her lip until the pain cleared away some of the fog in her mind.

She could feel the disaster she'd so dimly sensed that day in the spaceport bearing down on them like an onrushing wave.

"The *Terranan* guardswoman. The one who…shot…Coryn." She could hardly say the words. *Terranan* energy weapons. Here. It made her want to retch. "What happened to her?"

"What does it matter? She'll be dealt with." Amalie put an arm around her shoulders.

"It matters. Where did they take her?" Miralys shrugged off Amalie's arm.

"Comyn Castle. She's been arrested by the Hastur's own guardsmen." Donal reached toward her imploringly. "She went willingly. This can wait until morning, *chiya*. We've had enough of tragedy this night."

"No," Miralys said, forcing her voice to steadiness. "No, it can't. Amalie, Donal, I'm sorry. I have to go."

Miralys forced herself to wash and dress, to arrange her hair in a manner suitable for an audience with the Hastur. Her hands shook and every passing second crawled past like an eternity. There was a hot, tender lump on the back of her head where she must have cracked her skull against the cobbles.

Neemah Bell would have gone to Comyn Castle the moment

she heard what had happened. Probably without a guard. Miralys had only known the Interim Legate for ten standard days, but it was hard to mistake what sort of person Neemah Bell was. *And where she is, the Hastur will be.*

As soon as Miralys was presentable, she tossed a cloak around her shoulders and ran.

Despite the hour, Comyn Castle boiled like a disturbed anthill. Members of the Comyn Council in various states of dress shouted at each other in the halls. Guardsmen were mustering in the big courtyard with the loud stamping of booted feet. Servants, some still rubbing sleep from their eyes, bustled everywhere, trying to manage the chaos. It was easy enough for Miralys to slip in unnoticed. No one glanced twice at a *comynara* in a green woolen gown.

It only took a few minutes of listening at doorways to ascertain Neemah Bell's whereabouts, but it was simple blind luck that gained Miralys admission to the Hastur's private sanctum. Ewan, the guardsman at the door, was a man she'd known since childhood and a good friend of her foster-father's paxman, Daniskar. "I have to see him, Ewan," was all she had to say for him to hold the door open for her. Silently, she promised an offering to the Lord of Light for her luck when this was over, and stepped hesitantly through the door.

In contrast to the sumptuous meeting rooms in the rest of the castle, the small chamber was plain, almost barren. Nevertheless, the walls were paneled with costly wood, and the furniture was clearly the work of a master joiner. Beyond the red-curtained windows, the sky was still dark.

Neemah Bell sat, stiff-backed and silent, in a hard wooden chair. Two guardsmen in the Hastur livery flanked her, hands on their swords. Naked relief flooded her face for a fleeting moment when she saw Miralys.

Miralys's head throbbed dully and the room seemed to tilt a bit on its axis. *I probably have a concussion.* She ignored it and settled into a chair next to the Interim Legate.

Finally, after what seemed like hours but was probably no

more than a few minutes, the Hastur strode in, wrapped in a dressing gown thick with embroidery and wearing house shoes. His white hair was bound back in a neat horsetail. His expression was thunderous.

Miralys scrambled to her feet. Neemah Bell tried to do the same, but one of the guards put a heavy hand on her shoulder. The Hastur's eyes narrowed.

"I see your translator has arrived. But I will say this in *Terranan* Standard so that I can be sure you understand." The Hastur's eyes were fixed on Neemah Bell. The contained fury in his too-even voice made Miralys shudder. "Your guardswoman has transgressed our most sacred law. Coryn Ardais is dead. His father demands satisfaction."

Neemah Bell spoke before Miralys could shush her. "This has been a terrible tragedy. I assure you we will get to the bottom of this and Officer Petrie will face consequences."

"Indeed she shall," the Hastur agreed. "The penalty for the use of distance-weapons in violation of the Compact is death."

"She is under our jurisdiction," the Interim Legate protested. "You have no right to—"

"Be glad I do not extend the penalty to you, *Mestre* Bell. You are the head of the house of the *Terranan*. Your guardswoman was under your authority."

Neemah Bell opened her mouth to speak again, but Miralys caught her eye and shook her head. *Not while he's so angry. Later, he may be willing to be reasonable, but not just now.* She exhaled slowly in relief when the Interim Legate subsided, sinking wearily back in her chair.

"The Interim Legate understands, *vai dom*," Miralys said in *casta*.

"Then the Interim Legate may go," the Hastur said tightly in the same language. "I have said to her all I have to say on this matter for the moment, and I have much to discuss with the Council." He turned cold eyes on Neemah Bell. "Get out of my sight," he added, this time in Terran Standard.

Miralys hung back when the guards, taut-lipped, escorted the

Interim Legate from the room. "Uncle, wait."

The Hastur whirled to face her, and it took every ounce of courage Miralys could call up from deep within to stand her ground. Meeting his pale eyes, she suddenly understood why her foster-father had always regarded this man with a mix of awe and terror. "As a representative of the *Terranan* you have no standing here, Miralys Ridenow. You made your choice when you left Neskaya Tower and took ship to Vainwal."

"I know." She forced her voice to steadiness with an effort. "But I'm not speaking for the *Terranan*. I am speaking as your kinswoman."

"And what does my kinswoman have to say to me?" At least his expression had softened a trifle.

"Your kinswoman is hoping to keep you from making a terrible mistake." Miralys gripped the arm of the chair that stood between her and the Hastur so hard she could feel the carvings on it digging into her palms. The pain cleared her concussion-mazed head for a moment. "There's more going on here than it seems. I'm certain of it."

The Hastur slammed his hands, open-palmed, on the desk. Involuntarily, Miralys flinched back. "A *Terranan* killed a young lord of the Comyn with a forbidden weapon. What more is there?" Half to himself, he added, "Anjali Aldaran warned me years ago what would come of letting the *Terranan* bring their filth to Thendara. I should have listened then."

"There is a great deal more, *vai dom*. I don't understand yet how it's all connected, but I know that it must be." And she found herself telling him all of it. Her inexplicable foreboding at the spaceport. Kyro's hostility, after all the letters he'd sent her on Vainwal. The odd but undeniable sense that neither Coryn Ardais nor Officer Petrie had really been under their own control.

The Hastur steepled his fingers thoughtfully and regarded her. "*Laran*. Have you confided your suspicions to the *Terranan*?" His eyes narrowed dangerously.

"No, Uncle. I've kept my word to Keeper Ruanna." She suddenly found herself wondering whether she'd really understood the price of the promise she made so easily when she left Darkover for Vainwal.

"I know you have the Ridenow Gift, Miralys. And occasional flashes of the Aldaran, however unreliable, no thanks to your late father. But what you say you've sensed makes no sense. Who on Darkover stands to benefit from Coryn Ardais's death?"

"Anyone who wants to get rid of the *Terranan*." Miralys met his eyes unflinchingly. It hadn't occurred to her until just this moment, but now that it had, it made perfect sense. "Legate Hamilton was popular, even among our people. I know you and he were even friends after a fashion. So long as Hamilton represented the *Terranan,* the anti-*Terranan* faction on the Council would have a damnable time rallying any support. But with him gone, and a *woman* sent to replace him, and with a nudge here and there to make sure our people stayed angry and the *Terranan* behaved especially badly, even for *Terranan*..."

Finally the Hastur nodded, albeit slowly and reluctantly, annoyance mixing with approval on his face. "You sound like your foster-father. And much as I hate it, I have to admit what you're saying makes entirely too much sense. But *chiya,* what you suggest would take a full working circle to accomplish. The Towers are stretched so thin right now that they can barely staff the relays. Aldaran and Neskaya are empty but for the *kyrri.*" Now why did the Hastur's statement sit so oddly with her?

"I know, Uncle. But don't you think you should find out for sure before you sentence Officer Petrie to death?" *You should know by now that the* Terranan *won't just stand idly by and let you execute her. But maybe that's exactly what whoever is orchestrating this disaster wants.*

He sighed heavily, burying his face in his hands. For the briefest of instants, the Hastur looked very old and very weary. "I can give you until we inter Coryn Ardais to come to me with proof, Miralys. The mourning period gives me an excuse to defer an execution. But after that I'm not sure I'll be able to stave off the Council." He took a signet ring from a drawer in his desk and pressed it into her hand. "This will give you the authority you need to ask questions. But remember, you are working on my behalf and not for the *Terranan*."

"A seven-day."

"That's all I can promise you, *chiya*. I'm sorry."

All Miralys really wanted to do was to go back to her rooms, drink enough wine to forget the horrors of what had happened that night, and sleep off the pain in her skull, or maybe just die, but that wasn't what she did.

The Hastur's signet got Miralys access to the cell where Jennifer Petrie was being held. From the look of the woman, slumped against one age-darkened wall, the guards outside the cell really hadn't even needed to lock the door.

Officer Petrie raised lifeless, red-rimmed eyes at the sound of Miralys's footsteps. Miralys didn't need the Ridenow Gift to read what the other woman was feeling. Guilt. Shame. Grief. *Confusion*.

"I'm sorry, Miralys. Oh God, I'm so sorry. I killed him. I killed that boy." Her voice was colorless. She sounded like a corpse reciting a list of its crimes. "I don't even know why I brought my sidearm with me from the Legation. It's against regulations. I know it's against regulations. But I did it."

"What happened, Jennifer?" Miralys had expected to feel anger. This was Coryn Ardais's killer, however much or little responsibility she bore for her actions. But what Miralys mostly felt was pity.

"I don't know." Officer Petrie spread her hands helplessly. "I don't know. The boy tried to start a fight with me. He had a knife. He was just a kid. I know how to de-escalate a situation. I've had the training, you know. But I pulled my sidearm on that boy and I killed him." Officer Petrie didn't even try to stop the tears that ran down her cheeks, didn't try to wipe them away. Her next words gave Miralys chills. "It was like some kind of out-of-body experience. I did it. I remember doing it. I just wish I understood why."

Trade City and the Terran Zone were unnervingly empty the next morning. Most of the Darkovan-owned businesses in Trade City were shuttered, and the few whose doors were open sported hand-lettered placards in rough Standard declaring , with varying degrees of politeness, that the establishment didn't serve *Terranan*. None of the Darkovan staff at the spaceport or the Legation, save Miralys, had reported for duty. The Dockworkers' Union had called a special meeting later that afternoon to discuss their response to the situation. The Darkovans had been suspicious of the guilds and unions initially, but once they'd understood what a union was, they'd rushed to embrace them.

Whatever the Dockworkers' Union decided was liable to cause a major headache for the Portmaster, but it would be small potatoes compared to what would happen if the situation with Officer Petrie were allowed to fester unresolved for long.

Violence.

The only real question was whether the first salvo would come from the *Terranan* side or from the Darkovan.

When Neemah Bell came to beard Miralys in her office, she'd been staring at the same document for the last forty-five minutes, trying to force her battered brain to parse the colorless, passionless *Terranan* terminology. The Interim Legate's arrival was almost a relief, despite the deep frown on her face.

"I heard what you did last night, Miralys," she said. "Talking to Officer Petrie. I appreciate your loyalty, but I don't need you playing girl detective on my behalf." *I have enough problems as it is.* Miralys had tried to avoid reading Neemah Bell's mind, but her surface thoughts were so clear she might have shouted them from the top of Comyn Castle.

Miralys buried her aching head in her hands. "I know. I'm sorry. I thought I could find out something we didn't already know."

"Did you?"

"No." *At least not that I can tell you. I'm sorry.* Never before had the promise—the blood oath—she'd made to old Keeper Ruanna felt like such a burden. Neemah Bell deserved to know that someone might be wielding *laran* against her.

Fortunately or unfortunately, the Interim Legate misread Miralys's expression. "Don't think me ungrateful, Miralys. I can't imagine what this must be like for you, caught betwixt and between like this. That you would even think to help us—did you know Coryn Ardais well?"

"Hardly at all. I'd seen him once or twice at Comyn Castle. He would have been a small boy when I left Darkover for Vainwal." She took a deep, steadying breath, shoving the image of Coryn lying dead on the cobbles to the back of her mind. "It's just that I have this gut feeling that there must be more to this story than we're seeing." It wasn't a violation of her oath to say that much.

"Be that as it may, this is a matter for Legation Security and whatever investigators the Sector Field Office decides to send."

By the time they get here, Jennifer Petrie may well be dead. What Miralys said aloud was, "The friends who were with Coryn Ardais last night won't talk to a *Terranan* security officer. But they might be willing to talk to me."

Coryn Ardais's friends were easy enough to find. With the closure of the tavern across from Miralys's hostel, they'd decamped to the Rabbit-horn and Barrel in Old City to drown their grief for their friend in endless tankards of beer. Miralys knew their type: younger sons with far more money and time than purpose and good sense.

The two boys were uncomfortable at the thought of talking to an unaccompanied woman, and warier still about Miralys's association with the *Terranan*, but the signet the Hastur had given her two nights before gained her their reluctant cooperation.

The story they told was much like Officer Petrie's. Coryn had no real love for the *Terranan*, but he was no revolutionary and he certainly wasn't violent. He hadn't been deep in his cups on the night he'd been killed. And yet, halfway through a game of cards, he'd suddenly pulled his belt knife and jumped to his feet to confront a *Terranan* security officer.

"I know this sounds mad, *domna*," the younger of the two said into his beer, refusing to meet her eyes, "but it was like those old stories, the ones where the *leroni* used their gifts to control people."

The older one nodded. "The look on Coryn's face gave me chills. It was almost like he wasn't even there in his body."

It was at that moment that the Hastur's words came back to her: *"Aldaran and Neskaya are empty but for the* kyrri." But Amalie said Byrna Castamir had stayed behind at Neskaya.

Byrna Castamir had the Alton Gift of forced rapport, and she knew well how to use the strength of the circle—and Miralys's Ridenow Gift in particular—to amplify it. In the days when Miralys had still been at Neskaya, the circle had used that knack to alter the memory of a particularly troublesome *Terranan.*

But they couldn't possibly use me that way without my knowledge or consent.

Could they?

She remembered those strange moments of blurred vision, that unnerving sense of someone else looking out from behind her eyes. With Kyro Aillard. With Jennifer Petrie. She remembered suffocating sense of wrongness that had awakened her from a sound sleep and drawn her down to the street the night Coryn Ardais was killed.

She remembered the vision she'd had of Coryn and Officer Petrie as marionettes dangling from strings. Perhaps Coryn and Officer Petrie hadn't been the only puppets in this little drama.

What was it she'd heard Donal say when he thought she was still unconscious? *'She wasn't supposed to get hurt.'*

The splitting headache she'd nursed for the last two days could as easily be a reaction-headache as a concussion.

But surely this couldn't be any more than crazy speculation. Even if Byrna Castamir were in Thendara, for the remnant of the Neskaya Circle to have planned anything like this, Byrna and Amalie and Donal would have had to have known Miralys was coming home to Darkover.

Or they could have brought *me home.*

Miralys muttered what she hoped was a coherent excuse to the boys and got to her feet.

As soon as she reached the street, she broke into a run.

Miralys barged into the Interim Legate's office without ceremony and in violation of all protocol, Neemah Bell's secretary trailing behind her shouting useless and probably meaningless threats. Finally the man leapt in front of Miralys and tried to block the door. "You can't just go in there!"

"Watch me." Miralys pushed him aside and walked past, putting a just a touch of *laran* into the shove.

Fortunately Neemah Bell was alone. Miralys wasn't sure what she would have done had the Interim Legate been in a meeting.

"Miralys!" Neemah Bell studied Miralys's face and frowned. Miralys wondered what the other woman saw there. "Are you all right? We're not supposed to meet until tomorrow morning…"

"Am I all right? Yes. No. I'm not sure. But there's something I need to know. Why did you bring me here from Idyllwild?"

The other woman's brow furrowed with consternation. "I told you that day at the spaceport. Your qualifications—"

"No." Miralys knew her voice was too loud, knew she must sound half-mad, could 'hear' the worry mixed with fear in Neemah Bell's surface thoughts. The Interim Legate moved to put her polished wood desk between herself and Miralys. "I didn't apply for the post, and you had plenty of possible candidates right here on Darkover. Hell, Domenic MacAran was Legate Hamilton's translator for twenty years, and I'm sure he would have happily stayed on."

"Domenic MacAran doesn't have your academic background. Miralys, why don't you calm down? Have a seat. I'll make you some tea. We can talk about this later." Neemah Bell was an inch from summoning Security. Miralys could feel it. It didn't matter.

"Domenic MacAran knows a lot more about the political situation here than I do. He's lived it. For the last twelve years I've only read about it from the comfort of various places off-world. And Domenic wouldn't have been a political liability the way I am."

The Interim Legate just stared at her.

"Neemah, I'm a *woman*. You're too savvy not to recognize the implications of that here on Darkover. It doesn't matter what degrees I do or don't have. You'd have been far better off walking into the Comyn Castle with a man at your side—*any* man, even if he was low-class and stupid—and you must know that. So I ask you again: *why me?*"

Neemah Bell seemed to shake herself. "I—I saw your file in the Cultural Reconciliation database and it was…I guess it was a gut feeling." She sat down hard in her desk chair, blinking like someone emerging from a dream. "I don't know—"

Miralys didn't hear the rest of that sentence because that was when her vision blurred.

"No," she snarled, slamming down her psychic barriers and forcing herself to look away from the Interim Legate. Her neck muscles cramped with the effort "Not today. Not this time."

Even through her shields Miralys could feel the howling, killing rage on the other end of that psychic connection.

Miralys dared to follow that connection with a tendril of thought. The person at the other end slammed down her own barriers, but not quite fast enough.

Miralys knew where they were.

Legend had it that Ashara's Tower had stood for centuries before the founding of the city of Thendara itself, that Comyn Castle had been built around the Tower and not the other way around. Legend also had it that—among other things—Ashara's Tower was cursed. Perhaps that was why the small circle working in Thendara chose to use what everyone referred to as the new New Tower, leaving Ashara's tower to the *kyrri* and the birds that nested in the rafters.

And, it seemed now, to a renegade circle hell-bent on destroying what fragile relationship the Darkovans and the *Terranan* had managed to build over the years.

The corridors in this part of Comyn Castle were empty, and Miralys passed easily enough through the shields guarding the threshold to the Tower. She'd long ago learned the knack of it at Neskaya.

The stone walls of the tower were dark with age, and the tapestries and furnishings of the Tower time-faded and clearly centuries old, but the Tower did not look unoccupied. On the contrary, the floors were freshly swept, and someone had thrown a still-damp cloak across a chair.

Taking a deep, steadying breath, Miralys mounted the stairs to the Tower's Working Room. She wished she could believe that she didn't already know what she would find there.

A *kyrri* descending the stairs gave her a look that was more hostile than curious when it passed her, but it made no move to bar Miralys's way.

The Working Room in Ashara's Tower was much like its sister at Neskaya. The thick rugs, the matrix screens, the wide circular bench in the center of the room. For just a moment, despite her anger and her terror, Miralys felt a stab of homesickness so intense she thought her knees might buckle. *Funny to be homesick right here at home.* She had to work to suppress a bubble of hysterical laughter.

She'd hoped without really hoping that the circular bench would be unoccupied, but it wasn't. She'd hoped the forms occupying the bench would be unfamiliar, but they weren't.

Amalie. Donal. Byrna Castamir, thinner and grayer than Miralys remembered her, and with skin like worn parchment. Miralys could feel the rapport linking them as though it were a physical thing. It called to her like a river to a single drop of water, falling.

Byrna Castamir opened faded blue eyes. "*Chiya*," she said. "You've come home." Whether she'd spoken mentally or aloud, Miralys couldn't have said. Byrna's words seemed to resonate in her bones. Byrna held out her hands.

"Did you do this? Are you the ones who orchestrated Coryn Ardais's death? Are you trying to turn the Council against the *Terranan?*" Miralys spoke aloud, trying to close her mind to the irresistible pull of the circle's rapport. It had been so long since she'd felt that kind of acceptance, that kind of unconditional love. "Have you been using my Gift all this time without my knowledge?"

She remembered Jennifer Petrie's face, that night in the cell. She remembered Coryn Ardais, falling to the cobblestoned street, dead. Both of them no more than puppets in a play.

His death is a tragedy. That was Amalie, her mental "voice" like cool water, just as it had always been in the days Miralys had worked as part of the Neskaya Circle. *But it was necessary. As necessary as a soldier's death in war.*

All Miralys could get out around the tears crowding her throat was a single word. "*Why?*"

The images came in a torrent. Miralys gasped for air, as though she were drowning in water and not in thought.

Terranan tourists, descending like locusts, wearing their contempt for anyone with eyes to see. The Towers, empty, tapestries crumbling into dust on their walls.

Miralys herself, on the day she left Neskaya. A tall, thin girl with a head full of red curls, with a *Terranan*-style pack over one shoulder. Holding herself determinedly erect, with her hands clenched together so they wouldn't shake.

Give the Terranan another century here and there won't be anything left of us to call Darkovan. Was it Byrna or Amalie or Donal who spoke?

Tears pricked the corners of her eyes in the here-and-now. Miralys pressed the heels of her hands against her eyes. "You used me," Miralys shouted aloud. "You manipulated Neemah Bell into bringing me home and you used my Gift to do this!" And then another horrible thought occurred to her. *Legates aren't supposed to drop dead while playing cards on a restday afternoon.* "Legate Hamilton. Did you—did the circle kill him?" It would have been as nothing for a trained monitor to simply stop his heart.

We are fighting for our survival, Amalie said, all sternness now. *There will be a few casualties.*

When Miralys met Byrna's faded eyes, Byrna looked away. *Legate Hamilton was an old man. Older even than the Hastur.*

The Terranan have no right to seduce our children! That was Donal, rough edges with a core of solid stone, just as she remembered him. *They lured you away into that Empire of theirs, you and so many others. How long until there are no more Keepers left to bind the circles together?*

They didn't take me. And oh, it had been years, since Miralys had 'spoken' this way, years since she'd fallen headlong into the acceptance of a circle's rapport. It felt like coming home, and she almost hated them for it. *They didn't even lure me. I chose.*

Into the circle's rapport, she cast the memory of how suffocated she'd felt at Neskaya, the memory of how desperate she'd been for the privacy of her own mind. The relief, when she'd stepped onto the *Terranan* shuttle that took her away from Darkover for the first time in her life, had been so profound Miralys had nearly wept.

Miralys felt Byrna's horror but Amalie and Donal stood firm. *Without the* Terranan, *you would have been happy with us.*

Without the Terranan, *I wouldn't have known there was anywhere else to go! That isn't the same thing!*

Can't you see how utterly the Terranan have corrupted you? That was Donal's voice, warm and shot through with gold. *This is why we fight. For you. For the others they've taken or will take. Oh,* chiya. And Miralys could feel the circle's attention shifting, like the rumble and the flickering flash of lightning that preceded thunder-snow in the Hellers.

From Miralys, from Comyn castle…to Interim Legate Neemah Bell, who they'd first seen through Miralys's eyes. Miralys could feel the circle reaching out, reaching *through* her, touching her Ridenow Gift.

Miralys clapped a hand over her mouth to muffle the howl of anguish that threatened to burst forth. *What right do you have to use me this way without telling me?*

It was for your own good, chiya. *For the good of all of us. When the Terranan leave—*

"That's the part you don't understand," Miralys whispered aloud. The words felt as though they were being torn from her throat. "They won't just leave."

Won't they?

Through her rapport with the rest of the circle, Miralys could see, could feel, Neemah Bell rise from her chair and walk across the room, moving like a puppet depending from insubstantial strings.

If there had been a true Keeper in the circle, rather than Byrna Castamir playing the Keeper's role, Miralys could never have stood against the combined might of their *laran*. She would simply have been pulled into their undertow.

As it was, Miralys had barely more than a few seconds before they overwhelmed her. She reached for the first familiar mind she could find, sleeping restlessly in the castle below.

The Hastur.

Uncle! Uncle, wake up!

And then Miralys could fight it no longer. Helplessly, she fell into a rapport that had once been as familiar to her as breathing, and she remembered nothing more.

"I hear I have you to thank for resolving the matter with Officer Petrie." Neemah Bell was waiting for Miralys when Miralys returned to her office on the first day of the new work period.

Miralys just shrugged uncomfortably. The official story—the one the Hastur had given out to the *Terranan*—was that Miralys had fallen ill with some Darkovan fever on the night she'd barged into Neemah Bell's office. It was a story that excused an assortment of evils: Miralys's invasion of the Interim Legate's office that night and her subsequent behavior, her several days' absence from the Legation while she recovered—physically, at least—from the aftermath of what had happened in Ashara's Tower.

Miralys wondered if the pain in her soul would ever leave her. Once upon a time, Amalie and Donal and Byrna had been the closest thing she had to family other than her foster father.

"Well, whatever it is you said to that Comyn Council of yours, I'm grateful."

"I didn't say anything. I was too busy languishing in my bed with a fever." Yes and no. True and untrue. Like so many things. By the time Miralys had awakened in a bed at Comyn Castle, the Council had released Jennifer Petrie back to the *Terranan*, claiming that they'd discovered that Officer Petrie had been under the influence of a native hallucinogen on the night she'd killed Coryn Ardais. A violation of the Compact, yes. But mostly a terrible accident.

Thanks to the Keeper of the *real* circle at Comyn Castle, that was certainly what Officer Petrie remembered.

The Hastur had promised the Interim Legate that the Council would keep a closer eye on what went on in the establishments in Trade City. Neemah Bell promised that the Legation would take greater care to ensure *Terranan* weapons never made it out of the Terran Zone and into the streets of Thendara.

Miralys had asked the Hastur, dreading the answer, what would become of the tattered remnants of the Neskaya Circle. The Hastur had said it was up to the Council. She'd wanted to plead that they'd only been trying to do the right thing, but a look from the Hastur had turned the words to dust in her throat.

Miralys wished the Keeper had altered her memory, too.

Neemah Bell gave Miralys a penetrating look, clearly unsatisfied with the official story. Unsatisfied with the lies.

Finally the Interim Legate smiled, but her eyes were still searching Miralys's face. "You know, I had the oddest dream that night you fell ill. I dreamed I'd been turned into one of those puppets that children play with…"

"Perhaps you'd caught a touch of my fever." Miralys looked down at her hands.

Neemah Bell raised one dark eyebrow. "Perhaps," she agreed.

Miralys wondered how much longer they'd be able to keep the truth of *laran* from their Terranan cousins. *And what will the Terranan do when they know the truth? What will they do when they know Darkover has something to offer them beyond technologically-backward cousins lost to the First Expansion diaspora?*

What was it Amalie had said? *Give the Terranan another century and there will be nothing left of us.*

Neemah Bell asked her a question, but Miralys didn't really hear it.

She was too busy wondering if Amalie had been right.

DARK AS DAWN

by Robin Wayne Bailey

"Dark as Dawn" was one of the most morally complex stories I've received over the years. It reminded me poignantly of Marion Zimmer Bradley's novel, *Two to Conquer*. Her protagonist was a despicable character who used his *laran* to exploit, manipulate, and ultimately destroy anyone who got in his way. In the end, his punishment (and redemption) came about through being forced to experience the harm he had caused. Robin Wayne Bailey's character is as much victim as he is oppressor, and I leave it to the reader to decide whether he is ultimately a villain or a flawed but hope-filled hero.

Robin Wayne Bailey is the author of numerous novels, including the *Dragonkin* trilogy and the *Frost* series, as well as *Shadowdance* and the Fritz Leiber-inspired *Swords Against the Shadowland*. His short stories have appeared in many magazines and anthologies with frequent appearances in Marion Zimmer Bradley's *Sword and Sorceress* series and Deborah J. Ross's *Lace and Blade* volumes. Many of his stories have been collected in two volumes, *Turn Left to Tomorrow* and *The Fantastikon: Tales of Wonder*, published by Yard Dog Books. He's a former two-term president of the Science Fiction and Fantasy Writers of America and a co-founder of the Science Fiction Hall of Fame. His latest book is *Little Green Men—Attack!*, an anthology co-edited with Bryan Thomas Schmidt.

Garrett hugged himself as he stared out through the small window of his room into the cold night of Ardcarran. The town lanterns and torches were all extinguished in these late-night hours, and not even the pale light from two of Darkover's four moons, Idriel and Liriel, each at half-phase, could push back the shadows and chilly darkness.

Not a soul moved in the streets below. Even the brothels and bordellos for which Ardcarran was famed seemed quiet. *It is as if the entire city is holding its breath,* Garrett thought as he rubbed his smooth-shaven, hairless arms.

After a few long moments with nothing to see, he turned around and leaned against the wall. He winced at the contact and drew himself immediately erect. His back and buttocks still stung from the brutal lashes and welts newly administered by John Barron, who lay soundly asleep in Garrett's bed with an empty bottle of *firi* clutched under one arm and his whip half-coiled on the sheet that barely covered him.

Garrett gritted his teeth against pain as he closed the shutter. The fire in the room's small fireplace had burned down to embers and ashes, and he shivered as he selected a pair of slender logs to build the fire up again. He placed them quietly in the hearth place. Rising, he glanced once more toward John Barron. His *Terranan* lover didn't like the Darkovan cold, so, moving the whip out of reach, Garrett stretched out gently on the bed next to John and cuddled beside to him. He lay like that, unmoving, for a long moment, reflecting on how much his life had recently changed.

Then, with upmost caution, he placed one hand upon John's arm.

The world went dark for Garrett, darker than any darkness he had ever known. It frightened him at first, but then, a soft cascade of broken images and nonsensical memory fragments began to flow through his awareness. In some distant corner of his brain, Garrett struggled to remain still and not disturb John. It was so much easier if John slept, relaxed and unaware.

Yet these images and fragments were like a deck of cards thrown into the air. They made no sense to Garrett, and he was too new to the art of touch telepathy, too untrained, to find the patterns in John's mind.

He pushed a little harder, as Devin Ardais taught him. Ardais the Catalyst, who had slept with Garrett for a couple of nights and somehow awakened this latent *laran* ability. Ardais, who now demanded things of Garrett, things that Garrett wasn't always prepared to do, but couldn't always resist. Things like this–*mind rape.*

Devin Ardais was an information broker, a fancy word for blackmailer, among other terrible things. In his own way, he was more cruel than John Barron. He used people like Garrett thoughtlessly, and who better, he reasoned, to obtain information furtively than a prostitute? Pillow talk had toppled entire planetary systems. It was an age-old story, but on Darkover, a world of telepaths and people with special mental abilities, it had a whole new twist.

Suddenly a pair of those cards tumbled, spun, and fit together like pieces in a jigsaw puzzle. An image formed of a Terran starship now in orbit. Another pair of cards joined with the first pair. The starship departing for...*Samarra!* With John Barron in command.

Garrett shot bolt-upright in bed, breaking his contact with John's arm. Startled, John Barron also woke. He rubbed his eyes and stared at Garrett.

"What...what is it, Garrett?"

"You're leaving!" Garrett shouted as tears sprung from his eyes."You're leaving, and I'll never see you again!"

John sat up and gathered Garrett into his arms. "How do you know I'm leaving, boy? What's gotten you so upset?"

Garrett fought to make up a convincing lie. For all John's sadism and sometime-cruelty, Garrett genuinely loved John. The thought of losing him was a hot knife in his young heart.

"You told me just now," Garrett answered. "You were holding me close and tight and whispering things in my ear, and you told me!"

John frowned and, letting go of Garrett, swung his feet over the side of the bed. With his back to Garrett, he said, "I must have been talking in my sleep. That's all it was, just talk."

Garrett crawled across the bed and wrapped his arms around John, then laid his head on John's shoulder. He cried softly, knowing that John had just lied to him as he had just lied to John.

An ember popped in the fireplace, momentarily brightening

the room as it sent sparks up the flue. John shot a look toward the flames, and then stood up. "I've got to get back to base," he said abruptly.

"Will you be back?" Garrett asked.

Without turning around, John shoved his right leg, then his left into his trousers and pulled them up. "You ask that every time," he answered, his voice cold. "It sounds a bit desperate. You know I'm a Terran officer, that someday duty would take me away."

"But not tonight, John, not so soon! Please, if you have to go just stay a little longer. Stay until dawn!"

John hesitated, his bare shoulders still gleaming with sweat in the fireplace light. He turned toward Garrett, but already he was slipping into his shirt and buttoning it. "You're a beautiful boy, Garrett," was all he said.

Garrett's hand reached for the whip which was still coiled on the sheets. "Take this!" Garrett urged, thrusting the hard, leather-wrapped handle toward John. "Use it on me, if you like!'

But John shook his head and backed away from the bed. "Keep it," he answered. "Consider it a souvenir."

Garrett scowled, then hurled the whip at John. "The scars you made on my back are souvenirs enough! Now get out if you're going! Get out of my room and out of my life! Have a great new life on Samarra!"

John spun around, leaned across the bed, and grabbed Garrett in a choking grip around the throat. "How do you know about Samarra?" he demanded.

"I told you," Garrett hissed, barely able to get out words. "You talk in your sleep!"

John brought his face close to Garrett's, as his fingers squeezed harder into the boy's soft tissues. "I should kill you to keep you quiet. Prostitutes die all the time in Ardcarran, and nobody asks questions." He eased his grip on Garrett's neck and finally let him go, pushing him roughly back on the bed. "Just keep whatever you think you've learned to yourself."

Garrett rubbed his throat, and his eyes gleamed as he stared at John. "You do love me," he whispered.

John dressed as quickly as he could, then left the room without even a word of goodbye. Garrett watched him go until the door closed. The harsh sound of the lock falling into place felt like the breaking of Garrett's heart. For long moments, he wrapped himself in the sweaty sheets of their love-making, clutched the whip to his heart, and just cried.

When he was almost at the edge of sleep, someone knocked at his door. He sprang up, hoping that John had come back, but when he opened the door, he recoiled in fear and backed away.

Devin Ardais and two of his men walked into Garrett's room. One of the men closed the door again as Ardais went to stand before the fireplace. His black cloak was speckled with flakes of snow. He sighed as he pulled off thin gloves. "The weather seems to be turning foul," he said. "We were drinking in a bar across the street when we saw the *Terranan* leave. I trust you had your usual good time."

Garrett clenched his fists as he stood naked before the three men. "You're spying on me." he said. "I don't like that!"

Devin Ardais looked stern. "It doesn't matter what you like, youngster. You work for me now. I gave you a special gift, and you owe me. Now tell me what you learned from the *Terranan*. They're always so full of secrets, both military and personal, and a cunning man can turn a profit from those secrets." He smiled a wicked smile. "I'm a very cunning man."

"You're a parasite!" Garrett shot back as he tried to put the bed between himself and his visitors and still have a shot at the door. "And you're not even a good fuck."

Devin shrugged "Well, on that part, I'll bow to your expertise. As for the rest, my little minion, never doubt that you do work for me. And if you forget it again, my two large associates…" he indicated his thuggish companions, "…will be close at hand to remind you."

The larger man strode up to Garrett and, with a lightning-fast move, caught Garrett's right arm and twisted it up painfully behind Garrett's back. "Lord Ardais asked you a nice question," he said.

"Fuck you!" Garrett shouted, but the man twisted his arm

harder, and pain shot up Garrett's scapula and shoulder. Garrett screamed, then through clenched teeth, he gave Ardais what he wanted. "He's been promoted to commander!" Garrett hissed. "And he's the new ambassador to Samarra! That's all I got!"

Devin Ardais tapped his cheek thoughtfully. "Actually, that's quite good," he answered. "A Terran ambassador with a penchant for whipping young boys and having sex with them." He paced to the window, opened the shutter and stared outward. It was still dark outside. "Yes, we can make something of that, I'm sure. But I have a bigger plan as well, one specially suited for John Barron."

Garrett struggled against the grip on his arm. "You leave him alone!" he shouted. "I'm warning you!"

Devin Ardais looked genuinely surprised. "You are warning me?" he asked, incredulous. "That's so generous of you. I'm afraid that I have to leave now, but when I'm gone, Gant...," he indicated the large brute holding Garrett. "...Gant is going to spend a little time with you to make sure you understand your new place in my organization."

"I'm not part of your...!" Garrett started to say, but Gant slapped him in the back of the head.

"Behave yourself," Gant murmured as he increased the pressure on Garrett's tortured arm.

"Gently, Gant!" Devin scolded. "Don't break him! He's potentially a very valuable asset." He beckoned to his other associate, a man equally as formidable and intimidating as Gant. "Now, Garth and I must catch up to the newly promoted Captain Barron and make him a few offers he can't possibly resist. We'll see you again soon, Garrett."

Garrett writhed in Gant's painful grip. "If you hurt John, I'll get you!"

Gant slapped him in the head again, so hard that he saw stars and his ears rang. Devin and Garth paid no attention as they quietly departed the suite. Garrett screamed, both angry and afraid, not sure which was the stronger emotion. And Gant hit him again, across the mouth to silence him. A third blow to his midsection knocked the wind from him and sent him to his knees. When Gant drew back to hit him yet again, Garrett threw up his hands to protect himself.

But his hands closed around Gant's arm. The world went dark. Gant gasped and his powerful body went rigid. Something electric passed between Garrett and Gant, and images began to flood Garrett's mind, violent and cruel images. At first, they repulsed Garrett. He didn't understand them. But they began to take on meaning and context. He released his grip on the larger man and, in the darkness, he made fists. He felt an aggressive power flow through his muscles, a new confidence and strength.

And he liked it.

The deep darkness faded, and the spark between him and Gant flickered out. His room became just his room again. However, Gant still stood as if frozen. Garrett stared at him, feeling the bitter pain of Gant's slaps and blows. After a few more moments, Gant's eyes began to flutter, and he showed signs of waking from whatever sleep or coma Garrett's touch had induced.

Garrett didn't hesitate. He drove a perfect fist into Gant's solar plexus. Gant doubled over, only to meet Garrett's hard knee. When the big man crumpled to the floor, Garrett straddled him and pounded his face to a bloody pulp, stopping only when Gant breathed a final, ragged sigh.

Garrett held up bloody fists to the dim fireplace glow, shocked by what he had done, but strangely satisfied. He understood now that he had taken knowledge from Gant and used that knowledge against him.

It was a major step beyond just taking fractured bits of information from a sleeping John Barron.

The thought reminded him of John, who was in danger and unaware of it. He had to protect his lover from Devin Ardais, no matter what it took. He sprang up with a clear purpose, washed himself from a basin of water, dressed in clothes suitable for travel, And after donning a thin backpack, threw his only cloak around his shoulders. Before leaving his room, he glanced at Gant's body and stopped long enough to go through the dead man's pockets, finding cash and a small, sheathed, razor-sharp knife. The cash went into his pack, the knife into his waistband.

Without another look back, he exited the rooms that had been both his home and his place of work, descended a flight of stone stairs, and walked into the dark night of Ardcarran. As he went, he glanced up at the pale fragments of Idriel and Liriel. Although their light was weak, they created strange shadows that stretched across the narrow streets, crawled up the walls and sides of buildings, shadows that seemed to reach for him, entice him, menace him. Not far from his door, one of those shadows suddenly moved.

"Hey, little gutter-rabbit." The shadow came closer and transformed into a skinny, half-starved human with hungry eyes and a knife in its hand. "I'll take that pack you're carrying."

Garrett whirled toward the man, with Gant's knife suddenly in his hand. The moonlight glittered on the keen edge as Garrett brandished it. "Come take it if you can," he snarled in a voice more like Gant's than his own. "Or go find easier prey. Better club them in the head, though, before they see you. It's more your style."

The skinny man hesitated, his eyes on Garrett's blade. He feinted, pretending to lunge at Garrett, but Garrett stood his ground, his gaze cold and ready, his grip on his knife expert. Finally, the skinny man stepped back, licked his lips nervously, and bolted into the darkness without another word.

Garrett put his knife away and continued on his journey. He wasn't even sure where he was going, but someone else in his head knew–John Barron. The broken, dream-like images, the knowledge he had taken from the Terran without understanding any of it, were all becoming clear.

I am changing and growing, Garrett thought to himself. He just wasn't sure into what. He had beaten Gant to death with his fists, and he felt no remorse. He held up his hands, one to Idriel, one to Liriel, and studied them in the light as if to make sure they were his own hands.

After a time, he continued walking past empty markets and blackened warehouses until he reached the outskirts of Ardcarran. The city was little more than an oasis in the middle of a Darkovan desert. The moons shone brighter, and the sand sparkled under the faint light. An easy breeze whispered against his ear and rumpled his hair.

Garrett stopped and adjusted his pack. Ahead lay the new airstrip. Recently built by Terrans, lined and criss-crossed with colorful landing lights, it glimmered in the night, like a place of beauty and mystery, as if the stars in the heavens had scattered themselves over the ground. Garrett had never seen anything like it.

But John Barron had. John knew the way to the hard-packed road that led to the airstrip. John knew about the sentry post at the gate. John knew the lay-out of the entire facility because he had supervised its construction. So with John's guidance, Garrett avoided the road and the sentry post, and made his way across the loose sand until he came to a fence. Gant told him how to quickly scale that and how to avoid being seen in the glare of the field lamps.

Once inside, Garrett crouched low. Five Terran aircraft sat out on the nearest runway. A hangar stood nearby. Its giant rolling doors were open and light poured from inside, but there was no sign of movement. Keeping low, Garrett ran across a sandy expanse, then over the hard, smooth landing strip, and up to the hangar doors.

With the skill of an expert criminal, he slipped inside, hugged the nearest shadows, and looked around. A pair of dirty mechanics were busy over some greasy engine parts. He watched them carefully for long moments. No one else seemed to be around. But then, off to one side through the frosted glass of a lounge window, another figure moved. A pilot's lounge. John Barron knew it well.

Garrett crept toward the lounge. Then, as he reached for the door knob, he drew himself erect, carrying himself with pride and confidence as John Barron would have, and he stepped inside.

A fit, middle-aged man with lively eyes and thinning hair greeted him. "Nice to know I'm not the only soul up at this hour," he said, smiling. "Just get in?"

Garrett smiled back and let John take over. "Just landed," he answered, extending his hand toward the other man. "Long flight from Caer Donn, and boy are my arms tired."

"That gag must be in every pilot manual ever written," the other said with a grin as he accepted Garrett's hand and shook it. "I'm Veet Waylon...."

The darkness that engulfed Garrett felt familiar now, and welcoming. He had no fear of it. A spark flowed from Veet Waylon's hand into Garrett's, and Garrett sucked all memories and knowledge from the other man. He did it easily.

Veet Waylon was a pilot, a rare expert at navigating the fierce air currents around the Hellers.

Now Garrett was, too.

He let go of Veet Waylon's hand, breaking the connection, noting how Waylon stared blankly into space, how confused he looked, even frightened, when he finally blinked and woke up.

"I must be more tired than I thought," Waylon muttered with an apologetic grin. "I'm out on my feet." He looked around for a chair and sat down. "Aldaran, you say? Met another fellow passing through here when I first sat down for repairs. My magnetometer crapped out. Can't fly in those mountains with that. Anyway, handsome guy. *Terranan*, I think, and military, to judge by his bearing. He was headed for Caer Donn. A private plane picked him up a little over an hour or so ago."

Garrett searched through Waylon's stolen memories and found John Barron there, even more handsome than Garrett remembered him. Garrett allowed a slow smile. In one short meeting Waylon had developed a crush on John. A crush on Garrett's lover. Garrett's smile turned to a look of secret jealousy. The John Barron in Garrett's head beamed with egotistical satisfaction. The Gant in Garrett's head whispered, "Kill him."

For the first time in a while, Garrett felt the sting of the lashes on his back. He didn't like the pain, but it was part of his job and he had learned to tolerate it. But he also remembered the things John had said to him before leaving, and he recalled the thousand small humiliations the Terran had delivered in bed. And the lies–

he remembered every lie.

Garrett was no longer just a prostitute. He had changed, become more than that. Yet he still remembered a prostitute's first lesson, that men were only good for two things–fucking and lying, and most were better at lying.

Yet, he still loved John. At least, some part of him did.

"So tell me, Veet Waylon," Garrett said conversationally. "Did you also happen to see a Comyn nobleman pass through here earlier? He might have had a tall companion or bodyguard along with him."

"That I did," Veet answered. "Arrogant pair. Didn't talk to anybody, just demanded that traffic control give them immediate clearance, then out to their plane and up in the air."

"Thanks," Garrett answered. Moving closer, he put an arm around Veet in a friendly way and let his hand settle on Veet's bare neck. "There's just one more thing I need, Veet."

Once again, a thick darkness swallowed Garrett, and he felt the spark establish itself between him and Veet Waylon. It was so easy now, and he controlled it. He felt Veet stiffen as, effortlessly, he pushed deep into Veet's mind and stole every bit of aviation knowledge, then deeper still, as he stole everything about the city of Caer Donn and the Terran spaceport there.

Mind rape. He had used that term before. He felt guilty for what he was doing to Veet Waylon, but at the same he felt power–immense power. He felt Veet start to collapse from the onslaught. Still in the link, Garrett caught him and eased him back into a chair. Yet, the darkness continued to swirl in Garrett's mind, and the link between them grew stronger than ever.

Indeed, it felt too strong! Garrett tried to break the link, but the link resisted. He struggled, then he began to panic. Despite himself, he plunged deeper into Veet Waylon's mind, absorbing information that would never be useful, stealing things he didn't want. It was almost as if Waylon didn't want to let him go!

Then, he saw it–the deep well of loneliness and isolation that formed Waylon's core, the terrible insecurities, all the dark fears, the damaged child that Veet Waylon concealed from the world and even from himself with the jovial and carefree exterior he presented to the world. Garrett cried as the wave of Waylon's secret pain threatened to drown him. So much sorrow!

Garrett wanted to reach out, to embrace and comfort. Yet, on some fundamental level, he knew that if he did that, he would lose himself inside Veet Waylon forever.

Gant! John! Help me!

The link weakened, and the swirling darkness in his brain melted away. Garrett's hand still rested on Veet Waylon's shoulder. He snatched it away and stumbled back from the chair where Waylon sat, blank-eyed, staring at nothing. Gant whispered something in Garrett's head, and John Barron answered with a sadistic chuckle.

Garrett's heart pounded, and his breathing turned ragged. He looked at Veet Waylon, not knowing if the man would ever awaken or what he would recall if he did. With a choked sob, Garrett backed out of the lounge. The workers in the hangar, still oblivious to his presence, continued scrubbing engine parts. Taking a chance, Garrett ran for the door and out onto the airstrip. He spied a plane and knew it was the right plane. He broke into a run, no longer worried about being seen. Yanking open the cockpit door, he dived inside, threw his pack into the passenger seat, and settled himself behind the pilot's yoke.

He studied the controls with Veet Waylon's eyes.

He started the engine just as Veet Waylon would have.

Before anyone could stop him, he turned the plane, taxied out onto the airstrip, and took off. All as Veet Waylon would have done. When an angry air traffic control belched out of his radio, he turned the radio down.

John Barron. Aloysius Gant. Veet Waylon. All three men were part of him now. Garrett began to sweat. It was getting harder to find his own personality as his mind became more crowded and more fractured.

He remembered a verse from an old Terran bible John Barron had once shown him.

I am Legion, for we are many!

Garrett put his hands on the yoke and felt the throb of the

plane's engine. The vibration coursed through him, and he experienced a deep joy, a transcendence, as he climbed to twenty thousand feet altitude. He had never flown before. And he had been flying all his life. He didn't know the way to Caer Donn, but Waylon did. So did John Barron. And Gant? Gant knew exactly what Devin Ardais was after.

Off to the left through the cockpit window, the two moons shone with a brighter, crisper light. Off to the right, the Hellers could barely be distinguished as an impenetrable wall of darkness. Below, the desert sand gave way to grassland, then forest and hills and, finally, fields of snow. Garrett tried to relax. He let the Waylon and Barron parts of him handle the controls and navigation while Gant slept.

We have to find Ardais and stop him, Garrett thought. Terran and Samarran relations depended upon that.

Gant stirred. *Kill him,* he said. *He deserves it.*

Garrett found it completely weird, holding a conversation inside his head. *I killed you,* he said. *Did you deserve it?*

No man deserved it more, Gant admitted. *I know what kind of man I am, Garrett, and I know what Devin Ardais is. Kill him.*

Garrett considered Gant's advice. Kill Ardais. Kill one man and spare millions.

Why did you go along with this? Garrett asked Gant.

You know the ancient legend about the scorpion and the frog? Gant answered. *It's what I am.*

But you're part of me now, so what am I?

Gant gave a low chuckle. *That's for you to figure out.*

Garrett glanced toward the cockpit window and noted the sole reflection in the glass. It was a startling reminder that he was alone, the only one in the plane. His hands were on the controls, his eyes on the navigationals. He was talking to himself.

A voice came over the airplane's radio, a traffic controller at the first and oldest Terran airbase ever allowed on Darkover. "Pilot, turn right heading 300 to intercept the GPS instrument approach." Garrett and Waylon followed the control tower's instructions and, a moment later, Caer Donn traffic control took over the aircraft and brought him down for an easy landing.

You're no longer just a prostitute, Veet Waylon said. *You're a pilot.*

You think that's funny, John Barron said. Now the voices were talking to each other! *Garrett was never just a prostitute. He was the finest piece of ass in Ardcarran.*

Gant smirked. *You would know, Terran.*

Garrett pressed his hands to his head and tried to shut them all out as a pair of ground crew walked toward the plane. One shoved chocks under the landing gear while the other waited with a clipboard. Garrett pushed open the cockpit door.

"Veet Waylon," the groundsman asked.

"That's me!" Garrett answered, knowing the tower would have identified the plane and its owner long before allowing it to land. "Back again where I started from!"

"Just sign here, sir," the groundsman directed, holding out the clipboard. "We'll tow your plane into the hangar just as soon as there's room."

"Have some other fellas come through here?" Garrett asked in Waylon's tone and speech pattern. "A couple of nabobs probably acting like they owned the place? One even claiming to be an Ardais family member?"

The groundsman made a face. "Oh, that pair. They landed just before you about fifteen minutes ago. Real jerks, if you ask me. But one of them did carry the proper Ardais credentials."

"Well, proper or not, I think they're up to no good, and somebody should keep a close eye on them." Garrett scribbled Veet Waylon's name on the clipboard sheet. "Even if he is an Ardais, you know that lot isn't known to be the most stable brick in the building."

Kill him, Gant said.

The groundsman frowned. "Yeah, they're all about twenty degrees off true. Don't ever tell anyone I said so."

"One more question," Garrett asked. "A Terran military officer, name of John Barron. Tall, handsome. Has he passed through here?"

"Oh, sure! Commander Barron is in one of our conference rooms right now, awaiting a pick-up flight to the spaceport at

Thendara. Do you know him?"

Garrett felt the hairs on his neck stand up. John was here! And Devin Ardais and his henchman, Garth, were also here!

Kill them! Gant repeated as if they were the only words he knew.

Garrett didn't hesitate. He offered a handshake to the groundsman, and in the instant their hands touched, he leeched all the memories and knowledge from the groundsman's mind. He needed that knowledge of basic layout and field operations if he was to have any chance of stopping Ardais. He knew it was a cruel thing to do, the most intimate violation of privacy possible, and yet he did it anyway and felt powerful for it.

When it was done, the groundsman sank comatose to the tarmac. Garrett barely noticed. He felt beneath his cloak for Gant's knife. Ardais was going down right here at the airstrip, right here in the hangar. His heart hammered as he jumped down from the cockpit. In the chilly air, he sprinted across the landing field for the hangar's open doors.

The voice of John Barron spoke in his head. *Better move faster, little whore, if you intend to save me.*

Shut up! Garrett snapped. *It's not all about you!*

Garrett reached the hangar and shed his cloak. Next, he shrugged quickly out of his backpack. It only encumbered him. But Gant's knife came into his hand, and he felt Gant smile with a ruthless kind of mirth. Or maybe it was really he, Garrett, who smiled. He couldn't really tell anymore.

The hangar was filled with small aircraft and little room to move among them, but urgency drove Garrett as he sped to the far side of the hangar and to a hallway beyond with several rooms. Clutching his knife, Garrett checked them all.

No sign of John Barron, nor of Devin Ardais!

A hand closed on his shoulder. Instinctively, Garrett spun around and caught the wrist of a field security guard. He immediately regretted it as all the bright hangar lights turned dark. Blackness swirled around Garrett, filling his mind and senses. An electric spark flared between the guard and himself, and a new flood of memories, knowledge, skills spilled into

Garrett's already crowded brain.

The guard stared wide-eyed, as if seeing right through Garrett. Then he slowly sank down to sit like a child on the floor.

Garrett reached out, but then snatched his hand back. "You're going to be okay," he told the guard, trying to sound reassuring. But he didn't know if that was true. He wanted to think that he was only copying memories, not stealing them, not doing any real damage.

Could you use that power on a woman next? Gant said. *It's getting crowded in here, and not all of us are into men.*

Waylon chuckled. *Don't worry, son. You're young–there's time.*

"Shut the hell up!" Garrett screamed. He felt the guard's confusion, but the man did have a useful bit of information. Like the groundsman, he knew the lay-out of the hangar and its surrounding grounds, and so all the other personalities inside him knew it, too.

They're dragging me into an alley out back, John Barron said. *That's where they're going do it!*

Garrett raced down the hallway and slammed against the release bar of a heavy metal door. The door sprang back with surprising ease, and Garrett nearly tumbled out. Half in a panic, he started to laugh. He felt as if he were leading a team, but in reality he was very much alone.

There were few lights behind the hangar. He groped his way along the back of the building, moving with stealthy care as Gant would have done, following guard's directions, until he came to the mouth of a narrow alley between a pair of hangars.

Devin Ardais and the giant, Garth, stood over an unconscious John Barron. "Hold him down," Ardais whispered to his accomplice. "There can't be any mark. Even the commander can't know what's happened."

Ardais reached under his cloak and brought forth a slender black box. Opening it, he extracted a syringe. It gleamed suddenly as *Idriel* broke over a rooftop.

Garrett stepped into the alley. "Stop, monster. Gant told me everything about your genetic poison and your plan. I won't let you do it."

Ardais looked up. Even in the alley darkness his scowl was plain. "Gant told you?" He sounded incredulous. "You won't let us what?"

Kill him! Gant urged.

Veet Waylon concurred. *Kill him.*

Kill him, John Barron agreed.

Where am I? The groundsman exuded confusion while the guard remained quiet.

Garrett pressed his hands to his ears.

"We've been paid a fancy coin for this operation," Ardais hissed, "and you're not going to interfere. One drop of this into the commander's veins, and he becomes the unwitting carrier of a synthetic virus to Samarra."

"And with a six-month incubation time, he'll be in the Samarran courts when it activates and begins to infect everyone. It will topple the government and probably start war with the Terran Empire when they trace it back to your boyfriend."

The John Barron inside Garrett's head recoiled. "*Boyfriend?*"

Devin Ardais uncapped the syringe and bent over John Barron's still form. "That's what I'm being paid for. Now don't go away, little whore. I'll deal with you next, as I should have done back in Ardcarran."

Voices suddenly spoke behind Garrett. Not the voices in his head, but real, human ones, and the beams of flashlights stabbed into the alley.

"Don't touch me!" Garrett shouted as a dozen men rushed into the alley. They were ground crew, pilots, military men, led an Aldaran family member. Most of them stopped as Garrett held up his hands, but the military men pressed forward. Avoiding Garrett, they moved toward Ardais and Garth.

"Assaulting a starship commander is a capital offense, the Aldaran lord said, "and if what we overheard is true, and that syringe will determine that, you've committed a serious breach of the Compact. I think you'll soon regret your actions."

Devin Ardais stood up, still with the syringe in hand. "I am an Ardais," he proclaimed. "You have no authority over me!"

You saved me. John Barron's voice spoke inside Garrett's head. *My hero.*

Garrett pressed his hands to his ears again, but he couldn't ignore the voices. Nor could he shut out the arguments of the other humans now in the alley, nor the arrogant intonings of Ardais himself.

The Aldaran lord sidled cautiously up to Garrett. "My family would like to meet you," he said. "You sorely need training. You don't need to steal entire personalities. We can help you learn to focus."

Garrett looked up. "He's going to walk away, isn't he? He's guilty as hell, and you'll let him walk away because his name makes him above the law?"

The Aldaran lord shrugged and looked regretful. "He is an Ardais, from one of the ruling Domains of Darkover."

Garrett's left hand made a subtle move. Gant's knife flew across the alley space. But the Aldaran lord's move was quicker. He brushed Garrett's hand ever so slightly so that the knife missed its intended target. Garth's head snapped up, and his eyes filled with surprise as he looked at Garrett. Nobody made a move to help him he sank to his knees at Devin Ardais's feet.

Well done, Gant said. *I never liked him.*

"On the other hand, Ardais," the Aldaran lord said, "you are in Aldaran territory, and you have undeniably breached the Compact by attempting to use this virus as a weapon. These witnesses will attest." His face darkened. "I see no need for a court or a trial. You may easily have an accident or just disappear in the High Hellers never to be heard from again."

Garrett furrowed his brow as he watched Garth's slow collapse. "Did I do that?" he asked Gant. "Or did you?"

You made a decision," Gant answered. *And you acted. You've grown. You've changed.*

"But it was your skill. I still don't know who I am," Garrett said aloud, "or what I am."

You're a scorpion, Gant said. *Just like me. It's your nature. You've been used all your life. Now for the first time, you have the power–real power.*

The guard and the groundsman spoke up. *You're not a scorpion*, the guard said. *You're a young man with a chance to finally better himself.* The groundsman agreed. *To change and grow. You never have to go back to your old life.*

Gant, Barron, Waylon, the groundsman and the guard all drew closer inside Garrett's head to offer comfort. *Go with this Aldaran nobleman*, they urged. *Let his family train you. Remember, you just saved two worlds.*

Go with him, Gant scowled, the lone dissenter. *Then kill him for fun.*

The other personalities mentally dog-piled Gant as Garrett clapped his hands to his ears.

Veet Waylon chuckled. *I think this is the start of a beautiful friendship.*

THE CITADEL OF FEAR

by Barb Caffrey

This story combines a number of elements: a siege, a deadly enemy, a fortified place (for some loosely defined value of "fortified"), and a struggle for survival. Combined with the courage and resourcefulness of the Renunciate protagonist, the results are anything but predictable. This story has much in common with Diana L. Paxson's "Siege," but each author has woven together a very different, equally satisfying tapestry.

Barb Caffrey has written three novels, *An Elfy On The Loose* (2014)*, A Little Elfy in Big Trouble* (2015)*,* and *Changing Faces* (2017), and is the co-writer of the Adventures of Joey Maverick series (with late husband Michael B. Caffrey) Previous stories and poems have appeared in *Stars of Darkover, First Contact Café, How Beer Saved the World, Bearing North,* and *Bedlam's Edge* (with Michael B. Caffrey).

Miralys n'ha Camilla had been riding, like any other day. The sky was clear, the mountains were easily seen, and if the snow wasn't quite up to beauty, it at least seemed clean and fresh. "This is the life!" she called to her client, Jennella, a sensible woman she'd truly enjoyed shepherding into the mountains.

Jenella smiled, but said nothing. She wasn't quite used to riding, she'd said the night before at their meal of beans and kava. The lines of pain on her face that Miralys had noticed lately, though, had become far less; this trip had done Jenella a lot of good.

The pack animals were behind them, including her little chervine, Surefoot...they should be able to reach the City of Sorcery high in the mountains, the place she considered her second home, within a few more days.

Then disaster struck.

She saw a flash of white above, heard a rumbling coming from somewhere. She tried to call to Jenella to get clear, to save herself, but Miralys's voice couldn't be heard over the tumult. Her horse started to rear as an avalanche of snow, ice, and rocks came down; her mind screamed, but her body couldn't move due to the sudden pressure. And her *laran*—weak but usable, her mother Camilla had always told her—tried to reach anyone she could, in the hopes she didn't need to die here.

As she passed out, she hoped Jennella was all right. And that Surefoot had somehow managed to escape, too...

The next thing she knew, she was being dug out from the mountain of snow. Four hard-faced women pulled her out, put her on a pallet, and carried her to safety near the semi-permanent encampment outside the city. A healer exclaimed over her legs (both broken), told her she could set them, but...and then Miralys had passed out again. When she woke next, her legs were weak, but fully healed.

She knew there would be a price for that. There always was.

As she recovered, a young woman was always by her side. The woman's name was Gwennis. Miralys had never seen her before, but accepted Gwennis's ministrations—as Gwennis was obviously an apprentice healer of some sort—calmly. Best of all, Gwennis was able to tell her that Surefoot had indeed found a way here, though they'd not found a trace of Jennella, nor the horses, nor anything else.

Gwennis turned her face away whenever Miralys wept, as was proper.

Finally, the bill became due for her healing. She was summoned to see the city elders two hours after she'd gone to bed. Bleary-eyed, she was guided, without Gwennis, to a fire and a circle of stones. It was cold and clear, the smoke bracing with its piney smell. And as the women chanted, Miralys wondered what they would see.

Or at least what they'd tell her.

Finally, the elder closest to her beckoned her close with a

finger. Miralys went quietly, as if in a dream, and sat at her feet. She did not ask questions, only listened.

"You need to take several youngsters down to the Lowlands, including your healer, Gwennis. Two will go to Nevarsin immediately, to the Guildhouse there. The others, we're not sure where they'll go, except it'll be a long journey with many pitfalls...you're the only guide we trust, and we'll give you all you need to make the journey."

Then they sent her away to get more rest.

She spent the next two days acquiring provisions. She talked to other trail guides, who warned her of the various robber-bands about and where they were likely to be holed up. She also worked on getting to know the five girls she'd be escorting down.

They were all so young! Had she ever been that age? (She must've, but it seemed like it had been forever.) And only two had professions; Gwennis was a healer, while Betrys was a trained midwife...what was the Guildhouse to do with the rest of them?

Before she knew it, they were on the trail. A few of the girls didn't want to listen to her, but after one nearly fell off the mountain taking a piss (the girl had picked a bad spot, way too close to the edge for common sense), they'd listened a bit better.

The girls ranged in age from fifteen to twenty. The twenty-year-old, Betrys, was the aforementioned midwife; she was the steadiest by far of the lot, besides Gwennis. But three of them, Rakhaila, Elinora, and Margwenn, had no idea what they wanted to do. Worse, they'd never been around men whatsoever as far as Miralys could tell, and had the worst romantic notions about them. (Why they still wanted to become Renunciates, she hadn't any idea.) But as if that weren't enough, none of them had any idea how to protect themselves. None had any *laran*, either; only she had a bit, and it wasn't reliable except for her one talent...

So she'd have no true backup, this trip. *Thanks to Avarra, I must not need any,* she thought sarcastically. She figured the Goddess Avarra must know her well, and would forgive her bad feelings about all of it.

As she trudged down the mountain—she was taking point, as she was the only one likely to find fissures in the ice, or trail that wasn't solid enough for the girls' footing—she thought more about what she could possibly do if they ran into a bad situation. She wasn't all that tall, and while she was good with a quarterstaff, she knew she couldn't protect all five girls by herself from any determined opposition. And while she'd tried to show them some basic defense moves, only Gwennis seemed to have any knack for it, while Betrys—so steady otherwise—just shrugged, and said she'd roll into a little ball and hide.

Children!

She had snares, which might be useful in a pinch. (Just simple gut, as she didn't want to leave any precious metal hanging about; besides, that was just plain cruel to the animals at this time of year, dying like that.) She also had an axe to cut firewood, and…but it was pointless to speculate.

Still, her *laran* said trouble was ahead. And she listened to herself, even when she didn't understand why.

There was something niggling at her. Something about men. The robbers and thieves, she knew how to stay away from, and she thought she could keep them away from the girls. But if they got snowed in somewhere…

Too many men willing to travel in winter were scoundrels, if not outright reprobates. The only way any of them would go anywhere was if they were displaced, maybe turned off the great estates and had nowhere else to go; either that, or they were hermits who hated women, nine times out of ten. And that tenth one, while a good person, would perhaps turn one of these girl's heads…they didn't know yet about how a man could promise the sun, moons, and stars, and then proceed to break every promise he'd ever made.

Or maybe that was just her experience. But she didn't want these girls to go through the same things she did…she'd rather they knew their sisters, and valued them, and would become good women capable of taking—and upholding—the vows of a Renunciate down the line.

Not my call, she reminded herself. *Pay attention to the trail.*

The next two days were all right, save for the girls' intransigence about getting up in the morning. Snow, ice, rocks, etc., but all hazards she expected. No sudden thaws to make footing insecure or set off possible avalanches; no sudden freezes, either. The one pack animal she had followed her without complaint, and as little Surefoot was a bit of a weather chervine, that gave Miralys hope they'd all make it through.

But her nights, as usual, were plagued with nightmares. She was trapped, again, in a white-out blizzard, much worse than what had occurred at the time. Then, as she found her way to the trail, a huge wall of snow and ice fell upon her. She screamed, in nightmare, and felt her legs break...could barely breathe...felt scared out of her mind that she'd die here, alone, no one ever knowing where she'd fallen...

Back to the here and now, she reminded herself. *Just because the trail looks all right, that does not mean it is all right. Remember your lessons!*

So she tested the trail before she let the girls walk upon it. Surefoot didn't so much as sniff the wrong way. And they kept going another five days, with the girls either sacking out so completely they didn't hear her in the night, or courteously leaving her alone despite her nightmares.

Then the eighth day dawned, bright and sunny. There was a bit of a thaw in the air, which worried her; this was the wrong time of year for such things. Worse, as they continued down the trail, there was sign of a number of other travelers; by their copious litter—including deep foot tracks along with torn branches and once the remnants of a fire she, herself, had to put out—she believed it to be a bunch of ruffians she'd encountered before. Not truly *bad*, mind you—just careless fools, with none of them worth the least of Surefoot's hoof parings.

The girls, of course, chattered so much that they must feel it all a grand adventure. They'd obviously never been anywhere, except for Betrys, and even she had only been to see various women (and their families) with her own mentor. They kept looking down the mountain, wide-eyed, and she hadn't the heart to say much other than "Watch out, and stay away from men if you see them before I do."

She knew they wouldn't listen, but had to make the attempt.

Another two days went by. She stayed a reasonable one half-day behind the men by best estimate, allowing the girls to get up an hour later and then giving them more trail chores. She hoped they'd understand why she was hanging back, but couldn't count on it. All she could do, aside from keeping a weather eye on them, was to pray to Evanda, Avarra, and any other goddesses around that they'd not run into each other. She didn't even trust the peace of the trail-meet, as such men had violated such sacred compacts before if they felt the risk—in this case, defiling five innocent young women—was justified.

That was enough for all men's hands—and women's, too, no doubt—to be turned against them, if proven. Then again, if these men violated these girls, they deserved to be sent to the coldest of Zandru's hells.

But who would believe a Renunciate over a man, even if that man was one of a group of scoundrels?

Then, the weather worsened, just after they'd taken a break for the light afternoon meal. The girls looked worried, and rightfully so; this snow was sticking, and on top of the refreezing ice and snow was likely to make their footing too treacherous to continue.

Quickly she rigged a rope line, and tied it around her waist before going to Gwennis and doing the same there. Gwennis went to Betrys, who went to the next girl, and within a few moments, the six of them were roped together. Normally Miralys would want the pack animal roped with them for comfort, but Surefoot had proven her mettle so many times, she'd rather leave Surefoot alone.

As it stood, there was shelter under a deep underhang not too far from here, if they could reach it; that was perhaps the best place they were going to find tonight. But with the men ahead of them, on a long, dark trail far away from anyone…this was going to be trouble. She didn't need her *laran* to tell her that.

But first things first. We need to make it to the shelter, and then…may all the goddesses protect us. She normally was not so devout, or so superstitious, but something had her spooked; besides, asking for help was not wrong, even if expecting it was.

It took subjective hours of work to get there. But as they grew closer, even the sticky snow couldn't hide the boot prints of at least half a dozen men…the group she'd been trying to avoid was already in the shelter she needed, and now her luck had run out.

Why me? she thought. Fortunately, the girls weren't panicking; Surefoot was still pacing at her back; they had provisions to share, which might save them.

But her *laran* was pinging mightily, nearly screaming, *Don't go in there! Don't do it!*

She told herself to ignore this. There was no other choice. The snow was thick, heavy, and the terrain was studded with rocks, dead trees, and other detritus that may as well be considered traps due to the low light remaining.

She started composing work details in her head as they got closer to shelter. They'd need water, to build a fire (especially if the men hadn't done it; but even if they had, two fires beat one, and might give her and the girls some sort of dignity away from the uncouth men), start cooking so there would be hot food available in a few hours (or at least before they broke their fast the next day), someone would need to brush down Surefoot and check her hooves…

All these thoughts didn't take her mind off the gibbering fear at the back of her mind. She could control it. She knew she wasn't in an avalanche now. She knew if she got to the shelter, the chances were good they'd be able to get out again…why did she hate the idea so much, especially after she realized they needed to go there? And how could she possibly hold a brave face for the girls to see?

She did scout around with her weak *laran*, looking for banshees and other, assorted critters. The snow hid a multitude of things, however, and none of the characteristic smell of either *cralmacs* or banshees was about. That would have to do.

The girls were shivering. They couldn't see the shelter, but Miralys knew it was there. She realized she'd have to lead them in; somehow, Surefoot seemed to realize this, too, as the little chervine had come to the front. Miralys took Surefoot's reins and led them all inside.

It was dark. There weren't any fires visible, which didn't necessarily mean much; perhaps the men hadn't understood how to get a fire from green wood, as it took skill. As it was, they didn't have any fire-starters except some of Surefoot's dried dung she carried for emergencies; it smelled horrible, but it would start a fire even with wet wood, providing they had patience.

And she'd have to share with the men, if they had no sense...damn them to Zandru's coldest hell!

The girls were quiet behind her. Perhaps they were exhausted from fighting the snow. Fortunately, they hadn't tried to take the rope line off, and she could lead them...she did turn Surefoot loose, though, because there seemed no danger for the little chervine here.

No, just from the men, she thought sourly. *But where are they?*

This little shelter had been hollowed out by something since the last time she'd had to use it, ten full seasons ago. She could smell animals now, though perhaps not banshees...not unless they'd taken a bath recently, and did banshees do such a thing?

Banshees, she thought disdainfully. *Why am I thinking about them?*

Then, something—a shriek?—went straight through her body. She stopped, and the girls did, too; but something was not right about them. They seemed possessed.

She felt the fear, too. It shrieked in her bones, shocked her muscles, scared her sinews. It seemed even worse than what she'd been buried alive in snow for two days, and for a moment made her stand still. The girls would've bolted, if not for the rope line; only Surefoot seemed unaffected, but then, almost nothing rattled Surefoot.

And that helped to calm her enough to bring her back to a sense of her responsibilities. Miralys had to take care of the girls...even though whatever was here was bad, perhaps safety could still be obtained.

It was all she could hope for, as going back outside would be certain death. And maybe her small *laran* could help them stay alive.

Besides, as she settled herself, she realized that the shrieking seemed far away. Not close at all, as there were echoes. And if whatever it was, banshee or no, was interested in them, they'd already be dead—cold logic told her that, if nothing else.

She had to ignore how she felt, and set up camp. Control what she could. Help the girls. Help Surefoot. This was her purpose, and she would carry it out—the fear would not win, not if she didn't let it!

Methodically, almost blindly, she made her way toward where the wall of the mountain had been, the last time she was here. The girls followed in fits and starts, which wasn't easy or pleasant, but she could manage. Then, she sat them down, cutting each free of the rope line (she could always string another one, if need be), and took stock. None of the girls seemed alert; what was the *Terranan* phrase one of her off-world clients had used last year? "The lights are on, but no one's home," she thought it was.

That about summed it up. But it was better than the panic of before. Made it a little easier to care for them.

Too bad Gwennis and Betrys had succumbed, though. It would've been good to have their help. Maybe if she let them sit for a little, she could try to bring them out of their reverie to aid the others?

Still, first things first. Break out the waterskin. Care for Surefoot's hooves. Build a fire. Cook some dinner. And make sure the girls didn't bolt into the great white open.

And she needed to keep watch. Because those men had to be around somewhere, unless that's whatever the creature—she hoped it wasn't a banshee, but it probably was with her luck—had found for dinner. Much less breakfast and dessert.

Not that she'd miss them if they'd been eaten. Probably no one would. But no one should die that way.

Then the creature shrieked again, a sound that went right

through her. If she hadn't lived through an avalanche, she'd have been tempted to flee right now. She had no idea why the girls didn't seem any worse, though…but small blessings, no?

And the smell…it was foul, like rotten eggs had rolled in a midden. Yet not quite as bad as the one banshee she'd run into years and years ago…the one who'd inexplicably run from her.

Why? Miralys didn't know. But she hoped whatever it was would work for her again, as she needed a miracle to save these girls, Surefoot, and herself from it.

Too bad none of us have that see-in-the-dark laran talent I've heard about, she thought wryly. *Though that's probably just a myth…one day, though, I'd love it if we could get some of those Terranan flashlights up here.*

Again, she felt paralyzing fear. And the girls…they gibbered, their eyes vacant, unmoving, almost corpse-like.

What to do, what to do, what to do? She thought wildly. *I have a quarterstaff. I have my mind. And I have five girls to protect…Goddesses, help me now protect these young innocents!*

Then she saw the man shamble into the clearing she'd made. He was dark-haired, scarred about the face, and his arms and legs were bleeding profusely. He looked almost as if he'd been mauled, but had somehow survived. He didn't seem to recognize the fire, walking directly into it. As his clothing burned, something returned to his eyes briefly…and that something, whatever it was, caused her to act.

She used her quarterstaff to knock him out of the fire, and rolled him on the ground onto the dried leaf litter she'd found. Within a few moments, the fire was out on his legs, but he'd been badly burned. Fortunately, the man had passed out, probably due to the pain. But there was no time to waste.

Somehow, she had to rouse Gwennis from her stupor, to help heal this man…but how?

"Gwennis," she went to the young woman, taking off the girl's heavy woolen mittens and chafing her hands. "You need to help me. Your talents are needed!"

But the girl didn't stir. Her eyes remained vacant, unseeing. Gwennis's body, now that Miralys could feel it, shivered almost uncontrollably, which would not do. Gwennis herself wouldn't survive much longer if Gwennis couldn't wake up and tend to herself, much less anyone else.

Nothing for it but to try to use her *laran*. If it worked today, she might be able to help; and if it didn't work, well, she was no worse off.

But it had to work! It just had to.

Miralys closed her eyes, firmed her will, and did her best to speak into Gwennis's mind. *Wake up,* she commanded the small spark she saw. *Wake up, and help! You are needed!*

But I'm so tired, Miralys heard from a distance. *And it hurts. I'm afraid...I'll be hurt...rather die than feel that...how did you stand it?*

That last question was interesting. Sounded more like Gwennis than the rest. So Miralys decided to concentrate on that. *I did so because I had to,* she thought with asperity. *I didn't want to die like that. I needed to live, to be useful, to help others, and to do what I was born to do. So do you—shake off the fear, and wake back up! Do what you were born to do, and help me heal this injured man—much less your four friends!*

Then, Miralys wasn't sure how, she pushed at the small spark of light. She encouraged it into becoming a small bonfire, what she'd sensed from Gwennis before all this...a conflagration that was welcoming, healing, and gave succor from the storms, whether they were brought on from without or within.

Slowly, almost too slowly, Gwennis returned to herself. The color of her face, previously chalk-white, went back to its normal lively brown. Her eyes, no longer empty, looked around the dimly-lit cave with interest, saw the four girls slumped on the floor...and one dark shape, unmoving, at her feet.

"This the man?" she asked, deceptively calm.

"Yes," Miralys said shortly. "Can you help him?"

"Let me get my pack, and I'll see what I can do."

As Gwennis did that, Miralys went next to Betrys. She had no more energy to use her *laran*, but could and did chafe Betrys's hands and talked to her in a low, even voice. "You are needed," Miralys told her. "You are needed, and must awaken. Do not fear—I am here, and will help you all I can."

Then Betrys shook off her stupor, and got up. Smiling once at Miralys, dazzling even in this low light, she asked Gwennis if there was anything to do to help. And the two of them went about their business: they laid out herbs, put a small amount of water on the fire to clean the wound, and bandaged the man's leg.

Miralys had almost nothing left, and wasn't sure if she should try to rouse the other three just yet. The creature was still nearby, and she still felt the fear of before—but she would not let it stop her. She would watch the young women, and the injured man, and do what she could.

This was her life. This was her purpose. And she would do it, damn it, or die trying. Nothing else existed. Not even the fear.

Then a second man stumbled in. He, too, looked awful; his arm was broken, his legs were bleeding, and while he didn't walk into the fire, it was only because he didn't make it all the way there.

Gwennis and Betrys hurried over, and started working on him, too. Miralys, unbidden, went to the opening of the underhang, and tried to reach out with her mind...were there any other survivors? And had whatever it was finished with them?

She found an odd spark of life that didn't seem human or animal. It didn't speak, exactly. Instead, it was just there, orange-red. It needed warmth, and was tired of fighting...just wanted to live, and do its best.

Something moved within her. She didn't quite know what it was. But she used her mind, carefully, to draw the creature out, and offered a truce—warmth now, if the creature would leave them and theirs alone forevermore.

She hoped it understood. Sometimes, she could speak to animals, even though no one else around her had realized it. That was one reason she knew Surefoot loved her, as she loved the little chervine...when her talent worked, it was useful.

But was it working? Especially as she'd had to overextend, earlier, to reach to Gwennis and wake her up?

She tried to say something, anything, to the two young

women, but couldn't…as she fell into the darkness, she thought she heard someone—something?—say, *Daughter. Rest now.*

She did. She had to.

Three days later, they proceeded down the mountain again. The two men, Dontan and Marvelo, had formed friendships—platonic ones, it seemed—with Betrys and Gwennis. The other three girls were shaky, tired, overly anxious…perhaps because of the small banshee at the edge of their party, the one Miralys had spoken with. It smelled bad—but it had been through the fire, too, and no longer wanted to eat any of their party. (Miralys had the sense the banshee was in the mood for some *cralmac* instead, and wished the little thing well.)

That little banshee would protect them until they got to the tree line. Then, they'd be on their own.

Miralys was grateful for the small creature, even though it could not turn off its nature. The fear it exuded was palpable, and all five girls felt it to some level, as did the two men. *But there are worse things than fear,* she thought wryly, *such as knowing you could not stand up to it.* And she refused to live in that citadel of fear any longer.

She resolutely turned her attention to the trail, and her mind toward the future.

THE JUDGMENT OF WIDOWS

by Shariann Lewitt

Castles, towers, and citadels lend themselves to a Gothic flavor: a vulnerable character, often a young governess or bride, comes to an isolated, often ancient place, where dangers lurk in every shadow. In the following tale, a resourceful, perceptive young woman faces even more extraordinary challenges. When I put together an anthology, I want to the final story to be a resting place: memorable, emotionally satisfying, and with a lingering sweetness, like a fine chocolate left on the reader's pillow. "The Judgment of Widows" struck me as perfect in all these ways. I hope you'll find it so, too.

Shariann Lewitt has been wakened well before dawn by a jaguar while sleeping in a tent in the Ossa peninsula, gone SCUBA diving in a volcanic caldera, and been up close and personal with penguins on Antarctica—but when she wants a real jolt of adrenaline she takes a drive in the Greater Boston area where she lives. When not trying to play Indiana Jones in real life, she impersonates a mild mannered professor at a famous university. Since she has no spare time, she spends it sleeping. And she prides herself on stopping for those red shiny things at street crossings at least 75% of the time.

Leonie Storn knew a good offer when she saw one, and so she had written out her acceptance even before her family started to express their doubts.

"You don't have to do this," her mother said. "He's not offering you a full marriage."

Leonie wanted to say, *Like you and Father have?* But she held her tongue, since what she'd seen of her parents' marriage seemed like prison for her mother and an afterthought for her father.

Her eldest brother's wife, Callista, said, "You can't go. You're needed here, and you don't know, you might catch the eye of one of the local lads."

Which Leonie knew meant I want you do the work I don't want to do, it's useful for me to have a healer without having to pay for one, and I'd rather have you marry beneath us and continue as my help maid. Leonie was having none of that, thank you very much.

Her favorite brother, Mikhail, said, "South of Dalereuth? Nobody goes to Dalereuth. I'm not even sure anything exists south of there. Clearly Zandru has a hell of fish. Think of it, solid walls of frozen fish guts, with their innards hanging down in gutsicles that tear off and stab you through with their disgusting squirmy splinters with the stink of rotting fish blowing through on knife blade gales." He acted out the miseries she would have to endure, including pinching his nose and trying to breathe while vomiting. Mikhail's pantomime had always made Leonie laugh, but this one topped all the rest by a good ways.

"What a horrible hell," he continued. "Nobody ever thought of that one! I always said you deserved to go to the worst of them. I'll take you there myself. When do we leave?" And then he laughed heartily and embraced her

She always knew she could count on his support.

Father only cared that it was an offer of marriage, and from an Aillard. He never saw the long letter that had arrived to her alone, along with the formal offer addressed to her parents from his.

To be sure, the offer was not precisely what a *damisela* dreamed to receive, but then Leonie was no young girl of romantic nature. Kieran Ridenow-Aillard, the Lord of Hannoth, a fishing village south of Dalereuth, had written quite clearly of what he offered her and why it was she he desired.

To the most Vai Damisela Leonie Storn,

In seeking a wife, I have consulted deeply with the *leroni* at Dalereuth Tower, who have reason to know me well. I search for a companion who has spent more than a single season of Tower training and has skills to offer a fishing town, a woman of education with a good mind for business who can provide leadership and take on the aspects of our business as necessary, as I shall be out with the fleet much of the time.

I also know that you carry the Rockraven Gift, which I think may be of much benefit to my people and to my line. As *laran* has been decreasing among us, it is of great importance to me to marry a woman I believe will give me children with strong *laran* as we need in our Towers and among the Comyn. My branch of the Aillards is a minor one, but with strong *laran* users I believe that we may change that position.

I cannot offer you all my heart, for the depth of my love is claimed and while I can and do admire women of your type, my strongest love has always been reserved for men. I could lie, as many in my position might, but I prefer us to be good friends and that you come into this arrangement with an honest understanding of what I need and what I offer.

I offer you a place where you may use your mind as fully as you desire. You shall have responsibilities and leadership, and I have looked for a woman who has both the ability and desire for such. I would not deny you the opportunity to love fully, as do I, so long as you are discreet. The people of the village must never suspect and I must never lose their respect. Finally, you shall never light a candle to Avarra for anyone but me, and those children that come of our marriage shall be only mine, not only for my pride but for the reasons I have explained.

I hope that you and Rian, the one I love, will come to be good friends to each other as well, and that you will be able to regard him as a member of our family and an uncle to our children. He is much in favor of this agreement and thinks most highly of you among the ladies I have considered.

If you feel you can accept these conditions and live happily in Hannoth with us both, and my fishing people besides, we shall all be most deeply honored by your grace.

Your most humble and hopeful servant,
Kieran Ann'dra Ridenow-Aillard

She had read the letter through many times, but had shown it to only her mother. Who had at first been horrified by what she called a "cold blooded contract." But the more she read it, the more Leonie thought it fair and, better, appreciated the honesty with which Kieran had approached her.

She and her mother both were confused by the reference to her Rockraven Gift as useful. She sat in her mother's solar while her mother dismissed the other women, most notably Callista, who had campaigned most vigorously against this marriage.

"I do not see what you have to discuss," Callista shot just before she departed, tossing her rich copper curls over her shoulder. "This is ridiculous, to go south of Dalereuth, to a fishing village no less, when she has everything she could want here. And I think it most rude of you to ask me to leave."

Lady Storn and her only daughter counted together, silently, to twenty before they dared speak. And then Lady Storn said nothing of the proposal, but winced. "I do not know why I agreed to that marriage." She had said it far too often over the past five years.

Leonie patted her mother's hand. "Who was to know? She was pleasant enough until they locked the *catenas* on." Which is what Leonie always said in their little ritual.

"Much as I would prefer something better for you, I can only wish you away from her," her mother admitted, after having argued against the match for two days. "But the Rockraven Gift? I know you have it only in part, though stronger than I have. And we have never found any use for mine. Your father certainly has reminded all of that often enough."

Her mother stated it as simple fact, but Leonie winced. Her father often threw her "useless Gift" in her mother's face.

"Besides, the full Gift killed itself out, if it ever was as strong as legend says. Which I'm not sure I believe anyway," her mother continued.

"I just don't see why he thinks it would be any use," Leonie agreed. "Even at Arilinn no one could figure out any real benefit to knowing the coming weather a few hours or a day in advance. Maybe to tell the children to come in or put on warmer clothes, but everyone knows it's going to snow and close the passes in the winter and the streams are going to flood in the spring. No one needs *laran* for that."

"Well, he does talk about his branch of the family becoming more important," her mother said. "I would expect such a skill to be useful for a campaign. To know a storm is coming would be to know that there is cover for movement, or that one might not want to join battle the next day."

Leonie considered her mother's words. Her father refused to listen to his wife, though she had more insight and understanding than he, even of those things he considered only in the male realm. He lost so much by confining her to the solar and the nursery, and Leonie realized again how lucky she was to have an offer where her intelligence meant more than her looks. Especially since she had far more of the former than the latter, which had not much helped her in the Comyn marriage market, no matter her excellent *laran*. "Perhaps. But maybe he just likes the fact that I just have one of the known Gifts, although in a minor form. There isn't any particular Aillard Gift."

"That we know," her mother responded.

They sat in silence for a few minutes, and then her mother studied Leonie's face. "I am sorry you will not have all that I dreamed for you, but women rarely do. At least you will have more than most. And Father likes the grand names. He has been ready to accept from the moment he saw them." Then her mother smiled without much humor. "I am certain that is part of the reason why Callista is so upset. Not only will you leave, but you will rank higher than she. For that reason alone you should go."

Leonie's acceptance went out with the next rider, along with her parents' formal acceptance to his parents. Then it took a harried tenday for her father to gather her dowry in portable forms, her mother to inspect and refold her trousseau several times over, and for Callista to protest that she absolute required Leonie's presence with the children and that Leonie was the house *leronis* besides and could not possibly be spared. Mikhail mustered an honor guard that could see her safely more than halfway across the world, and they set out.

It took more than two tendays before they arrived at Dalereuth

Tower where they were to meet with the Aillard honor guard to escort her to Hannoth Manor. The days had grown warmer and the air had become thick and wet. Here at least they could rest, wash, and eat well.

Leonie's hair, straight as it was, didn't dry for a full day in the braids to make it appear thicker and wavy. At least the color wasn't bad, a pale gold barely kissed with the red of the morning sun. Not striking, but then she knew quite well she was no beauty. Still, Kieran Aillard had made it clear that she was exactly what he wanted. And he was not a man to seek a woman for her beauty in any case.

"The air smells of—something. And it is so heavy. But so much better in the Tower," She remarked to Mikhail.

"The air smells of salt. And fish," Mikhail said. "And it's heavy because it's wet. It's always wet from the sea."

The Aillard contingent, led by Kieran's mother and sister, met them at the Tower. They had brought her a gift of the local garments and insisted that she dress before they took one more step south. The striped skirt was red and white and gold, and trimmed in black, the blouse white and the bodice red, all trimmed with black and gold. Leonie recognized the Storn and Aillard colors mixed, though the gold had been added and there should have been far more black.

"We can't have more than a touch of black here, or they will think you one of the widows," *Domna* Margali said. "Or that you were trying to be seen as aligning with them, and that would never do."

Leonie was quite curious about this but had no time for questions, as she was immediately instructed to remount. Her own guard with her brother mixed with the Aillards and they rode out together under bright, streaming banners on a glorious day.

They arrived at the manor just before noon, having not yet seen the town. Leonie had never seen the sea, nor had she imagined anything like it no matter how people had attempted to describe it to her. So her first sight of her new home did not include the high black cliffside or the great ridge that ringed the town. She had no eyes for the manor house carved into that cliff, halfway up, terraced and polished with long winding steps leading to arched gates, nor did she notice the young men standing on the third step from the bottom to welcome her.

No, she had eyes only for the stretch of soft black sand leading down to endless sparkling water beating small white curls upon the dark strand. Above, the sea birds screeched out their cries as they dove into the sparkling surface and came up with a fish. She sat in the saddle, entranced, feeling the soft breeze touch her cheek, and smiled. Something reached from the endless water into her soul and comforted her. She belonged here in a way she had never felt at home in any place she had been before.

"Thank you, gentle Avarra," she whispered into the salt air.

"Well, then," *Domna* Margali brought her mind to the present.

Leonie turned quickly and took in both the great house perched above the ocean and the men now walking along the sand to greet them.

One, she saw immediately, bore a pleasant resemblance to the ladies. That must be Kieran, and he was well favored indeed. The sun had darkened his skin and lightened his hair, so he had the look of someone who spent most of his time outdoors, and his body showed the strength and power of one who had worked it hard. He had his mother's piercing green eyes and thick, bronze-colored hair.

The man who accompanied him looked to be of the same age. Also with the telltale signs of much time spent in the out of doors and the body of—Leonie could not quite figure it; neither of them moved like swordsmen, nor did they have the bulk of loggers or miners. Both had a kind of rolling gait that she could not place.

Kieran first greeted his mother, as was proper, and then came over to her, bent over and kissed her hand before lifting her from the saddle. "My lady bride, you do my house grace." He bowed again and this time held out his hand and led her up the long flight of polished steps into the majestic manor.

Except for the walls being cut into the black rock, the Great

Hall was much as at Storn, where she had been raised. The two fireplaces were so large she could stand in them and spread out her arms without touching the edges stood across from each other. Tapestries hung from the walls along with ancient weapons, shields and heraldic devices, most of them the red and gray feathers of the Aillards combined with other elements to designate subdivisions within the family. Many people waited in their Festival best along the walls, and flowers decorated the mantles. Kieran's father was there, but Lord Aillard himself was present to perform the ceremony. Not that he was the head of the Domain. That would be Lord Aillard's mother, who was by now too elderly to travel. Still, Leonie was quite aware of the great honor done them, for not only was he Lord of the Domain (though among the Aillards the Lady ruled) but a powerful *laranzu* as well.

Elaborately-worked copper bracelets lay on a cushion before Lord Aillard. Kieran led Leonie before the celebrant and the ceremony itself was brief. Mikhail spoke consent for the Storns and Leonie, Lady Margali spoke consent for her family as well as Kieran's, the bracelets were locked on their wrists, and Lord Aillard pronounced, "May you be forever one."

Then servants brought large trays of food to the trestle tables at the far end of the Hall, the end without windows, and musicians settled into their niche to tune their instruments. Just before he led her out into the first dance, Kieran turned to the young man whom he had brought out to greet them. Leonie read the glances between them, and then saw the half-hopeful and half-afraid stare *Domna* Margali gave her, and understood all too well why she had been chosen.

Then the musicians struck up a tune and the dancing must go on as if there were only joy.

That night, as was customary in the South, the married women dressed Leonie in a spidersilk gown finer than anything she had ever worn before. Her loose hair was dressed with ribbons and the sheets sprinkled with pink and blue and lavender petals. Then the women had withdrawn and Kieran entered with musicians and several friends at his back. At least he insisted that they not enter when he laughed and locked the door behind him.

And then they were alone.

Leonie waited for what she knew must come. He settled next to her against the heap of pillows edged with layers of bobbin lace, took her hand, and established a light rapport so she knew he spoke only truth.

She felt both the honor and kindness not only in his voice, but through the rapport they shared. And she also could tell that he found her as appealing and desirable as he had ever found a woman, and more that he had ever hoped to find a wife.

"I am not averse to women, though I have promised Rian that you shall be the only woman in my life. And that he shall be the only man. I would like you and Rian to get to know each other and, I hope, like each other. I should like our children to know him as an uncle, as my family does not come this far south. I expect that yours won't either."

The more Leonie sought the more she found, until she could no longer compare Kieran's talent to any she had probed. And as a monitor in Arilinn, she had taken the full measure of many who were the most Gifted in the land.

"Why didn't you stay in a Tower?" she asked. "You belong there. We need more *laran* users like you, when we have so very few now."

Their rapport was now so deep that he no longer needed to answer with words. Rian had *laran*, but not enough to stay at Dalereuth Tower past his season of training. Besides, neither of them wanted a life away from the sea. For the sea called to Kieran—and to Rian—a hundred, a thousand times more.

And she left herself utterly open to his probing as well. She let him see not only her thoughts, her past, but her Gift as well. Her utterly useless Rockraven Gift, the strongest part of her *laran*. And she felt his surprise and sudden respect at this great reservoir of talent without any reservation that it could be used for—nothing at all.

You are wrong, he said mind to mind. *It will have much use here. I do not know why you think so little of it. And besides, it will give our children much greater gifts to use for the good of Darkover.*

But they were linked deeply enough that, though she knew that was absolutely true, underneath there was also his own ambition. For the good of his branch of the family, for the combination of Ridenow with Aillard. And now Storn and Rockraven. Minor families, to be sure, but with histories of strong *laran*.

He wanted children. Badly. Children with strong *laran*, perhaps even a girl who would be a Keeper. She smiled. So he was ambitious, deeply so. Just with different tactics. And a long game.

Yes. And she felt the deep approval in him, that she understood both his desire and how he planned to achieve it. And that she agreed. *And your Gift? Why throw it out as if it were useless? Perhaps you disparage yourself too much.*

But she had tried over and over again and still had found no use for the ancient Rockraven Gift. It hadn't even been any use back before the full Gift had died out, or killed itself out more likely. More a curse than a gift, Leonie thought, for anything where a babe killed her mother at birth could be nothing good.

"Only an embroidery, an old legend," her mother had said. "We can't know what was really true hundreds of years in the past."

"People just want stuff like that to be true," Mikhail had told her. "Honestly. Calling killer storms before you're born? Do you think that's reasonable? Does that make sense?"

Because Mikhail always asked if something made sense.

Neither of them had the Rockraven Gift, though. Neither of them had ever felt a storm move through them, the gathering of the clouds thick with rain, the lightning poised to strike, seeking a target, desperate to erupt. None of them had felt both the fury of the storm and the glorious release, the wildness that she could embody as the storm moved through her and they merged.

She could easily believe it. And now Kieran believed it, too.

Then they both withdrew their hands slowly and let the rapport gradually fade to a comfortable background between them, coming back from a place where they had been far more intimate than had they merely shared their bodies.

"Tomorrow I will take you into town to meet my people. Your people now," Kieran told her when they had rested and adjusted to just the lightest touch of rapport. "And you must be careful to impress the widows. You cannot rule here if they judge against you. Indeed, you will be on trial here until they decide to accept you."

"There are so many of them?"

"They call the sea the widow-maker. I know that my mother and the *laranzu* at Dalereuth Tower think that I simply indulge myself by going out with the fleet, but if I did not go, the people here would lose all respect for me. A man goes to sea unless he is crippled or past the age to haul a sail in a storm."

"But I must leave now."

Leonie set her shoulders. "But..."

"I promised Rian."

Then he was gone. And she knew that all her life to come would be like this, second always to Rian, unless she made her own way. Kieran was a good and decent man and far better than most women in her circumstances could expect, but Rian would always come before her in his heart.

That had been the agreement. She had no reason for sorrow now.

The next day Leonie, fully braided, pinned, and polished, was instructed by her new maid, Dika, to dress in a riotously bright pink, blue, lavender and cream skirt and a plaid bodice to match with a four-colored woven belt with tassels hanging so thickly that she could barely see her skirt. "Only the *Domna* gets to wear four colors," Dika informed her as the woman tied a series of complicated knots to fasten the belt and another series in the ribbons falling from the butterfly clasp at the nape of her neck.

When she met her husband for a formal introduction to the town he admired the knotwork. "Fishing folk like good knots. There are over a hundred and we often decorate with them. The children learn the most important eight before they can are old enough to count."

So saying, they mounted a pair of sturdy ponies and rode into town. Or at least the two streets of town where the few businesses clustered. A pub, of course, and then Leonie noticed another one at the opposite end of the street. A chandler's shop, with nets and ropes neatly stacked outside the door, stood across from a bakeshop. Between the structures on her left Leonie could catch glimpses of the wharf, but then turned her attention back to the merchants and the others on the street. Though Kieran was about to ride through, Leonie dismounted and walked along the shell-paved path down the center of the first street, leading her pony until a groom took the reins from her. She wanted to peer into every shop and stall, to chat with the women and few men who watched her while pretending not to.

Young women in brightly striped skirts that grazed their ankles and bodices that left their large sleeves exposed curtsied self-consciously as she walked by. A girl of no more than six years wearing a solid blue bodice and lavender and blue and bright turquoise skirt was gently pushed by her mother from the vegetable stall with a bouquet bound in lavender and blue ribbons. The girl hid her face in her mother's skirts before an elder sister or cousin took her and led her into the street to present the flowers with a pretty curtsey and a deep red blush to Leonie, who received them seriously.

"Thank you," she said to the child.

"We're happy you're here," the older girl replied. "Mother said you are a healer as well as our new Lady, and we need a healer so you are doubly welcome."

"Chella!" the woman at the vegetable stall yelled.

But Leonie smiled broadly. "I am indeed a healer, Tower-trained, and I am honored to be among you. I hope to help the people Hannoth prosper."

Some small applause broke out and Kieran looked at her with approval, but Leonie noticed harsh expressions from some older women dressed all in black, their hair scraped back from their frowning eyes. Leonie shivered slightly. "Who are they?" she asked Kieran, indicating the three women with her eyes.

"The widows," he said under his breath. "You'll see more on the wharf. Fishing is dangerous business and men are often lost at sea. And the tradition here is that women do not remarry. They put on black and watch the sea. Some of them make the bobbin lace, those who need the money. We try to make sure that none starve." He had run out of breath.

Leonie turned her gaze from them and noticed the forge and a second pub at the other end of the street. From there they turned the corner onto the wharf, where the fishing vessels that were in port bobbed, tied up at the pier. Most had been painted brilliant white with trims that matched the women's stripes, and bore fanciful names.

She might have found it all very pretty except that everything smelled of fish. Women, many of them dressed all in black, sat on low stools as they gutted fish and discarded the viscera into buckets. Fish crowded drying racks in the sun and other, fresher specimens sat in cold water baths as merchants picked through the catch. Men mended nets on their laps and children, some as young as eight, carried buckets of entrails away and scrubbed out the great wooden trays that held the different varieties caught in the sea.

Leonie had never seen so many kinds of fish. Indeed, she had rarely eaten fish at all, only the small ones that came from the high hill lakes. Those they saved for special celebrations. She had never imagined so many fish existed, and she could never have conceived they smelled so awful.

No one here stopped working to offer a bow or curtsey. The men and women, and even the children working on the wharf looked up as she and Kieran passed and noted their presence, but returned immediately to their tasks.

And again, the women in black, with their severe hairstyles and their complete lack of jewelry, gave her hard looks. From the back she noticed that these women did not wear the butterfly clasps at the nape of their necks that all the women on Darkover wore for modesty, but instead covered their entire heads and hair past their shoulders with an unadorned veil to match their mourning. Leonie assumed it was held in place with hairpins but she dared get no closer to inspect.

She did notice that a number of the widows were not old, and some as young as she. Kieran said fishing took a great toll on the community, but Leonie thought it cruel that these young women, many of them lovely if one looked past their hard expressions and their unrelieved mourning, should remain alone. Surely after a year they should be able to remarry, at least as a freemate.

Then she scolded herself. Commoners did not marry *di catenas* as she had. Only Comyn, concerned with heirs and inheritance and genetics, locked on bracelets for life.

Still, these young women should have some hope in life instead of being imprisoned forever to a life of drudgery and mourning, poverty and hopelessness.

If Kieran died, would they expect her to don black forever, wear a veil, and walk the wharf?

If Kieran died, would she want to leave this place, this sea? Would she want to remarry? She had never considered those questions, but she had never heard of such a cruel custom before.

Now she resolved to put those questions aside for the moment. She needed to see this town. But something underlying the sea salt and sand added bitterness to the taste of Hannoth and chilled her even under the warm southern sun.

Spring became summer and Leonie found much good in her new life. She found that she liked Rian when he and Kieran were not fishing, and the three of them spent many pleasant evenings singing. Rian had a fine voice and Leonie played the *rryl* well enough, and often she could feel Kieran weaving them together as a Keeper would in a circle, so that their telepathic bond became natural and easy to access.

After three tendays she had to give instructions to the cook that they must have something other than fish every other day. Which drove Irmelin, the black-veiled widow who ran the kitchen like a captain ran a company of cadets, to a fury Leonie had never expected. "And what else do you think we should eat, *vai dom*na? Seaweed? I have a recipe for that somewhere." The spindly cook waved a giant ladle, which looked suspiciously like a Renunciate's knife, in her face and backed her out the door.

True to her word, the next evening Irmelin slammed a bowl of slimy green—to call it stew would be to give it far too much credit—on the table and left. Leonie went to the kitchen the next morning and apologized. Abjectly. They went back to eating fish and Leonie, properly chastened, dared not enter the kitchen again.

When the heat had become nearly unbearable and Leonie saw the benefit of her sleeveless bodices, one of the women from the wharf came to the manor with a message for her. No one from the village would enter the house even if invited; they stayed on the porch to speak to *Dom* Kieran.

But this time the petitioner wanted her. She went out from the cooler corner deep in the cavern recess the house into the heat of the porch to speak to a young woman who yet wore colors, a yellow, tan and green striped skirt and green bodice. Still, she had the beginnings of the hard look of the widows, expecting bad news at every turn.

"It's me Giley," she started with no preamble, none of the careful honorifics and courtesies that even at Rockraven the locals began a request. "He's been hurt bad with a fish knife through his hand. I washed it with sea water, but the knife was dirty, used all day with fish guts. It's already blown up and he's screaming, poor mite, and the old women say he'll lose his hand or his life and I'd best choose now or it'll be chosen for me. Widow Emelda is ready with her cleaver but I heard you were a healer and I asked her wait."

"Of course, let's go," Leonie responded without thinking.

The woman, whose name she didn't know, led her to one of the stone cottages at the edge of the town. In the one room with a loft above, the child lay on a bed against the wall across from the cook fire. His face was already ghastly pale and he held his hand and moaned. Leonie judged him seven or eight years old, one of the children she had seen running with buckets and ropes on her first day on the wharf.

She went directly to the bed and touched his hand. Already swollen, she could see the dark purple lines starting to form. The widows were right, without a healer they would have to amputate immediately or the boy would die. But she was a healer and this was something she knew how to handle.

Calling upon her *laran*, she sank deep into the cellular level of the boy's hand and his fluid systems. She merged her own rhythms to his, the flow of the blood and lymph, the cells that came to fight against the bacteria that multiplied so quickly that they couldn't possibly defeat it.

But she could. She poured energy through her own channels into his, clearing away the invaders in great sweeps as one would clear dust from a kitchen floor. They were wrong, they did not belong, and she added her trained strength to his flailing force and *pushed*. And continued to push and wipe and clean until suddenly she found no resistance and the wound was clean.

Exhausted, she sagged onto the beaten dirt floor. The boy's breathing had calmed and his hand showed no sign of injury. He slept and all Leonie wanted was to sleep as well. To sleep, and then to eat every morsel she could find, more than this poor household held.

She never quite remembered how she got back home and into her own bed. She had some vague impression of a cart. But when she woke she found the table laden with honeyed nuts and iced moon cakes and seed-paste candies she had never tasted before. And that night for dinner she and Kieran and Rian had duck stuffed with dried fruits on a bed of rice.

And that night, for the first time, Kieran came to her bed. He tried to be gentle and was awkward, but then so was she. And somewhere inside the telepathic bonding that went with their bodies, she felt Rian join them and approve and they were all three together. And then she slept.

After that, the widows in black no longer glowered when she passed. A tiny thing, but Leonie felt the tone of the town change. Others came to her for healing now and she could speak to a few people on the street, if only about their health.

And then the warm season began to turn cooler.

Excited and grateful by the coming cold, Leonie still noticed a new tension in the town. The women in black seemed almost to smirk at the women who wore colors. And the women in colors looked at the women in black in dread. The men seemed to fold in upon themselves and then stare out to sea, their eyes scanning the horizon as if it were not another perfectly clear, bright day. And the old men smoked their pipes and shook their heads and drank their pints outside the pub.

Happy as Leonie was, she could feel growing tension in Hannoth. Finally she asked Kieran why everyone seemed so afraid.

Kieran said nothing but Rian spoke instead. "Storm season is coming."

"Storm season? "Leonie felt as if all the ice in Nevarsin had pierced through her.

Rian nodded. "Every year at summer's end we have great storms. If we are lucky, only one or two and they are not too bad. In a bad year…"The man looked to the sea. "In a bad year we are lucky if anything is left standing. And when men are caught fishing when the storms come, many die."

So many women in black on the wharf, and many of them young enough to marry again. But they could never marry again if the men kept dying at sea.

Storms. She could feel the storms.

Day followed beautiful clear day and the fleet was out, Kieran and Rian with it in the boat that Rian had sailed with his father when he was a boy. The women and children worked on the wharf, drying fish and mending nets. Leonie stood on the cliff and studied the cloudless sky.

Then one day, as perfect as all the others, her *laran* reached out and touched a few clouds gathering. She didn't worry; clouds gathered and dispersed and she returned to the manor carved from rock to check with Irmelin on food supplies and then down to the stables on the animals. As she did every day, when she had finished her duties at the manor Leonie rode into Hannoth and told the women that she had spoken over the distance with *Dom* Kieran and the fleet was safe. She forgot the clouds.

When Kieran was out to sea Leonie went to the top of the

manor every evening when the first moon rose (tonight it was Liriel) and reached out with her *laran* to touch her husband. Just a small reassurance, a quick smile, a flash of pleasure at his hard work on the lines and the nets and his joy with Rian was enough for her to bring back to Hannoth. All was well with the fleet.

But tonight all was not well. Kieran seemed as always, but she sensed something far out to sea, well beyond their senses. Those clouds had moved and she felt the force of the lightning ripple through them, though it had not yet released far out to sea. On the high, rocky cliff above the strangely silent shore, she raised her arms with her spirit out to the gathering fury that matched the vast sea.

Kieran, she did the telepathic equivalent of scream. *Kieran, danger to the fleet. Storm, a big storm. Coming from...* she wasn't able to give words, but showed him the trajectory of the squall and let her own experience of the lightning rip through him as well.

She had caught him at an intimate moment, not that she cared. Nor did he. Already he answered her. *The fleet can hide. Let the people know. Take them to safety or many will die.*

Safety. But where would be safe? She had never seen such a thing, a hurricane they called it. She only knew of storms in the mountains, not one that came with the full power of the ocean behind it.

And then she turned around in the dark and faced the silence. For as long as she had lived in Hannoth she had become accustomed to the constant sound of the waves slapping sand and gulls screaming overhead. An ocean breeze always blew, kissing her skin and gently tugging at her fine hair.

Now there was nothing, nothing at all. The sea itself lay motionless and far, far out, well below the lowest tide Leonie had ever seen. No sounds, no flying things, not even any insects disturbed the deep silence. No breath stirred the immobile air.

Like an indrawn breath before a scream, the whole of the world had withdrawn power to burst out in a moment. The coiled, waiting force slammed through her as if it would toss her aside like a blade of grass.

Below, she could see a shadow where she knew the village of Hannoth should be, as still as the ocean, as dark as the sky. No one moved, no light shone from a single window. No one knew the horror that prepared to come among them.

Safety. Where would anyone be safe from a thing far greater than any blizzard up in the hills? What would have stood so long?

This manor, she realized. This rock, this face, so ancient as to be part of the forming of the world. It had caves, so many caves that the manor itself had been carved into them. And then she knew what she had to do.

She raced toward the village barefoot in her night dress, completely unaware of both, as she thought of how to organize her people and get them to the caves in time.

When Leonie arrived the wharf was deserted. Only two of the oldest widows came out of their doors, one waving a broom and the other telling the first that she must be a *chieri*. Leonie paused to catch her breath and saw the women look at her with confusion and disapproval.

"A storm, a very great storm, is coming soon," she said between gasps. "It will hit before morning I think."

"And how do you think you know that?" the woman with the broom asked, giving her no title of respect.

"She is a *leronis*," the other woman hissed. "She healed the Alban boy."

"Healing has nothing to do with storm saying, Mhari," the broom woman replied. "She's just a chit of a girl with city airs, if you ask me."

"Well, then, it's a good thing no one did ask you, Camilla. Since you haven't got the sense of a bird, not one of which is flying. And take a look at the sea, if you will." A third woman joined them, this one wearing a striped skirt, though Leonie could not make out the colors in the dark.

"You're making a racket out there when honest people need their sleep," an old man shouted and threw a large gourd vessel at the women, which bounced on the shell paved walk.

"Good thing you're up, Grandfather Gabriel, so you can help

out. *Vai domna* says a big blow is on the way," the woman in the striped skirt said. She had a loud voice that carried, and now more people joined them.

Another widow looked out to the sea and then up to the moons. "Aye, the signs are here. We'd best get the windows battened and hunker down. Better wake everyone now and get to it."

"Wait," Leonie stopped them. "What happens with these storms? Aren't people hurt? There is space in the manor, in the caves around the cliff, which should be safer than these." She gestured toward the flimsy homes thatched with sea grass.

"And what of the fleet?" the old man asked.

"They're warned. Something about a place to hide from the wind. An island?" Leonie didn't know a better way to explain it.

"Indeed, a hidey hole from the hurricane. We've a number of them over the fishing grounds. With enough warning they'll be as safe as can be."

"Now, *Domna* Leonie, you'd best get back home and get decently dressed," one of the widows said. "We'll wake the town and organize those here to pack their things and come up the cliff. But it won't do for you to greet your guests in a night dress."

Leonie shook her head and snorted. Life and death and all they cared about was that she was not properly dressed! Ridiculous. The widows stared and she tried to stare them down, but in the end she remembered the power the widows had, and that she had to win their respect.

So Leonie turned and stomped off back to the manor to put on boots and, very incidentally, a striped skirt and bodice. There, she was respectable. Down below on the beach path from the village she saw the families, women and children staggering under sacks, many with sheep or chervines carrying packs or even pulling carts. None had horses.

"Where in Avarra's good world shall we put them all?" Dika asked.

"In the caves, of course," Leonie snapped, a little more sharply than she had intended.

"They're disgusting," Dika replied.

"Better than dying," Leonie replied. "How many brooms do we have?"

"How would I know? Ask Irmelin." Leonie almost said that Dika's tone sounded very much like insolence. Instead, she turned and went to the kitchen.

"How many brooms do we have?" she demanded.

But Irmelin was too busy ordering the entire household as a general might order his troops to notice. "Secure the water cisterns first, and make sure to bring plenty inside for drinking and washing first. Drain as much as you can. We will try to capture as much as possible from the storm," she instructed two muscular men Leonie had never seen before.

"And you," she pointed to several young boys and a girl who, Leonie knew, turned the kitchen spit, ran errands, and generally made themselves useful. "You will fasten all the shutters as I showed you. Teams of two, every room. Make sure the rods go deep into the stone and lock, mind you, and if one single one blows open during the storm you won't sit down for a week, I promise you." The children nodded and ran off, each pair hand in hand.

"And you," Irmelin turned to her scullery maids, "you had better secure all the storage caves. Be especially careful of the blue-grain stores, for it that gets damp it will mold and we won't be able to replace it until Midsummer. Then all the dried fish and fruits and the preserves in glass last, for those should be safe even if the damp penetrates into the stone."

Then she turned to Leonie and scowled. "Why are you here? What do you want?"

"Brooms. And the location of the most habitable caves that we are not currently using for storage. The safest ones that are not sea-facing."

Irmelin laughed out loud. "They are all sea-facing. The sea carved them out." Leonie could practically hear her think, "you ninny." Still, the cook paused to give her request more consideration. "Do you plan to shelter people in them, then? There are the westerlies, the caverns that lie deep behind the cliff and have only the smallest entrances here. But you can't use them. No one would go there."

"Why ever not?" Leonie's frustration, fueled by her sense of the approaching winds, broke through her words.

"Because they do not believe you."

Leonie looked at her in stone silence.

Irmelin smiled." Oh, they've come up here, all right. Because you've offered shelter in the *manor*. Not the caves. And they expect that you'll feed them all, too. They don't like your high and mighty ways, Lady Leonie. You're not from here and you have no idea of these storms and what they do. You're just some outsider who thinks she knows better than us because she's Comyn and Tower-trained is all. You don't know anything about the sea or our ways."

Leonie strode out of the kitchen, through the hall and through her bedchamber to the balcony facing the sea. She had had no idea that Irmelin had held such contempt for her.

Already she could feel the tendrils of wind caressing her cheeks, tossing the neck strings of her shift around not quite wildly, but well enough that their tassels flashed.

She greeted the people of Hannoth in the courtyard of the manor, the open cliffside that overlooked the ocean, now still and withdrawn in a way that terrified Leonie. "You know a great storm is coming," she began with no preamble. "It is powerful and dangerous and could tear down every building in Hannoth. The only safe place in here in the manor, in the cliffs."

"How do you know?" one of the widows challenged her. "You are not from here. You don't know."

"The signs are right," someone in the crowd protested.

"Oh, there'll be a big blow, no doubt. But why abandon the town? Why listen to her that it's going to be so strong? Could be running from just a baby blow and this land girl doesn't know the difference."

"I am a *leronis*," Leonie said, and spread her arms wide. "And I carry the Rockraven Gift and I know the storm."

"You know nothing."

"You lie," another of the old women shouted."

"*I do not lie.*" The Rockraven power, driven by the storm, filled her and poured out of her slight form.

Although not one of the villagers in that cavern had any *laran* to speak of, everyone in that place, even the animals, had no doubt that Leonie spoke the truth. She opened herself to the storm as she had always desired and let the power of it surge through her. Her experience of the might of the winds, of the surging sea, filled the great cavern.

The hurricane rolled through her and over them for only a moment, but that moment was long enough. It struck to the heart of Hannoth.

"We stay," the eldest of the widows said in the silence, and the people set camp in the solid shelter of the obsidian cavern.

Leonie barely felt their presence, their feeble life- sparks against the eternity of the rock, the magnificent strength of the ancient cliff , and the fury of the storm. She wanted to go to the peak of the rock wall and open her arms to the storm, to become one with it, and draw strength from it. Sea and sky called her now and she wanted to answer. Rock and fire rose within her and all four merged in one glorious moment of perfect unity.

And then it was done and she was only Leonie again and had to come in from the rain.

The storm raged throughout the night and all the next day, and did not clear until just before dawn upon the second day. Leonie dared not venture to the cavern again, but stayed in the manor itself, mostly between her own chambers and the kitchen. Irmelin remained strangely silent as she served Leonie such delicacies as she could, the seed-paste sweets and tiny blue-grain cakes spread with some local fruit jam Leonie could not identify but found delicious.

Dika told her when the people left the manor in a subdued and almost deferential tone. But Leonie thought that they cared only to help her as she recovered from the backlash of the *laran* she had expended, over and over, with the storm. Though much of it, she knew, had been her own desire to explore her abilities with the storm.

True enough, she could control nothing of it. Nor could she

communicate through it. But she could feel it rise and fall, the nuances of many bands as they came together, and she understood that this single glorious and deadly tempest was, in truth, hundreds of smaller squalls united. She was driven to go into it again and again, to study and learn until it exhausted her, and she wasn't yet quite recovered when the fleet came in.

Kieran returned with the fleet, Rian at his side, both of them subdued but still pleased. "We lost very few for a hurricane of such strength," Kieran told her.

"Even in my father's life I think only one or two stories of storms so strong have be told," Rian said.

"And you! Do you not see the tribute?" Kieran asked.

"Tribute?" Leonie asked.

"Can you walk?" Kieran asked.

Leonie rose from her bed and found that she could hardly bear her weight. Kieran came to support her from her side, and Rian took the other. The three of them walked out of the door, down the stairs and through the Great Hall.

"Her shoes," Dika called after them, but Kieran and Rian kept going, past the door onto the great terrace before the sweeping steps downward.

The terrace and the steps were all covered with black cloth, some of it fine and most of it coarse and faded. Leonie was confused as Kieran and Rian helped her down the stairs, one after another, her bare feet treading on the long lengths of black, fiberplant for the most, with hard wool and some finely spun wool, and a very few lengths of deep black spidersilk. But all had one edge cut off.

Only near the very end of the stairs did Leonie recognize what they were. The veils. The widow's veils.

At the very end sat a thick package wrapped in a blanket against the black sand.

"From your people," Kieran said with awe.

"I have heard of this from my grandfather, who heard of this from his grandfather, but it has not happened in living memory. Everyone in Hannoth thought the custom dead," Rian explained.

Leonie opened the blanket and let it fall to the sand. Inside she found a veil of as many colors as she could imagine, each stripe separated with a strip of a different black cloth. From a different widow's veil. The front and sides, and a bit in the middle had been trimmed with bobbin lace in a riot of colors. On the fourth side, the long one, the various stripes were not sewn together, but fluttered apart as ribbons.

Leonie turned it in her hands, barely able to breathe.

Dika came up after her, looked upon the veil, and fell to her knees. *"Dom*na, may I put it on you?"

Leonie nodded.

"You will wear it always," Kieran said. "As a symbol of who you have become. Not simply the *domna* of this place, but as something far more."

"I don't understand," Leonie said after Dika had attached the huge veil to her hair. It fell to her feet and over her shoulders like a great cape, and the bobbin lace hung over her forehead like a ceremonial crown.

Kieran and Rian looked at each other. "You are become the Hurricane, the Mother Protector of Sea, She Who Will Never Wear Black, the Shield of the People. You will warn the people of the storms at sea, and there will be far fewer widows on the wharf."

"The widows approve of me?"

Kieran laughed. "The widows of Hannoth have declared you their demi-goddess, my love. My loves."

The three embraced on the shore as the white wavelets lapped the black sand.

ABOUT THE EDITOR

Deborah J. Ross is an award-nominated author of fantasy and science fiction. She's written a dozen traditionally published novels and somewhere around six dozen pieces of short fiction. After her first sale in 1983 to Marion Zimmer Bradley's *Sword and Sorceress*, her short fiction has appeared in *The Magazine of Fantasy and Science Fiction, Asimov's, Star Wars: Tales from Jabba's Palace, Realms of Fantasy, Sisters of the Night, MZB's Fantasy Magazine*, and many other anthologies and magazines. Her recent books include Darkover novels *Thunderlord* and *The Children of Kings* (with Marion Zimmer Bradley); *Collaborators*, a Lambda Literary Award Finalist/James Tiptree, Jr. Award recommended list(as Deborah Wheeler); and *The Seven-Petaled Shield*, an epic fantasy trilogy based on her "Azkhantian Tales" in the *Sword and Sorceress* series. Deborah made her editorial debut in 2008 with *Lace and Blade*, followed by *Lace and Blade 2, Stars of Darkover* (with Elisabeth Waters)*, Gifts of Darkover, Realms of Darkover*, and a number of other anthologies. She has served as Secretary to the Science Fiction Fantasy Writers of America (SFWA) and chaired the jury for the Philip K. Dick Award. When she's not writing, she knits for charity, plays classical piano, and studies yoga.

THE DARKOVER® ANTHOLOGIES

THE KEEPER'S PRICE, 1980
SWORD OF CHAOS, 1982
FREE AMAZONS OF DARKOVER, 1985
OTHER SIDE OF THE MIRROR, 1987
RED SUN OF DARKOVER, 1987
FOUR MOONS OF DARKOVER, 1988
DOMAINS OF DARKOVER, 1990
RENUNCIATES OF DARKOVER, 1991
LERONI OF DARKOVER, 1991
TOWERS OF DARKOVER, 1993
MARION ZIMMER BRADLEY'S DARKOVER, 1993
SNOWS OF DARKOVER, 1994
MUSIC OF DARKOVER, 2013
STARS OF DARKOVER, 2014
GIFTS OF DARKOVER, 2015
REALMS OF DARKOVER, 2016
MASQUES OF DARKOVER, 2017
CROSSROADS OF DARKOVER, 2018
CITADELS OF DARKOVER, 2019

Printed in Great Britain
by Amazon